THE FRAGMENT OF
SHADOW

By Ben Hale

To my family and friends,

Who believed

And to my wife,

Who is perfect

The Chronicles of Lumineia

By Ben Hale

—The Shattered Soul—

The Fragment of Water
The Fragment of Shadow
The Fragment of Light
The Fragment of Fire
The Fragment of Mind
The Fragment of Power

—The Master Thief—

Jack of Thieves
Thief in the Myst
The God Thief

—The Second Draeken War—

Elseerian
The Gathering
Seven Days
The List Unseen

—The Warsworn—

The Flesh of War
The Age of War
The Heart of War

—The Age of Oracles—

The Rogue Mage
The Lost Mage
The Battle Mage

—The White Mage Saga—

Assassin's Blade (Short story prequel)
The Last Oracle
The Sword of Elseerian
Descent Unto Dark
Impact of the Fallen
The Forge of Light

Table of Contents

Map of Lumineia

Prologue: Shadow's Intrigue

From the cliff's edge, Shadow watched the sun set, relishing the gathering darkness. The gold on the horizon dimmed to red, and finally the valley below was swallowed by night. A smile tugged at his lips as creatures crept from their lairs, unaware that he saw all.

Owls flitted in the night and great cats stalked their slumbering prey, the trees alive with motion invisible to any but one with shadow magic. He yearned to join them, especially on such a night, where clouds obscured the moon and stars, giving him nearly unlimited power.

Shadow glanced to the ledge at his feet, to the spot where he had first separated from Draeken. Two hundred years. That's how long he'd trained with Elenyr and the other fragments. He'd been impatient before, but tonight he felt compelled to escape.

"You're not ready to go out alone," Elenyr had said earlier that day. "You must learn control."

"You must learn trust," Shadow had retorted, and then stormed from the training hall.

Shadow scowled, annoyed that Elenyr seemed to trust the other fragments more than him. She had permitted each of the others small assignments, opportunities to leave and return alone. But to Shadow she cautioned patience. He was tired of patience.

On the darkened ledge he reached for the shadows, felt the magic caress his skin like velvet, shaping, twisting, merging into threads of darkness. They embraced his torso and lifted him off the ground, bending and turning into limbs and wings, claws and a spiked tail. He allowed his body to turn into its elemental form, the flesh joining the darkness and growing, until his head morphed into a tapered snout.

The predators below went still, the sounds of the night dying as the new predator appeared on the ledge above. In the darkness they could not see Shadow's body, but they sensed the arrival of a dragon.

"Flee, little prey," he murmured, sending a plume of darkness from his jaws.

He launched himself skyward and banked north, feeling the wind pressing against his wings, the rising air heated from the stony foothills. He flapped his wings for height, relishing the sensation of extreme power, yet, in the back of his mind, he heard Elenyr's voice of caution.

Each of the fragments could turn his body into its elemental form, but Shadow lacked the power of the others. His was the weakest of magics, harmed by any other element. But on a night like this, he was king.

Shadow soared above the villages and cities of Talinor, visible by spots of firelight far below. Clouds obscured the moon but did not herald rain, and he gloried over the sheer freedom. He was breaking Elenyr's first rule, but that knowledge only served to heighten his pleasure, and he imagined speaking to her tomorrow, listening to her words of caution and temperance, all the while knowing she was ignorant of his escapade.

The warm air flowed across his wings, smooth and inviting. He'd cast the dragon before but Elenyr had always restricted his movements. Not tonight. He flipped and dived, turning with every swirl of wind. Then he heard a faint chime of music and the beating of wedding drums.

The echo of amusement was a temptation Shadow could not resist, and he swooped toward the source. Men and women danced in a village, their distraction just begging to be interrupted. Shadow recalled a time he and Elenyr had traveled to a village in eastern Griffin. He'd discovered a couple that had slipped into the woods, their passion overcoming patience. Shadow had morphed his features to that of a demon, terrifying them out of their wits, and for years the village claimed a demon stalked the nearby woods. He'd thought their fear no end of amusing. Elenyr had not been pleased.

And here he was, with no Elenyr to chastise him. His features lighting with anticipation, he circled the village, spotting what was obviously a wedding. The happy couple sat beneath an altar of flowers and woven reeds, the ceremony beautiful in its simplicity. Shadow dropped to the ground and crept up behind the couple. He stayed out of the pool of light cast by the torches, while the attention of the guests remained focused ceremony.

Children danced as a bard sang, the couple eating their first meal as husband and wife while others shouted praise for their union. The girl was pretty, if a bit thin, while the man was obviously a farmer's son, his broad shoulders and lean frame speaking to a life of hard labor. They probably had little coin, but they seemed happy.

Shadow crept forward, his jaws passing through the smoke rising from the fire where a pig roasted, and the villagers froze, their fear holding them spellbound as a giant dragon materialized from the darkness. The firelight robbed Shadow's body of solidity, turning him nearly ethereal, but the villagers were too terrified to notice.

"I am the harbinger of night," Shadow growled, his voice booming over the village. "I soar in the sky and hunt below, and have come seeking prey to satisfy my hunger. But on this night I am pleased, and I approve of this union."

"You ap-p-prove?" the groom quavered, his bride hiding behind his body, as if it would protect her from a dragon's wrath.

"Would you prefer I eat you all?"

"No!" a woman cried, her tone desperate. "We accept your approval."

"Then burn a pig in my honor," Shadow said. "And I will be satisfied."

He retreated into the shadows, his laughter coming out in a rumbling growl as he soared upward anew. He imagined the tales that would spread, of a dragon that had appeared and blessed the union between a commoner and his new wife. Mischief was fun, but the rumors were better.

He imagined the potential rumors of his intrigue all the way back to the refuge. Although loath to leave the sky, his fun would not be nearly as enjoyable if he were caught, and so he reluctantly alighted on the cliff. He dismissed the dragon and the shadows fell away like a cloak. He turned to flesh and retreated from the ledge.

Casting a final, longing look to the sky, Shadow disappeared into the tunnel, again turning his body into shadows as he flitted back into Cloudy Vale. The tunnel intersected with others and he followed the one that took him upward, to his quarters. The corridor culminated in a tiny storage room. Empty except for dust, the room contained a trio of brackets for light orbs, but the magic had long since perished. Striding across, he touched the rune hidden beneath the first bracket.

In a whisper of machinery, the wall swung open, revealing a dim room beyond. It had taken Shadow months to build the secret door, and he had waited until tonight to use it. He imagined using it for many years to come.

The fragments of Fire and Water slept in their beds, their forms obscured by the gloom. Mind and Light were just visible beyond, the room lit by a single light orb set against the door. Shadow smirked and stepped through the door—

The light amplified, burning bright enough to scatter the shadows in the room. Halfway through the door, Shadow froze. Elenyr stood near the entrance, her arms folded, her expression tight with anger. For several seconds Shadow stared at her, struggling with what to say, some excuse for his absence. Fire was sitting up in his bed, a smirk on his face as he watched the exchange.

"I was just—"

"Don't," Elenyr warned. "Bed. Now."

Shadow grimaced. "Sorry."

"No you're not," she snapped.

He couldn't resist a smile. "Probably true."

Light giggled. "You're in so much trouble."

"Why do you have to always break the rules?" Water demanded.

"Why do you have to be so irritating?" Shadow shot back.

"Shadow," Elenyr said, stabbing a finger to the bed. "Sleep now. Punishment tomorrow."

Shadow sighed and sank onto his bed. To his dismay, Elenyr crossed the room and shut the secret door, and then turned her arm ethereal and reached into the wall. A dull clanking indicated she'd broken the mechanism. Then she withdrew her arm and departed, extinguishing the light. In the ensuing silence Shadow endured the laughter of his fragment brothers until Mind crossed the space and regarded Shadow with thinly veiled contempt.

"What?" Shadow demanded, rising to his feet as well. "Are you jealous I got a night for myself?"

"Be smarter next time," he said coldly.

"I suppose you could do better?"

"I already have," Mind said, his claim silencing the laughter.

"You've gone out on your own?" Light asked, his eyes bright with wonder.

Mind ignored the question and poked Shadow in the chest. "You think this is just a game, escaping from Elenyr to go play. But the next time, you might get caught by someone besides Elenyr. Then you won't return at all."

"So *now* you care about me?" Shadow asked.

Mind pointed to the now broken secret door. "I would bet anything Elenyr knew about your secret for months but *allowed* you to escape."

"She would never encourage breaking the rules," Water said, his tone condescending enough that Fire groaned.

"As much as I dislike Water's insufferable tone, I have to agree with him." Fire shook his head. "Elenyr would not do that."

"She does what is necessary for us to learn," Mind said. "And Shadow will always be one who stalks. The most important lesson for him is not how to fight, but how to remain free."

Stung by the truth to Mind's words, Shadow folded his arms. "You think this was just a lesson?"

"Shadow has to learn not to get caught," Mind said, and then leaned in. "Don't get caught."

Mind turned away and returned to his bed. The others continued to argue but Shadow stood in place, surprised and annoyed by Mind's observation. As he reclined in bed, Shadow wondered if Mind was right.

Chapter 1: Target

Present Day

Shadow watched the three figures in the valley below. Even with the distance, Lira was beautiful and exotic, explaining why Water and Light had a spring in their step. Shadow grunted in irritation, wishing he'd gotten the chance to spend more time with Lira.

As an Eternal, Lira had sworn to protect Lumineia. If that wasn't enough, the woman had lived for thousands of years—even more than the fragments or Elenyr. Shadow liked the woman, but even more, he wanted the secrets she undoubtedly possessed.

"Wishing you got to go with Lira?"

Shadow glanced to Fire, and found the fragment ascending the steps to the parapet. "What do you want?" Shadow asked.

Fire stepped to the edge of the balcony and looked over the ledge. "I've never seen you gawk like that before," Fire said.

"I wasn't gawking," Shadow protested.

Fire grinned. "Liar."

"Don't you have an assignment to get to?" Shadow asked, jumping down from the battlements.

"We're getting ready to leave," Fire said. "But Elenyr wants to see you."

"About what?"

"Who knows?" Fire said. "But you'd better hurry."

Shadow grunted in annoyance and descended the stairs. The small overlook set nestled between two peaks, affording the only exterior view from the refuge. The steps cut back and forth, merging into a short slope that reached the floor of Cloudy Vale. He spotted Mind next to the exit, sharpening his favorite sword. Their eyes met but Mind motioned to the door leading to the fragment's quarters when they were young.

She's waiting in there.

The thoughts pressed into Shadow's consciousness like a whisper over his shoulder. "Why?" Shadow asked aloud, but Mind merely shrugged.

Shadow followed the crushed stone across the refuge. Trees dotted the space while a small pond covered much of one side. Buildings were constructed into the cliffs, the doors and windows facing the tiny valley.

Nestled in the hollow between mountains, the refuge was thousands of feet above the nearest valleys. Treacherous slopes made it impossible for outsiders to ascend the exterior, and only Elenyr and the fragments knew how to use the secret tunnels that connected to Cloudy Vale.

Elenyr's quarters were on the north side of the pond, while the fragments each had their own quarters in the chambers that circled the space. Shadow glanced to Elenyr's quarters as he walked by, wondering about the discussion with Lira and Ero. They'd made it clear, the ancient race had returned to Lumineia.

Wylyn and her son Relgor had arrived with a handful of brutish soldiers called dakorians. While the other fragments had displayed concern over the threat, Shadow found a smile creeping onto his face. The prospect of a decent foe left him with a more obvious emotion—excitement.

Part of him wished he'd been selected to go with Lira, but he recognized that Water and Light were better suited to searching for Wylyn. If they found Wylyn, the battle would be severe, and they would need their magics. Still, he was grateful he would not be going with Mind, Fire, and Elenyr. Fire was usually fun, but the three tended to be too serious for Shadow's liking.

Shadow reached his old quarters and stepped through the open door. The room had belonged to him and the fragments for their first few centuries, until Elenyr had deemed them old enough to have their own quarters. Dust tinged the air, and the wood on the old beds had long since lost its color.

Elenyr stood at the rear of the room, facing the secret door he'd crafted to escape. She'd ensured it would never open again, and he smiled fondly at the memory of his first excursion outside Cloudy Vale.

"Are you ready for your assignment?" Elenyr asked.

Shadow shrugged and leaned against one of the beds. "All I have to do is find an ancient map. Doesn't seem so hard."

Elenyr motioned to the broken door. "Do you remember the first time you snuck out?"

"Of course," Shadow said with a grin.

She chuckled to herself. "Even after all these generations, there's still a family that talks about the dragon that blessed their ancestors. And they still sacrifice a pig at weddings."

Shadow recalled the early years after his excursion, when a small religion had arisen, seeking to worship the Divine Dragon. He'd thought their worship the pinnacle of amusement. The others had stopped him from appearing to his newfound followers to cement their worship.

"If you want me to be sorry, I'm not," Shadow said.

She cast him a soft look. "No. I always knew your mischief would be a part of you."

"So why are we here?" Shadow asked, motioning to the room.

"Because there's more to your assignment than I let on."

Shadow tried to keep the excitement from his face. "And?"

"I suspect Wylyn's son will seek the same map."

"Why do you think that?" he asked.

"Because Wylyn needs answers, same as us," Elenyr said. "She needs a power source and a certain ore to build her Gate. I doubt she'll go herself. She won't want to risk her own life. So I think she'll send

17

her son, which brings me to you. I want you to find the map, and then find Relgor."

"Why not tell the others?" he asked.

While keeping secrets from the other fragments was not uncommon, Elenyr always had a reason. Shadow knew Elenyr rarely spoke the whole truth, a habit from her days as an oracle. Despite her secrets, he'd had learned early that she always spoke what needed to be heard.

"Our focus must remain on Wylyn," she said. "And we cannot afford to be distracted."

"So you're sending me alone," he said.

"Don't pretend you're not excited."

He grinned and raised his hands in defeat. "I won't. What do you want me to do if I find Relgor?"

"Whatever you have to," she said. "But don't get caught."

Shadow glanced over Elenyr's shoulder at the wall, realizing why the woman had chosen this chamber to meet. He wanted to dismiss her concern, but the reminder of all the times she had caught him was too bright to ignore.

"I'm not about to let the outlanders catch me," Shadow said.

"That's what you said about me," Elenyr said.

He gestured to the wall. "How long did you know about my secret entrance?"

"I figured it out the day you stole a gear from the dwarven smith in Herosian."

"That was the first week," he said, shocked to realize that Elenyr had been watching him create his secret opening for months. "Why didn't you stop me?"

"Because I wanted to see if you could escape and return without my notice."

"I failed," he said, and then smiled. "That time."

She motioned to the secret entrance. "You could have departed the moment you repaired the mechanism, but you waited for weeks before slipping out. You waited for a night where the moon was dark, and your power would be at its greatest."

"I had to make the most of it."

"And that's why you were caught."

His smile gradually turned to a frown as he realized why Elenyr had caught him that night. She'd known the moonless night would be irresistible. He'd thought himself clever, but Elenyr had been wiser.

"What's your point?" he asked.

"Most think of magic as power," she said. "And it is, but knowing oneself is where true might is discovered."

He folded his arms. "Is this another talk about figuring out who we are? We already know we are the fragments of Draeken."

A faint smile passed across her features. "Despite all your talents, all your magic, shadows always give way to light."

"I already know that," he said, annoyed. "You've said it many times."

"Then why do you think yourself weak during the day?"

He gestured to the sunlight streaming through the door. "Do you see many shadows during the daytime?"

"You are *made* of shadow," Elenyr said. "But you stand in daytime as if it is night. Why do you suppose that is?"

"I'm not the one that knows magic," he said. "That's your domain."

"You are more than your magic, Shadow. And if you do find Wylyn's son, you're going to need more than darkness to stop him."

"I'll be fine," he said.

19

"Just don't get caught," she said. "These aren't soldiers with swords, or bandits with bows. These are foes that will burn you to ash."

"Don't worry," he said, unable to resist a smug smile. "They cannot catch what they cannot see."

"I hope so," Elenyr said, and then stepped into a warm embrace. "Because I need my Shadow."

Surprised by the effusive display, Shadow hugged Elenyr back. When they parted, Elenyr regarded him for several moments and then nodded. She then turned and slipped out the door, leaving Shadow in the chamber.

Shadow looked to the wall at the back of the room, his thoughts shifting to the decades of training. He'd kicked against the rules then, but over time gained an appreciation for the boundaries Elenyr had set. He would never admit that, of course, and not just because he'd have to endure Water's smug smile.

He turned and stepped outside, and watched Elenyr, Mind, and Fire, exit through the north tunnel. Mind paused on the threshold and looked back, and again their eyes met. Mind's thoughts whispered into the corner of Shadow's mind.

She's right. Don't let your arrogance get you killed.

You were listening? Shadow thought back, and made sure to insert his irritation.

Of course, Mind said, a ghost of a smile appearing on his lips. *You were never very good at guarding your thoughts.*

I am when I want to be.

Just be careful, Mind said.

I'm not going to get caught, he said.

She's not worried about you getting caught, Mind said. *She's worried about you getting killed.*

Shadow felt Mind withdraw, and then the fragment departed, leaving Shadow alone in Cloudy Vale. Shadow again ascended the stairs to the overlook, and shortly after, watched Elenyr, Fire, and Mind appear below. Shadow continued to watch them wend their way through the trees, his forehead creased with doubt.

Was Elenyr as concerned about the other fragments? Did she trust them as little as she did him? It rankled that they kept expressing concern for him, while they were the ones with the greater assignment. And what did Elenyr mean about knowing yourself being stronger than magic? He released a derisive snort and looked to the sky, annoyed at his own confusion.

Despite his annoyance, he found a thread of anticipation seeping into his thoughts, and by sunset he'd discarded the others' fears. He was a fragment of Draeken, a guardian of power. No cage could hold him. No foe could best him.

When the sky had begun to darken he stepped onto the parapet and gazed down the long cliff. Several thousand feet below, the cliff turned into a valley, the trees casting long shadows, obscuring the creek. Darkness mounted until the sun relinquished its hold, and the rays of sunset dimmed. Shadow smiled and spread his arms wide, and then leaned into the fall.

Wind buffeted his frame as he plummeted down the cliff, but shadows were already gathering across his arms, coalescing into wings of smoke. He drew in the billowing magic and the shadows answered the call of their master, merging and shaping into bones and sinews, muscles and claws, until his dragon became whole and he stretched his wings.

The wind caught and he banked out of the curve, soaring across the valley, his large body barely visible in the gloom. He flapped for altitude and released a thundering roar, a challenge that went unanswered. There was nothing Shadow liked more than arrogant prey, and the hunt was just beginning . . .

Chapter 2: Ilumidora

Shadow flew through the night, winging his way north to the capitol city of the elven nation. Just before dawn, he descended through the trees of Orláknia and alighted on an escarpment. Dismissing the shadows, he descended on foot, breaching the tree line just as the sun appeared on the horizon, illuminating the city of Ilumidora.

Known as the City of the Sun, the city had become the wealthiest of all the nations, and members of every nation sought an excuse to visit, if only to behold its beauty once in their lifetime. Shadow stopped to survey the city, suppressing his distaste.

A thousand-foot tree rose from an island in the center of a lake, its enormous boughs reaching to the far shores. Other great trees grew on the banks, their branches extending to the center tree, intertwining to create upper highways and streets.

Columns of water flowed upward from the lake's surface and fed the floating rivers, a network of glittering streams that ringed the central tree and expanded outward to embrace the branches of the outer trees.

Homes and taverns, inns, and factories, all were nested in the branches. With lightcast walls, aquaglass windows, and shaped branches for roofs, all three of the elven magics were on display, the upper throughways a beautiful labyrinth of floating creeks, graceful branches, and streams of light.

Small elven watercraft curved up the sweeping creeks, transporting goods and people, carrying them to the lofty perches above. Renowned for their artisans and enchanted goods, the City of the Sun could have been called the City of Gold.

The upper boughs of the center tree contained the queen's castle, the branches holding the fortress of aquaglass and hardened light, the height and enchantments allowing it to shine for miles in all directions. Ilumidora was beloved by the people of every nation.

Shadow hated it.

He could not deny the city's enchantments, but the sheer amount of light in the city—which endured throughout the night—made his magic nearly useless. Of course, even in a city of light, there were always shadows to wield.

Descending the slope, Shadow joined with a road thickened by travelers. Shadow had arrived on the western road, and Talinorians clogged the entrance to the city, the newcomers obvious for the shock in their eyes.

Two large trees were bent into an arch, with a host of smaller trees filling the gap to the neighboring giants. Archers dotted the branches above, the elven guard eyeing the new arrivals. On the latest trip to the city, Shadow had stolen a relic from a merchant, earning him a bounty. He spotted his likeness drawn on several posters fastened to the wall, pleased to see the reward had increased.

Being chased by elves was always fun, but Shadow slipped under a wagon carrying fruit from Keese and turned to his shadow form. Looking like any another shadow, he clung to the axle.

The wagon bounced over the city threshold and turned toward the nearest stream, and Shadow took the first opportunity to slip free. He threaded his way through the crowd to the edge of the road, where inns and taverns provided respite for travelers, the owners human and dwarven rather than elven.

The floating city of Ilumidora contained all elven structures, all fashioned of magic, while the structures that ringed the lake were built of stone and wood, crafted by other races that wanted a foothold in the city. All paid handsomely for the use of the land.

Shadow stepped onto the Outer Ring, the street that circled the lake. Inns and shops lined the space, their height restricted in order to provide a view of the road. Beyond them, a wall of trees surrounded the city.

The city's beauty hid impressive defenses. The lake could rise up, becoming a wall of solid water connecting the outer ring of trees. The five-hundred-foot fortifications would deter even the most valiant attacker, but the enchantments had never been put to the test.

Shadow threaded his way through the crowd and up the street until he reached one of the trees that formed the outer wall. The tree reached to the heavens, its branches weaving into the boughs of its great neighbors, the wood flattened to become streets and paths, turning through floating taverns, shops, and homes.

A staircase wound its way around the trunk, and many commoners chose the route to ascend. Adjacent to the tree, a plume of water lifted boats into the floating waterways of the upper city. Those with coin opted for a ride, and boarded one of the small ships bobbing in the stream leading to the geyser.

A richly dressed noble settled into his seat, his companions and guards filling the watercraft. The ship curved away from the tree as the group relaxed and rose up a plume of water to reach a floating creek above. It flowed above another creek going in the opposite direction, where another boat glided, its occupants a pair of richly dressed elven maidens.

Shadow leaned against the railing of the stairs and watched the common folk ascend until a noblewoman came to the ship about to ascend. She stepped into the boat with her daughter, and the woman motioned the guards to a halt.

"I wish to speak with my daughter alone," she said.

"Mother," the daughter said, exasperated, "I just kissed him."

"As you wish, my lady," the guard captain said, and ordered the soldiers to the steps.

The noblewoman sat and looked to her daughter. The young woman appeared to be nearing adulthood, and her expression was one of defiance. Shadow waited for the boat to glide away from the dock and then leapt the railing, landing in the boat as it accelerated up the slope.

The two women leapt in alarm, and the guards shouted, sprinting up the stairs in pursuit. Shadow tipped an imaginary hat to the young woman as he settled into a seat, his silence drawing a scowl from the noblewoman.

"If you seek to harm me, my guards will punish you."

"Relax, my lady," Shadow said. "I'm just catching a ride."

"Why don't you walk like the other poor," she said.

"*Mother*," the daughter exclaimed. "The poor do not deserve your condemnation."

Shadow nodded his approval and eyed the soldiers shoving their way up the curving stairs, rushing to get ahead of the boat. The ship rose up the plume of water and curved into a floating stream.

"You'll see the inside of a cell for your thievery," the noblewoman said.

"Who did you kiss?" Shadow asked idly.

The young woman raised an eyebrow. "A bold question."

"Serania," the woman said sharply, "do not speak to thieves."

"Why did you kiss him?" Shadow asked.

Serania raised her chin. "Why'd you steal a ride?"

"Because I can," Shadow said.

She grinned. "Because I could."

"Daughter!" the woman snapped.

"It's true," Serania said. "And he was attractive. Not as attractive as you," she said, pointing to Shadow.

Shadow smirked at her boldness, and at the anger on the noblewoman's face. "What house do you belong to?"

"I'll not have you—"

25

"Erlan," Serania said, raising her chin slightly. "I am the first daughter."

Shadow raised an eyebrow. House Erlan was currently second in line to the crown, with House Berania being the first. If the daughters of Berania perished, Serania could very well sit on the throne. Unlike most nations, the elven kingdom did not have a single royal bloodline, they had two, each rotating who had claim to the throne. Even though unlikely, it meant the young woman had a great deal of influence in the city, and it explained her mother's insistence on decorum.

"A lady worth pursuing," Shadow said.

"Come by anytime," Serania said, to her mother's fury.

"Perhaps I will," Shadow said.

The boat slowed, the river carrying it towards a branch where a dozen soldiers had gathered with blades drawn. Panting from their ascent, the noblewoman's guards stood with them. The captain's smile was triumphant as the boat approached her guards.

"I hope it was worth it," Serania's mother snapped.

"It was," Shadow said.

He took Serania's hand and kissed it, eliciting a shocked gasp from her mother. Above, another boat glided, its passage briefly causing a shadow to pass over them. Shadow reached for the darkness like it was a rope and allowed it to carry him free. The noblewoman leapt back as Shadow soared away, a curse on her lips.

Shadow blew a kiss to Serania and willed the shadow rope to pull him up to the boat. As he appeared over the edge, the quartet of merchants recoiled in surprise, but Shadow was already jumping free. Catching the shadow beneath a tavern, he swung up to a higher branch and disappeared into the crowd.

Entire taverns hung from giant branches, bordering an even larger bough that formed the street. Horses and wagons ascended the flattened wood, which veritably hummed from the volume of magic in the grain.

Shadow passed into a section of floating water, the buildings crafted of tinted aquaglass. One contained light orbs, each magically carved to form small creatures. The dragon glowed with inner light, while the green dragon at its side flapped its wings, the display visible through the wall. A current of water swirled above the structure, with large fish swimming over Shadow's head, the water curving in a graceful arch that wrapped around the street.

Shadow passed beyond the water to reach one of the limbs of the queen's tree. At thirty feet thick, the branch was also flattened, the bark a rough purchase for the soles of Shadow's boots. Buildings hung suspended from large branches above, the structures thickening as Shadow approached the central tree. He paused and leaned over a railing, and through the maze of hanging buildings, he spotted the lake glittering beneath the City of the Sun.

Soldiers walked among the crowd, but their passage was lazy, their occupation more to deter thieves and bandits than fight in war. Not since the bloodthirsty King Hackor had the elven nation fought a war, and the people had grown complacent.

Shadow slipped around a pair of soldiers, their rich clothing marking them as captains. He slowed at their arrogant conversation and cut their purse strings with a tiny shadow blade. Then he strolled away, and smiled when they discovered the theft. With his newfound coin in hand, Shadow ascended to a large inn close to the queen's castle.

Situated so the windows faced the aquaglass castle, the tavern catered to the wealthiest patrons of the city, and it cost one of the solder's coin pouches just to enter. Shadow paused beyond the guards and eyed the vaulted space, the living limbs that supported the roof, extending into graceful beams.

Leaves were enlarged and hardened to shape the walls, and a breeze rustled the barrier, the air cooling as it passed inside. Nobles sat in chairs of wood, inlaid with gold and silver, their glasses filled with rich liquid , their personal guards lining the wall.

Shadow made his way to the back, where a door led to the kitchens. He ducked through the opening and passed women and men shouting, the food carrying delicious scents to his nose. Then he reached the rear door and swung it open, revealing a small creek attached to the back.

Winding behind the rear of other buildings, the creek was nearly invisible from the main streets, allowing the taverns to carry trash outside the city without being noticed. A single boat rested there, but instead of boarding, Shadow pressed a hidden rune outside the door.

He frowned when the stream did not shift direction and pressed the rune again. Nothing happened except a dull glimmer in the grain of the wood, suggesting the magic was still present but had not been used in some time.

Shadow had not visited the Ilumidora guildhall in some time, years in fact, but he'd assumed it would still work. If this entrance was shut, he doubted the others were open, and he would have to find another entrance to the Thieves Guild.

"Move and I'll gut you."

Shadow smiled. "I need a guide, and one appears . . ."

Chapter 3: Thieves Guild

"Turn around," the voice said. "Slowly."

"You told me you would gut me if I moved."

The voice grunted in irritation. "Just do what I say."

"What you said the first time, or the second time?" Shadow asked. "If you are going to threaten, you need to do it right."

"Just turn around," he snapped. "I won't gut you."

Shadow rotated to find himself facing one of the cooks. The elf wore a dingy apron, his body a little rounded in the center, his arms flabby. No doubt a sentry for the guild, the elf had probably partaken too liberally of the rich meats and breads the tavern provided. Although his appearance did not intimidate, the blade did, and Shadow recognized the mark of a seeker on the glass blade. The small dagger seemed to bend of its own volition, pointing to Shadow's heart with every motion. The less-than-intimidating elf could be defeated, but the seeker blade could move at the command of its owner, making the small man a real threat.

"You don't look like one of the Ravens," the man said.

"You don't look like a thief," Shadow retorted.

The elf looked to his belly and his face went pink. He jabbed the dagger into Shadow's midsection, his eyes glimmering with hatred. A shout came from the kitchens and the elf reached out and caught Shadow's tunic, pushing him toward the small boat floating in the stream behind the tavern.

"Get in," he growled. "And bind your hands with those."

He used the dagger to point at the chains sitting on the ship. Shadow did as requested and watched the dagger bend to continue to point at Shadow's heart, the glittering point unwavering as Shadow sat on the bench and shackled his hands.

"Who are you?" the man demanded.

"Shade."

The thief tapped a rune on the boat and it glided away, joining a trio of trash-laden boats on their way to a descending plume of water. The thief may not have been skilled in combat, but he never took his eyes from Shadow.

"You belong to the Thieves Guild?" Shadow asked.

"If you are a Raven, the guildmaster will cut out your heart," he said.

"So you *do* work for the guild."

The man scowled. "I know you recognized my dagger, so I'll remind you that it obeys my will as much as my hand. Disobey me, and it will cut you to pieces."

"Is Guildmaster Sethig still in command?" Shadow asked.

The man glared at him. "You know the Ravens killed him. His son has taken his place."

Shadow frowned at the revelation. Such an assassination would have reached his ears, unless it was recent. It did explain why the entrance to the guildhall had been shuttered and showed that the Ravens had expanded.

"When?" Shadow asked.

"I ask the questions," the man said with a sneer.

The boat passed under a building, the creek narrowing to travel in a tight space. Darkness briefly swallowed them, and Shadow phased to his elemental form. The chains passed through his flesh to clank on the floor of the boat. In the gloom, the man's eyes widened, and the dagger leapt for Shadow's heart.

The blade passed through him and plunged into the wood of the boat, digging deep into the wood. The blade quivered, unable to release itself, while Shadow flitted through the darkness to the man's back, his arm turning solid to wrap around the man's neck, Shadow's own blade glittering on the man's jugular.

"I think it's time I asked the questions, don't you think?"

The man nodded vigorously. "What do you wish to know?"

"Seth is now leading the guild?" Shadow asked.

"For six days, now," he said.

"Tell me how to get into the guildhall," Shadow said.

"I can't allow a Raven into the hall," the elf said, his voice cracking. "It's the only one left."

Shadow spun him about. "What do you mean, the only one left?"

"The Ravens eliminated the halls in Herosian and Terros," he said.

"When?"

"Last week," he said. "We just received word, and Seth ordered the entrances here shut. But you would know all this if you were—"

"I'm not a Raven," Shadow said.

Shadow scowled and looked beyond the man. Six months ago, he'd been in the guildhall of Herosian, eating with allies after helping a pair of the thieves complete an assignment. Much of the talk had centered around the Ravens still controlling Keese, where they'd forced the Thieves Guild out a few years ago. And now they were down to just one hall?

"How do I get inside the Ilumidora hall?" Shadow repeated.

"In the under city," he said. "South side, last room on the right, behind the red wall. There's a rune on the light orb."

31

"You've been most helpful," Shadow said.

"I could take you there," the elf said.

"I work better alone," Shadow said.

The elf's hand twitched toward the dagger, his eyes dropping to the stuck seeker blade. He licked his lips. "You'll need my help," he said, his voice friendly.

Shadow smiled—and then evaporated. The boat had just passed into another tunnel, and Shadow used the darkness to escape. The elf snatched the dagger and swung, just as the boat passed into the light. Shadow was gone, and the chains were around the elf's wrists.

As the elf cursed, Shadow dropped off the river and plunged into a lower stream. The current carried him downward to a column of water that brought him even lower. He snagged the side of a boat and allowed it to carry him all the way to the bottom of the city. Then he pulled himself free, eliciting shouts from those on board, and slipped into the crowd. Weaving his way through, he reached a street that descended under the lake, the tunnel of aquaglass leading to the lower city.

Originally built as a place of training for the army and storage for goods, the underwater network of aquaglass tunnels and buildings had gradually been overtaken by others. In the darkened depth of the lake, and in the shadow of the enormous city above, the poor lived in squalor.

Many of the factory workers and outcasts from higher houses lived in cramped quarters, dirty rooms, and even the streets of the undercity. Stripped of the gilded lights of the upper city, the people turned to what mattered most.

Children laughed and flitted about, playing in the underwater tunnels. Fathers returned from working an overnight shift in the light orb factories while mothers washed clothes and cooked. The tunnels smelled of fried fish and lemon.

Shadow passed side corridors and small houses, all built inside large aquaglass chambers. Many rooms were built of scraps of wood and stone, an invisible city that the noble elves did not wish to see.

Nearing the heart of the lake, the ground rose upward, turning into the island the queen's tree rested upon. The tunnels came to an end a short distance from the royal tree. Unbeknownst to her, the Thieves Guild had defied the edict to not build too close.

Shadow entered a small chamber that had once been a storeroom. Water leaked down the walls, giving the air a musty feel, while fish swam in the murky depths beyond. The room was empty except for a pile of scattered trash and a dim light orb hanging in the corner. Shadow reached to the light orb and turned it. Spotting the rune, he pressed it, pleased the thief had spoken honestly. The wall adjacent shimmered.

He reached out and pressed his hand against the aquaglass. Its appearance remained solid, but his hand passed through the mirage, allowing him to step into the secret corridor beyond. Shadow smiled and twisted a matching light orb at the side, returning the wall to its former solidity.

The corridor was dark and silent, and Shadow advanced down the aquaglass tunnel until it turned to earth, and he entered the island. Massive roots suddenly appeared, wrapping around the tunnel, the limbs thick and gnarled. A light appeared ahead and Shadow slowed as he approached the cavity hidden beneath the royal tree.

Hundreds of feet high, the base of the trunk was hollow. With a dwarven ascender set against one wall, the many levels contained holes and gaps in the floor, with ropes and climbing walls connecting the levels. Thieves ascended and descended, using the maze to train.

Traps and pitfalls littered the climbing surfaces. One young man struggled where an anti-magic web had caught him. A woman worked to loosen him, her scolding words harsher than necessary, suggesting a deeper tension.

Roots were abundant, some as thick as a house, others as small as his body. All supported the sentient tree. Shadow reached out and caressed the bark nearby, murmuring his praise. Holding the castle aloft and hiding the Thieves Guild beneath, the sentient tree bore a mischievous streak that Shadow admired.

Foregoing the ascender, Shadow slipped to the shadows at the back and caught a thread of shadow. It pulled him up the darkened wall. He passed through a smaller gap in the floor and ascended to the next level.

A pair of thieves passed by, and he ducked into a storeroom, flitting to a small window at the back. He phased to shadow and leapt through as the women entered, their tense conversation referring to a thief that had failed a challenge in the past week.

As he ascended the interior of the tree, more thieves appeared. He flitted from shadow to shadow, even falling into step behind a burly troll thief. Phasing to his elemental form, he glided behind the troll all the way to the ascender.

The troll turned, and Shadow ascended the wall, using the gloom to reach the highest level of the guildhall. From there he scaled the wood to a small structure at the top, the guildmaster's quarters. Then he settled on the roof to wait.

From his perch he could see all the way through the patchwork of floors, so he watched the movement of the thieves. On previous assignments from Elenyr he'd worked with the Thieves Guild, but Shadow had not returned in years, and time had a way of changing things. Many he knew by name, and he would have even called them allies. He did not have friends.

His patience was rewarded when he spotted the guildmaster in another ascender, this one descending from the top of the guildhall, likely coming directly from the queen's own castle. He had a companion, one Shadow recognized as Gendor, feared member of the Assassin's Guild—the Blade Ghost.

"Interesting," Shadow murmured, leaning forward.

Clad in a burgundy tunic and dark cloak, Gendor was lean and muscular. He carried a thin sword at his side and an ugly knife with two prongs in the opposite sheath. His gaze was cold, his expression even more so.

Seth, the guildmaster at his side, presented a stark contrast. Affable and quick to smile, the man was part dwarf and had served under his father for nearly a century. His red hair had gone silver, and then gone completely, leaving him bald. His beard was thick and braided. Shadow knew Seth to be a stalwart defender of stealing only from the wealthy, and accepting thieves into his guild that did more than steal. Despite his infamous occupation, he sought men and women of honor. But this time his smile was gone, and his features were dark with anger.

"You mean to come to *my* guild and demand *my* allegiance?" Seth demanded. "My answer has not changed."

"Then you are a fool," Gendor said.

The ascender came to a halt and the two men stepped off, but Seth turned to face him. "You know, I've never liked you, and I doubt Guildmaster Loralyn supports what you are trying to do."

"The Assassin's Guild is evolving," Gendor said. "And it's time you found your true masters."

"The seven assassins?" Seth scoffed. "There are hundreds of thieves."

"Especially among the Ravens," Gendor said coolly.

Seth's eyes narrowed. "They may be gaining strength, but they will not last the century."

"They will with my support," Gendor said.

Seth scowled. "You would ally with the Ravens? They are thugs and brutes, and the Raven doesn't care if blood is spilt."

"Neither do I," Gendor said, tapping the hilt of his sword.

"I'll report this to Guildmaster Loralyn," Seth growled.

"Be my guest," Gendor said. "But I've been summoned to a full Assassin Council, and who knows what might happen." He chuckled and retreated to the ascender. "I do hope you will reconsider. I would hate to see your guild become my enemy."

"I will never bow to you," Seth spat.

"I thought you might say that," Gendor said, and his eyes flicked to the base of the chamber. "So I'll leave you with some encouragement."

Shadow followed his gaze and spotted a dozen black clad figures appear in the lower tunnels, at the entrance Shadow had used. Their faces hidden behind silver masks, they drew their blades and darted into the hall.

The thieves were quick to draw their weapons, and the shouts of battle rang under the roots of the great tree. Gendor smirked as he ascended out of sight while Seth pulled his axe and dropped into a hole in the floor. Unseen, Shadow dropped into a different hole and fell through the roots toward the base, a shadowblade materializing in his hand.

Chapter 4: The Bloodsworn

Shadow dropped through the labyrinth of giant roots and caught a patch of shadow behind a home, using it to swing closer to the conflict. The light in the guildhall was too bright to use much of his magic, but his advantage was anonymity.

He flipped to the top of the root and raced along its length, eyeing the battle below. Two score thieves were present in the guildhall, but the attackers were more skilled, and blood already darkened the floor.

Shadow reached the end of the root and slipped free, landing behind one of the attackers. He darted in, striking once, before flitting back into the shadows. The man slumped to the floor, the woman he was about to kill scrambling backward as her attacker perished.

Seth charged into the battle and struck at an assassin, bringing his axe to bear on the lithe figure, but the killer was too quick, and spun around the guildmaster, using their sword to wound a thief behind the guildmaster. The attacker slapped Seth on the side of his skull, making it clear he could have killed him, but chose not to.

"To me!" the guildmaster bellowed, and the thieves collapsed towards him, forming a defensive ring. A glance revealed that no thieves were dead, but many were injured.

"Three lives we must take," one of the killers said, his deep voice disturbingly cold. "One for each week Gendor has awaited an answer."

"You're not killing any of them," Seth snarled.

"And who is going to stop us?" another killer asked, flicking her sword at two young thieves, causing them to recoil. "You?"

"Actually, I will."

All eyes lifted to Shadow, who sat atop a nearby root. He flipped a knife in his hands, lazily, like the battle was already won. One of the killers stabbed a finger at Shadow, barking an order, and two of the assassins separated from the group, converging on him, both raising crossbows.

Shadow turned elemental, allowing the bolts to pass through his shadowy body, and plunge into a root. Shadow turned corporeal and smiled as the chamber shuddered, and dust rained down on all of them.

"Have you ever heard the story of why Seth's father chose this place to make his guildhall?"

Shadow dropped to the ground as the assassins looked about uncertainly. The chamber trembled again, and one of the giant roots shifted. Seth, a broad smile on his face, retreated toward the center of the hall, urgently whispering to the others.

"It was because he made a friend," Seth said, drawing the killers' attention. "She doesn't like many people—and hates those who hurt her."

"My apologies for not introducing you," Shadow said as one of the roots split open and wood reached out, forming large spears. "I'd like you to meet Urindilial, queen of all trees."

Wood groaned as the other roots split, shifting the levels of the guildhall and crushing rooms. A storeroom crumbled and barrels fell, shattering on the floor. Light orbs disintegrated, plunging the room into a network of shadows.

"Kill them!" the assassin shouted. "Quickly!"

The assassins darted in, but the spears of wood streaked forward, the spikes at the end impaling the two closest to the thieves. Men screamed as spears the size of a man's leg burst through their bodies.

Shouting orders, the assassins charged, weaving between the snapping wood in an attempt to reach the thieves, only to be met by Shadow. Using the newfound darkness, Shadow wrapped himself in the body of a silver reaver.

His body grew and widened, his arms swelling with strength, long spines rising from his spine. Releasing an excited bellow, Shadow lumbered into the fray, striking at the killers with the spikes extending from his hands. Assassins shrieked as they were thrown about, their bodies striking walls or caught midair by the roots of Urindilial, only to be torn asunder.

Shadow smashed a meaty fist into a woman, knocking her sprawling. Then he picked up a man and tossed him at the wall. More roots formed into claws that caught the man and crushed him.

One woman hacked at the limbs and didn't see the root rising like a scorpion tail at her back. It struck once, and the body flew all the way into an entrance tunnel. The remaining survivors turned and fled, only two making it to the exit, the third caught by another root as it wrapped around his throat, extinguishing his life.

"Urindilial," Seth called, "it's over."

The splinters of wood calmed and withdrew back into the roots, the bark sealing again. Shadow released his silver reaver and the shadows returned to the darkness, leaving him standing between a trio of dead killers.

The sudden calm settled upon the hall as the roots finally stilled, and dust stopped falling from the ceiling. Shadow turned a circle, his eyes sweeping the still forms, but none of the thieves were among the dead.

"Care for the wounded and deal with the dead," Seth said, and the thieves parted. Many reached out to touch a nearby limb, expressing their gratitude to the tree that had saved their lives. Then the guildmaster crossed the space to Shadow.

"Guildmaster," Shadow said wryly, "do you have to antagonize everyone?"

"Shadow," Seth said, a smile beneath his beard, "your arrival is most welcome."

One of the roots passed over Shadow's shoulder, and a flower blossomed at the end. The flower caressed Shadow's check before

39

falling into his hand, and then the wood retreated, the grain a slight shade of red.

"Urindilial," Shadow said, "you flatter me." He offered a bow and blew the limb a kiss.

Seth grunted in amusement. "It appears I'm not the only one happy to see you."

Shadow swept his hand to the nearest root. "It is me that is happy to see such beauty."

The red tinge returned to the tree, and Seth laughed. He clapped Shadow on the back and gestured to the dead killers. "What brought you here? Did you follow them?"

"Coincidence," Shadow replied. "I wanted to speak to you regarding an item I seek and happened to see Gendor's arrival. I was inclined to intervene."

Seth noticed one of his thieves waiting, a woman with the mark of a master thief, and gave a hand gesture for her to continue caring for the thieves in his absence. Then Seth motioned Shadow toward a darkened alcove. When they were out of earshot, Seth's smile faded.

"These are troubling times," he said.

"Like assassins wanting the allegiance of the Thieves Guild?"

"We aren't exactly friends with the assassins," Seth said, pulling on his beard. "But they've never displayed antagonism against us. This is the first time an assassin has attacked one of our guild in ages."

"When did Gendor first ask for your loyalty?" Shadow asked.

"Three weeks past," Seth said.

When Wylyn arrived.

The timing could not be a coincidence, but how were they connected? Realizing there was more at play than he'd first imagined, Shadow considered what the assassins had to gain with Wylyn's arrival. He doubted the entire guild was involved—the woman that led the

40

assassins was too honorable for that. But Gendor? The man's thirst for coin had no end, and Shadow knew he'd wanted to expand the guild for some time. Had he sought to do so without the knowledge of his guildmaster?

"Did you know Gendor had recruited others?" Shadow asked.

"First I've seen," Seth said. "There are plenty willing to kill for coin, but the Assassin's Guild has always been selective, only taking lives because they deserved to be taken."

"You sound like you admire them," Shadow said.

"I wasn't always an old dwarf," Seth said. "And when I was a child I dreamed of becoming an assassin. Alas, I was better with a lockpick than an axe."

"So who are they?" Shadow asked, gesturing to the dead men and women.

"Guildmaster!" one of the thieves called. "This one's alive."

Shadow and Seth hurried to the fallen man, arriving as his mask was removed. The man's features were scarred from combats, his eyes hardened from bloodshed. His features were Talinorian, so he was likely former military.

"Fetch a healer," Seth said, and the thief scurried off. Then he bent over the man. "What's your name?"

"You are fools," the man said, coughing. "And your fate was sealed the moment you refused Gendor's offer."

"Why?" Seth asked.

"Because the ancients have returned," he said, grimacing in pain. "And we have been waiting."

"Who's we?" Shadow asked.

The man met Shadow's eyes and he thought he would refuse to respond, but the man managed a dark smile. "The Order of Ancients has sought the return of our masters for eons, and now that time has arrived."

"What does this Order have to do with Gendor?" Seth asked.

"The Order commands," the assassin said. "And we are its Bloodsworn."

"Not this time," Shadow said, motioning to his other fallen companions, a smirk playing across his lips.

The dying man glared at Shadow. "You think to stop an ancient? They *created* us, and they created magic. They are our masters."

"Not my master," Shadow said.

"You will die like the rest, *fragment*."

Shadow blinked in surprise, shocked that the man knew his identity. Few knew of him or Draeken's origin, and to hear the truth from an assassin's lips inspired a disturbing amount of doubt. The man's lips curled into a sneer.

"Since your birth you have fought against an unseen foe, and now you find yourself surprised. You are known to us, as are your brothers and your protector. Enjoy your final days of freedom, guardian."

The man's body relaxed in death, a disturbing smile still on his face. Shadow rose to his feet, his thoughts leaping to the other fragments, and the chilling truths the assassin had shared. If an adversary did know of the fragments, they could all be in danger.

"Of what did he speak?" Seth asked, his voice uncertain.

"Rumors and suspicion," Shadow said, flashing a disarming smile. He turned from the body and walked past the healer that had arrived too late.

"He called you a fragment."

"He's a dead assassin," Shadow said with a snort. "And apparently one that serves a rogue member of the Assassin's Guild."

Seth nodded, but his gaze remained uncertain. "Why did you come here?"

"I need a map of the locations built by the ancient race," Shadow said. "It is an unrelated matter."

Seth glanced to the dead member of the Order of Ancients. He did not seem convinced. "Our archives were in Keese," he said. "Then the Ravens forced us out and took our guildhall."

The dwarf's features tightened, and Shadow saw the emotion written on his face. The Thieves Guild was under siege, with assassins demanding their loyalty, and a rival guild taking their territory.

"I'll see what I can do about the Ravens," Shadow said.

"Why would you do that?" Seth asked.

Shadow grinned. "Because it will be fun."

"You can't do it alone," Seth said.

"I always work alone," Shadow replied. "Good luck with Gendor."

Seth looked away to answer a question from one of his thieves. "Where do you intend to start?"

Shadow turned to his elemental form, and like dissipating smoke, faded into the darkness beneath a limb. Seth looked back and his voice faded. He turned about, shocked by Shadow's sudden disappearance.

"How does he do that?" the dwarf muttered.

From above him, Shadow slipped away. He climbed upward, and entered the ascender Gendor had used. The ascender rose through the tree and came to a halt at the back of a storeroom in the queen's castle. Slipping into a throng of cooks, he passed through the castle's great hall, pausing to steal the queen's crown from off the gilded pillow. Depositing it on the chair of a duke, he walked to the castle gates, reaching them just as men began shouting. While the flustered duke was surrounded, Shadow departed into the upper city, his thoughts on the Order of Ancients.

Chapter 5: The Angel of Death

As Gendor exited through the banquet hall, the servants paid him no mind, but one set of eyes watched him depart. From a perch above the chandelier, a woman watched, her scowl deepening.

Lorica's hand reached for the sword on her back, her calloused fingers wrapping around the hilt. She yearned to pull the blade free and drop it on the departing assassin, to cut him down and watch him die in the midst of shrieking servants and shocked guards. But killing another member of the guild was forbidden, and doing so would invite the condemnation of all the assassins. Even having her sister as guildmaster would not spare her life—at least without the right evidence.

She reminded herself of her purpose and released the hilt of her sword, allowing Gendor to depart unharmed. She settled back into her perch, wondering why Gendor had visited the thief guildhall.

Strictly speaking, Lorica should not be following Gendor at all. But Lorica had quietly watched the assassin for years. Three weeks ago he'd disappeared, leaving his contract unfulfilled.

Gendor had never failed to complete a contract, but he'd simply departed. A week later he'd appeared in Keese with the Ravens. Lorica had tracked him to Ilumidora, where it appeared he was meeting with the Thieves Guild.

She frowned, wondering why an assassin would seek a meeting with the Thieves Guild, especially when the guild was being hunted by the Ravens. Lorica suspected it was only a matter of time until the Ravens replaced the Thieves Guild, but that wasn't her problem. Her problem was Gendor.

From her perch on a ledge behind the chandelier, Lorica continued to ponder Gendor's behavior. Her vantage point, hidden behind the light of the great hall, could not be seen from below, affording her visibility and secrecy.

She withdrew the small coin from her pocket and traced her thumb across the skull symbol. Normally the coin looked like any other, but the skull had pressed outward from the metal, as had seven tiny blades around the surface. It was a summoning, one that required the entire guild. Gendor was obviously returning to the hall in Herosian, and a tremor of excitement ran across her flesh. A full council would be a perfect chance to reveal what she'd learned and confront Gendor, and finally exact her vengeance.

She stepped off her hiding spot and jumped down to a balcony overlooking the hall. Just as she landed, she spotted a new arrival. The striking man exited the kitchens and passed the banquet table. He deftly stole the crown, a brazen act that would merit losing a hand if not a life, and then deposited it on the chair of a duke. His smile was smug, and Lorica nodded her approval when the banquet hall erupted in shouts. Using the same commotion, she descended the wall and slipped out a side door. Curious, she stepped onto a balcony of the castle and watched the man depart across the bridge leading to the city. Guards closed on him and he raised his hands, and then evaporated like smoke, his body passing through them and materializing on the opposite side.

"Catch me if you can," he said.

The guards charged him, but the man slipped into the crowd and disappeared for good. Lorica found a smile on her face and shook herself, squashing the spark of attraction. He was probably just a thief with talent.

Lorica jumped from the chandelier to the nearest balcony and then descended the steps to the great hall. From there she slipped to an exterior balcony and leaned over the drop. A trio of enormous limbs held the castle aloft. Other smaller branches curved their way through the interior, supporting the upper, segmented portions of the structure.

A shout came from behind and she knew she'd been spotted. She ignored the rushing guards and leapt the railing, spreading her cloak wide. The material reached outward, the light catching it and spreading it further, morphing into wings.

45

The wings spread wide, shimmering in the light, beautiful and regal. She banked away from the fall, the wings pulling on her body so she soared across the lake. She relished the wind in her hair and then pulled her cowl over her features.

"The Angel!" someone cried, recognizing her from the bounty posters.

"The Angel of Death!" another shouted, and soon soldiers converged upon her, pushing their way through the crowd.

She banked upward, slowing as she streaked for the outer wall. Arrows reached for her, but she was moving too fast. As she approached the battlements, she closed her wings and spun, spinning over the wall and beyond the city.

She spread her wings again and soared into the trees, twisting and turning as the shouts faded behind her. Lorica continued to fly, outstripping the lightcast birds that were sent to follow. The small entities had eyes linked to their casters, allowing the elven guards to track their quarry, but she flew beyond their reach and then dropped to the earth.

She landed hard and dismissed the wings, and the threads of light folded inward, merging back into an innocuous cloak. Pulling her hood back, she departed the elven kingdom, all the while watching the trail at her back.

She could have escaped the city without becoming the Angel, without being seen. But she wanted Gendor to know she was there, and he would rightly assume she was following him. It was a warning, the only one he would get before she sank her blade into his corrupt little heart.

She turned away from the city and worked her way northward. Reaching the road, she traveled west, leaving the elven kingdom for Talinor. Now that Gendor knew she'd been in Ilumidora, he would be cautious, and she needed time to get to Talinor and speak to her sister. All the evidence she'd gathered would be for naught if she couldn't speak to her sister before the council began.

After a week on the road she reached Herosian, capitol city of the Talinor. Built in seven rings expanding from the central castle, the city did not compare to Ilumidora but it had its own beauty. The central circles were known for their rich occupants and grand estates, while the outer rings contained factories and homes for the common folk.

Arriving deep into the night, she made her way to a small entrance reserved for the military, and a guard in the guild's pocket ushered her through the outer wall. Once inside the city, Lorica made her way to a castle.

Built by the Verinai before their fall, the castle sprawled across an enormous area. Its walls were the thickest in Lumineia, it's battlements armed with dwarven ballistae and elven enchantments. But not even the king knew of the giant chamber hidden beneath the fortress, the birthplace of the Titans.

Lorica made her way to the moat that surrounded the castle and paused, eyeing the battlements above. Darkness had settled in and the outer wall was illuminated by large light orbs, the light failing to breach the water of the moat.

The water came from Blue Lake and flowed into a myriad of canals and streams throughout the city, including the moat. Lorica eased herself from the darkness and descended to the water, where a small eddy had formed.

The curl of water looked like any other, revealing an obstruction underneath. But instead of a stone, it hid a box of air, with an illusion for a lid. Lorica fumbled for the handle and then lifted the section of water, reaching in to retrieve the contents.

The pile of parchment came with a handful of memory orbs, the balls glittering dully in the moonlight. Two of the memories were her own, while a third came from a dying man, a simple guard that happened to witness Gendor with a group of shadowy figures. Gendor had taken his life, but not before she'd convinced him to share the memory. Others came from other witnesses.

She collected the parchment and the orbs before retreating up the embankment. She'd hoped to have a lot more evidence before forcing a confrontation with Gendor, but she had enough, and couldn't stand to let him live another day, not after what he'd done.

On impulse she veered away from an entrance to the assassin guildhall and made her way east, toward the seventh ring. It was late, but like many of the factories in Herosian, workers labored throughout the night, refining exports of ground flour, precious stones, and woven cloth.

The streets were nearly empty, only a handful of wastrels wandering about. A patrol of soldiers passed, but their gait was relaxed, their attention on the tale being told by one of their own. Like just another shadow, Lorica passed them by and ascended a sloped street to a weaver guildhall.

The dark structure sat empty, the weavers gone home for the night. She came to a halt on the threshold and looked up to the single spire, breathing in the scents of cloth and dust, scents of home.

Adjacent to the hall stood a ramshackle home. The paint on the walls had long since peeled away, leaving graying wood. The windows were cracked, and a hole in the wall suggested an animal had burrowed beneath the foundation.

"I'm sorry I haven't visited much," she murmured. "I know I said I'd come back often, but I believe I've finally found your killer."

She thought of the search, of the decade spent hunting, and now finally she was ready. All the evidence, everything she'd gathered, all pointed to Gendor, and she was done waiting. She'd become an assassin to find Zenif's killer, and it was time for Gendor to pay for his crime.

Lorica leaned against the railing and sighed, her thoughts shifting to the man who'd displayed such magic in Ilumidora. A smile spread on her face, barely visible beneath her cowl, and she faced east.

"I saw someone today," she said. "I think you would have liked him, even if he was not a weaver. He had magic I've never seen . . . and he was very attractive."

She chuckled lightly as she imagined Zenif's voice, his deep tone that inspired trust. Whenever she favored another, Zenif would be there to interrogate him. Although he'd chosen to be a weaver, he had the air of a warrior and could intimidate even hardened soldiers with merely a glance.

A flicker of movement caught her attention and she whirled, her sword appearing in her hands. But the figure that stepped out of the shadows was dressed in dark, supple armor and a matching cloak. When she removed her cowl, the features looking back at her were similar to her own.

"Sister," Loralyn said, her tone amused. "I, too, would like to hear about the man you met."

Chapter 6: Sister

"Lyn," she said, stepping forward to embrace her sister. "How did you know I'd be here?"

"You always visit Zenif's hall before you return to the guild."

"I miss him," she said.

"As do I," Loralyn said softly.

She leaned against the frame, and neither made a motion to cross the threshold. A drunken man wandered towards them, but he gave them a wide berth, as if sensing the lethality to the two assassins.

"Have you ever wondered what it would be like if he hadn't been killed?" Loralyn asked.

"He'd be a father first, and a weaver second," Lorica said. "We both know that."

Lorica looked away, her thoughts drifting to the night he'd been killed. He'd journeyed to the castle to make a delivery, a task for an apprentice, yet he'd wanted to see his two younger sisters in the guard. None of them had known that someone had taken a contract on a captain of the guard. Unarmed, Zenif had tried to stop the attacker, and paid for the attempt with his life.

In the home adjacent to the hall, a child coughed, and a light orb glowed to life. Through the open window, a woman appeared at his bedside, singing the young one back to sleep. From the darkness, the two assassins watched the woman until the child stilled, and then the light orb was extinguished.

"The boy has Zenif's eyes," Loralyn said.

"And by all accounts, his skill with a loom."

Loralyn laughed softly. "Remember when he told father he wanted to be a weaver?"

Lorica smiled. "I'd never seen father so angry. The oldest son of a high captain, opting to join the weaver guild instead of the army."

"Mother would have been proud," Loralyn said.

It was a reminder that, of their family, only the two of them remained, two sister assassins. Lorica had always thought Zenif would outlive them, probably by decades, yet he had fallen to an assassin's blade.

"Irenae invited us to dinner," Loralyn said. "She wants us to meet his son."

"You know our oath," Lorica said. "We do not cross the threshold until justice has been satisfied."

"Are we certain it is Gendor?"

Lorica patted the bag. "I have gathered everything. We can confront him at the council."

"That is not the purpose of the council," she said.

Lorica frowned and turned to her. "What do mean?"

"The krey have returned to Lumineia," Loralyn said.

"The ancient race?" Lorica asked in surprise. "Why?"

Lorica knew little of the krey but understood that the ancient race had been absent since the Dawn of Magic. Why had they returned? And why now? More importantly, how would it affect her hunt for Gendor?

"I do not know why they are here," Loralyn said. "But the council must decide a course of action."

"What about Gendor?" Lorica asked. "We spent years joining the Assassin's Guild, and searching its ranks, all to find Gendor. It is our oath."

"That was until I became Guildmaster," Loralyn said.

Lorica's voice gained an edge. "Surely you would not put your office above our oath. Assassins are only supposed to kill the target, and only when the target deserves death. After finally joining the guild, that was the first lesson we learned. Gendor broke his oath to the guild, and no one can punish him. No king or army can strike at the Assassin's Guild, because we are judge and executioner."

"There are things you do not understand, sister."

"I understand that Zenif's blood cries to me," Lorica hissed. "And if you were listening, you would hear it as well."

"I never stopped listening," Loralyn said, heat creeping into her voice. "I just hear more than you do."

"Like what?" Lorica demanded. "We became assassins to hunt Zenif's killer, not to actually be assassins."

"You can't tell me you don't like the craft," she said. "You *like* being the Angel."

Lorica frowned but could not deny it. "Before, we killed for the king. Now we kill those that deserve it—those that no judge can touch."

"The people love you, the nobles fear you. I may be the guildmaster, but it is the Angel of Death they know."

"Yet Gendor eludes us."

"Only because we were not certain."

"I am certain now," Lorica said. "We *know* he has taken contracts outside the guild. He even sent someone after the Hauntress."

"Many fear the Hauntress," Loralyn said. "And for good reason. She's more lethal than we are."

"She does not kill innocents," Lorica said. "Just like us."

"But why would Gendor do this?" Loralyn asked. "Why accept outside contracts? Why kill so many?"

"I think he's building a rival guild."

Loralyn swiveled to face her, surprise on her features. Lorica smiled, pleased she'd managed to reveal a truth her sister did not already know. As guildmaster, Loralyn had access to archives that none within the guild possessed, and it had been some time since Loralyn had shown such surprise.

"That's a serious accusation."

"I've seen him gathering with strange groups," Lorica said, withdrawing the memory orbs from her pouch. "They have the look of killers but lack the restraint of our guild."

"You get all that from their eyes?"

Lorica frowned. "Do not pretend otherwise. We both know the cost of a kill."

A dog barked and the home adjacent to the weaver hall lit up again. Lorica and Loralyn retreated from the fence, into the shadows next to a bakery. Wreathed in darkness and the scents of bread, Lorica watched Irenae exit with a small dog, the animal leaping about, tugging at the rope attached to his neck.

"I didn't know she'd gotten a pet," Lorica said, her voice quiet.

"For the boy." Loralyn smiled when the woman cursed. "I think she's begun to regret the choice."

The dog leapt about, clearly eager to play, while the woman sought to calm him until he could relieve himself. Lorica's smile was sad, and she wished it was her and her sister playing with the puppy, and the child that had yet to meet his aunts.

"How does she feel about our occupation?"

"She does not understand," Loralyn said softly. "But she keeps the truth to herself. The Assassin's Guild has its share of enemies, and if they knew her connection to us, she would be in danger."

Lorica scowled, her eyes flicking to the empty streets. "Gendor would not hesitate to kill them if he knew their identity."

The dog completed his business and bounded back inside, followed by the weary woman. Lorica watched them go with regret in her heart. Seeing Zenif's wife and son reminded her of her own youth, of playing with Zen and Lyn in the yard, of fighting with sticks. Even then, Zenif was more interested in cloth and textiles, and hated it when any of them muddied new clothing.

"Do you have any idea how much effort went into that thread?" he'd asked when Lorica returned from swimming in a muddy river.

Lorica looked down at her dirty and stained tunic and shrugged. "It's just a tunic."

The ensuing scuffle had left the tunic torn and bloodied, a fact that did not help Lorica's claim of innocence to their mother. She smiled at the memory, and the familiar ache of losing Zenif tightened in her chest. The door to his house shut and the light once again extinguished.

"Tell me about Gendor," Loralyn said.

"I've been following him."

Loralyn frowned. "I know we want justice, but if he had caught you . . ."

"Have more faith in your little sister," Lorica said. "I kept my distance, gathering memories from witnesses. Most of them didn't know much, but then I found a survivor."

She withdrew the memory orb and handed it to her sister. Loralyn activated the memory and the ball glowed to life, an image appearing within, showing a darkened stairwell. The memory was of a soldier standing guard. Clearly bored, he fidgeted and muttered to himself, until abruptly he crumpled to the floor, staring down at the blade protruding from his chest.

The blade was yanked out and the vision faded, the image failing to display the groan of the dying man. A shadowy figure appeared above, and then another, both flitting past his sight. Each glanced down, revealing silver masks and dark cloaks. Then Gendor appeared and knelt to examine the dying man. A faint smile appeared on his lips before he stood and strode away. For several seconds the image grew darker, the dying man's life fading. Then Lorica appeared, her expression intense, her words a silent request to keep the memory. Lorica held aloft a small purple orb and the man managed to touch it. Then the man relaxed in death, his vision showing the banner of Griffin on the wall.

"That looks like the king's castle," Loralyn said, a scowl on her face. "Who did he kill?"

"Just the guard," Lorica said. "They left the bloody sword next to the king, and a nick on the prince's arm."

"A warning," Loralyn said. "But why?"

"I assume Gendor wants the king to know he can be killed," Lorica said.

"And his companions?"

"I do not know," Lorica said. "But I spotted him in Ilumidora before he met with the guildmaster of the Thieves Guild."

"The Thieves Guild may be at war with the Ravens," Loralyn said. "I doubt he is seeking an alliance with the guild, but maybe the guildmaster wanted to take a contract on the Ravens."

Lorica had not thought of that, but she forged ahead. "Whoever his companions are, they are lethal. I managed to follow one to the dwarven kingdom, where he infiltrated and killed the wife of a clan prince."

Loralyn was silent, her expression hard and calculating. "We must tread carefully, sister."

"Why?" Lorica asked. "You've already summoned a council. Let us challenge him and claim our vengeance."

"And what about his companions?" Lorica asked, turning to face her. "What if he has trained more?"

She snorted derisively. "He is not one who trains."

Loralyn cocked her head to the side. "Indeed. He is one who controls. But the greater question is, how have we not noticed his followers?"

"I've seen two of the cockroaches," Lorica said.

"Where there is one . . ."

"There are more," Lorica said. "So tomorrow?"

Loralyn regarded her for several moments, and Lorica held her breath. After a decade of waiting, plotting, hunting, she sensed the moment had come, and desperately wanted to demand the truth from Gendor, and then kill him.

"Tomorrow," Loralyn said with a nod. "If the moment comes that I can confront him, I will do so."

"Finally," Lorica said.

"But be warned," Loralyn said, a small smile on her face at Lorica's anticipation. "He has friends among the council, and they will not handle a challenge well."

"Rest easy," Lorica said, her smile wide. "Tomorrow we kill Zenif's killer."

Her eyes returned to the weaver hall, and the home at its side. She wanted her family unified, not broken and alone. She wanted to see her nephew, to teach him a blade, to see him become like Zenif. Only Gendor stood in the way.

Until tomorrow.

Chapter 7: The Unspoken

Shadow took his journey west, across the plains of Talinor toward Keese. Instead of flying at night, he visited the taverns and inns, blending into the shadows in order to listen. When possible, he asked those with influence regarding the Order of Ancients. Few answered, but Shadow followed them afterward, and from their subsequent conversations he learned a great deal.

By the time he was passing Herosian he'd begun to discover the truth. The Order of Ancients had apparently been around for ages, but their hopes for a return of the ancient race were disregarded by most. After the Mage Wars, someone had united the various factions of the Order, and the Order had seen a significant rise afterword. Despite their gathering strength, the Order had quietly drifted into obscurity. Until now.

Shadow spoke to one man in Herosian, a minor Lord too into his drink to notice the questioning. He didn't give any answers to Shadow, and actually had him thrown from the tavern. But Shadow crept back inside, and from the darkness, listened to the man's boasts. When he'd learned all he could, Shadow cut the wood beneath his chair, so that when the man went to rise, he fell on his backside. Smiling to himself, Shadow departed, and pondered what he'd learned about the Order and its connection to the Bloodsworn.

He'd heard one of the killers in the Thieves Guild say the name, but the term was new to him. Unlike the Order, the Bloodsworn had only existed for a short time. At first, Shadow heard only rumors, until he found a man in a small village a day's ride from Herosian. There he overheard a captain in the Talinorian army talking of an absence of mercenary killers. Overnight, hundreds had simply disappeared from the cities of Talinor. The captain assumed they had moved on, but Shadow got a different impression.

They had been gathered.

On impulse, Shadow turned aside from Keese and returned to Herosian, this time at night. The moon was too bright for a dragon, so he cast a tigron, and rode the great cat across the plains, arriving well before dawn.

Shadow forewent the closed gates and sent a thread of shadow up the outer wall. Dismissing the tigron, he ascended the wall to the battlements and crept across the parapet. Two soldiers stood talking nearby, while a third, a woman, stood a short distance apart.

"Why won't you come to the tavern with me?" one of the two men said, leering. "I can show you a good evening."

"I already said no," the woman replied.

"What about me?" the second man said arrogantly. "Too pretty for us?"

Shadow paused and crept up behind the two men, who had taken a step toward the woman. With great care, Shadow attached a thread of darkness to the boots of the men, and then tossed it over a pole of a banner. From there he attached it to a heavy stone intended for repairing a section of the wall.

One of the men reached for the woman's shoulder, calling her by name, and the woman flinched away. Shadow took that moment to kick the stone from the battlements. The two men yelped as they were flipped upside down and knocked into the wall, their helmets striking the stone. Their cries of surprise went silent and their bodies slacked in unconsciousness.

The woman turned to find Shadow at her side, and her eyes flicked to the two unconscious men. "You're not supposed to be up here," she said, a small smile on her face.

"My apologies," Shadow said. "I noticed some insects that needed squashing."

She smiled and then suppressed it. "I can take care of myself."

"Perhaps it was I that was uneasy," Shadow said.

The woman laughed. "Who are you?"

"Shadow."

"That's not a name."

"That's what they call me," Shadow said.

"Well, they call me Indra."

"Did the beauty come with the name?"

She grunted and pointed to the two men. "You're as bad as they are."

"You wound me," Shadow said, feigning indignation. "I'm much better at it than they are."

She laughed and motioned to him. "I live in the sixth ring, north side, by the Ram's Horn Inn."

"Is that an invitation?"

"Maybe," she said.

He grinned and walked toward the back of the parapet, and then impulsively turned. "Do you know anything about the Bloodsworn?"

"A dangerous question," the woman said, her smile fading.

"So you know about them?"

"We are told not to ask."

He frowned. "They are a threat against the people. Surely the guard have been informed of them."

"The Bloodsworn are a mystery," she said, glancing about as if merely speaking their name would invite retaliation. "But all the guard know the truth. In the last three decades men and women have gone missing, disappearing without a hint as to their fate."

"And you think it's the Bloodsworn?"

"The taken have one thing in common," she said. "They were those that spoke against the Order of Ancients."

"That's the second time I've heard of a connection between the Order of Ancients and the Bloodsworn," Shadow said.

"We are told not to investigate the disappearances."

Shadow looked to the city sprawled out beneath them—the seven circles progressively smaller until the castle at the heart of the city. It seemed impossible that word of the Order and the Bloodsworn had escaped Elenyr's notice and the notice of the other fragments. After spending so much time among the people, they knew a great deal, but the Order's gift for silence had kept the truth from reaching even the fragment's ears.

Such an effort to keep a truth hidden implied intent, but who did they want to keep the secret from? If the city guard were being instructed not to investigate, someone high in the kingdom was involved, a general, a prince, or even King Porlin.

Shadow frowned when a flicker of suspicion crept into his thoughts. The Order and the Bloodsworn behaved like they were afraid of discovery, but who did they fear? If not the wrath of kings, who was more dangerous?

Draeken.

The thought came quickly, and Shadow sensed its truth. The ancients may have returned to Lumineia recently, but the Order had set themselves against Elenyr and Draeken's fragments long before. The only question was why.

"You have been most helpful," he said, inclining his head.

"Speaking their name will invite reprisal," she warned.

"Perhaps that is exactly what I seek." He stepped to the edge of the battlements.

"Will I see you again?"

"If you're lucky."

She snorted in amusement and he stepped free. Catching the shadows on the wall, he slowed his momentum and dropped to the ground below, his thoughts already shifting to the Bloodsworn.

It was late, but not so late that the taverns were empty. Curious to exploit what he'd learned from Indra, he made his way to a group of taverns in the sixth ring, an area known for being frequented by soldiers.

He paused at a guard tower and cast a line of shadow to a window, using it to slip inside. Several beds were in the room, and he retrieved a guard uniform from a chest next to one. Then he fastened a web of shadows across both men's faces, so that when they awoke, it would feel like they had a spider on their noses. Smiling to himself, he slipped outside and dropped to the earth to don the persona.

He entered a tavern called *The Dented Helm* and settled at a table with a group of officers. Slurring his speech, he demanded answers about the killers that murdered his father. One of the officers looked at him with disdain.

"And who killed him?"

"The Bloodsworn."

The word echoed in the suddenly quiet room, and several officers recoiled, a trace of fear on their faces. Others at nearby tables stood and ambled out, as if the mere mention of the Bloodsworn would invite retribution to all present.

"Hold your tongue, man," one officer hissed. "You know our orders."

"They killed my father," Shadow yelled, and stumbled to the door. "I mean to find them and show them the edge of my blade!"

They retreated from him like he had a ravenous plague, and Shadow disappeared into the alley. When he was out of sight, he straightened and a smile appeared on his face. At the next tavern he repeated the performance, and then the third, where he was unceremoniously tossed into the street.

Shadow rose to his feet and brushed the dirt from his trousers, and then retreated into the darkness next to a shuttered brickmaker's shop.

From there he scaled to the roof and chose a perch that gave a view of the three taverns.

As he waited, he cast a ball of shadow and tossed it into the air, morphing it into a spinning blade. Catching it, he sent it twirling again, the deadly dagger spinning through his fingers like a coin.

Time slipped by and Shadow grew bored, his thoughts drifting to Indra. The woman was interesting, and he found her courage appealing. She'd been surprisingly forthright with information, making him wonder what she would do if he arrived at the end of her watch. Just as he began considering returning to Indra's post, he spotted a knot of shadowy figures appearing at the end of the street.

Four in number, they strode with purpose, obviously headed toward the castle. Another appeared from the darkness, and then another. Soon there were a dozen. Shadow frowned. He'd kicked a beehive, but this many was unnecessary.

Then a new figure appeared, one of the soldiers that had been present in *The Dented Helm*. Wringing his hands and twitching, the man darted into the street and whispered to the leader of the group. Too far away to hear the entire conversation, Shadow heard enough to realize the man was an informant, so Shadow slipped to the adjacent roof to listen.

"We have other business this night," the leader said, his voice deep, hard.

"Will I still receive my payment?"

The silence was deafening, and the man scurried away. Shadow expected the men to laugh, but their discipline did not waver. When the informant was gone, another of the cloaked figures stepped closer to the leader and lowered his voice.

"We cannot afford to let the guards speak without repercussion."

"Secrecy is our weapon," another intoned, her cowled head bobbing.

The leader motioned to the tavern. "Be quick about it. The council has already begun, and we must meet with the others."

The man nodded and separated himself from the group. He entered the tavern, and for the second time that night, the patrons fell silent. A moment later he exited and followed Shadow's track to the other two taverns. The rest of the Bloodsworn continued to advance down the street, where they met the seeker.

"Your blade is dry," the leader said, his tone disapproving.

"The man has departed," the seeker said, bowing his head in apology.

"Probably sleeping in a ditch somewhere," a woman said.

"We'll kill him after our work with the council is complete," the leader said. "We have waited decades for this moment. We shall not turn aside."

The group fell into step and worked their way down the street, their path taking them into an abandoned warehouse, where a secret entrance in the basement permitted entry into a network of tunnels. Their robes whispered against the stone, sending rats scurrying away in fear, all the while, a flicker of movement appeared at the back of their number. As the Bloodsworn made their way toward their target, a new figure had joined the group, his cloak not made of cloth, but of shadows . . .

Chapter 8: A Fallen Guild

Shadow followed the Bloodsworn into the underbelly of the city. They were all cloaked and cowled, their gait purposeful. Shadow wanted to listen, but none spoke, and there was an air of stillness about them, of killers approaching their prey.

An abandoned sewer, the tunnel curved downward without fork or turn, gradually descending into the earth. Occasional light orbs provided illumination, and Shadow made certain to keep one of the Bloodsworn between him and the light, which would rob his cloak of solidity, and strip him of anonymity.

He drifted among them, allowing the shift of position to grant him access to their ranks, where he used the proximity to learn about his foes. As the cloaks parted, he caught glimpses of matching warrior garb, with many bearing the hallmarks of battlemages.

One was a light mage, his sword hilt glimmering with enchantments. Another carried a small crossbow, the bolts marked with the symbols of fire. The handle was unique and hand-crafted, suggesting the woman had built and enchanted it herself. Oddly, all were human, and he wondered if the Bloodsworn did not like the other races.

The group slowed, and Shadow drifted to the back, melting into the darkness of the tunnel. At the lead, the man reached into his cloak and removed a silver mask, an unspoken order that the others followed.

The mask was solid, even over the eyes, suggesting light magic was threaded into the material so the wearer could see. The features of the mask were dispassionate and cold, the face of one with no fear, no compassion. It was the mask of one who wanted the victim to know their end had come.

"We are sworn to the spilling of blood," he said.

"For the ancients," the group intoned.

The leader nodded, and then turned the corner, leading the group into a giant cavern. Shadow stopped on the threshold, his gaze lifting to the massive space. Directly beneath the king's castle, the secret chamber was as large as the citadel above.

A small stream entered the chamber from one corner, feeding the lake that dominated the chamber. An island sat in the center of the lake. A giant statue, easily fifty feet tall, stood on a pedestal in the center, the warrior muscled and armored, its features visceral.

Seven towers ringed the pedestal, each bearing a single flag that faced the statue. Shadow realized the number, and recalled Elenyr describing a location with seven towers, the refuge of the Assassin's Guild. He frowned as he recalled Gendor telling Seth of a summons to an assassin council.

Shadow noticed a light coming from the base of the statue and peered at the opening. Then he realized that the footstool of the statue contained a room, likely a council room where the assassins could gather.

He stepped off the stairs and fell, casting a thread to slow his descent. As he dropped into the chamber, he spotted the group he'd followed lining up behind one of the towers, using it to hide their approach. Then Shadow noticed the others.

More Bloodsworn had entered the chamber from other entrances, and they surrounded the island, each group gathering behind the towers, many joining the group Shadow had followed. As shouts came from within the council room, Shadow heard the distinct sound of a blade being drawn.

Shadow dropped to the base of the bridge and sprinted across in shadow form, little more than a streak of darkness. He reached the group and came to a halt, just as the Bloodsworn charged into the open—only to be met by two newcomers.

Fire and Mind.

Shadow came to a halt when he spotted his fragment brothers barring the entrance, battling the horde of Bloodsworn. Fire cast a pack of moordraugs out of fire. At ten feet tall, the beasts had circular jaws with teeth all the way down their throats. The fearsome entities charged, swallowing cloaked figures like they were an afternoon meal.

Mind had his sword in hand, and fought with unparalleled skill, his blade deflecting sword and arrow, magic and might, weaving a pattern of death against the killers that sought to get past him. He knocked a spear high and then spun beneath the shaft, snapping the wood and catching the remainder before hurtling it at the wielder. The woman ducked, and spun—into Mind's next strike, his sword piercing her frame even as another fell, the broken spear having entered his heart. Their bodies hit the ground in unison.

Despite the skill of Mind and Fire, Bloodsworn leaked through the opening, entering a chamber where the sounds of battle echoed. But if Elenyr was absent outside, that meant she was likely inside.

Shadow came to a stop, his eyes sweeping the battlefield. He could dive into the fray, but with so much fire and light, he would be a liability to the other fragments. Or he could strike from the outside, giving them an advantage without their knowing it. The tactic appealed to him, so he ripped a cloak from a fallen Bloodsworn and swung it about his shoulders before diving into the midst of the attackers.

He had a blade in hand, and shouted like one in battle, but in the other hand he held a whip of shadow. A trio charged Fire's flank, and Shadow sent his weapon out, striking at their feet, making them stumble. Fire heard them hit the ground and whirled. He spotted the trio and smashed his hammer into the earth, blasting them all backward, their cloaks burning.

Shadow avoided a rampaging moordraug and kicked one of the Bloodsworn in the back, knocking him sprawling. Then he touched the curve of a bow, the arrow releasing and driving into the fallen man's back. The archer stared at the buried arrow in dismay, her distraction costing her dearly when a moordraug approached her from behind, its jaws closing above her frame, her scream lost in the din.

Shadow smiled and joined a troll that had a floating bow above his head. The weapon had two arcs, and it fired on its own, suggesting a sentient weapon. The troll caught the jaws of a moordraug with his hammer and held it open, allowing the bow to fire a bolt down its throat. The bolt exploded inside, sending smoke and cinders out the now slack jaws. The moordraug detonated, sending fire and smoke blasting outward.

Shadow used the smoke to leap into the air and catch the floating bow, dragging it to the earth. It struggled so he released, and the bow leapt into the smoke, whirling to take aim at him. It fired three bolts, each passing through the shadows he'd created to impact groups of Bloodsworn, knocking cloaked bodies flying.

The troll scowled and the crossbow turned about as if hunting. Before Shadow could be spotted, he blended into a group charging Mind's flank. He cast a handful of long daggers, and sent them spinning into the cloaks, pinning them to the ground. The leader was yanked backwards, while others merely stumbled, their cloaks tearing. Mind stabbed the first in the chest and then kicked him into the others, knocking them all sprawling.

Another figure burst from the interior, followed by a dwarf. They were not dressed as Bloodsworn but they joined them regardless, and Shadow recognized Gendor and Thorg, an assassin known as the Dark Dwarf. The man and his companion spun, barking orders for the Bloodsworn to close ranks. As the last of the moordraugs disintegrated, the Bloodsworn gathered. Then Elenyr and two female assassins joined Fire and Mind at the chamber's threshold.

With the conflict now stilled, Shadow realized he was at risk, so he slipped backward, working his way out of the circle of Bloodsworn assassins. He paused in his retreat when he noticed a trio of Bloodsworn rushing around the pedestal. On impulse, he turned to follow.

As Gendor gathered his ranks, the three Bloodsworn dropped small spheres onto the ground, each pulsing a red dot. Spaced out around the giant statue's pedestal, it was obviously an attack, but what did they intend?

Shadow shrugged as he realized it didn't matter and began collecting the spheres. He gathered seven before shouts of alarm came from the front, and then he attached the seven spheres onto shadow squirrels. The little rodents skittered into the mass of Bloodsworn. Shadow slipped to the corner of the council chamber and listened to the conversation.

"Your army will die with you," Loralyn snarled.

Gendor released a mocking laugh. "Only two of you remain. And even with the Hauntress, you cannot stop me, or the master I serve."

"Do you ever stop talking?" Fire wiped the blood from a cut on his cheek, flames licking at his fingers. Shadow stifled a laugh, grateful for Fire's belligerence.

Gendor glowered at Fire and raised his hand to reveal a small, spherical object. He touched a rune on its surface and it glowed to life. Then he tossed it toward Elenyr, his sneer one of disdain. Gendor and his Bloodsworn retreated, the soldiers tossing other spheres onto the ground around the council chamber. They all glowed into life, growing brighter by the second.

"You are a relic from a dead age, Hauntress," Gendor said. "And it's only fitting you die by another ancient weapon."

"Go!" Elenyr barked. "Inside!"

The group sprinted into the council chamber and Fire summoned a wall of flames, closing off the doors and forming a barricade. Shadow retreated, darting away from the council chamber and the strange glowing spheres.

Shadow had given himself plenty of space, or so he'd thought. The explosions rent through stone, sending Shadow tumbling between two towers and into the water. Dazed, he clawed his way to the bank and watched the Bloodsworn stumbling to their feet, confused and angry at the craters in their midst, those caused by his shadow squirrels.

Then a great groan echoed in the cavern, and Shadow looked up to see the Titan teetering. In a creaking of stone, it tilted to the side and fell, crashing into the outer wall and sliding into the lake. Water fountained upward before settling, revealing the crushed pedestal. Where Elenyr and the fragments had been . . .

A rare sense of concern ignited in his heart, and Shadow scrambled forward. To his relief only a portion of the pedestal had caved in. The north side, the part where Shadow had removed the spheres, remained intact, while several craters were now visible in the space where the Bloodsworn had stood. With half his army dead, Gendor ordered the remaining Bloodsworn to depart, and the cloaked figures swept away.

Gendor surveyed the damage with a smile of triumph that Shadow yearned to erase. Torn between following and searching for Elenyr, Shadow watched the Bloodsworn leave. Then his choice was made for him when a grinding of dirt signified someone had survived. Shadow hurried to the edge of the fallen building. Elenyr, Mind, and Fire all emerged, as did two members of the Assassin's Guild, but the first carried the second.

The assassin laid the inert body on the ground, and then crumpled to her knees. Silent tears dripped down her cheeks, only visible to Shadow from his vantage point. The agony and rage were palpable on her features, and when she looked up, Shadow recognized her as Lorica, the Angel of Death.

"Sister." Lorica's voice was barely a whisper. She looked to Elenyr, her eyes desperate. "Do any of you have healing magic?"

"We do not," Mind said softly.

Lorica cradled her sister's head, and the dying woman reached up to clasp her hand. "You must rebuild the guild," Loralyn said. "The assassins must continue."

Shadow drifted as close as he dared, drawn to Lorica's grief. He'd seen many die, but the anguish on the assassin's features seemed to strike at his soul, and he could not tear his gaze from the dying woman.

"I can't do it without you." Tears dripped onto the fallen assassin's chest. "I'll get you to a healer. There's enough time."

Elenyr grimaced in helplessness, and Shadow realized there wasn't enough time. Loralyn would die, and her sister could only cling to her

69

final moments. Mind and Fire were also quiet, their silence a mark of respect that normally Shadow would have broken. But this time his desire for mischief had waned, and he disliked the strange ache in his chest.

Loralyn smiled up at her sister. "You have always been the strong one."

"That's not true and you know it," Lorica said.

"Rebuild the guild," Loralyn repeated, her voice fading.

"Gendor's guild is too strong," Lorica said.

"It is not the Bloodsworn you must fear," Lorica said, her eyes flicking to Elenyr. "It is his master. Be wary, for the Order of Ancients has risen . . ."

Loralyn's body relaxed in death, and Lorica screamed her rage, the primal sound reverberating in the chamber. Elenyr reached out and placed her hand on the woman's shoulder, but Lorica jerked free of Elenyr's grip.

"You must leave."

"We can help you against the Bloodsworn," Mind said.

"Your help got my sister killed."

Elenyr glanced to Mind, and Fire shook his head. Elenyr sighed and motioned them away, and the trio retreated to a bridge. Shadow watched them depart, uncertain if he should reveal himself or continue watching Lorica.

Shadow had intended on joining the other fragments, but then he realized they still had not acknowledged his presence, giving him a rare opportunity. As Elenyr and the other fragments disappeared into a tunnel, Shadow eased back into the darkness, and waited for Lorica to lift her sister into her arms and trudge away. In silence, Shadow fell into step behind her and followed her from the ruins.

70

Chapter 9: Trapped

The assassin carried the body of her sister to one of the seven towers, the one bearing the flag of the star. She eased the door open and entered, and Shadow slipped through the gap, darting into the rafters before the door shut. From his perch he watched Lorica gently lay her sister on the bed.

With great care Lorica positioned the body of her sister, laying her arms across her chest and putting her sword hilt in her hands. Then she brushed the dust off her clothes, a tear dropping into the dirt on the dead woman's tunic.

"I'm sorry, Lyn," she whispered. "It should have been me . . ."

The ache and anger in the voice cut Shadow to the soul, and he abruptly sought for a point of egress, unwilling to witness the assassin's grief. But there was no window in the tower, just a small bedchamber and a set of stairs rising out of view. Although spacious, the room contained few adornments, most of which were paintings. A easel sat in a corner with a partially completed canvas.

Lorica sank to the floor, her back against the bed containing her fallen sister. She stared into space, her eyes distant, broken. Perched on a beam in the corner, Shadow did not move, and wished he'd waited outside.

"First Zenif and now you," she murmured. "Both dead by the same man." Her voice had turned bitter, and anger briefly tightened her features. "You should have trusted me. I *knew* he was gathering a rival guild, but you had to adhere to the tenets of the guild."

Tears leaked from her eyes and she angrily brushed them away, and for several seconds there was silence. Bound in place, Shadow watched the hardened assassin cry. The woman had probably not shed a tear in decades. Although young, she had the look of a seasoned warrior, the hardness to the gaze that bespoke training and experience.

Her frame was equally as hardened, her arms muscular, but that strength was now absent. Shadow realized the woman was showing a piece of her soul that had been buried for much of her life.

"You've always watched out for me," she said, her voice distant. "Even when we were in training for the army. I remember that officer that tried to force himself upon me, and you dragged him into the night."

A quiet chuckle escaped her lips, the tone filled with admiration and regret. "You made me come to where you'd bound him to the stockade wall and stripped him to the waist. You told me you wouldn't always be there to protect me and handed me a sword. That's when you cut him loose."

"He nearly killed me," Lorica said softly. "And you just stood there, watching. I remember being so angry with you, but I turned that anger on him, until I stood over him as he wept, his blood on my blade. I was so angry I wanted to strike at you, but you smiled and told me you were proud of me. I cursed you then, but it was the last time I felt fear."

She sighed and wiped a hand over her face, as if the memory had suddenly become painful. Every time Lorica talked, her voice gained more control, her features turning more rigid. Shadow did not envy Gendor when she caught up to him.

"We were supposed to cross the threshold together," Lorica said, her voice distant. "But now you will never get the chance. Because of Gendor."

Her features hardened anew, and the window into her soul shut, the fragment of vulnerability sinking deep. Lorica rose to her feet and reached down to her sister's hand, removing the ring on her finger.

At first the ring appeared like an ordinary black jewel, but as Lorica slid it onto her finger, the surface of the jewel glowed, the symbol of the Assassin's Guild appearing, the light illuminating the stone and Lorica's rigid features.

"I know you would want me to rebuild the guild first," she said. "And I know that is the duty of the Guildmaster, but I don't care. I'm going after Gendor first."

Lorica looked away, as if she could no longer bear to see her sister's body, and Shadow thought she might cry again. But the tears were gone, and it was obvious Lorica struggled with saying goodbye.

"I will kill him," Lorica said. "For the guild. For you. And for Zenif."

Lorica leaned down and kissed her sister's forehead, and then trudged to the door. She lingered on the threshold before casting a final look at her dead sister. Then she reached up and tapped her ring on the stone above the door.

A rune glowed to life, and Shadow's eyes widened. The rune was a type of fire rune, a trio of sharp lines extending upward from a single center, all red, all growing brighter. It was a warning for a single type of charm.

A detonation spell.

Shadow dropped to the ground and stepped into Lorica's shadow as she stepped through the door. Following an assassin so closely was a quick way to lose one's head. Even silent and in shadow form, he knew he would be caught if Lorica was not distracted, but he wanted to see what the assassin would do next.

Lorica made her way to the second tower and touched a second rune before moving to the third. At the first opportunity, Shadow slipped to the shadows next to the destroyed council chamber and watched from there, his eyes on the assassin.

The woman made her way to each of the towers except one, activating identical runes on all. Then she retreated to the center council chamber, coming to a halt just feet from Shadow's hide. He retreated deeper into the darkness between two fallen stones and waited.

She stood silent, but anger and grief wafted off her frame. When red lines of light appeared in the towers she did not turn, even when the light brightened, rising to the point of blinding. Shadow shielded his eyes as an ominous whine came from the towers.

The detonation ripped the stones asunder, fire engulfing the breadth of the first tower and spilling to the sides. It swallowed the paintings, the furniture, and Loralyn's body. White fires devoured the tower, the stones shattering into chunks of rock that flew in all directions, some sizzling into the lake beyond. For an instant the fire raged, and then the second tower detonated.

Shadow flinched as the tower erupted, the stones also disintegrating, the flames ripping through beam and support to rend the tower to ruins. It collapsed from the strain, landing on its side in a plume of sparks and fire.

The third detonated, and then the fourth, each expanding the wall of fire around the island. Shadow's hiding place quickly evaporated as the flames extinguished the darkness in the cavern, and he was forced to retreat deeper into the fallen stones of the council chamber.

Even a hundred feet away, Shadow felt the heat as the fifth and sixth towers shattered. The ring of fire was nearly complete, with only the seventh tower remaining intact. The banner flapped in the gust of fire-heated air, the symbol of an angel.

The woman stood in place, watching her world burn. Then she took a step towards her own tower—before drawing her blade and spinning to face Shadow. Before he could blink, he found her blade on his throat.

Trapped by the stones, Shadow leapt high, but she swept her free hand, sending a ball of pure black to strike his chest. Chains of anti-magic burst from the sphere and expanded around his body, binding his legs and arms, sending him crashing onto the rubble.

She stepped forward and caught the chain at his shoulder. Without a word, she turned and dragged him toward the final tower. Shadow struggled in his bonds but the anti-magic proved impervious, so he resorted to diplomacy.

"I'm not with the Bloodsworn."

Silence.

"I serve the Hauntress," he continued. "I do not stand with Gendor."

Still silence.

She dragged him across the stones like he was nothing more than a sack of flower, her strength intimidating yet admirable. Shadow continued to speak his cause, all the while he worked at the bonds, managing to get a hand free of the chains.

She dragged him to her tower and tossed him on the floor. The interior resembled her sister's, albeit with even more weaponry. They also contained a pair of great wings, the feathers ornamental, yet unfinished. Then he noticed that each contained a name, and realized it was the list of her kills.

"Is that the Duke of Summerfell?" he asked, using his chin to point at the newest addition.

Lorica was standing at the wall. She drew her sword and placed it in a large stone chest against the wall. One by one she retrieved the other weapons and placed them in the chest, the daggers and swords disappearing until only one blade remained, a sword of blood red.

"Word was he beat a farmer's daughter six months past," Shadow said. "And rumor had it she was far from the first. I wager he incited the ire of one with coin to issue an assassin contract."

She gently lifted the red blade down from the wall and examined the dark metal. It was a sword meant for claiming a single life. To don it was a promise, an oath of revenge. She slid the sword into her scabbard, the sound of scraping steel a chilling proclamation, a death knell for Gendor.

"I heard he died in his bed, with a hundred guards in his castle, all untouched. They claimed his heart gave in to age. How did you do it?"

She lowered the last of the supplies and placed everything in the stone chest, stripping the walls of everything of value. She briefly disappeared up the stairs and returned with more weapons. She placed everything in the stone chest, until the tower lay barren.

"I've seen the duke's castle," Shadow said. "Your infiltration skills are impressive. Did you use poison? One not known to the healers?"

She added the last of the items, and then stepped to the wings on the wall. From a small wooden box, she collected two feathers. One she inscribed with Gendor's name, adding it to the wings. Then she took another and tossed it to Shadow, where it settled on the floor. As Shadow stared at the feather, she lowered the lid of the chest. She stepped to the door and reached for the detonation rune, and Shadow called out to her.

"I am not your foe," Shadow said.

She finally met his gaze. "I don't care."

She slammed her palm onto the rune and then stepped outside, the door shutting behind her. From the inside, the rune glowed to life, sending threads of heat into explosive charms embedded in the stones. They spread, arcing from one to another until they had all been ignited. As Shadow struggled against his bonds they glowed to life, growing ever brighter.

Outside, Lorica departed the assassin refuge, her wings carrying her over the fire and billowing smoke to reach an exit. She did not look back when the charms reached their pinnacle, and the final tower detonated, exploding into broken stone and raging fire.

Chapter 10: Shadow's Request

The tower burst into flames, the stones shattering, the interior filling with fire and ash, cinders and smoke. The door burst apart, the burning fragments of wood clattering into the courtyard still littered with dead Bloodsworn.

The tower crumbled and collapsed, falling onto the first level, piling onto the couches and walls, burning the feathers to ash, the names flitting away. Only one feather remained, the feather enchanted to endure the flames, the one bearing Gendor's name. The feather fell and swirled one way and then another, the heat brushing it across the room and back, before it gently landed on the stone chest, remaining there as the fires consumed the beams.

With little wood to fuel its hunger, the fire burned low, until only the wooden supports continued to blaze, the stones blackened and scorched. From inside the stone chest, a dull clanking sounded, and then the lid shifted. The feather slid across the surface as the lid lifted, and a hand appeared.

Still bound in anti-magic bonds, Shadow rolled from the chest and fell to the scorched ground. He coughed at the lingering smoke and then began to laugh. He withdrew a dagger he'd found in the chest and finished cutting his bonds. Then he stood and discarded the anti-magic bonds.

"Well played," he murmured as he looked to the devastated assassin stronghold.

He picked his way through the broken tower and exited the ruined island. He crossed a bridge and ascended the stairs to the exit where he'd entered. From there he paused and looked back upon the secret refuge.

Smoke still climbed from the seven towers, obscuring the view of the fallen Titan. The waters, once clear, were now filled with broken stones, and ash darkened the pristine lake. In the midst of the fallen refuge, the bodies of the dead also burned, the vestiges of the Assassin's Guild gone. Except for Lorica.

He turned away and departed the fallen refuge, hurrying down the tunnel. Lorica had sought to kill him, but he found the woman intriguing, her passion as commanding as her prowess. He wondered if the woman would survive, for she was about to hunt Gendor until he died, or she did.

He reached the end of the corridor and escaped outside, leaving through an abandoned inn in the sixth circle. It was night, but the remnants of sunrise touched the horizon, the colors nearly swallowed by the ominous clouds.

The streets were filled with people. Merchants called out, hoping to sell their wares before the coming deluge. Bakers rushed to return their goods to the shelves, while patrons completed their purchases and departed, their pace hurried. Lightning crackled in the distance and thunder rumbled, hastening their steps.

Shadow ascended to the top of the abandoned inn, the roof tiles creaking with his passage. When he reached the top he drew on the growing shadows and cast a compass, the needle of which pointed north.

He frowned. He'd expected Lorica to have departed west, toward Keese. Instead, it directed north and east, deeper into Herosian. When she'd left, she'd been intent on seeking Gendor, so what gave her pause?

He hesitated and looked west, torn between following Lorica and continuing to the Ravens Guild for the ancient map. The assassin could be a powerful ally, but Shadow preferred to work alone. Shrugging, he took a step away from Lorica before Elenyr's words returned.

Again he hesitated, and considered the possibility that on this assignment, it would be better to have such an ally. He was also curious, and ultimately he turned after Lorica, deciding that if she proved too much of a bore, he would just disappear.

Shadow dropped into the streets and followed the compass, passing though knots of rushed patrons. His pace was unhurried, and he ignored the surrounding haste, even as drops of rain passed through his compass and splattered on his boots.

The compass led him through the fifth ring and back to the sixth. The streets emptied as he walked, and windows were shuttered. For a long moment the street was silent, and then the storm broke, sheets of rain battering the city, sluicing off Shadow's cloak and filling the gutters that lined the road.

The needle wavered and he frowned, for the first time accelerating his step. He turned several corners, ignoring the patches of darkness for the sheets of rain that obscured his path. When the needle began to point downward, he slowed and drifted to an overhanging roof, where he shook the rain from his cloak. Then he eased to the corner and peered down the street.

He stood at the end of the road, the view of a weaver hall and home. Light orbs were visible through the windows, while the weavers continued to labor on their looms. Outside, the street was devoid of life, except for a cloaked figure standing in the shadows of a neighboring structure.

Shadow watched Lorica observe the weaver hall, confused and intrigued. Why would the assassin come here instead of going after Gendor? What would give the assassin such pause? Then Lorica began to speak and Shadow drifted close.

"I'm sorry, Zenif," she said, her voice distant. "Please tell Lyn I'm sorry."

"Who's Zenif?"

She whirled, her red blade at his throat. Shadow remained in place, leaning against the wall. The woman glared at him, the blade so close that Shadow could see the blood channels in the red steel.

"Do you seek death?"

"You already tried that," Shadow said, his lips twitching with amusement.

"How did you find me?"

Shadow motioned to her boot, but she didn't take the bait. He chuckled lightly. "Your caution is admirable, but this is not a ruse."

She scowled, and then glanced to her boot. Her scowl deepened and she kicked the wall, dislodging the small rune of shadow attached to her ankle. The brand rolled into the rain and disintegrated.

"You branded me when I was about to kill you?" she asked.

Her tone was incredulous. But there was also anger and rage, the fury of one whose home had been violated by an intruder. She wanted to kill him, and only curiosity held her in check.

"Who's Zenif?" he asked.

She leaned in and put the tip of her blade on his throat, her lips curling with hatred. "You are indeed a—"

He faded to his shadow form and slipped along the wall. Her eyes widened in shock, and then she spun to strike, but he darted through a window into the warehouse. She followed with agility that matched his own and pursued him to the open space inside the warehouse.

"Who's Zenif?" he asked.

"Do you know who I am?" she asked, her voice soft and dangerous.

"The Angel of Death," he said, and then offered a smirk and a bow. "It's truly a pleasure."

"You *dare* to mock me after witnessing what I have endured?"

She darted in, her sword swinging for his heart. Shadow drew his own dagger, the short blade deflecting her sword wide. He stepped to a stack of barrels and raced up the wall, flipping over her and landing behind. She did the same, but her cloak flared outward and the wings allowed her to swoop wide, before she dropped like a hawk.

He retreated, racing backwards up a stack of barrels as if it was flat ground, the shadows of his boots bonding to the shadows on the wood. Again surprise flickered across her features, and Shadow used the momentary hesitation to cast his own wings out of darkness, the dark material allowing him to soar above the assassin.

She deflected his strike and landed her own, the weapon bouncing off a second blade, this one appearing in his free hand. The new dagger carried a feather on the blade, and her eyes went wide as she saw the name.

"Is there nothing you will not desecrate?"

"Who's Zenif?"

She glared at him, her wings flaring as if sensing her anger. Then she charged, her blade whirling at him, seeming to come from all sides. He fought with both daggers, and the ring of steel echoed in the confines of the warehouse, blending with the sound of rain on the roof.

Shadow retreated, twisting and turning, avoiding the lethal blade by a hairsbreadth. He'd trained for thousands of years, yet in her found an equal. Of course, he'd skipped much of his training, especially in his early years, and he found a touch of regret.

"I'll cut that arrogant smile from your face," she growled.

"Forgive me," Shadow said, weaving into a collection of barrels before leaping above them. "My smile was one of chagrin, for I realize now how much Elenyr was right. I should have trained with more diligence."

"Your lie will not make me spare you." She bounded after him, and the two fought above the barrels.

"It will if you are wise," Shadow said. "Because you face an enemy you do not understand."

"Gendor?" she spat. "I've tracked him for a decade, yet you presume to know him better than I?"

"I know not the man," he said. "But I hunt who he serves."

"I do not believe you."

The menace had returned to her voice, and she slashed a rope binding several barrels. They collapsed and rolled across the floor, taking Shadow with them. He managed to keep his feet and cast a shadow whip that he sent into the rafters. A tug sent him soaring out of sight. She launched herself after him, her wings allowing her to gain height, joining him in the beams.

"Your guild is gone," Shadow said. "Your sister is dead, and you have no ally to speak of. To strike directly would be foolish."

"And *you're* going to help me?"

"No," he said, and then smiled. "*You're* going to help *me*."

A hint of amusement appeared in her gaze, but she quashed it with a scowl, and leapt eight feet, rebounding off a beam and catching another with her free hand, allowing her to swing around Shadow, forcing him closer to the wall.

Shadow brought his feet together and dropped, eluding her flashing blade. He flared his wings and alighted on a stack of barrels before leaping free. The light in the warehouse was dim but not dark, and he glided through the gloom to the floor. She followed, falling faster than he, and leaned into a strike that would plunge her sword through his back—but the weapon passed through his wings, cutting empty air.

From within a gap in the barrels behind her, Shadow flitted away, evading her gaze as she banked and landed hard, searching for where he'd escaped. Shadow phased to his elemental form and glided along the walls, circling.

"If the circumstances were different, I would not interrupt your quest for vengeance," he called, causing her to spin. "Or your mourning."

"You know nothing of mourning," she growled, her tone harsh.

"True," he said. "But that doesn't mean I'm wrong."

She spun, her blade pointed at him. His daggers sheathed, Shadow stood in the open, his arms wide, vulnerable. He waited for her to strike but she did not, and Shadow accepted the tiny opening.

82

"You know the Bloodsworn are dangerous," he said. "But they have connections to a greater threat, the Order of the Ancients. Both link to the Ravens in Keese."

"All I want is Gendor."

"Then join me," Shadow said. "We can hunt together."

She stared at him, and he wondered if she would try to kill him again. The woman was truly lethal, a fact he found appealing. He recognized that she might kill him. Perhaps not here, perhaps not today, but she could claim his life.

"One condition," she said.

"I usually ignore rules," Shadow said.

She growled. "Speak Zenif's name again, and I *will* kill you."

"Only if you tell me who he was."

She released an explosive breath. "You never quit, do you."

"It's one of my best qualities."

She glared at him, and then looked away. When she looked back there was such heat that he saw the truth. He was her family, maybe a husband—no—a brother or a father. He'd been killed and she felt the pain, a pain she had not shared with anyone except Loralyn.

"Speak on this again and I kill you," she repeated.

"I'll meet you outside the western gate, after the storm." He inclined his head and then retreated into the darkness, his body joining the shadows he owned.

Chapter 11: Requiem

"I'll take the first watch," Elenyr said.

Fire yawned. "Are you certain?"

"I don't sleep much anyway," Elenyr said. "Not anymore."

Fire nodded and absently cast the wolf of fire that set to prowling. Then he reclined onto his bedroll and was asleep in seconds. Mind regarded Elenyr with a curious expression, but she kept her expression neutral, unwilling to let him see her thoughts.

"Do you think Lorica capable of rebuilding the guild?" Mind asked.

It was just one day since the assassin battle, and the trio were camped a day's ride north of Herosian. As they left the city, Elenyr had thought often of what they had witnessed, and wondered about the sole survivor.

"She is strong," Elenyr said. "But revenge sought in grief often ends in ruin."

Mind inclined his head in agreement, and for a while there was silence. Elenyr continued to watch the fire, her thoughts shifting to the foe they faced. Elenyr and the fragments had fought many threats, but this was different. A storm was coming, and she feared for her fragment sons.

But how to protect them? She wanted to shield them, but she'd spent lifetimes teaching them to stand and fight, to defend those that needed aid. They would not stand idle against such an enemy—nor did she want them to. But she still yearned to protect them. She only had one plan, and she could only hope it would succeed.

"I'm going to take a walk," Elenyr said.

Mind regarded her from across the fire. "You've departed before. Where do you go?"

"I'll be back by morning," Elenyr said.

She rose and strode away from the fire, allowing the night to swallow her frame. The moment she was out of sight, she morphed to ethereal and accelerated, worry compelling her to action.

Wind and brush, stone and grass, all passed through her ethereal body, which moved more by will than muscle. Miles passed as she drove herself faster and faster, streaking across the dark countryside on her way south.

The walls of Herosian rose up in the distance, approaching at shocking speed. Elenyr didn't slow, and sped into them, passing through the stone to enter the street beyond. She slowed and turned west, along the outer wall of the city, breathing hard from the run.

The midnight hour had come and gone, and the streets were devoid of life, with only a handful of drunken wastrels or soldiers ambling about. Elenyr made her way through the streets, avoiding contact with all.

In the third circle of Herosian, she slowed and came to a halt, her eyes lifting to the spherical structure. Unique in all of Lumineia, the building was perfectly round, its base partially sunk into the earth. Fashioned of purple, clouded glass, the shop had taken a fortune to build, a fraction of the owners' earnings each year.

Requiem

The name hovered in shining letters above the glass door, a name that linked to her time as an oracle, although few knew of the requiem trees built during the Age of Oracles. They'd been all but destroyed in the Mage Wars.

Elenyr strode to the door and passed within, her ethereal body moving through the door to enter the room beyond. The giant space contained curved walls all the way to the ceiling, filled to the brim with small glass orbs. Pedestals dotted the center of the room, where other

85

orbs rested, the memories of their long dead owners floating in the glass.

Memory mages were uncommon, making their talent highly valued. The wealthy paid to have their memories placed into a sphere of glass, allowing them to see and witness moments of note from their past. Cheaper memory orbs were no more than a single image frozen in time, while expensive orbs revealed a full memory, including sound.

The owner of Requiem came from a long line of memory mages, but what made the orbs unique was their second talent of sound magic. With both magics, they were able to capture moments with such exactness that many were brought to tears.

A circular desk sat in the center of the floor, and Elenyr stepped to it, ringing the bell on the counter. A faint groan sounded from below, and then stairs appeared, recessing into the floor in the center of the desk, revealing a spiral staircase to the living quarters of the owner.

An older man trudged up the steps. Dressed in a nightgown and soft shoes, he brushed his white hair back against his head, yawning as he reached the desk. He rubbed his face, his grey eyes rising to regard Elenyr.

"Moren," Elenyr said, "it's good to see you. How is your daughter?"

"Close to surpassing my skill," he said. "Do you know what time it is?"

"My apologies," Elenyr said. "But I have a task for you."

"You always do."

The man sighed and retrieved a decanter from beneath the desk. Filling a glass with ale, he took a swig and yawned again. Then he rubbed his eyes and leaned onto the desk, swirling the liquid in his glass.

"One rule," he said, his tone of regret. "That's what my father said when I took over. Always serve the Hauntress with exactness. I didn't realize it meant you'd be arriving at all hours of the night."

"My business cannot be conducted in front of others."

The man took another sip and shrugged. "I have many clients with such needs, but you are the only one for whom my father required an oath. From what I understand, my grandfather, his father, and who knows how many generations beyond, were all required to make the same oath. What did you do that made my entire lineage beholden?"

"Are my tasks onerous to you?" Elenyr asked, her lips twitching with amusement.

"Of course not." The man swept his hand to the room. "Making memory orbs is what I do. But why us? Why use my family?"

Elenyr thought of the fragment of Mind, of his ability to reach into another's mind and extract memories. To keep a secret from someone with such magic was nigh impossible, unless she used another powerful memory mage.

"Because you are the best at guarding secrets," she said.

The man shook his head, obviously not satisfied with the answer. "Another memory?"

"Indeed," Elenyr said.

Elenyr reached to her throat and removed the pendent she always carried. At the end of the silver chain hung a flat section of glass, cut to resemble a large diamond. It was a simple keepsake, not expensive, yet it contained more value than any treasure.

Elenyr passed the pendent to the man and he examined it critically, a flicker of purple appearing in his eyes. He yawned again and placed it on a small pedestal on the counter, positioning it so it pointed to her.

"The glass is nearly full," he said. "If you wish to record much more you'll have to get a second one."

"Does the quality of the pendent not permit more memories to be imbued in the glass?"

"Of course," he replied. "And this is of the highest craftsmanship, the glass as pure as anything I've ever seen. But even this has limits."

"I suspect the time of its use will soon be at hand," she said.

The man inclined his head. "You know what to do. Clear your mind of anything except the memory you wish to imbue. Breathe it in, feel it, hear it, and then lower your mental barrier enough that I can retrieve it."

"You cannot breach my mental shields yet?"

He chuckled at her amused tone. "I suspect you guard your thoughts as a matter of routine, to keep secrets from one with magic that matches mine."

"Perhaps." Elenyr allowed a small smile.

She cleared her thoughts and recalled the battle in the Assassin's Guild. Time was limited, so she recalled a moment when she'd looked to Mind and Fire, and saw the two battling side by side, both protecting each other.

Then she recalled the moment the assassin had cradled her fallen sister, the pain, the anguish written on her features, and Fire and Mind standing over her. Fire looked stricken, while Mind's features were inscrutable.

The man reached up and touched her temple. Purple light curled around his finger, swirling down his hand. He withdrew his hand and touched the pendent, leaving a stream of purple light between her and the necklace.

The memory seeped from her, coalescing inside the glass, showing a flurry of images, of blades and fire, and two fragments fighting as one. Elenyr relived the moment until its end, and then closed her mind again. The memory thread faded, and the man sealed the magic into the glass, the images disappearing.

Throughout the process he did not look at the memory or allow it to enter his own thoughts. His discretion was part of what made him so expensive. When finished, he held the pendent aloft and returned it to her hand.

"You have my gratitude," Elenyr said.

She donned the necklace, and then tucked it into the folds of her tunic, out of sight. Moren's ancestor had cast a charm to hide the object from Mind's notice, but she didn't take any chances. If Mind didn't know it existed, he could not attempt to break the barrier.

"Why do you do want to remember this moment?" he asked, motioning to the pendant.

"Do you ask all your customers the same question?"

"Actually I do," Moren replied, smiling faintly.

"And what do they say?"

"That they do not wish to forget," he said.

"You know as well as I," Elenyr said. "Memories shape our identity, and they protect us from falling to our weaknesses. If we want to conquer ourselves, we must simply remember."

"I might use that on my door." Moren nodded his approval.

"Say hello to your daughter," Elenyr said.

He yawned. "I will."

Elenyr withdrew a pouch of coin and dropped it on the counter. Then she turned and strode to the door. The clink of coin sounded and Moren chuckled, calling out as Elenyr reached the exit.

"You know you don't have to pay," he said.

"It's for your daughter," Elenyr said. "Tell her to buy a dress for the fall festival."

He smiled and hefted the coin pouch. "I'm sure she will be grateful."

Elenyr inclined her head and then turned ethereal before passing through the door. In the street, she turned north, returning the way she had come. The streets were still empty, with only a handful of guards patrolling.

Foregoing the closed gates, she went straight to the wall and passed through it before accelerating across the farms and fields. The stars had turned during her foray into the city, and she saw that sunrise was imminent. Feeling the need to return, she flew across the countryside until she spotted the pinprick of light next to the road. Turning to it, she slowed and phased back to flesh.

Gasping from the sprint, she took a moment to calm her breathing. Then she approached the fire. The sentry of fire padded toward her, and she patted his head before entering the pool of light, claiming her previous seat by the diminished fire. Mind stirred and sat up.

"A long walk."

"Lots to think about," Elenyr said.

"Anything you wish to share?" Mind asked.

"In time."

His features tightened. "Why do you keep secrets from us?"

"Do you remember the first time Draeken shattered?"

"It is not a memory I can forget."

"You were not the only one present," she said. "And your shattering left a scar on me as well."

"What does this have to do with your secrets?"

Elenyr leaned against the log. "A father does not burden a child with the knowledge of an impending war, nor does he share his worry over the yield from his crops. He does not speak of his fear regarding a bandit attack, or the dread when his wife falls ill. All this he retains, so the child may know the joy of his young life."

Mind bristled. "I am not a child."

"Are you certain?"

Anger tightened his features, and the grass nearby began to bend. The ground trembled, making the logs in the fire spit sparks. Elenyr

90

watched Mind regain control of the magic she knew he feared, and when the ground settled, she sighed.

"You are no child," she murmured. "But to be whole you must accept the parts of you that you fear the most."

Mind would not meet her gaze, and she regretted provoking him. Mind rarely succumbed to anger, but when he did, the very earth trembled. It was a magic beyond his reach, one even Elenyr did not understand. But she knew that one day it would make him the most powerful.

"Will you ever trust me?" Mind asked.

Elenyr smiled. "Will you ever trust yourself?"

She held his gaze, knowing that he kept his greatest fears to himself. He was the eldest fragment, the one gifted with power and intelligence. He had nothing to fear, except what lurked within his own flesh.

Mind reclined on his bedroll and rolled away, and Elenyr lay on her own blanket. She watched the stars gradually lighten with the approach of dawn, wondering if she could have prepared more.

And hoping it would be enough.

Chapter 12: Shadow's Truth

After Shadow's departure, Lorica wrestled with the choice to join him, and throughout the storm she failed to make a decision. But when the time came, she found herself at the appointed place—to find him absent.

She waited, her annoyance rising. Travelers glanced at her as they exited the city. The minutes ticked by, and just as she was considering leaving, he appeared through the city gates astride his own mount. He yawned and smiled, as if he'd expected her to be there.

"Overslept," he said, his tone unapologetic. "Ready for revenge?"

"Are you always this irritating?"

"Always."

She grunted in annoyance and cast a look back at the city, already regretting her choice. Then she reluctantly flicked the reins and joined Shadow. She kept her distance, and sat back in her saddle, watching her strange companion. The man was an enigma and inspired an ocean of fury. He'd watched her grieve and come closer than anyone else in figuring out her truth.

He said his name was Shadow, and she'd assumed that was his persona. But he also wielded magic of the same name, and with greater skill than she'd ever witnessed. In addition to his magic, he possessed the swordcraft of a master, defying her as if it were a game. Abruptly he cast a look over his shoulder.

"Have you figured me out yet?" he asked.

"What makes you think I want to?"

"You keep staring."

She made to argue but his smile merely widened, and she scowled and looked away. He'd witnessed her at her most vulnerable, defied her attempt to kill him—twice—yet he still smiled like the labors of life held no weight.

"Who are you?"

"You already know my name."

"I know the name you have given me," Lorica said.

"It means more than you think," he said with an impish laugh.

"Do you always speak in riddles?"

"You shouldn't scowl so much," he said. "It will give you wrinkles."

She scowled, but that only made him laugh again. She resisted the urge to draw her oathsword and plunge it into his back, and then stifled the surge of attraction. How could a man so aggravating be so captivating?

She swore to ride behind him, to watch in case of betrayal, but he made no motion to attack, and seemed not to care that an assassin of the guild rode at his back. Indeed, he behaved like they were on a weekend ride, without a care to weigh down his shoulders.

The road stretched away from them, muddied from the storm. The air had cooled and the overcast sky heralded more rain, a fact that had driven the travelers to the inns. Trees dotted the landscape, marking the creeks that wound through the rocky hillside. On impulse, she flicked the reins and her horse accelerated to join Shadow.

"Where did you get your magic?"

He raised an eyebrow at her tactically inferior position. "So you trust me now?"

She snorted in disgust.

"I was not born with magic," he said, smiling. "Magic gave birth to me."

"Your riddles grow tiresome."

"Yet it causes your blood to rise," he said.

"Is there *any* truth you will speak?" she asked.

He seemed to consider the question with great difficulty. "I do serve Elenyr," he said with a nod.

"The Hauntress," she stated.

"Indeed," he said.

"Who is she?" she asked.

"I asked you about a name," he countered. "You seek what you are not willing to give."

She scowled, and then recalled what he'd said earlier and forced her features to relax. She'd been an assassin of renown for years, and now she was guildmaster, so why did she let him make her feel so intimidated? They rode in silence, the miles slipping away until finally she settled on a neutral topic.

"Tell me what you know of the Bloodsworn."

"Assassins of nearly equal skill to your guild," he said. "But they seek to usurp your throne of skulls."

"I already knew this," she said.

He inclined his head. "The Herosian city guard are forced to look aside while the Bloodsworn commit their murders."

Lorica raised an eyebrow. "They seek to retain their anonymity."

"You are formidable," he replied. "But it seems that Gendor did not found the Bloodsworn. He merely inherited it."

She nodded, grateful that her earlier assumptions were correct. Gendor was a fearsome killer, and ambitious, but he lacked the tactical mind required to plan and hide such a collection of assassins. That suggested there was another he served.

"How are they connected to the Ravens? And the Order?"

"I do not know," he said. "But I saw Gendor depart the Thieves Guild in Ilumidora moments before the Bloodsworn attacked. He spoke as if the Ravens were his allies."

Her eyes widened in surprise as she recognized him. She'd thought him familiar in the assassin refuge, and again afterword, but then his features had been cast in shadow. Now as she rode beside him, she recognized him as the same one she'd spotted leaving the hall.

"How old are you?"

He burst into a laugh. "Older than you suspect. Younger than my age."

"More riddles?"

"More truth," he said. "But truth requires a key to understand, and I'm afraid you have yet to merit such a key."

Loathe to return to his riddles, she motioned west, toward their destination. "And the Order of Ancients?"

"A mystery all its own," he said, his smile bordering on excited.

"They worship the krey, and the krey have returned," Lorica said.

"You know of them?"

The question was light, but she noticed a flicker of need, eliciting a smile. "So there *are* truths you lack."

"Perhaps." He allowed a smile. "What do your records speak of the Order?"

The question revealed his need to understand, and she recognized it as one of the reasons he'd followed her out of the assassin refuge. He wished to know about the Order, to understand their identity and the threat they posed. It also gave her leverage. Unfortunately, she didn't have access to such leverage.

"I do not know," she admitted, and showed the ring on her hand. "I have the key to the archives, but their location has not been revealed to me."

"I assumed you would know."

"The Assassin's Guild sees many upheavals," she said. "But the seal of the guildmaster was crafted by an oracle, and it only reveals the archives to one with honor."

"An oracle?" he asked, surprised. "When?"

"Ages ago," she said, waving her hand. "When I prove my honor, the seal will open, and I will become the guildmaster my sister was."

Her throat tightened and she looked away, her thoughts flashing to Loralyn's body and the council chamber crumbling above them. Then she recalled the krey weapons, the ones that had failed to destroy the entire council chamber. Why had Gendor spared them? She then glanced to Shadow, wondering if he had intervened . . .

"The council chamber," she said slowly. "You were there."

"I tipped the battle in your favor," he said. "Until they trapped you inside and sought to destroy you."

"You stopped the krey weapons," she stated.

"Is that what they were?"

His surprise was genuine, and she realized that he'd stopped the council chamber and the Titan from landing on their heads. They would have been crushed without his intervention, meaning he'd saved her life.

The idea that she owed Shadow her life rankled, and she fell silent, realizing that she'd repaid his act by binding him in a tower set to explode. And then sought to kill him just hours later.

Her grief surged to the fore, bright and bitter. Shadow had also stalked her as she stood over the body of her sister. He'd followed her to the home of her brother's widow, watched her as she grieved, seen her at her most vulnerable. He'd taken as much as he had given.

Tears welled in her eyes, but she forced them away. She was an assassin, trained to kill those who deserved death, those unclaimed by justice. But the tears defied her will, and she looked away, unwilling to let Shadow bear witness.

Whether he saw or not, he remained silent, and for several miles they did not speak. When she was certain her emotions had been caged anew, she shifted the conversation back to the Bloodsworn, and they talked of their foes.

Throughout the journey to Keese, Shadow made no mention of Zenif, or Loralyn, and she studied his demeanor as much as his words. She wanted dearly to hate the man, to have her suspicions proven right. But she was wrong.

Shadow was inquisitive and clever, with a sense of mischief that lacked compassion, but still retained a sense of justice. When they passed through a tavern, Shadow cut the leg from a chair beneath a man berating his children, and when he fell, they burst into laughter. Shadow merely smiled and slipped the dagger back into its sheath.

There was also an air about him that seemed timeless. He made comments about a village's history, but not as one who had studied, but as one who had been present. It was an odd form of speech that made her notice other oddities, a twist of a word here, a flicker of an accent there. It was as if he came from everywhere and nowhere, a man with no homeland, yet one that still fought for home.

After a five day ride they crested a hill and Keese came into view. The walled city, half the size of Herosian, bordered the South Sea, and the glittering water stretched to the horizon. The city's occupants were comprised of every station, all ruled by a duke. The sun was bright, the summer heat beating down upon them.

"I'm ready for a bath," Shadow said, wiping his forehead.

"You need one."

He chuckled and motioned to her. "I smell as you do, assassin."

She fought to suppress the smile and failed. His expression became triumphant, as if her smile was a victory all its own. It annoyed her that

Shadow had gotten her to drop her guard, and she clenched a fist on the pommel, the contact serving to extinguish the emotion.

"You call me assassin because you know my identity," she said, angling her horse down the road. "I think it's only fair I know yours."

"You want the truth?" he asked.

"Doesn't everyone?"

"Perhaps," he said, "but in this, I do not believe you're ready for the truth."

"One question then," she said. "Just one."

He swatted a fly that had landed on his arm, his features pensive. "What will you ask, I wonder. My name? My origin? Or perhaps the identity of the Hauntress is what you seek."

"Are you afraid?" she challenged.

"Hardly," he said. "But you present an intriguing game that I am inclined to pursue. One question, one answer. Do make it a good one."

She saw in his gaze that he meant his words, so she leaned back in her saddle and considered the choices. Knowing his name might prove useful, but names could be anything. The truth about his companions might also be of use, but in the end one question found its way to the surface, one that seemed to have an obvious answer, yet might hide a wealth of knowledge.

"I wish to know your age."

"Ah," he said, his eyes lit with delight. "A clever question indeed."

"Will you answer it?"

He reined his horse and she did as well, both halting a mile from the city gates. He held her gaze, his dark eyes arresting, his smile pleased and mischievous. Then he inclined his head and swept a hand to himself.

"At the close of the Age of Oracles, my life began."

A crease lined her forehead. "That would make you over five thousand years old."

"You asked a clever question, you got a clever answer."

"How is that possible?"

He laughed lightly and nudged his horse. As he passed, he winked at her. "One question, one answer."

She watched him pass, confused and intrigued. Was he mad? She jerked her head, dismissing the thought. The truth to his statement was evident, and explained a great deal about his language and knowledge, but it also left her with a host of new questions. As they approached Keese, she realized that she knew his name and age, but his identity remained a mystery.

Chapter 13: The Raven Guildhall

Lorica pondered what Shadow had revealed as they entered Keese and made their way to one of Shadow's hides. They both possessed places of refuge in the city, but Lorica was loath to reveal hers, least of all to one that had lived for so long.

His hide proved to be an attic. Built into the house of a noble, the attic was only accessible from the roof, suggesting the occupants had no idea that Shadow used their home as a sanctuary. With a host of guards patrolling the gardens around the house, the house was a veritable fortress, but those very fortifications became protections for Shadow's hidden refuge.

Leaving their rented steeds at a stable, they flew to the roof at night, soaring over the oblivious guards. Alighting at the pinnacle of the large roof, Shadow undid a secret latch and led her inside. Shutting it behind her, he revealed a chamber surprisingly well stocked.

Spacious for an attic, the room contained no light orbs at all, and only moonlight through the window illuminated the space. It was not clean. Instead, the space was cluttered with various items, all likely stolen. A small access in the floor led to the noble's kitchens, and a number of foodstuffs had clearly been pilfered from the stores.

"Do you ever clean?"

"Not if I can help it," Shadow said. He opened a case of dried meat and tossed her a piece before claiming his own. Settling into a comfortable chair, he tossed a leg over its arm and began to eat.

"You've lived five thousand years, yet you don't know how to sit in a chair?"

"I know how to be comfortable," he said, and swept a hand to the room. "Why don't you relax?"

"I'd rather be hunting Gendor," she said flatly.

"All work and no play makes an assassin not very much fun."

"That doesn't rhyme."

"It wasn't supposed to," Shadow said. "I'm a fragment, not a poet."

"Fragment?"

Shadow merely smiled, and she realized he'd revealed a piece of information he might not have intended. Shadow changed the subject to the Bloodsworn and she did not press the issue. Instead they talked of the Ravens.

"What makes you think Gendor is in Keese?" she asked.

"Things he said at the Thieves Guild in Ilumidora," Shadow said. "I suspect if we find the Raven, she can tell us where to find Gendor."

"Then what are we waiting for?"

"Sunset was just an hour ago," Shadow said as if it was obvious. "Thieves aren't really active this early."

"In my experience, that's the best time to kill them," she said.

"We aren't trying to kill them."

He pulled a lever on the chair, allowing him to recline. Settling in, it was obvious he intended to sleep. He was so relaxed that he could have been taking a nap next to a lake, instead of an intruder in another's home.

"How can you be so relaxed at a time like this?"

"Like this." He closed his eyes and smiled.

"People get killed for being this irritating."

"Hasn't happened yet," he said.

She resisted the urge to draw her blade and remind him who she was. But she wasn't going to kill him, and he knew it. She sighed and scanned the attic for a bath, but the room lacked a second room.

"If you're looking to bathe, just use the house of our host," he said, using his chin to point downward. "They don't mind."

"They don't know."

He smiled again, and again she wondered at the man's sheer brashness. He'd obviously snuck into the noble's house and used their bath, and probably enjoyed the prospect of getting away with the act.

She considered foregoing the bath, but the stink of the road was too great, so she reluctantly lifted the trapdoor and dropped into the kitchen storeroom. It contained two doors, one to the kitchens, and one to a back entrance of the house. When shut, the secret trapdoor was invisible with the rest of the ceiling, the seam lost to the shadows, which had likely been cast by her companion.

Slipping into the back corridor, she checked several rooms, searching for the bathing chamber. Night was just setting in and the house prepared for sleep, only the cooks and servants going about their labors, along with the guards, of which there seemed to be an abnormally high number.

Everywhere she looked she saw wealth. Gold and silver marked the wood, and the walls were made of finely polished marble. On soft feet she searched the house and then found the bathing chamber, a room as large as a commoner's house. Steam rose from the water, wetting the walls.

She left her gear in an obscure corner and then disrobed before striding into the water, obviously heated by dwarven fire stones. The warmth seeped through her bare skin and into her bones, and for a moment, she relished the sense of solitude.

It was clear why Shadow had chosen this particular house to hide his refuge. The house was so large the nobles would rarely use so much space. The bathing chamber was in a corner where one could hear approaching footfalls, giving plenty of time to escape through the servant's entrance. Shadow had all but stolen their home.

She wanted to think of Shadow as impulsive and brash, but the more she saw, the more she realized he had a brilliant and clever mind. She imagined him floating in the bath like he owned the house.

Finishing her bath, she dried and dressed from clothes in her pack, and then returned to the secret attic. When she arrived, she found Shadow asleep in his chair, his body relaxed, as if he didn't care that he traveled with an assassin of the guild.

She shook her head and reluctantly claimed the bed, fleetingly wondering if he'd used the chair so she could have the bed. Reclining with her sword in hand she fell asleep and dreamed of her fallen sister.

She woke to find the room dark, and Shadow absent. She gathered her gear and ate some of his food until Shadow slipped through the hidden window. His eyes lit up when he found her sitting in his chair.

"You're awake," he said.

"You were kind to let me have the bed," she said.

He laughed lightly. "If I wanted the bed I would have taken it. I'm not the one with honor."

"Then who is?"

"One of my brothers."

"Another fragment?"

"You are more clever than I gave you credit for," he said, wiggling a finger at her.

"I did ask a clever question."

"Is that a sense of humor I hear?"

"No," she said, and then smiled. She wondered how she could smile under the circumstances, but the humor found a chink in her sadness.

He laughed lightly. "We should go. The Ravens will be out and we should scout their stronghold."

"You know where it is?"

"Of course," he replied, flashing a knowing smile.

He led the way through the secret window and onto the roof. From there, they both used wings to soar across the estate. Shadow passed over the outer wall and descended to a roof, and then an alley. From there he slipped into the rear of a small caravan of merchants. Lorica followed, joining him at the rear of the wagons. The small caravan made their way down the street and then turned, passing the main entrance of the estate.

"Where's the Raven guildhall?" she asked.

He came to a stop and motioned to the gates. "Right here."

She frowned. "You jest. We did not spend the night in the attic of the Raven guildhall."

"How did you like their bath?" he asked innocently.

She scoffed, and then looked to the guards. She'd thought them vigilant the night before, more so than normal noble guards. Their skills could not stop an assassin of the guild, but they had been formidable. She'd also noticed the interior of the noble's house, its wealth and opulence, as if the owner had as much coin as the duke that controlled the city.

"You let me walk into their bathing chamber," she said, her tone rigid with anger. "They could have killed me."

"Then you wouldn't have been a very good assassin," he remarked.

He turned and made his way to an expensive inn across the street from the entrance. As Lorica followed, she wrestled with the surge of anger, but oddly recalled the chair he'd subtly cut from beneath the man in the tavern two days past. He'd done the same thing to her, leading her into a game where she did not know the rules.

They ascended the stairs of the inn and he slipped out a window before scaling to the roof. As she joined him, she abruptly caught his throat and slammed him into the chimney. Rather than surprised, his expression was merely irritated.

"This tunic is new."

"Let's see how it looks with bloodstains."

"Those don't come out," he lamented. "You should know that as well as I."

"I don't like your games," she said.

"Yes you do," he said. "Because you haven't been dwelling on the loss of your sister."

Her teeth snapped together, not because he was wrong, but because he was right. She'd been so preoccupied with understanding her companion, she hadn't mourned her fallen kindred. Guilt flared, and then oddly a sense of amusement followed. The ache remained, but it was a shade dimmer than it had been before.

"No games," she said, removing her hand from his throat.

"No promises."

She growled and stabbed a finger at him. "Why do you behave like a child?"

"When you've lived as long as I have, you learn an obvious lesson. Life is more fun when you decide to have fun."

"That didn't rhyme."

"It wasn't supposed to."

He flashed his oh-so-irritating smirk and then stepped around her. Ascending to the top of the roof, he took a seat that afforded a view of the Raven guildhall. Uncertain, Lorica followed, and together they surveyed their target. Then Shadow began to talk, and Lorica listened to his description of the Ravens.

The estate was owned by a minor noble, a man by the name of Dentis. He had a great deal of business in Erathan and was rarely present. Situated just a few blocks from the Duke's manor, the estate boasted spacious gardens and its own wall, much like that of the neighboring estates.

The Raven's Guildhall had more guards than neighboring houses, and they were better trained. Although they resembled soldiers, they looked subtly different than those at other noble's homes—more tattoos, more scars.

"The guards are not soldiers," she said.

He selected a pair of cookies from a pouch at his side, and then proceeded to eat them both. "The owner claims privacy and employs only those she trusts."

"Thieves from the Raven's guild."

"Indeed."

"Then who is the Raven?"

"Lady Dentis," Shadow said. "Or that is what I believe."

"Does her husband know?"

"She keeps her dealings private from all," he said.

"Is that praise I hear?"

"Of course," he replied. "For one who deals in shadows, it's a pleasure to encounter one skilled in the art of anonymity."

She realized the description applied to her as well and wondered if he found her attractive. Then he stood and stepped to the balcony, obviously intent on leaving her behind. She rose to her feet.

"Where are you going?"

"Does it matter?" he asked.

"You're leaving now?"

"Don't tell me you've grown attached."

"Never," she said.

He smirked and strode to the edge of the roof. "I know you're going to try and follow me, but when you fail, meet me back here at midnight."

"What if I was going to stay here?"

"Were you?"

He grinned at her silence and then dropped off the roof. She darted to the edge and saw him alight on the alley floor as if he'd dropped two feet, not fifty. She shook her head and tried to resist the urge to follow. With a sigh, she dropped into the alley after him, and then pursued him, but he disappeared not a hundred feet away. Even with her considerable skill, she could not find his trail. With a sigh of irritation, she returned to the roof of the inn to watch the Raven guildhall and wonder about her companion.

Chapter 14: The Strange Master

Shadow and Lorica watched the Raven's home, the days gradually turning into weeks. Shadow frequently grew bored and left, searching the city for something of interest. He always returned to find Lorica annoyed, and she muttered curses about his patience, only serving to make his jaunts more amusing.

They saw no sign of the Raven, or Gendor, but Shadow was confident they would appear. He had stalked enough targets to discover a simple truth—one always returned home. But watching a home could be rather boring, unless one's companion was an assassin.

Lorica often brooded, obviously thinking of her sister, but there were times she smiled, and he caught glimpses of a sense of humor beneath the desire for revenge. He enjoyed irritating her because it frequently resulted in exasperation, and occasionally a faint smile.

Three weeks after their arrival, Lorica abruptly stood to leave. They'd moved their vantage point several times, and now resided in an upper floor of an expensive inn. She stepped to the door and swung it open.

"Where are you off to?" he asked. She'd never left her post before.

"Does it matter?"

He grinned as his words were hurled back at him, and asked, "What if I follow?"

"Don't," she said flatly.

Her voice was filled with warning, but to him it sounded like an invitation. The moment she was gone, he slipped out the window and descended the wall to the street. Her choice of timing was obvious, and the midday sun beat down upon the streets, preventing any shadows.

Lorica slipped into the crowd and wove her way into the heart of Keese, and then the poorer section at the northern end of the crescent shaped city. Shadow kept his distance. Lorica had noticed him before, and he didn't want to get caught again.

She reached a small hut adjacent to an overgrown garden. Glancing backward, she scanned the empty street and rooftops, failing to notice Shadow sitting on the roof directly above her head. Then she knocked softly, and a moment later the door swung open.

"Lory," an aged voice said in surprise.

"Sentara," Lorica said, embracing the woman and then entering. "It's good to see you."

"What brings you to my door? How are the wings?"

"Perfect," she said.

Shadow hung from the roof and peeked through the window. The room was tiny, little more than a bed, a tiny stove, and a door to a second room. With no decorations and dust on the floor, it had the air of a space rarely used.

"Would you like to eat?" the aged woman asked. "We just arrived, but Rune went to fetch supplies."

Lorica glanced about and seemed to notice the sparse furnishings. "You weren't already here?"

The woman shook her head. "We were in Erathan, until King Numen and his daughter were kidnapped."

"When?" she asked. "Who took them?"

"No one knows," she said. "But guards are searching the country, and I thought it best to depart."

Lorica seemed to want more, but she shook her head. "I don't have much time. I need your help."

The woman's eyes lit with curiosity. "You came with a question."

"What can you tell me of the one they call the Hauntress?"

109

The woman's smile faded and her features darkened. "A dangerous question."

"So you know of her?"

"You should go," the woman said, rising and stepping to the door.

"But Master Sentara—"

"Lory," the woman said. "I trained you, and so I ask you to trust me on this. Steer clear of the Hauntress."

"And the fragments?" she asked.

The woman closed the gap in a burst of speed uncharacteristic for one her age. "They are more dangerous than the Hauntress—more dangerous than any threat you have encountered."

"How do you know them?" Lorica asked.

"A story from another life," she said.

"Go," Sentara said, her tone filled with reproach. "And never speak of this again."

Lorica regarded her for a moment and then sighed. Instead of leaving, she shifted to another topic, and for a moment the two spoke of Rune, the girl that was apparently Sentara's charge. But the conversation was forced, and Shadow knew Lorica still wanted an answer.

"Lory," Sentara finally said. "I cannot tell you what you seek. I need you to trust me."

"I do," Lorica said, obviously unhappy with the exchange.

Shadow peeked into the window and watched the consternation on the woman's face. She seemed like she wanted to say more, and then shook her head. She rose and embraced Sentara before stepping to the door.

"It was good to see you."

"You as well," Sentara said. "Please give my regards to your sister."

Lorica's hand tightened on the door, and when she spoke her voice was quiet. "I will."

She swung the door open and departed. Shadow eased back onto the roof until she had disappeared into the street. Then he leaned down and examined the old woman with renewed interest.

Sentara had obviously trained Lorica at some point, and probably her sister. She seemed old and harmless, but the glint in her eyes bespoke an unpredictable nature, and Shadow's curiosity compelled him to remain.

Sentara abruptly whirled and strode to the door at the rear of the hut. Swinging it open, she entered a small bedchamber. Sentara shook off her cloak and then tossed it onto a hook in the corner. Then she stepped to her bed and lifted the bedpost, flipping a tiny lever.

The floor dropped into the ground, turning into steps that disappeared into darkness. Shadow, his eyes wide with delight, flitted through the door and down the steps before Sentara turned around.

On soft feet, Shadow hurried down the stairs into a large, secret chamber. The room contained a central training circle, as well as a pair of comfortable beds and dozens of blades about the wall. The lights brightened as Sentara descended into view, and Shadow leapt to a large case of swords, ascending to the perch at the top. Hidden in the shadows, he settled in to watch.

Sentara drew her sword and swished it through the air, cutting and slicing imagined foes, the bladework fine enough to be one of the Bladed. Intrigued, he watched her flow through blade routines like they were in her blood, until suddenly she came to a halt. Her chest heaving from the exertion, she flicked the blade as if in irritation.

"Are you going to come down from there?" she asked softly. "Or did you just come to watch?"

Realizing he was caught, Shadow drifted out of the darkness and dropped to the floor. He kept his distance and eyed the evidently

111

dangerous woman, intrigued by her behavior. The woman studied him in turn. She seemed frail and weak, yet held the sword in a hand like granite, the blade never moving. Her eyes, too, betrayed a resolve that could have bent steel.

"Who are you?" she asked.

"You do not already know?" He sniffed as if he expected better.

A scowl appeared on her face and she pointed her sword at his heart. "You are the fragment of Shadow, the mischievous one that should know when he's met a better."

"And you're my better?" Shadow asked.

The woman stepped to the wall and tossed a sword to Shadow. Then she took up a stance and waited. Shadow flicked the sword back and forth, testing its balance, a smile forming on his face. He recalled the first few months after Draeken had fractured, when he'd realized that during the day his magic was all but useless. Elenyr had given him and Mind blades, to which Shadow had complained.

"I already have magic."

Elenyr shook her head. "You're capable of more."

The comment had been an irritant that had driven him to learn the sword, and then other weapons. His frequent bouts with laziness aside, he'd been practicing swordcraft for thousands of years. How hard would it be to defeat an old woman?

"Besting one of your age will hardly be a triumph," Shadow said.

"If you win, I'll let you paint my blade whatever color you want."

Shadow burst into a laugh and glided forward. "Done."

"But if I win," she said, bringing him to a halt. "You must answer my question."

Shadow hesitated, sensing the confidence to the woman's words. She believed she could best him and wanted to use the wager to withdraw his secrets. Still, the chance to paint her sword was impossible to resist.

"Get ready for a purple sword," he said, darting in.

He feinted high right and then rotated, bringing his sword at her left side. The woman blocked the blade and stepped in, using her free hand to strike Shadow in the face. He recoiled from the strangely powerful blow.

"Is that the extent of your skill?" she taunted.

Shadow growled and lunged, driving his sword for her chest. At the last moment he halted and flicked the blade toward her leg. Belying her age, the woman leapt into a flip over the flashing weapon and landed on her feet, driving her sword at Shadow. He parried and tossed the sword upward, catching it in a reverse grip before spinning and blocking the next blow. He struck the weapon aside and flipped the blade in his hand, sweeping it across her hair as she ducked and twirled—into his fist. She recoiled, and it was his turn to taunt. She grunted in annoyance and they began to circle, each gauging the other for an opening.

"You're younger than you look," he said.

"You have no idea," she said, her eyes gleaming with amusement.

They came together in a clash of blades, and the ring of steel reverberated in the secret chamber. Shadow allowed himself to be driven backward but curved his path to the rack of weapons. When they reached it, he rolled along the wall, snatching a second blade on his way. With both swords in hand he lunged, swinging one high, one low.

Sentara leapt into a horizontal spin, her boots striking Shadow in the chest. Coming out of the spin, she kicked a sword off the rack, the blade spinning through the air, missing him by inches and plunging into the cabinet on the wall.

Shadow expected her to protest at the second weapon but she did not, and instead continued to fight, whipping her sword across, down and up, blocking his strikes while adding her own. Again forced to retreat, Shadow left a snare on the ground, the darkness catching the woman's boot.

The shadows were not enough to grip her tightly, but they were enough to cause a stumble. Sentara tripped and went down, and Shadow darted in. But her move was a feint, and she carried her momentum into a roll, rising to bring her sword into his hand, knocking his second blade free. Dismayed, Shadow retreated toward the wall.

Shadow reached the wall and placed his boots on the surface, and ascended backward up the slope, scaling it to the ceiling. The woman smirked at the display and fought the upside-down Shadow, her blade swinging for his head.

"You are not the first shadowmage I've known," she said.

He flipped off the ceiling and landed on the ground, hurling the sword at his opponent. She twisted, and the blade spun past her. When she rotated back he reached for the blade with a thread of shadow, the end forming a hand that allowed him to yank the weapon free. It hurled towards her back. Sentara raised her sword to strike—and then ducked.

Shadow had thought victory in hand, and the sudden sword spinning toward his chest was a surprise. He flinched and managed to catch the blade, but she used the distraction to spin around him, and place her blade on his neck.

"Now," she said coolly. "The truth. Where is Elenyr?"

"In Herosian, I expect," he replied, blending the truth with a lie.

"Hunting the krey," Sentara said.

Hiding his surprise at her knowledge, he asked, "How do you know Elenyr?"

"She was once a friend," Sentara said, lowering her sword and turning away.

"You have a gift for mystery which I applaud," Shadow said, and then pointed to her sword. "And a gift with the sword."

She regarded him for several moments. "It was not my first gift," she said. "But most considered my first blessing a curse."

114

He raised his hands helplessly. "Why speak riddles you know I cannot understand?"

"You're not the only one that likes to have fun," she said, her lips twitching. "Now leave. You may return if you like, but I will be gone."

Shadow couldn't shake the feeling that she'd known the truth before he'd said a word—and knew a great deal about him and his companions. Still, the mysterious woman was a puzzle he wanted to solve, so he offered an exaggerated bow.

"As you desire, but first a truth from you."

"You did not win," she said.

"Perhaps," he replied. "But call it an indulgence for a respected foe."

"And I respect you?"

"Don't you?"

She regarded him in silence and then gestured in invitation. "One question. One answer."

"What do you want with Elenyr?"

The woman cocked her head to the side and then shrugged. "I want her to return my mind."

He groaned. "Another riddle?"

She stabbed her sword to the steps. "I gave you an answer. It's not my fault you don't understand it."

"That's all you're going to tell me?" he asked as she forced him toward the steps. "Why did you even come to Keese?"

She cocked her head to the side. "I followed your brother," she said, and then poked him in the back with her sword.

Realizing he would get no more from her, he ascended the steps. When he reached the top, he phased to darkness and crept to the edge of shadow, poking his head out to where he could view the strange woman.

She stood where he'd left her, only instead of a sword she held a small glass orb, one she was arguing with. Shadow withdrew before Sentara could spot him and left even more confused.

Chapter 15: Brother

Shadow crossed the street and watched Sentara's hut until a young woman approached, one Shadow assumed was Rune. Within moments she and Sentara departed, their packs suggesting they would not be returning. As much as Shadow wanted to follow the old woman, he had a more pressing need, to find out which brother Sentara had followed to Keese.

If one of the fragments had come to Keese, he should connect with them. But Sentara had said *one*, not *some*, so who had arrived? The other fragments had departed Cloudy Vale in pairs. Curious, he returned to the top floor of the inn, opening the door to find Lorica pacing.

"Where have you been?" she demanded.

"Looking for someone," he said with a shrug.

"If you followed me . . ." Her hand twitched towards the hilt of her sword. "Doesn't matter. Several carriages just entered the estate. I think the Raven is here."

Shadow stepped to the window and eyed the carriages coming to a halt outside the stables. With dozens of horses and guards, it was obvious someone important had arrived. Then he spotted the woman stepping out of the middle carriage and nodded.

"She did indeed. Do what you need to get ready. I'll be back tonight."

"You're leaving now?" she asked, exasperated.

"I told you," he said. "I'm looking for someone."

She caught his wrist, her voice turning dangerous. "Did you follow me?"

"Of course not," he lied smoothly. "You said not to."

She measured his gaze, and he idly wondered if she believed him. Ultimately, she released him and he strode away. As he crossed the threshold, she called out to him, her voice turning cold.

"I don't like people poking around in my life."

"Too bad," he replied, and then grinned.

Shadow used the stairs to descend, leaving Lorica standing in the open doorway. He offered a mock salute before descending to the kitchens and then the alley. From there he slipped into the streets, his thoughts turning to what he'd learned.

The Raven's arrival and one of the fragments coming to Keese could not be a coincidence. But who had arrived? The woman had asked about Elenyr, who'd been with Fire and Mind, suggesting either Water or Light were in Keese. He guessed Water, simply because Light was hard to follow. But why had he come here? And what did his arrival have to do with the Raven? He glanced to the sky. The gathering storm clouds heralded rain, but it was not dark enough for him to find his own answers.

He stepped into an alley and approached a group of children. Street urchins were common in Keese, and watched him warily until Shadow withdrew a silver piece. He held it aloft. The oldest of the boys advanced several steps, his eyes flicking between him and the coin.

"What do you wish to know?" the boy asked.

"Anything strange happen in the city today?"

The boy inclined his head and reached for the coin, but Shadow held it back. "Truth first."

The boy's eyes flicked to the coin. He licked his lips and nodded. "A group of bandits attempted to relieve a man of his coin, but he froze them in ice before wanting to know about the Ravens."

The fragment of Water. He was the only one that used water to freeze his foes—one of his boring yet effective tactics. Shadow

118

scratched his chin in thought, wondering what would have brought him here, and how he could exploit Water's appearance.

"Where were they headed?" Shadow asked.

"The *Shark's Tooth*," he said. "On the docks."

Shadow lowered the coin and the boy snatched it away. He scurried into the crowd, and Shadow turned toward the Raven hall. He half expected Lorica to appear, but there was no sign of the assassin, and he wondered if she'd remained in the inn.

It wasn't that he didn't trust Lorica. She would do everything in her power to find Gendor, and he could count on her skills as much as her anger. But revealing too much about himself could be dangerous. She was perceptive and skilled, a potentially lethal combination. Plus it was more fun to keep her guessing.

He found his way back to the Raven's home. Avoiding the inn, he made his way to the servant's entrance and used the gloom from the storm to slip over the wall. Once inside, he worked his way through the gardens, listening.

" . . . really think he will come?" a guard asked as he and his companion patrolled the grounds.

"If he does, we're ready for . . ."

Shadow drifted to another group, and then another, gathering snippets of information. The Raven had already entered her house and her carriage was stored, but Shadow noticed a subtle increase in the guards, and they were all on edge.

One of the guards mentioned a cellar, and Shadow slipped through a door and made his way to the basement. Raven guards were everywhere, but he managed to slip by them unnoticed. At the cellar door he looked down and saw Thorg laboring over a cage of fire.

A sly smile spread on his face as he realized what lay in store for Water. For whatever reason, they knew Water was coming, and had set a trap, one that would contain even a fragment of Draeken. No doubt they intended on luring Water into the cellar, a task not entirely difficult, since he was not the fragment that possessed strategy.

"Let's not disappoint you, shall we?" Shadow murmured.

His steps hastening with eagerness, he returned to the gardens. The storm had darkened further, and Shadow used the growing darkness to reach the wall. A smile on his face, he withdrew from the estate and headed towards Water's destination.

He wove through the city to the *Shark's Tooth*, a tavern and inn on the shore. Recently built, the inn was known for its exotic quarters, chambers of aquaglass walls that allowed a unique view of the underwater shoreline. A single night would seem a fortune to a commoner, and on impulse Shadow sidled up to a haughty woman buying a broach. He cut her purse, and that of her husband, disappearing into the crowd as both cried out in dismay.

He listened to the sweet music of chaos as he entered the tavern. Spotting Water and Lira, he took a seat just behind his brother. With Water's attention on Lira, and hers on him, Shadow suspected he could start a brawl and they wouldn't notice. The closeness between them was telling, and he wondered if their relationship had pushed past friendly.

He kept a pattern of shadows on his features and hair, making himself appear taller and wider. Then he ordered a meal of fine cheeses, fruit, and seared fish. As he relished the food, he listened to them talk, a faint smile appearing on his face as he realized they were there seeking the Ravens as well, confirming his suspicions that Water had been lured to Keese.

As he finished the meal, he plotted how he could use them for his own aims. He considered the noble's home, and where the Raven would be. He needed to speak to Lady Dentis, and they needed to talk to someone named Serak.

As the two finished their meal, Shadow dropped a few coins for the barmaid and then made his way to the man near the front door. After a whispered conversation, Shadow paid for a single room and sent the key to Water. Then he went to their room and picked the lock. Minutes later, Water entered the room and spotted him.

With his feet on the desk, Shadow flashed a smile. "Hello, brother. What brings you to Keese?"

"Shadow," Water said with a laugh.

Water dismissed his staff weapon and stepped forward, and Shadow rose to embrace him. When they parted, Shadow rotated to Lira and caught her hand, lifting it to his lips. He was rewarded by a light flush to her cheeks, and a touch of irritation in her expression.

"I hope my brother has been treating you well," Shadow said.

"He has," she said.

"Not as well as I could, of course," Shadow said with a sniff. "But he'll do."

"What are you doing here?" Water asked.

"Still looking for the ancient map," Shadow said. "I've tracked it to Keese and happened to spot you in the tavern." He didn't mention the additional admonition to seek Relgor.

Water shared their tale, including encountering Serak and the battle with the Order underground. He finished by describing the kidnapping of King Numen, and then spoke of Grena, the woman that had told them to come to Keese. Shadow suspected Grena to be a member of the Ravens, but said nothing.

"So you think Wylyn is with the Ravens?" Shadow asked, frowning as if in thought.

Water's tale provided more than Shadow had expected, and he pondered the ramifications of Serak, the father of guardians. Was he part of the trap at the Raven guildhall? Or merely a part of the Order? Either way, they needed answers.

"Do you know where they are?" Lira motioned upward. "We were told to speak with Wenta."

"She is a low-level informant for the Ravens," Shadow said, even though he'd never heard the name. He rubbed his chin in thought. "Since we both want the Ravens, perhaps we can help each other."

"What do you have in mind?" Water asked.

"The Ravens and I are not friends," Shadow said, "but I need time in their archives, undisturbed."

"How do we help with that?"

Shadow flashed a smile, trying to keep the smugness from his expression. Water was always so willing to help, and his sense of honor easy to manipulate.

"I need you to get caught," Shadow said. "While they interrogate you, I can sneak in and find what I need. Then I'll help you get out."

"I get my answers, you get yours," Water said.

"An interrogation usually involves sharp objects and blood," Lira said.

"They won't know who you are," Shadow said smoothly. "I need ten minutes, no more. The Raven won't be so hasty to harm you."

"And if she realizes I look like you?"

"You would be so lucky," Shadow said with a laugh, stepping to the door. "Just feign ignorance. You're good at that."

"Where are you going?" Water asked.

"I have my own room," he lied, and then pointed to the single bed in their quarters. "And there's only one bed here. I guess you'll have to share."

Water flushed. Shadow smirked. Then he departed and shut the door. Feeling confident with what he'd learned, Shadow exited the tavern and turned toward the inn where Lorica waited. Outside, he worked his way through the streets. He found her on the rooftop of the inn and sank into a seat at her side.

"Was she pretty?"

"How do you know it was about a girl?"

"It's always about a girl."

He laughed and shook his head. "We have an ally in the city. And they will provide the distraction we need."

"Just like that?"

"They're a good ally."

"And you trust them?"

The doubt in her voice made him smile. "He's the one with honor."

She regarded him with hard eyes, and he realized she, too, was used to working alone. She didn't have much trust for anyone. Over the last few weeks, he'd wondered if she would simply disappear and go after Gendor alone. But she'd surprised him by staying.

"I have yet to see Gendor," she replied. "I think we should wait."

"He's inside," he said smoothly.

Her eyes narrowed. "I did not see him enter."

"My ally saw Gendor with his own target."

"Would you lie to me?" she asked.

"Yes," he replied.

She chuckled, the sound annoyed. "Then how do I know I can trust you?"

"You don't," he said. "I thought I'd made that clear. We aren't here because we trust each other. We're here because we need each other."

She scowled, an expression that was quickly becoming his favorite. It pulled at her lips in a way he found captivating, but he did his best to hold her gaze. With Water's aid, they could breach the guildhall and get what they needed. And waiting would mean losing their quarry.

"We'll do it your way," she said. "But know this, if you lied to me, you get a scar. You won't survive a second lie."

"Then I'll make sure to make it count," he said with a smile.

She grunted in irritation and gestured to the guildhall. "What's your plan?"

Chapter 16: The Raven Archives

"Ready?" Shadow asked.

Lorica grunted in answer, causing Shadow to grin. Taking her answer as agreement, he crossed the street to the estate wall. They'd argued about going in at night, but Shadow had pointed out that the Raven might depart, and they should act quickly.

The storm gathered in the sky above, casting looming shadows in the street. Trees grew close to the wall and Shadow leapt into the branches, using them to cross the wall and enter the estate grounds. Lorica followed, and the pair worked their way through the roving guards to the Dentis home.

"Good luck," Shadow said.

"I don't need luck," she retorted.

He grinned and separated from her, threading his way towards the grand home. Guards patrolled the grounds, but their attention was on the outer wall, and Shadow reached for the patches of darkness beneath windows, using them to scale his way to the bedchamber of Lady and Lord Dentis.

Turning elemental, he slipped through the gap in the window and darted to the closet. He knew the room well, and had even slept in the regal bed, which was surprisingly uncomfortable for such wealth. Ignoring the rich trappings, he left the closet door cracked open and retreated into the dark folds of cloth.

For anyone else, sitting in absolute darkness would have been unnerving, but for Shadow it was like a warm blanket on a cold night, and he reclined against the wall of the closet, feeling the wood at his back. With his magic, he could see the interior of the closet as if a dozen light orbs hung in the small space. But his vision could do nothing about the smell.

Doused in perfumes and scents meant to rob sweat of its rank, the closet reeked, and several times he had to fight a sneeze. He'd explored the entire manor of the house of Dentis before and never located Raven's archives. He suspected they were located close or in the bedchamber. The only question was, would the Raven access the archives before Water was trapped?

It didn't take long for the sounds of conversation approached, and he shifted to peer through the crack. The bedchamber contained a large bed with sheets flowing from above. Vivid tapestries adorned the walls, while a single desk sat against the north wall. Two doors connected to the space, one that led down a corridor to a bathing chamber and another to the private receiving room.

Through the doorway to the receiving room, couches and tables were visible, the room lit with a trio of cats fashioned of brilliant light. The creatures were small and obviously sentient. They prowled around the summit of the anteroom, the chains of light clanking quietly.

". . . cage is in place," a male voice said. "The trap will work as planned."

"Well done," a female voice said. "You may inform Serak."

"You will not be joining us?"

"I have other business to attend to," she said. "I will join you in a moment."

An armored dwarf and a woman stepped into view and the dwarf gave a curt bow before retreating from sight. Alone, the woman stood in the center of the receiving room before turning and striding to her bedchamber.

Short and unassuming, the woman looked like any other noble. Her bright red hair was as captivating as her figure, her skin lovely and soft. In public she smiled often, her eyes igniting with amusement and delight. In private, her smile was absent, her gaze cold and calculating.

126

Her dress was a beautiful red accented with black, augmenting the fire of her hair and the lightness to her skin. She slipped free of the dress as she walked into the room, revealing fitted armor beneath. The material was obviously dwarven made, the slight luminescence suggesting it had been enchanted for strength.

She tossed the dress onto the bed and made her way to the closet, forcing Shadow to retreat into a thousand cloaks. His nose tickled and he struggled not to sneeze as the door swung open. Instead of reaching for clothing, she touched a release on the inside of the door and a panel swung open, revealing an abundance of daggers hidden in the wood. She removed the one she wore and picked up a curved blade, and then a small hand crossbow. Sufficiently armed, she closed the door and returned to the receiving room, unaware that her shadow had gained a passenger.

She strode across the bedchamber to the arched doorway leading to the anteroom. Stepping outside, she entered the small room separating the bedchamber from the hallway. The room contained a pair of paintings on either wall, and the shining cats prowled the ledge at the top of the walls. The Raven came to a halt at the door to the hall and used her dagger to reach up and tap the keystone.

Standing just inches behind her, Shadow's eyes widened when the silver light gathered in the keystone, and then flowed downward, expanding to fill the opening, obscuring the door. The silver liquid finished taking shape and then flickered, showing the Raven's reflection. Without hesitation she stepped through the Gate.

As Shadow followed her through, he realized two things. First, the reason the receiving area was guarded by three sentient cats was not for the safety of the Raven, it was to protect the Gate, and second, the Gate was hidden over an actual door, so one would always see the opening and assume it was merely that.

The room on the opposite side of the Gate was very different from the manor. Stark stone walls greeted him, the material faintly illuminated by a blue light orb hovering at the center of the circular chamber. The room was completely enclosed, without any windows. Instead it contained more Gates around the exterior wall, each with a symbol above that marked the destination. A glance back revealed that

127

they had entered through one of them, and the symbol above the Gate was of a bird. A raven.

Four corridors extended away from the central hall, but they too lacked windows, the light emanating from ensconced light orbs. The smells of earth and stone were prominent, suggesting they were deep underground.

Lady Dentis was focused on a Gate across the room, and Shadow used the opportunity to slip to one of the shadows next to a supporting beam. From there he watched Lady Dentis withdraw a letter from a pouch at her side. She reached the center of the room and came to a halt, and a moment later the Gate across from her opened.

Shadow expected a human or elf. Instead the individual that stepped free looked vaguely humanoid and had grey skin and black eyes. Shadow recognized him immediately as Relgor, Wylyn's son, and examined the krey with interest. A dark elf stepped into view beside him, and both strode to meet Lady Dentis.

The Raven inclined her head. "The fragment of Water is on his way. It won't be long now."

Relgor unrolled the parchment, a scowl appearing on his face as he read. "This is all the information you have? A copy of a map? I cannot build a Gate without the right material."

The Raven motioned to the parchment. "That map shows the location of a mine in the dwarven kingdom, where I believe they have the material you seek."

"Let me pursue the Gate material," the dark elf said, casting a sneer at the Raven. "I will not fail."

"After your failure in the Deep?" Relgor scoffed. "You aren't fit to accompany me."

The dark elf flushed. "The fragment of Water was more powerful than Serak described."

"You failed," the Raven said, a touch of smugness in her tone.

"And you think to use the Dark Dwarf to trap Water?"

128

"Gendor has faith in Thorg," the Raven said. "His fire magic will contain the fragment."

The dark elf growled and jerked her head. "What of the other fragments? We have been preparing for them for ages."

"All will discover their fate soon enough," Relgor said. "Now go below and prepare for Water's arrival. Shadow will undoubtedly be dispatched into the Deep, and you must have your trap ready."

"He is the weakest of the five," she said. "He will not escape."

Shadow grinned at that statement and resisted the urge to reveal himself and strike at all three to prove them wrong. The light at the center of the chamber would not allow his magic, and he guessed there was more to learn.

"See that it's done," Relgor said. "I'll take my journey to what you call the dwarven kingdom."

"Long live the ancients," the Raven said.

Relgor smirked. "Long live the krey."

The Raven bowed to Relgor, and then retreated the way she had come. The dark elf and Relgor departed as well, leaving Shadow alone in the crossroads. In the empty chamber Shadow waited, wanting to be certain the Raven would not return. When he was satisfied, he detached himself from the shadows and looked to where the Raven had departed, pondering what he'd learned.

The existence of the crossroads, and Relgor's presence, confirmed that the Ravens served the Order. It also revealed how the Order had kept themselves hidden from Elenyr and the fragments, for they could go and depart with ease.

The knowledge that the Raven took orders from the krey made it clear that Relgor already had access to the ancient map, altering Elenyr's assignment. Shadow mentally altered the assignment to stopping Relgor from getting what he wanted.

Shadow resisted the urge to explore each of the Gates and reminded himself that he needed the map first. Making his way to the four corridors pointing away from the Gate room, he followed each.

The first contained private quarters and offices, likely those reserved for the leaders of the Order. The second led to an armory large enough for a king, with a host of weaponry that had not been made on Lumineia. Shadow spotted a crate of the explosive weapons used at the Assassin's Guildhall and couldn't resist dipping his hand into the treasure, stealing one. The side of the crate had strange runes, but someone had written words in the common tongue.

Deton Spheres. Use with caution.

The third corridor led to a balcony, likely the only outside entrance to the hidden crossroads. The tiny ledge contained a railing and a shocking view. A mile off the earth, Shadow looked out over an endless vista of snow and ice, of great mountains that resembled foothills. It seemed he stood on the tallest mountain on earth, and when he returned to the crossroads he saw it with new eyes. It had not been built by the Order.

It had been built by the krey.

The stone was old, ancient even, probably as old as the Dawn of Magic. The Gates connected throughout Lumineia, and then he spotted the inscription circling the light orb in the ceiling, marking the location as the Forge of Light.

A chill washed over Shadow as he realized he stood in the birthplace of magic, where a spread of power had touched every soul in Lumineia. His curiosity mounted, but he made his way to the fourth and final corridor.

He expected a dead end, but instead it led to a set of stairs. Shadow descended to another balcony, only this one overlooked the largest cavern he'd ever seen, as if the entire mountain was hollow. The balcony contained an assortment of bookshelves.

Shadow stepped to the railing and looked out over the giant cavern, feeling the cool air against his face. It was so large that, even with

Shadow's vision, he could not see the opposite side. He would have marveled at the krey structure if they weren't trying to kill him.

Turning away, he stepped to the bookshelves and worked his way along. The archives contained few tomes, and instead it was memory orbs and strange objects that stood on the shelf. All were protected by curses, so he kept moving until he located what he sought.

The map did not look like much, only a flat piece of smooth white with an assortment of runes. He retrieved the anti-magic knife he used for such purposes and cut threads of light that surrounded the map. Then he gently lifted it free and stuffed it into his bag. With a final, wistful look, he left the rest of the items behind and made his way back to the crossroads.

Although he heard no one, he kept his pace slow, his caution proving necessary when a man appeared through one Gate and disappeared through another. Shadow grunted in irritation, feeling like he was surrounded by treasure with no time to steal.

He returned to the Gate leading to the Raven's home and activated it as he'd seen the Raven do. The silver liquid flowed into shape and hardened into a mirror, and Shadow stepped through, expecting the room to be long empty. He was wrong.

The Raven stood in the receiving room, all three of the cat sentinels arrayed around her. She smiled like she'd cornered her prey, and the cats went up on their hind legs, a chilling snarl escaping their lips.

"Hello, Shadow," the Raven said. "It's a pleasure to finally meet you."

Chapter 17: Lady Dentis

Shadow gestured to the woman. "With one so beautiful as you, the pleasure is mine."

The Raven smiled, but it did not touch her eyes. "I assume you know we have your brother trapped in the cellar."

"How is he faring in Thorg's cage?"

Her eyes narrowed at his knowledge, and she motioned the cats to surround him. The beasts circled him, the hackles on their backs rising as they herded him to the center of the room. Shadow did not resist, unperturbed by their presence.

"Relgor and Serak want you alive, you know."

"That's reassuring," he said.

"They think they can cage you, but we both know the truth. You would escape, and so you cannot be permitted to live. I will do what must be done and kill you here and now."

"You assume you can," he said.

She shook her head. "Always so arrogant, but I suppose that is part of your fragment."

"You seem to know a great deal about us."

"Serak knows your identity," she said. "And we follow him."

"And the ancients?"

"We knew they would come to claim this world eventually," she said. "So we made sure to prepare for their arrival."

"You invite a scorpion into your bed."

"A scorpion with more power than all the races combined," she said.

Shadow glanced to the cats, but they rotated around him, always moving, their eyes never leaving his body. They'd grown, and were now as large as wolves, their claws scraping the carpet, their powerful limbs coiled to attack.

"Does your husband know of your . . . hobby?"

Her features hardened. "My husband is a fool and lacks the vision of the Order."

"Why not kill him?" Shadow asked.

"You think to judge me?" the Raven asked, taking a step forward, a dagger appearing in her hands. "You've lived for ages but know nothing of life."

"I know he finds comfort in the arms of other women," he said. "But living with you would probably drive anyone into the arms of others."

Her eyes widened with fury, the cats slowing, as if sensing the coming order to kill. But the anger in her expression gradually cooled and she cocked her head to the side. She regarded him with curiosity.

"Did you know that under krey law, infidelity is tantamount to murder?"

"Is stupidity also punishable by death?"

She ignored him, and motioned north, towards the poor section of town. "Under krey rule there is no poverty, no sickness, no ignorance. Mankind lives in peace."

"Slavery is not peace."

"We are all slaves," she said. "Some to poverty, some to pride. Others are slaves to their carnal cravings, while others are slaves to ambition."

"Do you talk all your intruders to death?" he asked, groaning in annoyance. "Why tell me all this?"

"Because I want you to die knowing you chose the wrong side."

"I won't," he said. "I'm too arrogant."

She snorted in disbelief. "So be it. Goodbye Shadow. Know that the other fragments will suffer a worse fate."

"As fond as I am of cats ripping my throat out, I'm afraid I must decline."

She laughed lightly, the sound causing the cats to drift forward. "Your magic is useless against my pets, and we both know you are not as fast as the fragment of Light."

"I don't have to be," he said.

He opened his hand to reveal the krey explosive he'd taken from the crossroads storeroom, and the light was already blinking. The Raven registered the weapon and her eyes widened. She shouted an order just as Shadow dropped the deton sphere. It struck the ground and detonated, the force of the blast catching the three cats and slamming them into the walls. One struck an ornamental sword, the blade cleaving the sentient in two. It burst apart, the light disappearing into smoke and dust.

Standing on the chandelier above, Shadow dusted himself off and spotted the Raven, who'd dived into her bedchamber to avoid the blast. She pulled herself to her feet, smoke rising from tiny fires on her armor. Ash and dirt covered her face and littered the receiving room. Couches were gone, their supports burning, the tapestries also on fire.

"I would say send me a bill," Shadow said. "But I never clean up my messes."

He smirked and darted to the door, slamming it shut as the remaining cats lunged. The first clawed at the door, the second ripping into the wood with its teeth. As Shadow sprinted away, he listened to the Raven's furious shouts.

Shadow reached the stairwell at the end of the corridor and leapt, catching the bracket holding a light orb against the wall. Then he dropped to the lower floor, landing before a trio of guards. All three stumbled to a halt and drew their swords, but Shadow was already among them.

He kicked one guard in the chest, knocking him into a second. Then he reached for the third man's sword, catching the hilt as the man pulled the blade free. Twisting, Shadow spun and hurled the man into the wall, where he crashed into the floor. Then Shadow drew his small crossbow and took aim.

One of the men stumbled to his feet and laughed at the tiny weapon. "You think that's going to hurt us?"

"Of course not," Shadow scoffed, and fired.

The tiny bolt launched into the air, the charm causing it to swerve and aim for one of the light orbs bracketed against the ceiling. It shattered the orb into tinkling glass and passed on, hunting another target. One by one, the bolt shattered the light orbs, piercing the last orb as the two soldiers got to their feet.

The corridor plunged into darkness, causing the men to shout— until the gags formed around their lips. Shadow slipped through them, ropes of darkness coiling about their legs, yanking them to the ground. Silently struggling, they fought to break free, but in the absence of light, Shadow was king.

More guards appeared at the end of the corridor, only to be met by more ropes and more gags. The floor grew crowded so he lashed some to the ceiling, others to the walls. Shadow picked his way past the struggling men and left a handful of traps behind. Lightning crashed outside, briefly illuminating the line of struggling men. Then Shadow descended into the lower level of the manor.

Over the crashing rain, the sound of struggling guards did not reach the lower levels, and Shadow sauntered towards the cellar door. It was open, so he slipped into the darkness beyond and leapt the railing into the darkness below.

The cellar was the size of the manor and contained barrels and crates along the walls. The center of the room had been cleared, allowing for an unbroken view of the cage. Instead of steel, the bars

135

were made of fire chains. The enchantment spit sparks, the heat warming the cellar. The cell contained two occupants, Lira and Water.

Around the room, dozens of Ravens leaned against the walls or sat on barrels. The thieves were dressed like mercenaries, and wore light armor and carried swords. In their midst, two dakorians stood, their hulking figures towering over the humans in the room. Shadow recognized them from Lira's description and gave them a wide berth.

Next to the cage, an unknown man stood beside a dwarf, and Shadow recognized the dwarf as the assassin that had escaped with Gendor, the Dark Dwarf. The conversation had grown heated, commanding the attention of the spectators. Shadow slipped between the dark barrels and ascended to a high perch to listen to the conversation.

Serak may have been a mystery before, but his identity quickly became apparent. The way the other Ravens and Order members showed deference, the way the dakorians stood, as if ready to receive orders. Serak wasn't just part of the Order.

He was its head.

The conversation itself proved very interesting and supported what Water had implied in the *Shark's Tooth*. Serak had lived for as long as Draeken, an unseen adversary that had fought against the fragments since the Age of Oracles. A smile spread on Shadow's face as he realized the identity of their foe.

"How intriguing."

His murmur caused a woman to turn, but he had already let the shadows swallow him and flitted along the outer wall. The assassin Thorg stepped away from the cage and returned with a brand, and Shadow realized he was out of time.

He spotted a collection of small barrels containing various paints. Apparently the Raven had been preparing to repaint the walls of her manor, but Shadow saw a different purpose. Collecting several, he threaded his way through the group of enemies, his leaving a patch of pink here, a swash of purple there.

A woman spotted him leaving a bright pink smile on a man's helmet, so he sent a thread of darkness over her mouth. Her shout went unvoiced, and her body was yanked from view. Shadow slipped behind her companion, lashing him to the stone wall as well. A Raven turned, his eyes going wide. He yanked his sword free but Shadow closed the gap in a rush and silenced him with a single blow.

He spotted Water through the bars of the cage and noticed his stance. Although he seemed calm, Shadow noticed his hands, the tension to his palms and fingers. Shadow had seen that tension before, when Water gathered his magic, summoning unseen water. By now Water knew Shadow was present, so what was his intent?

Shadow noticed the moisture gathering inside the cell, the air in the cellar turning dry. It wouldn't be enough to destroy the cage, but the water would become steam on the bars, darkening the room from the light of the fire. And giving Shadow power.

Realizing Water's intent, Shadow smiled, and spread his arms wide, readying himself for the battle to come. The steam would not last long, but it would give him tremendous power for a few minutes.

"Before you mark me there's something you should know," Water was saying.

"What's that?" Serak said, raising a hand to stop the Dark Dwarf from branding Water.

Water released the magic he'd gathered, and moisture expanded into the bars of fire. The water burst into a plume of steam that engulfed the cage, obscuring everyone from view and plunging the room into darkness.

Serak's chuckle was mocking. "Your attempt to escape is woefully disappointing."

"I wasn't trying to break free," Water said, his voice triumphant. "I just wanted more darkness."

The soldiers shifted uneasily when a quiet laugh escaped Shadow's lips, causing those nearby to turn, catching a glimpse of him as he swelled in size, wrapping his body in flesh of shadows . . .

Chapter 18: The Darkened Cellar

In the depths of darkness, Shadow could have cast anything, but the confines of the cellar did not permit a dragon. Instead, he wrapped himself into the body of a reaver, and just for fun, added a scorpion's tail. And two extra arms sprouting from his back. And a second head.

Twenty feet long, his body was armored in steel-like plates, his tail bearing a lethal spike. In the midst of foes, he crouched low and released a rising growl, the sound betraying his eagerness and sending the people stumbling away.

He charged into a group, lashing out with his tail, skewering a man and tossing him across the room. His great jaws snapped shut and crates splintered, the wood smashing into Ravens and an Order member. Screams and shouts filled the cellar as Shadow rampaged in their midst.

He reached a dakorian and warped his claw into a giant hand that wrapped around the fearsome warrior's throat. Lifting him free, Shadow slammed him into a pillar, and then into the opposite wall. The soldier swung his hammer against the shadow body, cracking plates of armor.

The other dakorian swung his hammer at Shadow's second head, but Shadow whipped the scorpion tail at the soldier, the blade at the end smashing into the dakorian's chest and knocking him tumbling away.

"You are as strong as they say," Shadow said, bringing his jaws to the dakorian's armored skull.

"And you're just an ugly human," he sneered, struggling to break free of Shadow's grip.

Indignant, Shadow's voice dropped. "Ugly?"

Shadow reared back and slammed him into a pillar, snapping it in two. Then he picked up the dakorian's legs and held him up to the ceiling, before bringing him down on the broken pillar. The beam had formed a shard of wood, and it pierced the dakorian's armor, driving into his flesh.

He cried out as Shadow pinned him to the floor, and still reached for Shadow. But the mist had begun to dissipate, and with each passing second, Shadow's body lost its solidity. The dying dakorian's arms went limp, allowing Shadow to dart away, narrowly avoiding the hammer of his companion.

Shadow threaded his way through the enraged Ravens. Those with paint on their features were furious, their anger making them foolish. Shadow ducked an axe, the blade slicing deep into an Order member's side. He screamed in anger and struck back. Another sword came for Shadow, and he slipped to the side, poking the swinging blade with his finger, sending it into a woman's helm. The steel held, and the *clang* echoed in the cellar until the woman slumped to the floor.

Shadow leapt above the battle, smirking as he passed over the chaos below. He leaned over the edge and cast a group of shadow soldiers. They lacked the ability to do much harm, but they sewed chaos in the ranks of the Ravens.

He spotted Thorg approaching Water in his cage and veered in his direction. Just as the dwarf spoke, Shadow reached out and wrapped a clawed hand around his torso. Then he picked him up and launched him across the room, his body bouncing off the stairs and colliding with several Ravens.

The remaining dakorian struck Shadow's flank, hacking at his armor. Whirling, Shadow merged his two heads into one giant one, and chomped on the soldier. He continued to fight even with his upper body in Shadow's jaws, so Shadow launched him at the cage of fire. He crashed into the bars, his sheer weight cracking several bars before he bounced over and struck the ground, burn lines on the bones of his back.

The duel had permitted the rest to converge on Shadow, so he cast a horde of gremlins in the darkness. The smaller creatures of shadow burst through the darkness, jumping to women and pulling their hair, tearing into the clothing of the men, and clawing at feet. Women shrieked and men howled, and Shadow laughed in delight.

Shadow paused when he spotted Serak. The father of guardians had retreated to the side of the conflict, where he stood watching. His expression was calculating, almost triumphant. Annoyed at his expression, Shadow stepped free of his entity and sent it into the melee. Then he leapt to the ceiling and snuck behind Serak.

"Enjoying the conflict?" Shadow asked, driving a shadow blade for his back.

The man twisted, spoiling Shadow's aim. "Shadow," he said evenly. "You weren't supposed to be here."

"I like to be where I'm not wanted," Shadow said, circling the man.

"Since you are here, allow me to give a piece of advice," Serak said. He calmly withdrew a small light orb, blunting Shadow's knife as he struck again.

"What's that?" Shadow asked, circling back in case Serak attacked.

"When the time comes, remember that a piece is never as powerful as the whole."

"I will remember that," Shadow said. "Just as you should remember what it's like to be swallowed."

Shadow had directed his giant beast behind Serak, and it dipped its head. Serak twisted to evade but the tongue slapped across his cheek, rising up his head and sticking it on end. Serak sputtered and attempted to wipe the moisture away, but his hand came away with paint. Shadow laughed at his dismay and leapt astride his beast.

Serak bellowed for light, and someone ignited a light orb. The mist was clearing as well, and with each spark of light Shadow's beast faded. In moments he would be vulnerable, and he cast about for a place to hide. Instead he saw Water on his knees inside the cage, and the wall at the back of the cellar beginning to tremble.

A wicked smile on his face, Shadow retreated, letting the chaos die, permitting Serak to return to his place at the cage. A faint cracking of stone indicated a wall was about to break, but none but Shadow seemed to notice.

Serak stepped into the pool of light by the cage and Shadow stifled a laugh. The guardian's features were painted bright orange, his hair spiked in one direction from where Shadow's beast had licked his face, the saliva holding the hair straight upward. Paint dripped down his face and onto his body, staining his fine tunic.

"You'll pay for that," Serak growled, his eyes on Shadow, who stood on the threshold of darkness.

"Not before you do," Water said. He brought his hands together, and the back wall exploded.

The wave crashed over the cage, cooling the bars until they disintegrated. Parting around Water and Lira the wave flooded the basement. When the bars disintegrated, he caught Lira about the waist and the water picked him up, carrying him into the room.

Thorg and the thieves still on their feet converged upon Water, and Shadow leapt to join his brother. Serak's orders had been followed, and soldiers continued to ignite light orbs. Bereft of darkness, Shadow found himself in the midst of a dozen foes. Drawing his dagger, he fought for space.

Steel rang on steel, echoing in the cellar, and then Shadow spotted Water astride a wave of water. As a man swung his blade, Shadow flipped over his head, and came down close to Water's wave. He leapt aboard, his taunting laughter echoing back to the defeated enemy.

The wave carried them up the stairs and into the house, where Water had to bank them to the side. They crashed into a cabinet and glass shattered, fine dishes shattering on the floor. He caught a glimpse of Lorica through an open door and swiveled to watch as the Ravens mounted pursuit. Lorica burst into view and cut them down, surprising Thorg, who appeared on the stairs. Catching him by his tunic, she launched him into the dining hall and smoothly shackled his wrists.

Lorica leapt into the dining hall and shut the door before anyone else appeared. The rest of the guards flooded from the cellar, filling the corridor, with Serak at their back. Shadow offered a mocking wave as they blasted through the front doors and disappeared into the storm.

They streaked across the grounds and through the gates, where Water banked them into the road. The storm had picked up while they were inside and rain battered against them. Water used the extra power to accelerate, speeding them away from the Raven's manor.

"They were ready for us," Water said.

"It appears that way," Shadow said.

Water nodded, but Shadow noticed the anger in his gaze, and realized he thought Shadow had sent him into a trap. He had, of course, but Water's anger was a nice reward. Water sent a burst of water beneath them, carrying them to a rooftop garden and sending the makeshift river speeding out of sight. Riders appeared and gave chase, but they failed to notice Water's escape, and they carried on.

Water motioned to the disappearing river. "That should keep them occupied until we are out of Keese."

"Well done," Shadow said, shaking water off his arms.

"Couldn't have done it without your aid," Water said, but his features were tight, like he was upset.

Shadow bowed and swept his hands wide. "I live to serve."

"I thought you lived to play," Lira said.

"That too," Shadow said.

Lira was drenched, her hair in disarray, her clothing sodden. But there was a smile on her face as she dismissed her sword. Water murmured to her and dried her clothes, and Shadow used their distraction to glance at the manor. He hadn't thought Lorica would stay and fight once she knew Gendor was absent. But she'd stayed to fight Thorg. Now she was in a hornets' nest of foes, and he was surprised to feel a pinprick of worry.

"Serak was ready for us," Lira said. "He was ready for Water."

"I thought the same thing," Water said, glancing to Lira. "That cage would have taken a year to build, and multiple mages."

"But Wylyn has only been here for a few months," Lira protested, shaking her head in confusion.

"It appears Serak planned to trap you before Wylyn appeared," Shadow said, feigning confusion.

"In the Gate Chamber," Water said, glancing to Lira. "He did say he wasn't ready to meet us." Then he frowned and swept a hand to Shadow. "Did you know it was a trap?"

"Perhaps." Shadow couldn't resist a smile.

"I could have been branded," Water growled.

"We got what we needed," Shadow said, pleased to see Water angry. He didn't often lose his temper. "And it was a pleasure to see you so furious."

"*You* got what you needed," Lira said, her expression tight with disapproval. "And we paid the price."

"You were *supposed* to get caught," Shadow reminded them. "And you *did* get the chance to speak to Serak. From what I heard, you learned a great deal."

"You lied to us," Water said.

"Serak would have noticed if you were prepared," Shadow said. "You aren't very good at assuming a different persona." He stole a glance into the street, and spotted Lorica at the corner. "It's been a pleasure, brother, but my assignment awaits. Have fun with Lira."

"Where are you going?" Water asked. "Did you get the map?"

"Do you even know me?" Shadow asked. He reached into a pouch and tossed the map to him. "Something came up—I'll meet up with you later."

Without waiting for a reply, Shadow dropped to the ground and darted away. Lorica appeared from a nearby alley and joined him, and the two disappeared into the city. He noticed blood on her clothes and a nasty gash on her arm, as well as a cut on her stomach. A third injury marked her leg, and burns scorched her armor and clothing.

"You're supposed to leave *him* looking like that."

She scowled. "Gendor wasn't there."

"Too bad," Shadow said, a shade too flippantly.

Lorica caught his arm and pulled him into an alley, where she pushed him against a wall and drew her sword. The blade touched Shadow's throat, pinning him to the wall. Her glare was more than anger.

"Gendor was never there," she snapped. "You lied to me."

"Are you saying you found nothing?" he challenged.

"I didn't find Gendor," she said. "But I did find Thorg . . ."

Chapter 19: The Missing Target

Lorica watched Shadow disappear through the window into the Raven's bedchamber, still wondering if she could trust him. His plan to infiltrate the Raven guild hall seemed solid, but she got the impression he was withholding a great deal of information, and she didn't like being left in the dark. The Ravens were the best lead she had for finding Gendor and Thorg, but the way he'd spoken of Gendor's presence did not leave her feeling confident.

Lightning sparked in the clouds above and thunder rumbled. The rain had started but the full storm had yet to hit, and water sluiced off her clothing. She grunted in irritation and wished her traveling companion was more reliable.

She retreated into the darker shadows of the oak tree, positioning herself next to the bushes. Guards patrolled the grounds, the security augmented with the forces that had arrived the previous day. She hadn't seen any sign of Gendor, but she'd seen Thorg.

The thought of the dwarf assassin betraying the guild tightened her gut, and anger ascended her throat like bile. She stifled the emotion, reminding herself that it could get her killed. She waited for another group of guards to pass and then hurried to the outer wall of the manor.

Like most noble houses in Talinor, the windows were shuttered, the bars on the two lowest levels preventing entry by thieves. Shadow had scaled the exterior wall like it was easy, that annoying smile fixed on his face.

She grunted and strode to the back door of the manor. It was guarded by a burly human, and she crept up on his flank, using the rain to muffle her approach. Just as he turned, she stepped from the bushes and struck his helmet. She caught him as he slumped and dragged him back into the bushes. Then she eased her way through the now unguarded door and passed through the storerooms to the kitchens.

She was still irritated that Shadow had let her unwittingly infiltrate the manor, but it now proved very useful, and she already knew the layout. She ducked into a storeroom as a pair of cook women rushed by, obviously intent on finishing a meal in time for the Raven.

Lorica poked her head out of the doorway and then eased into the corridor. The smell of bread and roast meat wafted from the kitchens, the savory scents drifting down the hall. She slipped into the kitchens and donned an apron over the dress she already wore, both obscuring the armor she wore beneath.

"You look nice in a dress," Shadow had said as they'd prepared to infiltrate the manor.

"Why aren't you donning a persona?"

Shadow had laughed. "Why would I need to?"

As she strode down the corridor, she kept her gaze on the floor, irritated and impressed by Shadow. His magic made him arrogant, but was his pride not earned? She wondered if any strongroom on Lumineia could not be breached, simply because he was so adept at bending darkness to his will. For the first time, she considered the idea that Shadow was actually his name.

She made her way into the dining hall, and then ducked into a closet filled with brooms. She left the door ajar, allowing herself a view of the grand table. Through the far doorway she could see the door to the cellar, where the distant sounds of voices were audible.

Shadow had refused to name the ally that would provide the distraction but insisted they would infiltrate below, while he ascended to the top of the manor. With Lorica entering on the first floor, the trio were able to see the entire breadth of the large home, allowing each of them to find their intended target. She fleetingly considered ascending to the top floor and spying on Shadow but wondered if even she could sneak up on the man. Reminding herself of her purpose, she settled in to watch the dining hall.

The dining hall was large enough for a castle, with a lofty ceiling and hand-woven rugs. The table itself had been cut by magic, the large surface smooth and polished to reflect the many light orbs hanging from the ceiling.

Two great paintings occupied opposite sides of the room, one of Lord Dentis, the other of his wife. Lady Dentis wore a bright red dress in the depiction, accenting her beauty and lighting her hair. Her eyes were soft and delighted, a slight smile on her lips as if she knew a secret the viewer did not.

She examined the room with a critical eye, preparing herself for the coming battle. Thorg was as dangerous as Gendor, and if they came together, she would be hard pressed to fight them both. She thought of Gendor's face and her hand tightened on the hilt of her oathsword, her mind returning to Loralyn's body. She would not fail to exact revenge.

A flicker of movement drew her eye, and she spotted a group of Ravens appearing in the entrance corridor. They followed the man that had arrived yesterday, the one she knew as Serak. At the rear of the group, Thorg strolled with his hand on his axe hilt.

Her heart quickened, her breath growing harsh. She recalled his expression when he'd sided with Gendor, and his sneer of pleasure as he'd killed the other members of the council. He was a dwarf who loved the shedding of blood. He too had killed Lyn, and Lorica wanted to kill him, to drive her oathsword through his traitorous heart.

She reached for the door of the closet but her hand froze on the handle, the cold metal reminding her of her purpose. She was here for Gendor. She gripped the handle so tightly her fingers turned white, but the moment passed, and Thorg disappeared into the cellar with the others.

She forced her hand to unclench and then retreated into the closet, her breathing coming in ragged gasps. Thoughts of her sister were fast and hard, and she struck the wall with her fist, fighting to hold them in check.

Seething in silence, she waited. Every moment she wanted to descend into the cellar and grab Thorg by the throat, to squeeze Gendor's location from the assassin before plunging her blade through his heart. She fought the desire with logic, and told herself that she was an assassin, trained to be patient. But patience hadn't lost its family.

147

Through the cellar door she heard a muffled *thump*, and she welcomed the distraction. From the ensuing sounds she assumed Shadow's friend had been caught in the trap, and she wondered if Shadow had considered the possibility that Serak would kill them. It rankled that Shadow had not given the identity of his ally, and she was tempted to cross the corridor and look for herself. But if she were noticed . . .

She listened to the conversation, the snippets of heated words rising from the cellar door. Her heart had stilled, her breathing calm, and she felt a fleeting gratitude for the point of focus. She thought of her target and again glanced across the dining hall. A scullery maid had passed inside and dusted the cabinets before she passed out of sight, scurrying with a furtive glance to the cellar door.

Her attention on the dining hall, Lorica almost missed Shadow's appearance. The man appeared and disappeared, entering the cellar like a wisp of smoke. After all the effort to keep herself hidden, she felt a touch of envy at the casual ease with which he moved.

The seconds ticked by while she watched, and she retrieved the anti-magic shackles she used against mage targets. Gendor was not a mage, but Thorg was very powerful, and surprise would be her ally.

Sound erupted from the cellar, of bones and bricks breaking, of wood snapping and cries of pain. In the darkness Lorica smiled faintly. Shadow might be a mystery, but he certainly knew how to wreak havoc.

She eased from the closet and crept along the wall to the doorway. Just feet from the cellar door, she watched the barrier, her attention tuned to her surroundings, to the chance a random maid could enter the room, or a group of soldiers rushing to the sounds of battle. Then suddenly the door burst open, and out flowed a wave of water.

Shadow rode the wave with a man bearing his same features, except for the eyes, which were bright blue. With the door open a crack, Lorica watched them, shocked to see one that could have been Shadow's twin.

A woman rode with them, all three astride the wave. It banked into a cabinet against the wall of the corridor, shattering glass and snapping wood. Then the wave turned down the corridor, accelerating towards the door. In their sodden wake, guards rushed in pursuit, shouting for aid.

Lorica caught a glimpse of Shadow before they departed and their eyes met. He offered a cheeky smile.

Secreted in the doorway, Lorica opened the shackles and tensed. Thorg burst into view and sprinted down the corridor, his furious gaze fixed on departing foes. Lorica stepped into the open and caught his arm, smoothly attaching the anti-magic shackles to his wrist. With a deft twist, she rolled him around and fastened the second binding before shoving him into the dining hall.

Shutting the door behind them, Lorica turned to face the rising assassin, and withdrew a small orange orb which she tossed against the door. The ensuing *ping* echoed, and then all sound closed off from the room, ensuring that none from the cellar would hear.

"Lorica," Thorg sneered. "I thought you were dead."

"I'm not easy to kill."

"Your sister was."

Lorica's jaw tightened and she started forward as the dwarf retreated. He worked at the shackles that bound his wrists and magic, but they were forged by dwarf and enchanted by gnome.

"Where's Gendor?" Lorica asked, stalking him, her oathsword in hand.

"With Relgor," Thorg said. "In the north."

"I was told he was here."

"Are you certain your source told the truth?"

She thought of Shadow and her lips tightened. Flicking her blade, she held it aloft, showing him the red steel. His eyes hardened as he recognized the oathsword and he retreated another step, still trying to dislodge the bindings.

"Before I kill you I want to know why," she asked, closing the gap another step. "Why did you betray the guild?"

"We were mired by tradition," the dwarf said. "And if we continued to follow your sister, we would have been as poor as the seventh circle of Herosian."

"Better poor with honor than rich without."

The dwarf sneered in disgust. "So says the rich. You and your sister hated killing, and I will never understand why Thaden named your sister as his replacement."

"Because she was better than all of you," Lorica growled.

"Yet Gendor defeated her."

She continued to stalk forward, and her blade trembled in her hand. "His victory will be short lived."

"The assassins have evolved," Thorg said. "And you are a relic. In a year, the people will live in terror of Bloodsworn blades, of the mark we will leave on a target set to be killed. Kings will obey our commands, and all will scatter at the mention of our name."

"And the Order?"

"We are the hand of the Order," he said. "And the time has come for us to take our rightful place."

"Not if you are dead."

The dwarf came to a halt and held up his bound hands. "You think to kill me bound and helpless? You are indeed a fool."

He reached up to his beard and withdrew a small silver blade hidden within. Lorica's eyes widened and she darted in, but the dwarf caught the knife and stabbed the shackles. A piercing whine erupted in the dining hall and the shackles disintegrated.

Chapter 20: The Dark Dwarf

Lorica drove her sword towards his chest, but the blade struck a wall of stone rising from the floor. She reached for the top and leapt over, but Thorg had sprinted away. She dived to the table and rolled across, just as a shard of stone pierced the table. Like a sharp tooth, it rent the table and cut her side. Dishes shattered on the floor.

She rolled to her feet and spread the wings of her cloak, sprinting up the painting and kicking off the Raven's face. She banked to the side, narrowly avoiding a spear of fire that plunged into the painting. Flames licked at Lady Dentis, spreading away from the spear.

"You should have killed me when you had the chance," Thorg said.

She angled her sweep and spotted him standing near the door. He raised a hand and the stones of the floor ground together, shaping into a giant hand that reached up for her. She folded her wings and twirled through the fingers of the stone hand. She slipped through the hand and spread her wings, diving at the dwarf.

He cast a whip of fire and snapped it, burning through her armor and sending fires scorching her clothing. She dropped, collapsing her wings so she could roll across the floor, into Thorg's reach.

Her sword sliced across his shoulder as he ducked and drew his axe. The searing blade swung low, grazing her leg before swiping back, catching her on her side, her armor saving her life.

She stepped in and caught him by the beard, yanking his skull into her knee. He cried out as his nose broke and he reared back, bellowing at her. She swung her sword, but he leaned down and struck the floor, sending a wall of fire billowing outward.

She dived under the table as the flames rippled across the chamber, melting gold and burning wood, the expensive table igniting. The Raven looked pitiful, everything above the waist now burned except for a portion of one eye and an ear. Lord Dentis had lost the lower half of his painting, the flames climbing upward.

Thorg's giant stone hand came down on the table like he was trying to swat a fly, crushing the wood and the chairs beneath, the other end swinging upward. Narrowly missing being crushed, Lorica rolled out from under the table and leapt to the tooth of stone sticking through the middle of the table. Crafted from the stonework of the floor, the surface was far from smooth, and she caught a grip near the top, using it to swing herself into the air.

Thorg was on his knees, clenching his nose and shouting. He spotted her diving at him and opened the floor, dropping from sight. Lorica folded her wings, passing through the narrowing hole and landing in the cellar.

Pools of water were everywhere, and the shattered beams, crates, and barrels bore testament to Shadow's skill. All had departed in pursuit of Shadow, and the demolished cellar lay empty. Lorica only had eyes for her adversary, and she landed hard, driving her blade for the dwarf.

He rolled aside, her sword glancing off the stones. Then he used the momentum to come to his feet and hack at her arm, the axe blade leaving a gash. Hot pain lanced up her arm but she snarled and darted in, deflecting his next blow and kicking him in the chest, knocking the dwarf into a barrel that had miraculously survived. Thorg bounced off it and rolled across the ground.

"You think you can betray the guild without consequence?" Her raspy voice echoed in the confines of the cellar, harsh and brimming with fury. Lorica lunged and swung her blade. He managed to block, but the force of the blow knocked him into the wall. "You think to kill *my sister* without consequence?"

Lorica again grabbed him by the beard and hurled him sideways, sending him spinning towards the burning cage. The dwarf rolled to his feet and stumbled backward, raising a wall of stone between them. But Lorica leapt off the body of a dakorian and flared her wings, soaring over the wall to kick the dwarf in the cheek. He flew backward and struck a pair of burning bars extending from the floor, crying out as the flames touched his skin. She leveled her sword at him, the blade trembling at his nose.

"I am the Angel of Death! The sword of justice. But today I bring only vengeance, and I deem you unworthy of your life."

He brought his axe up, striking at her sword before calling on the flames of the bars. They formed a soldier of fire, the entity stepping between Thorg and Lorica. With an enormous greatsword in his hands, he swung, the blade coming for her head.

She ducked and rotated inside the entity's guard, and then drove her sword through the fire entity's stomach, and into Thorg's body. He cried out in pain, and the soldier crumbled around the blade, smoke and sparks dissipating to reveal Thorg's features twisted in shock.

Lorica gazed with unflinching eyes on the dwarf that had betrayed the guild. His jaw worked in disbelief, and he looked down at the end of the oathsword in his chest. He tried to speak but his strength abandoned him, and he dropped to his knees.

"You cannot stop the Order," he groaned.

"I don't care about the Order," she spat the words at him. "I'm here to claim the price of your betrayal."

"By killing me you've chosen a side." He coughed and grimaced. "You've sealed your fate and that of everyone you care about."

She leaned in until they were inches apart. "I don't have anyone left."

Thorg's eyes closed and he slumped, and she pulled her sword free. Flicking the blood from the blade, she sheathed it and stared at the assassin's body. Her fury faded, allowing the pain of her wounds to the fore.

Turning away from the body, she ascended the steps out of the cellar, quickening her pace when she heard shouting. She stepped into the hall, and at the same moment a dozen guards appeared at the opposite end. One spotted her and bellowed an order, and soldiers burst into view.

She turned away from the guards and sprinted up the nearby stairs, weaving her way down a corridor and up a second set of stairs. There she entered a corridor so dark she could barely make out the struggling bodies on the floor and walls. There was even a woman bound to the ceiling, her face furious as she fought the gag on her mouth.

Lorica stared in bewilderment until a shriek came from above, followed by the crashing and splintering of wood. Lights appeared at the opposite end of the corridor, rising to illuminate the stairwell. Two fearsome cats of pure light bounded down the stairs, followed by the Raven herself. The sudden brilliance caused the shadow bonds to disintegrate, and bodies fell.

A woman cried out as she was set free and crashed into the head of a guard below, the others thumping off each other to land on the floor. The Raven stared, her mouth agape as her guards rained down from the ceiling, and then spotted Lorica at the opposite end of the hall. Trapped between the dozen guards behind and the sudden army in front, Lorica drew her sword.

"*Shadow*," Lorica spit the word like a curse.

With no other option, she leapt a thief struggling to rise and then launched herself over a pair of guards reaching for their swords. Holding her momentum, she sidestepped a hasty lunge and elbowed him in the back, knocking him into another.

"Kill her," the Raven barked, and the cats burst into motion.

The two felines streaked through the guards, the leader lunging for Lorica, its claws scraping her armor. She twisted to avoid the first cat and then ducked the swipe from the second cat—but caught its tail. She drew a knife from her side and slammed the blade through the tail, embedding the steel into the floor and momentarily pinning the threat.

She leapt back as the cat spun, but the dagger held, and the claws stopped short of removing Lorica's face. The second cat skidded to a halt and charged again, driving for Lorica, its body low to the ground.

Lorica flared her wings, curving one to block the cat's view. Then she sidestepped and plunged her sword into the floor. The cat moved with her, swerving and diving through the wing—into the embedded sword. Its sheer momentum split the creature from whiskers to tail, and the two sides disintegrated to either side of Lorica, bursting into sparks of light. All present shielded their eyes as the blinding light filled the hallway, and when it dissipated the corridor was empty. An open door led to guest quarters, and the window beyond.

The Raven picked her way to the window and stared into the rain. "Find them," she barked to the guards behind her. "Or it's you I'll feed to the cat."

"Yes, my lady," a man said.

The man barked an order and the other guards scurried from the room. In their absence the cat approached, pressing its flank against her leg. She struck it on the head, and the enchantment whined like a real feline before shrinking back to the size of a house cat. Then it plodded away, leaving the Raven to glare at the rain.

From the roof above, Lorica retreated. She crossed to a far edge of the roof, careful of the wet tiles, and then dropped off the edge. As guards streamed out of the front entrance, she soared over the back wall and into the storm, allowing it to swallow her.

Rain pummeled her wings and battered her frame, and lightning appeared in the heavens, the thunder rumbling across her. Flying in a storm was a risk, but she wanted to find Shadow. To punish him.

She curved over the city, scanning rooftops until she spotted Shadow with his two companions. Then Lorica dropped into an alley and folded her wings behind her, waiting for Shadow to appear. She paced in the alley, her triumph over Thorg replaced by a simmering anger. Shadow had lied to her. He'd said he would but she'd still trusted him, a choice she now regretted.

She pulled out a strip of cloth and methodically bound her wounds, grimacing as the bandage tightened on the raw flesh, her anger continuing to mount. She'd followed Shadow to Keese, trusted him when her instincts said otherwise, and then he'd lied to her. She'd managed to kill Thorg, a death she'd wanted, but not until she'd fulfilled her oath to kill Gendor.

155

She watched Shadow drop from the roof into an alley and stride in her direction. With not even a scratch to mar his body, he strode towards her with the same arrogant lilt to his lips. When Shadow turned to her, she stepped into the open, and palmed the hilt of her oathsword . . .

Chapter 21: A Game of Truth

"Is that it?" Shadow asked when Lorica finished. "What's with the blade on my throat?"

"You lied to me," she snapped.

"I said I would," he replied, and grinned. "And you did say the first was free."

Her eyes darkened, and her sword trembled in her hand. He wondered if he'd gone too far, and then she tightened her grip and leaned forward, her voice hardening, a cold reminder of her occupation.

"I didn't say it was free."

Shadow grimaced as the blade slid along his neck, splitting skin, spilling blood. The cut was deep enough to sting, not enough to kill, but her gaze made it clear it could have. When the blade withdrew, Shadow reached up to the wound, his anger rising.

"What was that for?" he demanded.

"I said I'd give you a scar," she said.

"I didn't think you meant it," he said. He pulled back his hand to reveal the blood. "Are you mad? I handed you Gendor on a silver plate."

"He wasn't there," she said, stabbing her sword toward the manor. "And you knew it."

Despite his obvious lie, he hadn't thought she'd actually cut him. He'd survived the battle in the Raven's manor unscathed, only to be cut by one he thought an ally. He held up the blood on his hand as if it would prove his point.

"You're a hunter of men," he said. "Gendor may not have been inside, but Thorg was, and he would know how to find him. Did you make him talk before you killed him?"

She opened her mouth, but no answer escaped her lips. Shadow saw the failure in her expression and stabbed a finger at her. "You failed? I thought you were supposed to be good. The Angel of Death, the sword of justice."

"I *am* good," she said. "I killed Thorg, and he said Gendor was in the north with Relgor."

"That's it?" Shadow pointed that direction, his voice dripping with scorn. "You didn't ask for more detail?"

"Did you learn anything?" she asked.

"I learned Relgor is looking for a particular ore in the dwarven kingdom," Shadow said. "I can only assume Gendor is with him, since you killed your source."

She scowled. "I wasn't here to kill Thorg."

"Then why are you here?" he challenged.

She held the sword up so he could see the blade. "Do you even know what this sword is? An oathsword is meant for revenge, to claim a single life. I swore over the body of my sister that the next life I took would be Gendor's—and you made me break my oath."

"You could have told me that," Shadow said.

"*You* could have told the truth," she spat.

"I *never* tell the truth," he said, sweeping his hands wide. "I get the job done. That's what *I* do, and I try to have fun while doing it."

She closed the gap, bringing her face inches from his. "This isn't a game to me."

"It's always a game."

"Says the one that just put his brother's life at risk."

"I didn't say he was my brother," Shadow said.

"He looks just like you," she said. "Who else could it be? And if he is another fragment, I assume he is the fragment of Water?"

Shadow's anger turned to amusement. "You really are clever."

"So I'm right?" she asked, and shook her head in disbelief. "Yet you sent him into a cage."

"Water was never in danger," he said, waving a hand in dismissal.

"Would you say the same if he was dead?"

Shadow regarded her for several moments, and then he reached to the shadows of the alley. Breathing the darkness in, he sealed the wound on his neck, causing her eyes to widen. He flashed a humorless smile.

"I don't scar."

"When you get your family killed, you will."

"You know nothing."

"Do you even have a heart?"

He waved his hands in disgust and turned away, striding into the storm. He wanted to reject her accusation but fleetingly wondered if he really had risked Water's life. He'd risked all the fragments before, including Elenyr, and never given thought to the consequences. He half expected Lorica to simply depart, but then he heard her footsteps.

They made their way to the edge of the city and procured horses from the stables at the northern gate. Mounting, Shadow flicked the reins and left Keese in his wake, ignoring the assassin that continued to remain at his side. Neither spoke, but they made their way north.

The miles dragged by as they worked their way across the rain soaked hills of Talinor. When they reached the border, they crossed the Blue River into the kingdom of Erathan, and the rain finally let up. The clouds remained dark but lacked the hint of danger that had been present in Keese. The lightning pushed south, leaving them in their campsite in the trees.

She started a fire and Shadow cast a bow of shadow. Leaving his pack, he stalked the forest until he found a bird hiding under the bushes. An arrow of shadow pierced its body, and its companions took flight. Retrieving the bird, Shadow returned to the fire, annoyed that today the hunt held no pleasure.

He'd always liked hunting. With his gift, he could see the animals like it was broad daylight, even sense their shadows as they sought to hide. He could send an arrow through the night, bending its path to strike a target well out of sight. But today he couldn't shake the assassin's words. Shadow dropped the bird by the fire and began preparing it, yanking the feathers out with such vehemence that Lorica grunted.

"It's already dead. You don't have to mangle the poor creature."

"Do you want to eat?"

She raised her hands, and he finished preparing the bird. Adding some spice from his pack, he hung it over the fire with a few sticks and made sure the other end of the stick was in darkness. He then crafted a wheel that let the stick rotate, allowing the meat to turn.

"That's very clever."

"Now you want to be nice?"

"I'm sorry," she said softly.

"For cutting me?"

"Actually, I don't regret that." She flashed a faint smile. "But I'm sorry for not telling you the truth about my sword."

He sank into a seat by a tree. "I probably didn't give you much of a reason to."

"Was that an apology?"

"Not really," he said, and then swept a hand to her. "I guess neither of us is accustomed to trust."

"Then let's start with a game of truth," she said, settling into a seat across from him.

He raised an eyebrow, intrigued. "How many questions?"

"Three each," she said.

"The rules?"

"None," she said.

He watched the meat begin to sizzle, considering her proposal. He wanted answers, but it would cost him as well. Still, she didn't know enough about him to ask his greatest secrets. With a smile, he inclined his head.

"I believe its custom to let the lady go first."

She shook her head. "I already know one truth from before Keese. It's your turn."

He shrugged and then swept a hand to her. "Who's Zenif?"

Her jaw clenched, the firelight dancing across her features to reveal anger, grief, and then regret. She'd threatened his life if he ever spoke the name again, and he idly wondered if she would draw her blade. Instead she sighed.

"My brother," she said.

"And the weaver hall you visited?"

"Was his," she replied, staring into the flames. "My family were all soldiers except for him, and he wanted to be a weaver. He was good at his craft and married a good woman. Then one day he was delivering cloth to the castle in Herosian the same day Gendor was there for a target. Zenif was killed."

"I assume that's what made you become an assassin."

"The Assassin's Guild has always balanced the scales of justice," she said. "They kill those who think they stand above the law, those who merit death. The nobles do not fear the people, they fear assassin

161

blades. But killing an innocent is forbidden, and it took years to figure out that Gendor was the one who slew him."

"So that's how two sisters became assassins," Shadow said.

She leaned back against a fallen log. "I think that's enough of that truth. It's your turn."

"By all means," Shadow replied, motioning in invitation. "What would you ask?"

"Are you human?"

He laughed lightly, the sound fading into the trees. "Do I not look like a man?"

"You do," she said. "But you can turn your body into shadow, and you wield shadow magic as if it's part of your being."

"Very perceptive, assassin. I am human, but not entirely. In fact, I am the product of the guardian charm."

A flicker of fear tightened her features. "I thought they were all destroyed."

"Not all," he said. "Most guardians die because so much magic corrupts the flesh, eventually causing madness."

"Why have you survived?"

"A question all its own," he said. "For the answer is not what you expect."

The statement was a challenge, all but daring her to use her second question to ask. He realized he was giving her more information that he should, but the game was too captivating to resist.

"Then it's your turn," she said.

"Have you ever been in love?"

She blinked in surprise. "Why would you care about that?"

"It's the only thing that matters," he replied, sweeping his hands outward. "People live this life hoping to fall in love and have children, so they can also love and continue the cycle. Wars end, ages expire, but love always continues."

"I didn't take you for the sentimental type."

"I'm not," he said. "But you haven't answered my question."

The meat spit, the juices dripping into the fire. "Once," she finally said.

"What happened?"

Her lips tightened. "My affection was . . . unrequited."

"Did you kill him?"

She snorted and jerked her head. "If you must know, he told me I was intimidating. He said I was too strong to love."

"That's the very trait I find most attractive," he said.

She motioned to him. "You know my next question. How have you survived?"

"Because I am unique," he said, leaning in so the fire illuminated his dark eyes. "Guardians are made of flesh and magic, but I was torn from the flesh of another, and in that sense, I am more magic than man."

"Still," she said. "There were never guardians made of shadow magic." Her eyes lit up with understanding. "You and Water, you're fragments of the same guardian."

A smile spread on his face. "A truth few on this world know."

She regarded him as if seeing him for the first time. "In the Assassin's Guild, Elenyr traveled with two others that looked like you. Just how many fragments are there?"

"Five," he said. "You met Mind and Fire. The last is Light."

She looked in the dark trees and he could see the weight of knowledge settle upon her. Magic was an enigma to many, and to learn that beings existed with such powerful magic was hard for most to digest. Shadow took the opportunity to remove the cooked meat from the flames. Using a knife, he severed a section and passed it to her on the blade. She accepted it with a nod of gratitude, her eyes distant.

"They are your family," she said slowly.

"As much as one like me can possess."

He stabbed his own meat and began to chew, savoring the succulent flavors. For several moments they ate in silence, and he waited for her to accept what she'd been told. He had no doubt she understood far more about his past. She was clever enough to perceive more than the words that were spoken, but he did not regret the answer. Elenyr frequently warned about revealing the truth of their identity, and he'd never done so, until now. He found it freeing.

"You may ask your final question," she said.

"Will you remain an assassin after Gendor is killed?"

She stopped eating and her tone turned doubtful. "If I do not, the guild will die with me, but I am uncertain as to my path beyond Gendor."

It was evident the question cut deep, and Shadow found his amusement gone. He'd thought to hear of a life beyond the Assassin's Guild, but now realized the question carried more weight than he'd thought. Suddenly wanting the game to be over, he swept his hand to her.

"Ask your final question."

She hesitated, as if she had two questions and was uncertain which to ask. "Are you capable of feeling remorse?" she finally asked.

He laughed lightly. "*That's* what you wish to know?"

"Yes."

His laughter faded, his smile going with it. He wanted to reply with an easy answer but found the words difficult to speak. He considered how she would have seen the events in Keese. He'd placed his brother at risk and lied to her, and done so without a second thought. As a fragment of Draeken he'd always known he did not possess all the emotions, but he'd thought he had a piece of everything. Perhaps he was wrong.

"I think you know the answer," he said, his tone irritated.

She nodded and continued to eat. Both weighed down by the revelations shared, they did not speak again, and the truth finally drove them to their beds. With the fire dying nearby, Shadow looked to the stars, and wondered if he even had the capacity to feel.

Chapter 22: Office of Taxation

They departed their camp the following morning and neither made mention of the conversation, or its ramifications. Despite the obvious avoidance, Shadow felt oddly connected to the assassin, a kinship he could not define.

At night Shadow hastened their journey, the cloudy skies allowing him to fly. Lorica flew at his side, and the two soared in the dark heavens, her white wings contrasting with his dark ones. He often found his eyes drifting to her, trying to explain the growing attachment.

At first he'd found her attractive, and although she was undeniably beautiful, it was not desire that stirred his blood. Instead it was an odd mix of confidence and trust that he'd never felt before.

After a week's journey, they reached the dwarven mountains. The Tyndrik range of peaks stretched across the northwest, many covered in snow even in summer. Small fortresses dotted the peaks and cliffs, entrances to the mighty cities hidden beneath.

Shadow and Lorica ascended a canyon to a citadel. Little more than a gate in a cliff and battlements above, the entrance boasted a full company of armored dwarves. Shadow and Lorica quietly joined the rear of a caravan arriving from Erathan and slipped away the moment they were inside the tunnel.

Like many of the tunnels of the dwarven kingdom, the entrance had once been a mine and followed a meandering path as it plunged into the underside of the mountain. Shortly after entering, they reached the labyrinth of tunnels that comprised the dwarven kingdom.

While mining, the dwarves had discovered an enormous cavern at the heart of the mountain range and had decided to build a new capitol. The tunnel exited onto a ledge overlooking the city, and Shadow and Lorica came to halt to survey the view.

"The city will be enormous," Lorica said.

"When it's finished," Shadow replied. "But it will take lifetimes to build."

"You'll get to see it," she said.

"Probably," he said with a shrug.

He didn't really care about the rise and fall of cities. To him they were all the same, especially those built by the dwarves. Still, he could appreciate the effort the dwarves were making for Torridin.

Rolling underground hills were dotted with structures, the sounds of new construction echoing and reechoing off the walls. Artisans labored on a section of the cavern wall, shaping a great fire dragon. It would take centuries to complete yet would cover just a fraction of the walls of the cavern. Other artwork was just starting, and Shadow guessed that the bearded race would not be satisfied until the walls of the cavern were adorned with fire.

In all their irritating custom, the dwarves had forsaken the building of taverns, inns, and other common structures in favor of blacksmith shops, and the ring of hammers on steel added a backdrop to the shouts and the construction.

"Where do we go from here?" Lorica asked.

Shadow descended the road to the burgeoning city. "We know Relgor is looking for a certain mine," Shadow said. "One with a particular material." He swept his hand to the city. "Someone down there knows where it is."

"So I'm just supposed to talk to people?"

Shadow grinned at her frown. "Of course not. We steal the information."

"Do you always steal?"

"It's more fun," he said. "And in my experience, much faster."

She grunted and swept a hand to the city. "Lead the way."

Shadow descended the wide slope that entered the new capitol, advancing up a street dominated by dwarves. A handful of other races were browsing the wares of the smiths, so their presence was not unusual. As they passed a smith, Shadow pilfered a favorite hammer and used threads of shadow to place it on a neighboring anvil. As he departed, he listened to the accusatory shouts and laughed to himself.

"Is that necessary?" Lorica asked.

"You would begrudge me a little fun?"

"A young dwarf is being disciplined because of your fun."

"That's what makes the dwarves so tough," Shadow said, coming to a halt and leaning against a statue of the current dwarven king.

"Perhaps," she said. "But it's still unnecessary."

"Of course it is," Shadow said.

Shadow watched a young dwarf be cast out of the smithy. He scrambled to his feet and hurried northward, a pack on his back. Lorica frowned when Shadow fell into step behind the messenger.

"You knew that would happen," she accused.

"Guilty," he replied. "That forge is owned by Grund, a particularly grumpy individual, even among his kind. He owns a quartet of mines to the west. Every day at noon he dispatches a messenger to retrieve a report on the progress of his properties."

Lorica looked up at the giant orb hanging from the stone ceiling, the light bright enough to fill much of the enormous cavern, but not quite so bright to be noonday. She began to chuckle, the sound tinged with recognition.

"Grund sent the messenger early as punishment."

"I didn't want to wait," Shadow said.

"So this is immortality?" She swept a hand to the city. "You know a great deal about everyone, but are still impatient?"

"Patience is overrated," he replied.

168

The messenger slowed to a walking pace when he was well out of sight from the smithy and paused to grab a meal of deep fish. Dropping a few coins in the vendor's hand, the messenger munched on the meal as he ambled west and then south, unaware that he had two shadows in his wake.

Shadow came to a halt and watched the messenger enter the mining hub on the southern side of the growing settlement. Mine tracks exited nearby tunnels and intersected beneath the structure. Others curved into the city. Dwarves used the uncomfortable carts for transportation, and several were unloading. They passed through the structure and parted for their homes, the dirt on their faces revealing their occupation. Adjacent to the intersecting tracks stood the mine archives, a tower rising from below, connecting to two curved towers descending from the ceiling.

Shadow pointed to the structure. "All the mines issue a daily report to the king's treasurers, who in turn send a report to the clan houses. Grund doesn't like to wait, so he gets the report directly from the treasurers."

"And you didn't know its location?" Her voice was mocking.

"I don't know everything," he said with a grin. "And I've never experienced the soul crushing activity of reading tax records."

"You get an opportunity now," she said. "Unless you can think of a better way to find the right mine."

Her teasing smile on her lips, she led the way down to the treasurers, and Shadow had no choice but to follow. He caught up to her on a set of stairs. As it rounded a bend and passed through a tunnel, he motioned to her sword.

"How do you stalk your targets?"

"I watch and listen," she said.

"But how do you find them?"

"Most contracts contain a target and a location," she said, stopping at the end of the corridor, her eyes lifting to the office. "Those with just

169

a name require pressure. A few well-placed threats are usually sufficient to garner the truth."

He watched the guards in the office. "Unfortunately, the dwarves guard the location of their mines with surprising vigor. It is not uncommon for a rival clan to force the miners out and claim possession. The records here are used to help resolve disputes."

"Which explains the army," she said wryly.

The office was more a fortress, albeit inverted, with two curving turrets that descended from the ceiling of the cavern. Both intersected with a tower rising below. Mine tracks dominated the bottom level of the tower, the vaulted ceiling and open walls permitting an unbroken view by the hundreds of dwarven guards. Through the barred windows in the upper levels of the tower, dwarves could be seen toiling over archives, with axes and hammers on their backs.

"Dwarves," Shadow said with a snort. "Even the tax collectors carry a weapon."

"The paper must be made of mithral."

"Probably," she said, stifling a laugh as a guard ambled nearby. "The records are held in those curving towers?"

"I would assume," he said.

"The only access to the archives is through the tower," she said. "And there's too much illumination for you."

"They always think shadows hide thieves," he lamented. "They do, of course, but still. Do they have to be so paranoid?"

"They are stopping you," she said. "I'd say they're being rather smart."

He grinned and pointed to the top of the central tower, the access point to the inverted towers of records. "We'll need to go through there."

"See if you can keep up."

170

"I'll do my best," he said, offering a mock salute.

She stood and made her way to the nearest wall. She paused, and then sprinted between the lines of sight for two groups of guards. Then she crouched and looked back—to find Shadow hiding in her shadow.

"That's cheating," she murmured.

"I kept up, didn't I?"

She flashed a faint smile and her cloak unfurled, her wings filling the view. Launching herself off the ground, she wrapped herself in her cloak, soaring above the tower and disappearing above the top battlements.

Shadow admired her sleek approach and then pointed with his gauntlet and pressed a rune. A dim cord streaked up to the support and attached next to the top of the tower, yanking him off the ground. Soaring up the wall, he caught glimpses of barred windows before he too reached the summit.

"What was that?" she asked as he clambered over the tower's battlements.

Shadow grinned and detached the lighthook. "We all know shadow magic is the best, but other magics serve their purpose."

She raised her eyebrow. "I didn't think you'd be so versatile."

He smirked and ascended past her. "Try to keep up."

She grinned and scaled the side of the room with him, and together they reached the top, where two ironbound doors led to the base of the inverted towers. Barred and littered with curses, it would not open easily, so Shadow reached for the exterior of the inverted tower. As he reached for a curve of stone, she tossed him a coin, which he caught.

"What's this for?"

"A bet," she said. "I find the record, you buy me a drink. If you win—"

"I get a favor."

171

She raised an eyebrow. "What sort of favor?"

"You'll find out when I ask it."

She smiled at his challenge and inclined her head. Then she lunged for the second tower. Shadow did the same, hastening up the exterior of the curved structure to reach the barred windows. Although the ground below was illuminated, the towers were darker, allowing Shadow to fasten his shadow magic and accelerate. Reaching a window, he morphed to darkness and passed through the bars.

The inverted tower housed an abundance of shelves, all containing tomes of records dating back for thousands of years. Some tomes were so old the smiths had been forced to protect them by magic in order to retain the pages.

Shadow cast a quartet of gremlins, the tiny creatures scattering to begin their search. Shadow then searched as well, looking for records from the current age. The Raven had spoken as if the mine had been discovered recently, and he hoped the clue would bear fruit. On the third level, he located the right room, and then set to work finding the right record.

Despite his haste, he paused at a gilded tome inside a glass case. The tome was ancient, and the script on the cover indicated it contained records from the lost first capitol of the dwarven race. Xshaltheria.

Reminding himself he had a bet to win, he passed it by and continued his search. As he began considering looking in another tower, one of his gremlins returned with a book, and Shadow flipped through the pages. He smiled when he found a record describing what he sought, and then snapped the book shut. Tossing it on the floor, Shadow darted to the window and slipped outside. He dropped down the exterior of the tower, but spotted Lorica leaping out her own window.

He grinned and accelerated, the wind whistling in his ears as he plummeted toward the roof. He landed hard and rolled to his feet, but she landed almost at the same moment. Both breathless, both claimed victory.

"I was first."

"I win," Lorica said.

He frowned. "But I found the record of a strange dark ore in a mine to the south."

She shook her head and held aloft a page from another archive. "Then I guess there are two mines with the right ore."

Chapter 23: The Burning Tavern

They escaped from the tax collector's office and made their way to a small tavern, *The Red Beard*. Named for its owner, the structure rested on a small shelf of rock abutting the great cavern wall. The front was open, allowing an unbroken view of the growing city.

A set of stairs ascended to the ledge, which contained the tavern, a pair of homes, and what Shadow had come to see as required in all dwarven homes, a blacksmith workshop. All were illuminated by torches placed adjacent to the stairs. Fueled by dwarven firesap, the torches burned bright, the flames glowing in the darkness.

The interior of the tavern was all stonework, likely carved by the owner or a member of his family. Arches and beams were covered with intricate runes. Shaped like a large V, the tavern contained the kitchens at the center, allowing the serving maids quick access to the entire tavern.

Shadow claimed a seat with a view of the entrance and the blacksmith, and ordered a meal. Lorica scowled at his casual air, and the moment the barmaid departed she lowered her tone and leaned in.

"Why are we stopping?" she asked. "We have the location."

"I'm hungry." He said it like it was obvious.

He hated traveling on an empty stomach, and although the dwarves were known for their steel and stone, their skills in the kitchen were second to none. Besides, *The Red Beard* was renowned for its food.

"Relgor and Gendor could be arriving at the mine as we sit here and eat," she said. "We must hasten."

"It appears I'm not alone in my impatience," he said, his tone teasing.

She released an angry breath. "We have our target."

"We have two," Shadow reminded her. "And more questions than answers."

"Gendor is serving the krey," she said. "And Thorg said he would be here."

"He is serving Relgor," he corrected.

"That's the same thing." She folded her arms and sat back.

"How many have you killed?"

She raised an eyebrow at the turn in conversation. "What does that have to do with this?"

"Everything."

Shadow smiled to the barmaid that dropped a plate in front of him and he breathed deep of the savory scents. The steam curled around his face, briefly obscuring her scowl, and he realized he'd seen the scowl less since their conversation in the woods. He missed the expression.

"Still not hungry?" he asked.

Lorica regarded Shadow for several seconds, so he shrugged and reached for the fork. She sighed and ordered a plate for herself. When the barmaid moved to another table, she lowered her voice again.

"Assassins don't share how many they've killed."

"I'll show you my hand if you show me yours."

She regarded him as he ate, and then looked away. "Twenty-seven targets in ten years. A score of others when I was a soldier. You?"

"I've lost track."

"You lie."

He shrugged. "Honest. After I passed a thousand I stopped counting."

"You've killed a thousand," she said slowly.

Shadow shrugged. "I stopped counting a long time ago."

She looked away, clearly uncertain how to accept the information. He'd killed more than the entire Assassin's Guild combined, and it had never bothered him. He was curious about how an assassin dealt with the legacy of their craft.

"You have taken many lives," she said quietly.

"I have taken the lives of those who needed killing," he said, using his fork to point to her. "Same as you."

She cocked her head to the side. "Ever killed an innocent?"

He chuckled sourly. "The first lesson Elenyr ever taught. We do not kill innocents. The second lesson was how to tell if they were innocent."

"I bet that was a hard one for you to learn."

"It was," Shadow said fervently.

He thought back to their conversation in the woods, and how it connected to Elenyr's early teaching. Of all the fragments, he'd struggled the most with the endless lessons on morality, a topic he found to be intensely boring. He didn't feel anything when killing a foe, and at first he'd assumed he didn't feel anything when killing at all. Elenyr had made the difference clear in a way he would never forget.

"But it's a kitten," Shadow had said, holding the tiny animal aloft. "What do you want me to do with it?"

"Kill it," Elenyr said.

Shadow shrugged and placed the dagger on the throat of the kitten. Just as he started to pull the blade, a twinge tightened in his chest, and his hand came to a halt. He tried again, and again, the twinge coming each time.

"I don't want to," he said, surprised at his own reluctance.

"I know," Elenyr said, relief coloring her tone.

Shadow recalled cradling the small body and feeling the strange twinge in his chest. He didn't like it, and whenever it returned, he stayed his hand. Water and the others might look on the exterior and know, but Shadow could never tell if someone deserved death, and relied on instinct.

"What does this have to do with Relgor and Gendor?" she asked, drawing him from the memory.

"You've spent your life battling enemies of your country, and then hunting targets within that same country."

"One of my targets was a dwarf," she said.

He continued as if she hadn't spoken. "But our foe is a krey, one who has lived several times my own life span."

"Your point?"

Shadow withdrew a scrap of parchment from his pocket and placed it on the table. At the top he drew three lines, each converging on a single name. Then he spun the parchment so she could see the inscription.

"You have Serak at the top," she said.

Shadow pointed to the three lines. "The Bloodsworn are the assassins, the Ravens are the thieves, and the Order of Ancients is the army."

Her eyes widened. "You think they all serve Serak."

"They do."

"How can you know that?"

"Three keys to controlling the populace," he said, raising his hand to count them off. "Subdue the common folk with an army, steal from those that can be manipulated, and kill those who stand against you."

"It's a government," she breathed, examining the parchment with wide eyes. Then she snapped a look at him. "When did you figure all this out?"

"At the tax collectors," he admitted. "Sitting in that office reminded me that kingdoms are run on control. Commoners might go about their lives without thinking on it much, but control greases the wheels of commerce, industry, construction, even war."

"But this was all set up long before the krey arrived," she said, her voice pensive.

"What do you mean?"

She held her tongue until the barmaid delivered her plate and a mug. Then she leaned in. "I think they were setting this up because they *knew* the krey were coming."

Shadow pushed his empty plate away, pleased with the insight. His instincts said she was right, and the implications were dramatic. When Shadow had spoken to the fragment of Water in Keese, Water had described Serak's meeting with Wylyn in the Gate chamber beneath an abandoned temple. Now Shadow wondered if the krey had been communicating with Serak for much longer. An ageless being like Serak would be patient, and would have prepared Lumineia for their arrival.

He cocked his head to the side, his thoughts shifting to what Serak had said in the cellar of the Ravens. Before he could study it further, a group of dwarven guards appeared on the steps and ascended to *The Red Beard*. Their features fixed, their hands on their axes, they were obviously not there to eat.

"Looks like we have friends," Lorica said.

"Here for us?" Shadow asked.

The dwarves entered the tavern and stepped to the bartender, a woman that cast a furtive look at Lorica and then pointed to their table. Lorica scowled when the dwarves spread out and drew their axes, the captain pointing a meaty finger to his soldiers to cut off an exit through the open windows. Other dwarves vacated their chairs and retreated to the back of the two wings of the tavern. The captain came to a halt and used his axe to point to Lorica.

"The Angel of Death," he growled. "You should never have come back to Torridin."

"I told you I killed a dwarf," Lorica said.

The captain's eyes flicked to Shadow, eyeing him as he drained the last of his ale. "You and your companion are to be brought before a tribunal, who will likely issue an order of execution."

"Me?" Shadow protested, his mouth full. "What did I do?"

"You share a meal with an assassin," another dwarf spat. "One that killed a clan prince."

"A clan prince selling orc children to slave traders," Lorica said mildly. "He should be glad I only took his head."

Shadow swallowed and wiped at his mouth, causing the dwarves to shift uncertainly. "You take the north target," he said. "I'll take the south."

"You aren't going after any targets," another dwarf sneered, opening a pair of anti-magic shackles.

Lorica ignored them. "I'll meet you at the river crossing where you almost fell in."

"I did not almost fall in," Shadow protested.

"You said it was the moss," Lorica said, her eyes sparkling with amusement.

Shadow pulled a coin from his pocket and dropped it onto the table. "I do owe you a drink," he said.

"And I owe you a favor," she said.

"I'll collect another time," he said. "Do be careful."

"Are you actually concerned for my wellbeing?"

"I'm the one who can't feel anything, remember?"

The dwarf captain glanced between them, his bewilderment rapidly turning into anger. "Enough!" he barked. "Step out of the chairs and place your hands on the table."

"If you insist," Lorica said.

She stepped out of the booth slowly, the tension in the room mounting as she put her hands on the table. Shadow did the same, taking up position on the opposite side of the table. The dwarves shifted their feet and glanced to each other for support, and then the captain motioned the one with the shackles forward.

"One thing," Shadow said, bringing them to a halt. "You knew she was an assassin, yet you only brought a score of soldiers?"

"I brought a company," the captain said, his eyes lit with triumph as he made a hand signal.

A great rushing of feet heralded the arrival of a hundred additional guards, including several bearing the mark of fire mages. They sprinted up the stairs or dropped down from the roof, so many that the glare from the axe blades reflected in the tavern. Many carried nets in their hands, ready to cast over someone with wings. They even brought a ballistae, the bolts carrying more nets.

"You planned well for me," Lorica said, nodding her approval. "But you couldn't have known about my companion."

"He doesn't look like a killer," a female dwarf said, eyeing Shadow.

The guard captain glared at her and she flushed. Shadow grinned and winked at the woman, deepening the red in her skin. Then he used the distraction to slip his hands to the edge of the table, and Lorica did the same.

"Get them in shackles," the captain barked.

Two dwarves shifted forward and approached Lorica and Shadow. Surrounded by soldiers and looking across the table at Lorica, he sensed the same kinship as before, and a smile spread on his face.

"You always think this is fun," Lorica said.

"You don't?"

"Perhaps I'm beginning to."

"Quiet!" a dwarf barked. "And don't move!"

"What if I have an itch?" Shadow protested.

"Don't move!" the dwarf barked, his hands extending with the anti-magic shackles. "If you move to attack we will—"

Lorica groaned. "Kill, harm, maim, make bleed, we know. Can we get on with this?"

"I thought you'd never ask," Shadow said.

The two dwarves with the shackles exchanged a look, and then reached for Shadow and Lorica. Shadow winked to Lorica, and the two heaved the table off the ground. The edge struck the two dwarves and they were knocked backward, preventing a sudden charge by the captain, who raised his shield for the expected blow. But the table was not aimed at him.

Like most taverns in Torridin, *The Red Beard* contained a light orb in the rafters, filling the breadth of the tavern with light. Its position and magic covered the tables at the front of the tavern, while a second and a third glowed in the two wings. The table flew upward and crashed into the orb, shattering the charm into sparks and shards of glass.

As the sparks faded, the front of the tavern was lost to shadows, the sudden darkness punctuated by the captain's shouts and the thudding of rushing boots. The dwarves converged on the broken table but both Lorica and Shadow were absent. The captain whirled and shouted for quiet, allowing all to hear a rising laugh echoing in the gloom . . .

Chapter 24: Demons at Dinner

Shadow's laugh of anticipation reverberated in the tavern, sending a ripple of fear into the ranks. With two light orbs still active, Shadow could not cast a solid form. A sword would be almost ethereal, leaving him near defenseless, but the gloom was sufficient for a different sort of weapon, and Shadow cast a pair of demons.

Darkness welled up from the floor, swelling to become flesh and body. Each demon gained four arms and a dragon's head with two sets of jaws. Like creatures from a nightmare, they flexed their arms and growled, sending the dwarves into a hasty retreat. The demons were twelve feet tall, each arm as thick as a dwarf's torso. Their jaws snapped and they stalked forward, beasts of terror that elicited a scrambling panic.

"Kill the demons!" the captain bellowed, his voice tinged with fear. "And find the assassins!"

The dwarves converged on the demons, the axes hacking at their shadow flesh. The blades passed through the shadow magic, striking tables and chairs into kindling. Bursts of fire also passed through the demons, their bodies swirling like smoke from the passage, the balls of fire scorching more tables, even striking other dwarves.

One fireball struck a dwarf in the shield. The dwarf was knocked out the window, his armored body colliding with a charging dwarf beyond. Shields and weapons went scattering, and one dwarf tripped another into the stone.

A lieutenant howled and hacked at the demon's leg, the blade passing through the shadow and striking the dwarf at his side, the blade cutting a shallow line across the dwarf's leg. The injury was not serious, but the dwarf glared at his companion and struck him on his helmet, knocking him sprawling.

"Watch yourself!" he growled.

The demons released a roaring snarl that galvanized the dwarves to action. The soldiers inside the tavern charged the beasts, while the ones outside leapt through the windows and charged at their backs. The two sides crashed into each other, a tangle of shouting and struggling bodies.

Lounging on the arch of stone above the broken light orb, Shadow watched the pandemonium with a smile on his face. Lorica released a quiet chuckle and crouched at his side, pointing to the demons.

"It's not going to take long for them to figure out those demons are harmless."

"So?" he asked.

"So we are still trapped," she said.

In the dim light she pointed to the windows, where hundreds of dwarves blocked the way to the outside. Nets and crossbows were mounted, ready to strike at anyone flying out of the structure, and there were enough soldiers to prevent them fighting their way out.

"Enjoy the show," Shadow said.

"We have a target to get to," she said.

"You want to know the secret to life?"

"You're going to tell me even if I say no," she said.

He grinned and pointed to the chaos below. "Don't mourn what you lack. Love what you have."

Her smile faded and her features hardened, and he realized she was thinking about her fallen sister. "We need to go," she said. "Gendor has already lived too long."

"As you will," he said with a sigh.

The dwarves had begun to calm, the officers realizing the demons were not corporeal. The captain finally restored order and the dwarves came to a stop. He took a cautious step forward and reached up, his hand passing through the beast's arm.

"They're just smoke," he shouted. "They can't hurt you."

Shadow drew his small hand crossbow and fired toward one of the two remaining light orbs. The sudden tinkling of glass echoed, and the darkness mounted. Lorica drew her own hand crossbow, the bow expanding into place. She fired at the remaining light orb, plunging the tavern in darkness.

"Stand fast!" the captain bellowed. "They cannot harm you! They're just—"

A giant hand wrapped around the captain and lifted him off the ground. The dwarves surged back as the demon issued a snarl so visceral that hardened soldiers recoiled in fear. The demon reared back and hurled the captain across the room, his body landing on a pile of his soldiers. Then the two demons charged, plowing through the armored dwarves on their way outside.

"Where do their voices come from?" Lorica murmured. "Or do you have sound magic as well?"

He held up his gauntlet, where a series of small runes were embedded in the leather. Each bore a different symbol, the orange coloring that of sound magic. He smiled as he pressed one of the runes, and a demon bellowed a warning.

"Care to try?"

She hesitated, and then shook her head. "I want to find my sister's killer before he dies of old age."

"Love what you have," he admonished.

"Says the guardian who cannot feel."

The statement stung, and his smile faded. He turned and slid down the slope of the arch, irritated that her words had landed heavy. Reaching the bottom, he threaded his way through the beams to the exterior of the structure, where one of the demons continued to rampage.

The entities looked like demons, but they were more like brawlers, knocking dwarves aside before charging into the hacking blades. Pieces

184

of shadowflesh were left in their wake, the demons growing weaker by the second.

The dwarves not battling the demons were outside, hunting for the assassins. Shadow and Lorica dropped into their midst, taking the dwarves by surprise. Shadow evaded a hasty downward slash and ducked a blast of fire. Then he returned to his shadow form and slipped through their ranks.

Dozens of dwarves converged upon them, but Lorica swept her wings wide and leapt into the air. Nets were raised and dwarves aimed stubby crossbows. But the leap was a feint, and she dropped back to the ground, slamming into a pair of dwarves before rolling beyond, reaching one of the large mounted crossbows.

With nets hanging from the bolts, the weapon could fire nets into the air at shocking speed, the machine designed to ensnare a flying adversary and bring them to the ground. Lorica reached it and raised her sword, but Shadow caught her elbow and turned it aside.

"What are you doing?" she demanded, her blade sparking off the ground.

"Why destroy it?" he asked.

He sidestepped the blow from the machinist and brought his knee into the dwarf's face, knocking him backward. Then Shadow kicked him down the steps, into the dwarves rushing upward. The distraction allowed Shadow to grasp the controls and lower the weapon to point at the dwarves rushing their position.

A smile split his features as he pulled the lever, firing into their ranks just feet away. Nets exploded outward, instantly collapsing over the dwarves and leaving them entangled. Dwarves cried out as they found themselves caught in their own traps, their struggling bodies piling upward as others attempted to leap over, only to be caught anew.

"You enjoy this far too much," Lorica said, fending off the stragglers.

"You enjoy this far too little," he replied.

A dwarf cast a fire golem and the beast charged their flank. Shadow spun the machine and fired, but the net was too small to slow the golem, which came to a halt and reared back, bringing both arms down upon Shadow's position. Shadow darted backward, retreating with Lorica for the blacksmith shop. Lorica reached her blade out and sliced one of the controlling ropes, disabling the machine just before a dwarf reclaimed the weapon.

Shadow leapt over a flashing axe and sprinted for the blacksmith shop as the dwarves closed in. "What now?" Shadow asked.

"Now you follow me," she replied.

"We can't fly out of here," he said.

"We don't need to fly," she replied. "We need an escape tunnel, and its right there."

She pointed at the exhaust shaft. Several of the machines in the blacksmith used stonesap, and the exhaust was funneled through a large pipe system into the stone ceiling above. Lorica stepped on the anvil and leapt to the roof. Pulling herself up, she jumped to the shaft and kicked. The metal screeched and bent, and she kicked again, knocking it askew. Shadow picked up a bucket of water and hurled it on the fire, filling the room with steam and mist. Then he followed her up.

Smoke billowed up from the hole as Lorica swung the metal shaft to the side and ducked beneath. Shadow held it for her and then followed, cramming into the confines of the shaft. He cast a line of shadow upwards and then grabbed her wrist.

"Hang on," he said.

They shot up the chimney, disappearing as dwarves burnt the mist with blasts of fire. Shadow held his breath as he passed through the smoke at the top, where the chimney curved and merged with the wall of the great cavern. The end of the shadow rope sprouted spider legs and continued to pull them up the shaft, through the curves and out of Torridin.

The sounds of battle faded when they reached the top, and Shadow coughed in the smoky room. Smoke from the chimney and other chimneys entered through holes in the floor and filtered through small pipes to reach the surface above. Fortunately for them, at the back of the chamber sat a small access door, a method for dwarves to maintain the ventilation system. Lorica slowed in the absolute darkness, but Shadow cast a giant fist and struck the door, blasting it from its hinges.

Shadow tumbled into the hallway, coughing at the dust and smoke. Lorica did the same, and the two leaned against the walls, sucking in great breaths. Shadow wiped at the dirt now staining his tunic.

"I prefer to escape without getting so dirty," he said.

"You're afraid of ash now?"

"My clothes are ruined," he said.

"I don't care," she said, rising and pointing down the corridor. "I want Gendor."

"Don't be so hasty," he said. "We find Relgor, we'll find the Bloodsworn. Find the Bloodsworn, and we'll find Gendor."

"We should have left Torridin, but *you* wanted to eat." she said.

"What's with the anger?" he asked, his own anger rising. "We got out, didn't we?"

"I'm tired of you slowing me down."

He bristled. "Sure it's not the other way around?"

She closed the gap in a single step. "Have you *ever* lost someone you love? Or do you even know how to love?"

He folded his arms, feigning nonchalance even as heat crept into his voice. "Do you even know how to have fun?"

"I don't *want* to have fun," she shouted. "I *want* to kill the one that slaughtered my family."

"You'll get to them eventually," Shadow said.

"*I* don't have the time you do," she said. "Do you know what I would do if I had your life? I'd help people, not treat them like their purpose is worthless."

He laughed, the sound so filled with rancor that she flushed. "I've heard others say the same," he said, "but do you know what people would do with a longer life? The same thing they do with a shorter one. You would hunt and kill, because that's what you are. And warriors lose family members and friends. Don't you see? You're the reason your family is gone. You should have been a weaver."

She glared at him, and when she spoke again her voice had turned a dangerous calm. "It appears I was mistaken, thinking you an ally."

"Perhaps you are right," he sneered. "For once."

"I'll message you if Relgor comes to the north mine," she said. "Then we part ways."

Whirling, she departed. Shadow scowled and watched her leave, annoyed and angry. Turning down a different corridor, he left Torridin behind, trying to shed the pall Lorica had left. He'd thought they were drawing closer, but then she'd returned to her previous animosity. He knew he'd reminded her of the loss of her sister, but he'd thought she'd gotten over the loss.

His scowl deepened when he noticed again his lack of remorse or sympathy. The woman had lost her family just weeks ago, and he'd been talking about focusing on a fleeting amusement. As he made his way down the silent corridor, he wondered why a hard knot had appeared in his chest, and why it reminded him of his blade on the kitten.

Chapter 25: Axehead Mine

Once in the tunnel, he morphed into a jungle cat, the large shape giving him speed and power. Surging down the dark corridor, he accelerated into a run. Shortly afterward, his corridor intersected with a tunnel containing mining tracks.

He came upon a cart full of dwarven miners headed to work. They talked and laughed, drinking ale as they shared tales of their labors to a young dwarf in their midst. Shadow snarled, the sound echoing in the confines of the tunnel. The dwarven laughter died as they scrambled for their axes, spilling ale in their haste. Shadow streaked by, allowing just enough of his body to be seen to inspire terror.

Shadow flashed a smug smile as he departed but heard Lorica's disapproval. Accelerating, he sought to put distance between himself and Lorica, hoping it would allow him to return to the pleasure of working alone. He'd always enjoyed it before and saw no reason why he could not return to solitude. Despite his efforts, a strange hitch remained in his chest.

The tax record led him to the southwestern end of the Tyndrik mountains. The record had described a mine that contained an odd, black material that was neither metal nor rock. It lacked the known properties of other stones, but the dwarves, being dwarves, set about mining it anyway.

Shadow found the offshoot and sped down its length. The complete darkness allowed him to add to his entity, and his jungle cat grew to become a black reaver. As a black reaver, his body was larger than a lion's, his massive, muscular arms strong enough to rend armored men in two. Large spines extended from his back, and if he were real, would have been made of metal, which was part of the reaver's diet. He passed through several junctions and slowed as he reached the mine. All four types of reavers were feared, and Shadow used the cloak of a great predator as if it would shield him from the lump in his chest.

Axehead mine, so named for the prominently shaped cliff above the entrance, extended straight under the mountain. Then the mine curved and wound its way lower, following the initial silver vein.

Shadow reached the top of the mine and slipped into the depleted silver vein, following it downward. Relinquishing his hold on the black reaver, he turned back to human form and stopped in a storage alcove to pick up the clothing of a dwarven miner. Donning the helmet, he manipulated the shadows on his face so it looked like he had a beard. He was shorter than the other fragments, so he could pass as a dwarf. Although he could infiltrate the mine in his elemental form, doing so would leave him insubstantial, and the first light he passed would reveal the illusion.

His disguise complete, he followed the winding mine until he reached the deep shaft. At four hundred feet across, the shaft was an enormous cylinder that plunged straight down. A scattering of lights pierced the darkness, most set around a dwarven ascender that clung to the side of the shaft, a platform large enough to contain several mine carts. A glow came from the base of the shaft, and he heard the faint tapping of hammers.

Shadow snorted as he gazed into the depths. The dwarves had spent a fortune to dig the shaft, just to explore what they did not understand. Foregoing the ascender, he leapt into the void and cast a pair of shadow wings that slowed his descent.

The shaft was deep, deeper than he'd first thought. Easily five hundred feet down, its walls were rough and scored from dwarven mining equipment. Shadow stuck to the dark side of the shaft. As he approached the collection of miners at the bottom, he slid down the wall and alighted next to a section of machinery.

The base of the shaft contained a single towering piece of black stone. The miners had likely noticed it by scanning the earth and had dug down to reach the strange ore. They had nearly unearthed the whole of it, and half a company of dwarves crawled over the scaffolding they had erected. Side tunnels split off from the base of the shaft, leading to living quarters and a meal hall.

The dwarves were shaping the stone, carving it into a giant dwarven warrior, the helmet and shoulders already completed. Other dwarves were busy cutting the statue's axe, while still others labored over the intricate armor of the statue.

Unnoticed, Shadow landed against the back wall and picked up a hammer. Then he ascended the scaffolding and joined the throng. After all the fighting and mischief, he found the honest labor refreshing.

For four minutes.

Growing bored, he retreated to the dark well of the shaft and ascended to a crevasse thirty feet off the floor. It was dark enough that he could carve out the stone inside the crack, the scraping of stone blending with the dwarven hammers and chisels.

He carved out a tiny chamber and cast a bed out of darkness. Reclining on its surface, Shadow settled in to wait, annoyed that his thoughts continued to return to Lorica, and why he felt so vexed.

While the dwarves labored, Shadow slept, and when he awoke he slipped into the mine and explored. He searched the meal hall and the sleeping quarters, even rifling through the large trunks at the foot of their beds while the owners slumbered, their snoring reverberating off the rough stone walls.

When he'd explored everything, he returned to his hiding place, but remained restless. As the hours grew into days, he realized he needed a distraction. Fortunately, the dwarves were a surly group, prone to quarreling, so Shadow decided to provide himself some amusement.

He stole a hammer from a dwarf and left it next to his neighbor. A shouting match ensued, and Shadow retreated to watch the display. While other dwarves stopped to survey the argument, he subtly shifted a chisel in a dwarf's hand so, the next time he struck, it would break a piece rather than carve a line. Distracted by the argument, the dwarf hit the chisel, only to see a small chip form in the otherwise smooth carving. His look of dismay brought a burst of laughter to Shadow's lips.

"Is someone *laughing*?" the mine captain barked, causing the other dwarves to retreat to their labors.

The dwarf, a grey-headed captain the others called Hort, grunted in irritation and sent the others back to work. He then surveyed the workers, a scowl forming on his face. Shadow kept his attention on the crate he was unloading, the food set out in a neat row atop a dwarf's warhammer.

Throughout the day, Shadow gradually heightened the tensions in the mine, and since Relgor did not arrive, into the next day. By the end of the week the dwarves were on the verge of mutiny, with a stubborn brute insisting their wages had been short.

Sitting inside his little alcove, Shadow leaned against the stack of gold coins he'd pilfered and listened to the argument about lost wages. Then a new dwarf barreled into the argument and raised his no-longer-fearsome axe.

"My axe is pink!" a black-haired dwarf growled. "PINK!"

"Look at what someone did to my tools," another shouted, shoving the hammer at the mine captain. "The wood was soaked in water overnight."

"My seat was set to collapse!" another cried, rubbing his backside.

"Someone shaved part of my beard!" one bellowed, reaching up to tug on the half beard that remained.

"At least your beard isn't pink!" the first roared.

"Dwarves!" the mine captain called, his voice gaining a dangerous edge that subdued his workers. "I suspect someone has infiltrated our mine and thinks to use us for their amusement."

"Aye!" the one with the pink axe shouted. But he eyed his companions with suspicion in his gaze.

The mine captain organized them into groups and sent them hunting, leading one group into the kitchens. Shadow dropped from his alcove and followed them inside, keeping to the shadows against the wall.

The door to the kitchens was open and Hort led the way into the food stores. Unfortunately, his search led to a conspicuously large crate, large enough for a person to hide. The captain carefully opened it—releasing a trap Shadow had left. His head disappeared in a plume of purple dye. The liquid splattered the mine captain, turning his grey hair purple and staining most of his armor.

He whirled to face his companions, several of whom were struggling to suppress their laughter. The one with the pink axe could not, and his roar caused the mine captain to scowl, his face so red that Shadow thought the dye would burn off his skin.

"I want the intruder found!" he barked.

The others continued their hunt while the captain made his way to the sink. Unable to resist, Shadow snuck up behind the soldier to where he'd placed his helmet and used a knife to cut several words into the dye on the back.

For a moment he watched the dwarf furiously attempt to remove the dye, the effort only spreading it. Abruptly giving up, he jammed his helmet on his head and rejoined the others. Shadow followed at a discrete distance, arriving just as one of the patrols shouted that they'd found evidence of the intruder.

"He's been eatin' our food!" the dwarf with the half-shaved beard shouted. "And look what he did to Urink's memory orb of his wife."

The dwarf flushed and pocketed the orb before it could be seen. Fire gathered on his fist as his anger flowed, and he was not alone. The stone rattled underfoot as the dwarves with earth magic struggled to contain their anger. Hort shoved his way to the forefront.

"He's still here," he growled. "I bet my life on it. Find him and drag his empty carcass back to me so I can—why are you smirking?"

There was a great shifting of feet and then the captain seemed to realize they were avoiding looking at his helmet. Yanking it from his head, he spun it around and read the text about his backside, and the apparent size.

His nostrils flared like a beast's, fire curling around his lips. Sitting in the space between the great statue's axe and his neck, Shadow noticed the dwarf's insignia on his shoulder, marking him as a member of the guild of fire magic, and a first-class master. He idly wondered if he could get the dwarf to burn his companions.

"Is that necessary?" Lorica seemed to ask, and Shadow brushed his hand over his shoulder, flicking the words aside like they were flies.

A distant shout caused all eyes to look upward, and a moment later the distinct clash of steel reverberated from above. Hort barked for silence, and then a small knot of dwarves appeared on the dwarven ascender, the one leaning over the edge sporting a gash on his forehead.

"We're under attack!" he shouted.

The captain barked an order and the group retrieved their weapons. "Humans?"

The dwarf jerked his head. "They're the size of rock trolls but don't look like them."

"Dakorians," Shadow said aloud.

He'd forgotten all about his mission. Grimacing at the lapse, he stepped from hide and descended. Then he stepped from the shadows next to Hort, his body turning solid. His sudden appearance caused the dwarf to whirl and instinctively raise his axe.

"Captain," Shadow said, "although you're not going to like it, you really need to trust me right now."

"You're the one that did all this," the dwarf growled.

"True," Shadow admitted, causing the dwarves to bristle. "But if you don't listen to me, you'll all be dead in a few minutes."

Chapter 26: The Purple Dwarf

The captain scowled and his fist filled with fire. "Who are you?"

"That's not important," Shadow replied. "What matters is that a group of outlanders are about to descend upon you and they won't leave anyone alive."

"And you want us to trust *you?*" one growled and stabbed an axe at Shadow. "Look what you did to my axe!"

"Maybe your wife will like it," Shadow said.

"I *am* a wife," she shouted.

Shadow blinked in surprise and realized he'd mistaken the female dwarf for male the entire time. Her beard didn't help, and her stocky frame resembled that of her male companions. Shadow managed to suppress the obvious comment with difficulty.

"You may want to kill me," Shadow said, "but remember, if you die here, your people will find your bodies. Is this the way you want to be remembered?"

He swept a hand at them, the one with the half beard, the one with the pink axe, the captain with purple hair. The fury in their eyes would have scorched steel, but Hort leveled a finger at him.

"If you lie . . ."

A distant shout came from above and light blossomed in the shaft, momentarily filling the breadth of the mine to illuminate the group of dakorians crowded on the ledge above the pit, with Relgor in their midst. As the ascender approached the ground, the dakorians leapt from the ledge.

"Weapons," Hort shouted. "And shields." As he retreated he growled to Shadow. "What do they want?"

"That," Shadow said, pointing to the partially carved statue. "It's a mineral they need."

Two of the dakorians stepped off the ascender and plummeted down the mine shaft, their boots glowing bright, causing them to slow. Shadow wondered if he could steal a pair of their boots. Maybe off their bodies? Others jumped free as they reached the black statue. Like boulders of flesh, they landed on the ground, the scaffolding, the upper walkways along the outer wall, and even on the statue's head. Then Relgor landed on the uppermost section of scaffolding and surveyed the dwarves.

Gathered behind machinery, scaffolding, and mine carts, the dwarves were arrayed for battle. To their credit, they'd gathered weapons and shields in seconds, and stood ready to engage the unknown enemy, but they glanced between each other, clearly uncertain of the identity of the new intruders.

"Exterminate them," Relgor said. "And prepare the extractor."

"With pleasure," the dakorian at his side exclaimed.

The dakorians dropped to the ground, their landing sending a shudder through the stones. In all his purple glory, Hort stood and spun his axe, leading the charge into the dakorian soldiers, his axe chipping the bone before he held his shield high for the incoming blow.

The dwarves wore armor as normal clothing, and their shields overlapped to form an impenetrable wall. The lead dakorian swung his hammer, the weapon crashing into the shields and unleashing the interior power, sending dwarves and broken shields in all directions.

The dwarves instinctively employed their tactics against rock trolls, joining into tight knots and using overlapping shields to prevent attack. Closer dwarves lashed out, digging their axes into the legs of the dakorians, succeeding in chipping bone and drawing blood. One managed to drive his axe into the joint between the bone armor, the blade carving into the knee. The dakorian fell, and the dwarves rushed in, only to be brought to a halt by the powerful dakorians.

Shadow leaned down to Hort. "I don't think that went very well."

"And you were supposed to help," Hort snarled, shouting an order for the others to retreat.

"Not much I can do with all the light," Shadow replied, following him as he retreated behind a trio of overloaded mine carts. "I only have shadow magic."

"Which explains your blasted intrigue," the female dwarf spat from nearby.

Shadow spotted a trio of dakorians setting up a sort of machine that pointed at the statue. It resembled the drills the dwarves used to bore into stone, but this contained threads of power emanating from the inner workings, the energy brightening as it pointed at the stonework.

"Can you destroy the lights?" Shadow asked.

"That would blind us," Hort snapped. He cast a soldier of fire and sent it at a dakorian, but the hammer blasted it into useless curls of flame and sparks. Other entities fared as poorly.

One dakorian spotted Hort. "The purple one is their leader!" he shouted.

Hort looked daggers at Shadow and he shrugged apologetically. Both sprinted away as a dakorian charged through the mine carts. The heavy metal bent as the hulking soldier slammed into it, and dirt and rocks were scattered across them all.

Other groups of dwarves were being herded into tight corners, with dakorians closing off the exits. A glance showed that the dakorians had only suffered a single loss, while several dwarves lay dead on the floor. In minutes the trapped dwarves would be eliminated.

Stone rose up and fire was cast, but the magic shattered on the empowered hammers, leaving dirt and sparks littering the ground. Working in perfect unity, the dakorians forced the dwarves into tight groups, leaving Shadow and Hort close to the dwarven ascender.

"Captain?" Shadow asked, "If you want my help, now's the time."

Hort cursed and conjured a spear of fire, which he flung at a small tube that extended from the sleeping quarters. The fire tore through the tube and a dark liquid burst out, the stonesap exploding into a fireball that scorched a dakorian. Then every light in the shaft winked out except for the light emanating from the extractor and the dakorian hammers.

Shadow drew on the darkness and cast a ballistae, handing the controls of the weapon to the dwarven captain. Then he cast a charm on the dwarf's vision, allowing him to see. The dwarf gasped as the mine shaft lit up as if it was midday, and then he looked down at the giant ballistae in his hands.

"Now it's your turn to cause some mayhem," Shadow said, his voice tinged with amusement as he slipped away.

Momentarily stunned by the loss of light, the dakorians stood around the dwarves, blinking their eyes as they sought to adapt to the sudden gloom. The soldier nearest to Hort squinted in the gloom and suddenly noticed the giant weapon pointed at his chest. He swung his hammer just as Hort fired.

The *thrum* of the weapon was followed by a grunt. The giant bolt slammed into the dakorian and sent him across the shaft and into the wall. His hammer tumbled from his fingers and clattered to the floor, the embedded runes going dark.

"Strike that weapon!" Relgor shouted.

The dakorians converged on Hort but they stumbled in the darkness, struggling to find their adversary. In their midst, Shadow darted about, casting the shadow sight onto every dwarf he crossed. Answering the call of their captain, the dwarves raced to join him, striking at the dakorians milling about.

Another shadow bolt leapt from the weapon, blasting another dakorian into the far wall. Then another. The dwarves used the darkness to fight, digging their axes into the dakorians as they fought to reach the captain.

Shadow conjured a pair of bears and unleashed them, the animals lumbering about, swiping at the soldiers. Deep lizards added to the din, their shadowy bodies brushing against the dakorians, who shouted in dismay.

"Something touched my leg!"

"It's on my arm!"

"Kill it!"

"It's so slimy!"

Another shadow bolt crossed the chamber, crushing another dakorian. Three of the dakorians tripped, shocked to find their boots tied to each other. Another lifted his hammer but it was tied to the feet of his companion, causing the second to fall when his legs were yanked from beneath him. Shadow relished the sounds of sweet chaos.

Dakorians, shadow entities, and dwarves littered the battlefield, striking at each other, confused and disoriented. One dakorian went down, felled by a host of wounds. Another that had been struck by the shadow ballistae would never rise again.

But the lights from the extractor were still brightening, and it took the edge from Shadow's creatures, just enough that they did less damage. Hort relinquished the ballistae to one of his soldiers and dived into the fray, leading the charge against the outlanders.

Shadow paused on the scaffolding and snuck close to Relgor, hoping to overhear his words. His attention on the battle, Relgor hissed orders to his companions, urging them to extract what they needed from the statue. Several dakorians loaded large chunks of the rock onto the dwarven ascender.

"Take it to the swamp fortress," he barked. "We'll follow behind."

Relgor turned back and froze, his own shadow turning into a soldier that drew a weapon. He squeaked in surprise and recoiled. He scrambled to retreat but could not escape his shadow, and it plunged the blade into Relgor's upraised arm. He gasped in disbelief then stared in shock as the shape morphed into Shadow.

"Sorry," he said. "Couldn't resist."

"The fragment of Shadow," he hissed in pain. "You are more clever than I gave you credit."

"Where's Gendor?" Shadow asked.

"Why do you ask?" Relgor retreated, trying to put distance between them.

"Asking for another," Shadow said, wondering why he was still trying to help Lorica after the rift.

"In Herosian," Relgor said. "Do pay him a visit."

"I will," Shadow said.

Shadow raised his dagger, but Relgor's gaze looked behind him. Shadow whirled—and found himself facing a dakorian. The large figure caught him about the throat and lifted him up. Shadow struggled to release himself as the dakorian brutally struck in him the chest with his armored fist. Shadow cried out as ribs snapped.

"You think your magic is so powerful," the dakorian snarled. "But you are like mewling children, incapable of knowing when your death is near."

Shadow phased to his shadow form and slipped through the dakorian's fingers, causing the dakorian to stumble forward. Holding his side, Shadow hooked the dakorian's horn to spin around and alight on his shoulder.

"That's the thing," Shadow hissed into his ear.

The soldier whirled but Shadow leapt into the darkness and rebounded off the statue, again landing on the dakorian's shoulder.

"Magic is so much more than you realize," he said.

"Are you too afraid to fight?" the dakorian growled, spinning and shredding the darkness with his illuminated hammer.

Shadow retreated onto the higher scaffolding and warped the darkness so he was visible, so he looked like a demon. The dakorian blinked, surprise abruptly washing across his features before he charged, chasing Shadow deeper into the darkness of the upper scaffolding.

"Why would I fight you?" Shadow asked, his tone light despite the pain in his chest. "You're like a mewling babe that doesn't know its death is near."

The dakorian snarled and spun, striking at the scaffolding supports, knocking several down in a clatter of steel. The extractor had brightened enough that the bottom of the shaft was illuminated, but up here there was a wealth of shadows, and Shadow slipped into his domain.

"I'll kill you," the dakorian snarled.

"I'll kill you," Shadow repeated.

"You are nothing to me."

"You are nothing to me."

"Stop that."

"Stop that."

The dakorian snarled and fell silent. He spotted Shadow darting away and lunged, chasing after. The dakorian swung his hammer, tearing through the supports as he chased his quarry to the extreme summit of the statue, and then leapt, releasing a cry of triumph when his hammer came down—on thin air.

His shout changed to dismay when his hammer landed on nothing, the shadows that had shown the end of the platform dissipating to reveal the edge. The dakorian teetered above the statue's enormous axe. He reached for the scaffolding bar but it too was just a figment of darkness, and his hands passed through it.

"Sleep well, little babe," Shadow said from his back, and poked him in the knee.

Already off balance, he spun and desperately sought for a grip, but there was nothing, and he toppled over. His bellow of dismay pierced the din until he landed on the statue's axe, the sharpened stone piercing his back and claiming his life. His hammer tumbled from his lifeless

201

fingers . . . and fell into the extractor, shattering a portion of the machine.

Instantly light began to brighten, filling the mine as the machine began to tremble. Relgor looked on in horror before turning and sprinting to reach the ascender. The dakorians abandoned the extractor and leapt to join Relgor.

Catching the hint, Shadow dropped from the scaffolding and cast wings, but the light robbed them of substance. He landed hard and hurled himself into the tunnel, rushing to escape the blast he guessed was coming. Hort and the dwarves raced with him, all seeking to escape the rising wail that came from behind . . .

The detonation shook the earth and cast them all to the floor, the blinding light so bright that Shadow grimaced in pain as the light seared his flesh, leaving dozens of burns. He dived through the open door of the kitchen, smoke rising from his body. The black statue was erased in the blast, tearing the grooves from the lower part of the ascender and the bodies of the slain, and devouring thirty feet of the tunnel leading to the sleeping quarters.

When it finally subsided a welcome darkness returned, and Shadow limped to the dwarves. Hort and the other fire mages cast fire in their palms, providing light as they picked their way over the rubble to reach the main shaft. Instead of a statue, they found a pile of shattered stone.

Despite his injuries, Shadow grinned. "That went better than expected."

"Better?" Hort demanded, his voice rising. Then he controlled himself and stabbed a finger upward. "You should go, before I remember what you did to us."

Shadow noticed the menace in the surrounding dwarves and shrugged. "When you sing songs of tonight, make sure everyone knows about her pink axe."

The dwarf released a strangled shout and Shadow grinned before retreating from sight. His ascent slowed by his injuries, Shadow worked his way up the mine and back to the surface, but the dakorians were gone. Satisfied at the fun he'd had, Shadow limped his way south, wondering about Relgor's swamp fortress.

Chapter 27: Friend

From her perch in a tree, Lorica watched the entrance to the mine. She shifted to get comfortable on the small platform she'd constructed, but couldn't seem to get a good seat, the boredom of waiting seeping into her flesh.

She'd once waited a month for a target, yet never felt such discomfort on a hunt. She kept telling herself it was because of Gendor, but deep down she recognized it had less to do with her target and a great deal to do with her traveling companion.

It had been almost a week since she'd left Shadow in the tunnel outside of Torridin. Upon arriving at the mine, it had been clear the miners had not been disturbed, and she'd settled in to watch and wait.

Her chosen hiding spot overlooked a shallow canyon, where the entrance to the mine was located. Aside from a handful of traveling dwarves, she'd seen nothing, and had begun to guess that Shadow had been the one fortunate enough to intercept Gendor.

She tried to hold on to her anger, but on the third day of waiting she was tempted to sneak into the mine, just to prove she could. The impulse for fun was new and she stifled it, recognizing its source.

"I'm here for Gendor," she murmured to herself, a cold reminder of the target she hunted.

Eight days after leaving Shadow, a small black cat climbed into her post, and rubbed its fur on her face. She snapped awake, nearly shearing the entity in two with her oathsword. But the cat merely deposited a sealed letter and then evaporated.

She recognized the messenger as sent by Shadow and picked up the letter. She unwrapped the parchment and scanned the contents, grunting as her suspicions were confirmed. Shadow had indeed encountered

Relgor and fought the dakorians. Jealousy reared up and she was forced to quash the emotion.

She looked to the horizon and found it to be almost dawn, the touch of light above the mountains indicating the approaching sunrise. She gathered her things and then dropped to the ground, leaving the mine and working her way south until she reached a cliff. Her cloak unfurled and she stepped off an edge, falling into a curve that would carry her through a pass.

As she flew south, she watched the mountains scroll by, wondering if she would hold true to her promise and part ways with Shadow. Part of her wanted to simply pass Shadow and leave him wanting, but they were both hunting the same targets, and she would likely encounter him anyway.

She could also meet with him long enough to learn what he knew, and then leave, but the prospect left a bad taste. It wasn't just that she would see him again. He could follow her with ease.

She also had to contend with the fact that she'd started to grow attached to the fragment of Shadow. Without him, her gaze would have been fixed on Gendor, and the anguish of losing her sister would have remained bright. Instead, Shadow brought a smile to her lips, his constant need for amusement irritating, yet oddly healing.

As she passed beyond the mountain range and descended toward the trees, she spotted the river, and followed it to where a distinctive oak curved its trunk over the water. There she spotted a figure in the shadows, taking a nap.

Light from the rising sun passed through the leafy canopy, illuminating a bright forest and reflecting off the gurgling stream. The nearby road passed through a ford, the rocks covered in moss that Shadow had slipped on when they'd descended to fill their water skins and rest. Birds tittered in the trees, adding music to the bright forest. She dropped to the ground and furled her cloak, the sound of her boots drawing a look.

"Took you long enough," he said, not moving.

"I got your message this morning," she said. "How long have you been waiting?"

"Three days," he said.

"Your messenger took a while to get to me," she said.

He shrugged, and winced.

"Are you hurt?" she asked.

"Almost healed now," he said. "The dakorians certainly like to leave a mark."

"I thought you could use shadows to heal."

"Now you care?" he asked, raising an eyebrow.

She took a step toward him, concern lifting her hand. Then she came to a stop and her hand returned to her side. "Was Gendor there?"

"No."

The disappointment was sharp and she tried not to blame Shadow. "What did you learn?"

"That Relgor is gathering supplies to a swamp fortress."

"The krey are hiding in a swamp?" she asked, incredulous.

"I suspect Mistkeep," he said. "It's an old Verinai fortress in the Evermist."

"Anything about Gendor?"

"Relgor said he was in Herosian," he said.

"And you believe him?"

"Does it matter?" he asked. "You know you'll go there. Or maybe you'll go to Mistkeep first."

He eased himself down from the branch. She watched the controlled motion, the tightening in his jaw, and realized that although the injury had healed, he was still sore. It was disconcerting to see him in pain, but more disconcerting to find that she cared.

"Are you sure you are well?"

He cocked his head to the side. "I expected you to be ecstatic upon learning the location of the Bloodsworn."

"I expected you not to be limping."

Shadow chuckled wryly and lifted his shirt, revealing a deep bruise across his side. The purple mottling on his flesh surrounded a long wound across his ribs, making her wonder if his ribs had been broken.

"Everything can be killed," he said. "And shadows don't heal as well as the other elements."

"I thought you said you couldn't be hurt."

"I said I don't scar," he said. "I never said I couldn't be hurt."

"I'm sorry," she said.

"For me being hurt?" he asked. "Or what you said?"

She looked away, watching the leaves rustle in the wind. Then she sighed and looked back. "Both."

"The mighty assassin brought to humility," he mocked. "I bet that's unpleasant."

She scowled and pointed to him. "Don't you have something apologize for?"

"I didn't do anything," he said. He stooped to the stream and refilled his water skin.

She drew in a breath and almost walked away. She knew of Mistkeep and could probably locate the fortress on her own. If the rumors were even partially true about the swamp fortress, it would be an ideal place for Gendor to hide his Bloodsworn. Now that she knew the target, she could leave Shadow behind and hunt Gendor on her own.

But that wasn't what she wanted.

"I'm sorry," she said quietly. "What you said about my sister was harsh, and it's hard to remember that you are just a fragment of a person."

"What's that supposed to mean?"

"That one of the other fragments may have gotten the emotions you lack."

Shadow regarded her, his features tight with annoyance. She wondered if he felt that way because she was wrong, or because she was right. Then he closed his water skin and flashed a sour smile.

"Apparently I have no empathy."

"I could teach you," she said.

He burst into a laugh that sent a bird out of the trees. "I'm going to learn empathy from an assassin?"

"Why not?" she asked. "I'm learning how to enjoy life from a fragment of a guardian that shouldn't exist."

He seemed to be considering the idea, but she could see in his eyes that the prospect intrigued him. She'd offered a challenge, and that was one thing Shadow could not resist. She could have invited him to steal a dragon's egg and he would have had the same look.

"It will require us traveling together."

"I'll have to endure it," she said.

He grinned and reached for his pack. "I wondered if you would return at all."

"I had to," she said, falling into step beside him as they turned onto the road. "You knew about Gendor. But you could have put that information into the note."

"Couldn't risk it being intercepted," he said, but there was a sparkle to his eyes that implied he was lying, making her think that he too, had wanted her return.

"You could just admit you wanted me to come back," she said.

"And why would I admit to that?" he asked.

"I'm not used to having friends either," Lorica said.

"Is that what we are?" Shadow asked.

"Perhaps I misspoke."

He grinned. "Perhaps."

She noticed a strange look in his eyes, a surprise at the word, as if he'd never heard it before. The way Shadow fought, the way he planned, the way he talked, all bespoke one used to being alone. He had his fragment brothers, but they were his family, and he didn't care much for his connections in the Thieves Guild. It left her wondering if he'd ever had a real friend.

As they worked their way south again, she realized that her initial attraction for Shadow had dimmed. She still found him handsome, but the connection between them went deeper. As a rule, assassins made occasional allies that helped them reach their targets, but allies were not necessarily friends.

"So what's our plan?" he finally asked.

"You're asking me?"

He pointed to her. "You're the assassin hunting an assassin. Surely you know the best method to reach him without being killed."

"Have you ever been in Mistkeep?" she asked.

"A few times," he said. "But not in ages, and it was abandoned then."

"What do you make of the fortress?"

"Delightfully creepy."

She raised an eyebrow. "That's not exactly inviting."

He shrugged. "It sits on an island in the middle of the most lethal swamp in Lumineia. It's filled with darkness and dust, perfect for me, not so perfect for anyone else."

"If the Bloodsworn call it home, they've likely made it livable, and Gendor would have taken precautions against an assassin's blade."

"I could get in," he said.

"Probably," she said. "But Gendor serves Serak, who's been watching you for five thousand years."

"Which means he's probably ready for me as well." He released an annoyed grunt. "I hate it when it's hard."

"Because it's less fun?"

"Exactly," Shadow said.

She cocked her head to the side as a thought occurred to her. "Why don't we give them what they want?"

"What do they want?"

"You," she said.

"You want me to get captured?" he asked. "That doesn't sound very friendly."

"But it was brotherly?"

The reminder of the events in Keese brought a smile to his lips. She hoped it suggested that he could trust her as much as Water trusted him.

"Water was unharmed when he came out of the cage"

"I'll get you out as well," she said.

"So I'm supposed to trust you?"

"That's what friends do."

"If I get killed the first time I trust a friend, I'm going to lose faith in this friendship thing."

"So that's a yes?"

"That's a no," Shadow said.

210

She blinked in surprise. "I thought you'd like my plan."

"I do," he said, "But you should be the one caught. I know the fortress and have the magic to find you. It only makes sense."

"So I'm supposed to trust you?"

He smiled broadly. "Isn't that what friends do? And it sounds like fun."

She hesitated, and then inclined her head. "Perhaps you are right."

He laughed in delight, and she couldn't resist a smile, partly because it sounded like fun, and partly because he was right. She still wanted to kill Gendor, but the bloodlust had started to wane, and she found a contrasting desire. As they made their final plans, she found herself stealing looks at Shadow.

Lorica still didn't trust Shadow completely, not yet. But despite her best efforts, her trust was growing. It oddly reminded her of Loralyn, who'd always had the gift of knowing who to trust. Except for Gendor, a mistake that had cost her dearly.

Her smile faded, and she reminded herself that Shadow had his own goals. Although their friendship was forming, what would Shadow do if their goals were not in alignment? She hoped it didn't happen, if only because she had no desire to kill Shadow.

Chapter 28: Lorica's Gambit

"You really think this is going to work?" Shadow asked.

"It was your idea," she said.

"Then we know it's a good one."

She laughed, the sound tense. The entire journey to Herosian they'd talked about the best way to infiltrate the Bloodsworn, a challenge made difficult because Serak knew Shadow's magic, and personality.

"I don't see another option," she said.

The tactic they'd devised was dangerous, but it was the only approach she thought would outsmart their foes. Of course, their plan could very well kill them both, but as Shadow declared, "That's what makes it fun."

She surveyed the noble house from their vantage point on a nearby roof. The sun had set hours ago and Herosian lay steeped in darkness. The streets were well lit by elven light orbs, illuminating the seven rings of the city. The third circle boasted the most light, the homes of the nobles glowing in the night.

"Do you trust Indra?" Lorica asked.

Shadow's smile indicated a growing attraction for the girl he'd met on the wall of the city. Lorica had watched while Shadow asked for her aid, a request that earned him a kiss. She thought she would be jealous, but that emotion was surprisingly absent.

"She gave us what we needed," Shadow replied.

"And the kiss?"

"A bonus," Shadow replied. "She's very attractive."

Her grunt said it all, and he grinned. Then Lorica's eyes were drawn to the young man exiting the front of the large house. He was hardly an adult, his features still boyish, despite the haughty gleam to his eyes.

Ostensibly the cousin of a count, Yolan secretly housed the Bloodsworn that came to the city, and his house guard were all Bloodsworn. Indra had pointed them in the direction of Yolan's home, and Lorica and Shadow had been surveying it for the last few hours.

"You think he will take the bait?" Shadow asked.

"He's young and brash," she said. "He won't be able to resist."

Shaped like a horseshoe, the house wrapped around a fountain at the center. Elven cast, the water flowed upward into intricate spirals, a quartet of trees providing shade for the inverted waterfall. Flowers and other shrubs lined the structure, extending into gardens all the way to the exterior wall.

On the outside, the wall looked like any other barrier around a noble's house. But Yolan had subtly fortified the wall of his home, and when a gardener opened the hut to retrieve a tool, Lorica spotted the armory within.

"I'll see you on the other side," Shadow said.

She looked to him, measuring the certainty in his gaze. Their plan risked them both but required her to take the first plunge. Shadow still needed her, so she doubted he would abandon her to her fate. Still, it was the first time she would fully trust Shadow.

"Friends don't leave friends to die," she said.

"Lesson one of an assassin's guide to empathy?"

"Lesson one," she said with a faint smile.

"I'll be there," he said.

She measured his dark eyes, the set to his jaw, and believed him. Nodding, she turned and dropped off the roof, flaring her wings to descend to the ground. Then she stared at the doors across the way, readying herself for the show she needed to put on.

She recalled Gendor's face, his arrogance, his guilt. Then she thought of Loralyn as she'd died. The embers of anger and guilt fanned into flame, growing hotter as she relived a moment of such anguish. Gendor had killed her brother, her sister, and now he needed to be avenged. Drawing her oathsword, she stepped from the dark alley and crossed the street.

Her gaze fixed on the door, she approached the opening. The two guards spotted her and called out a warning, but she continued to close the gap, until she passed into the pool of light around the door and they recognized her.

"The Angel of Death!" one cried.

He yanked his sword free but Lorica was faster. Her blade flicked out, slicing once across his chest before she spun and grabbed the throat of the second. Dragging him through the opening, she put her blade at his stomach and raised her voice.

"I'm here for Gendor."

Raspy and laced with menace, her voice reverberated off the bricks of the house, summoning the attention of all the guards. In the shocked stillness she plunged her sword through the Bloodsworn in her grasp.

"How many of you do I have to kill before he comes?"

She dropped the assassin's body on the ground and whirled, avoiding a crossbow bolt that streaked toward her side. Then she surged into motion, charging the fountain. The Bloodsworn guards converged upon her, weapons clearing sheaths, crossbows being loaded.

The first to reach her attacked with two blades, but Lorica ducked the first blow and rotated into his guard. She drove her free hand into one wrist, knocking the weapon free. Then she used her blade to slap the man across the jaw, the motion filled with contempt. The dazed man fell onto his back, a bloody line across his jawline.

Lorica continued walking. "You think to kill me?" she snarled. "I am an *assassin*, and you are just common *killers*."

Her hatred for the group welled up like a geyser, compelling her to action. A trio of Bloodsworn closed on her and she leapt into the air, her cloak expanding into wings that carried her aloft. Just as she cleared the trees she dived into their midst, leading with her blade.

One man went down, never to rise, a woman was knocked into a tree, the brutal impact driving the air from her lungs. The third managed to strike at Lorica, cutting a shallow line across her shoulder.

Lorica ignored the sting and kicked him in the chest, sending him tumbling into the woman behind. Both went down in a tangle. Lorica continued to advance upon the grand home. She spun left and right, leaving dead and dying in her path.

"You hear me Yolan!" she roared. "I want Gendor!"

Bloodsworn converged on her from all sides, and she took to the air. Drawing her crossbow with her free hand, she unleashed a blistering volley, the bolts embedding into shields and flesh, driving deep and claiming three more killers.

They unloaded their own crossbows, forcing Lorica to dive though the fountain. Water splashed across her frame, the mist briefly obscuring her from sight. She landed on the opposite side of the fountain, her weapons out. By blade and bow she unleashed the fury she'd caged since Loralyn's death, the bodies of her foes falling to the ground.

But there were too many, and the Bloodsworn converged upon her, their shields preventing her from striking deeper into their ranks. Trapped in a ring of steel, she again took to the air, but this time they were prepared, and a large bolt streaked at her, enchanted nets hanging from the shaft.

She ducked and swooped over one, folding her wings to split the gap between two nets. The fourth caught her, the net wrapping around her, the bolts slamming into the outside of Yolan's home.

Yolan appeared in the doorway, where he'd probably been watching the conflict, out of reach of her weapons. He sneered at her and stepped into the open, just as she twisted her sword and sliced the bonds, pulling her crossbow free and taking aim.

"Kill her!" Yolan screamed.

Crossbow bolts thudded into the wall, missing her by inches as she dropped to the ground. She rolled to absorb the fall and came to her feet, her sword flashing. A Bloodsworn died and she used his body to absorb more bolts. Then she tossed him away and leapt to Yolan.

He turned to flee, but she grabbed him around the neck, her arm snaking around his throat. She spun, putting the man between her and the dozens of crossbows pointed at her. He fought to break free but the red steel on his neck discouraged movement.

"Where's Gendor?" she hissed.

"Gone!" Yolan shouted.

"Where?"

"I can't tell you that," he pleaded.

The army of Bloodsworn crept forward and she tightened her sword against his neck, drawing blood. He winced, and the killers came to a stop. Lorica sneered at them and lowered her voice.

"It would be so easy to kill you, Yolan. You and your Bloodsworn killed my sister, my whole family, and I *yearn* to return the favor. But you have information I need. If you tell me where Gendor is, you get to live a little longer. So what's it to be? Death now? Or death later?"

"Mistkeep," Yolan cried. "He's in Mistkeep."

Lorica shoved him into the dirt and leapt into the air, her wings unfurling and carrying her upward. A glint of steel drew her gaze, and she spun to see a mounted crossbow on the roof. She dived to avoid the bolt, but the bolt split apart, the enchanted ropes wrapping around her and tightening her cloak about her body.

She hit the ground and nearly lost consciousness. When her vision cleared, she felt pain from all the cuts and the impact. She tried to reach her sword, but it was bound at her side, and the Bloodsworn advanced upon her bound figure, one catching the sword hilt and pulling it from the net.

216

"You were a fool to come here," Yolan said, approaching the net. "But I cannot deny the chance to gain favor with Gendor. He will reward me handsomely when I present him your corpse."

She managed to regain her feet, and the surrounding soldiers retreated a step. Even caged, they feared her reach, and she allowed a grim smile. Instead she locked eyes with Yolan and spit into the dirt.

"I am the guildmaster of the Assassin's Guild," she snarled. "The archives have told me everything about the Bloodsworn, and those that now follow me will not rest until you are exterminated. They will hunt you and your master until your hearts are stilled, the memory of your faces forgotten."

A flicker of doubt appeared in Yolan's eyes. "What did the archives tell you about the Bloodsworn?"

Lorica managed to keep the smile from her face. "Enough to know *you* housed the Bloodsworn."

They'd gotten that answer from Indra, but Yolan licked his lips, his doubt turning to fear. Gendor would never have been convinced, but Yolan was young and impulsive, and so he ultimately did what an underling did best and yielded to a higher authority.

"Bind her," he ordered. "And throw her in the prison cart. I want her halfway to Mistkeep by dawn."

"But my Lord," a Bloodsworn protested. "We were told to kill her on sight."

"I know what Gendor said," Yolan barked. "But if we deliver Lorica, we'll give him access to the Assassin's Guild archives."

"As you order," the Bloodsworn said uncertainly, and then motioned the others to deal with Lorica.

Obviously reluctant to get within reach, they used poles to grab the net and drag her to the waiting prison wagon, a fortified wagon lined with anti-magic. She was forced inside at spearpoint, and they took her sword. Only when the door shut did she allow a small smile.

Dozens of Bloodsworn mounted horses to accompany the wagon on its way south. The driver snapped a whip, starting them into motion. Lorica stepped to the rear of the wagon and peered through a crack in the wood. The Bloodsworn were dragging the bodies of the dead out of sight, others attempting to heal the wounded. Above the house wall she could just make out the roof of a nearby inn, and a flicker of movement in the shadows.

She nodded to herself. "Let the hunt begin . . ."

Chapter 29: Mistkeep

Shadow watched the net bring Lorica down, and winced when she struck the earth. He'd grown fond of the assassin, and disliked seeing her take a blow, even if that was the plan. She'd fought with fury born of hatred, and he'd almost been convinced it was real. But she'd subtly turned into the final blow, allowing the nets to wrap around her body.

Lorica was loaded into the cart and a guard assembled, and Shadow noticed the captain take possession of the oathsword, which he strapped into a scabbard on his steed. Within minutes, the wagon was sent into the streets of Herosian. Although the battle at Yolan's home should have attracted attention, no Talinorian soldiers appeared, reinforcing what Indra had said. The guard did not interfere with the Bloodsworn.

Shadow worked his way from one roof to another, following the cart until he could get ahead of it. Lorica's cart trundled down the street, aiming for the southern entrance to the city. The road would cross over a handful of bridges, passing over the creeks that crisscrossed the city. Shadow made his way to one and dropped to the ground. Just as Lorica's cart came into view, Shadow ducked under the bridge and waited.

The clatter of horses came first, the Bloodsworn steeds passing over the narrow bridge. Shadow had chosen this crossing because the passage was narrow, and did not permit horsemen to ride next to the wagon. As it rolled above, Shadow rolled over the lip of the bridge and darted between the wheels. The light orbs that illuminated the street shined on the moving horses and wagons, filling the bridge with so many shadows that he passed unseen.

As the wagon passed above him, Shadow leashed himself to the wood, the threads of darkness picking him up and forming a hammock. The wagon bounced over the end of the bridge, but Shadow was hidden comfortably beneath and smiled as the Bloodsworn carried them to Mistkeep.

The wagon was carefully constructed, the wood molded and threaded with anti-magic to contain any prisoner. It was not so well built on the exterior, and Shadow scribbled a note onto a piece of parchment before inserting it through a crack.

The note was pulled from his fingers, and a moment later returned. Shadow smiled before tucking the note into his tunic and settling in. They had several days ride, and he had to avoid discovery for the duration.

The cart passed through the seventh circle of Herosian, the sounds of the outer factories fading, and the lights dimming even further. The echo of voices was gradually replaced with the plodding of horse hooves, and the murmuring of the guards.

Night was just beginning, so Shadow yawned and reclined in his hammock. There was always the possibility they would stop and discover him, but he doubted they would. So he allowed the rocking of the wagon to lull him to sleep.

Throughout the next few days, he spent most of the time in his hammock. At night he emerged. Fighting boredom, he studied the soldiers, resisting the urge to drive them to terror. These were not common townsfolk and may even suspect an intrusion to be him. Annoyed, he resigned himself to waiting and returned to his hiding spot each dawn.

Despite his decision to remain invisible, his boredom eventually drove him to act, and he was almost caught several times. The first came when he reached out to a horse striding by, and carefully unlatched the buckle of his saddle. The man rode for another mile before shifting in his saddle and dropping into the road. His pained shout drew the attention of all, and the leader berated the man for his not checking the binding.

From beneath the wagon, Shadow stifled a laugh at the man's confusion. He was clearly a killer, with dozens of marks on his shoulder, all beneath the symbol of a skull. The tally of his kills revealed a brutal nature, as did the other runic tattoos on his face and neck. The chastisement left him red with anger and indignation, and he yanked the strap before remounting.

"Let's move," the leader barked.

A scrap of parchment passed through the crack, but he ignored the bold lettering, and at the next opportunity he slipped from his hiding spot and undid the bundle behind a rider. When it fell, the leader responded with even more anger, even going so far as to threaten a bloodletting.

Shadow watched the exchange, and the eyes of the other companions, identifying those in the lead, learning the order of authority. Swordsmen were trained to fight and to follow orders. The Bloodsworn were no exception, except these were all men and women who had been cast out by their respective commands. All bore tattoos of kills and the eyes of those who killed for sport. But as Shadow watched their response, he noticed a current of resentment among the Bloodsworn. They followed Gendor, but was it possible that not all supported the Order?

Lorica rammed a piece of parchment through the crack, the scrape of the paper loud to Shadow's ears. He pulled it out and unfolded the heavily used parchment, and found the new message written in bold lettering.

You're going to get us caught!

Shadow wrote a quick message and stuffed it back to her. **Know your adversary.**

Lorica didn't respond, and he couldn't be certain she believed him. Although he had learned from the reaction of the company leaders, he'd done it for fun and only afterword had noticed how he could learn.

He wanted to do more but resisted the impulse. Two accidents on a ride were unusual enough, a third would likely spark a search, one that could very well lead to Shadow's discovery. As the miles dragged by, he amused himself by crafting tiny flies out of shadow, and sending them into the night, where they worked their way into the shadowed folds of the saddles and the clothes of the riders. They bit the Bloodsworn, repeatedly.

"Blasted flies," one muttered, slapping his arm.

Another grimaced and struck his neck. "I swear they have teeth."

Shadow stifled his laughter with difficulty, and swore he heard Lorica do the same. Through the tiny window in the door she would be able to see the killers, and probably suspected Shadow was to blame. This time, she did not warn him to stop, and he guessed that she enjoyed the spectacle.

Six days after departing Herosian, they reached the Evermist. The bog stretched for hundreds of miles, an enormous swamp that had claimed the lives of entire armies. The Evermist marked the southern border of Talinor and separated the claimed lands from the Dragon's Teeth.

Steeped in shadows and mist, the road disappeared the moment they entered the swamp, and the wagon bounced over a makeshift trail. Much less comfortable, Shadow passed a note through the crack and then slipped into a bush. From there he leapt into the tree and scaled into the branches.

Green mist filled the air, permeating clothes and lungs, causing men and women to cough. Great predators stalked the bog, the beasts frequently drawn to such a company. But Shadow spotted subtle runes placed in the trees along the winding path, an invisible line that silenced the passage of the riders, protecting them from threats.

The difficulty of the road slowed the wagon to a crawl, and the riders muttered to each other, casting furtive looks into the dark mist. When the sun set a distant howl rent the stillness, and the men cursed and drew their weapons. Shadow again resisted the urge to drive them to madness. In the swamp, such an act would be almost too easy, but would probably get Lorica killed.

Shadow followed the wagon as it made its way through the mist, the trail swerving repeatedly, avoiding the patches of crocodiles, snakes, and the haunt of a scaled reaver. Like all reavers, scaled reavers were sentient, with a mind both cunning and devious. Scaled reavers lurked in lakes, bogs, and the sea, and were sworn enemy of sailors. Occasionally one attacked a ship, leaving wreckage and flotsam, but no bodies.

Shadow heard a faint splash in the murky pond, and glided to the canopy overlooking the water. At first the greenish water was still, and then he spotted what looked like a trio of bumps in the water, the three nostrils of a scaled reaver. Crocodile bodies littered the exterior of the water, the flesh consumed, the scales left to rot.

Shadow slipped away before the beast spotted him and returned to Lorica's wagon. The scaled reaver's lair was just a few hundred feet from the trail, suggesting it had recently moved in. He frowned, considering a course of action, but the wards on the trees held, and the sounds of the riders' passage did not pass beyond the limits of the trail.

Shortly after passing the reaver's lair, the lead rider came to a halt next to a lake and led his horse onto a bridge. Shadow dropped to the brush and flitted under the wagon, disappearing just as the wagon passed into the open.

Although the sun hung high in the heavens, much of the light failed to breach the mist of the lake, the darkness hanging over the lake and the keep, cloaking the fortress in the swirling green mist.

Shadow poked a head out and eyed the fortress, pleased at the change. In his youth the citadel had been left by the Verinai, and some sought to claim it. But the Evermist had expanded, swallowing the fortress and making passage difficult. It had lain all but empty until Shadow had discovered it and walked its halls like a lord. But since his last visit, the structure had been cleaned and renovated, the walls dotted with small light orbs, as if protecting the exterior against the shadows hiding in the mist.

As the wagon passed through the fortress gates, Shadow smiled. The orbs were not there to stop the mist from touching the fortress walls, they were there to prevent him from entering. And here he was, entering.

The wagon came to a halt in a courtyard, and the Bloodsworn parted to care for their horses. The wagon was wheeled through a second gate and into the keep. Shadow used that chance to slip away, darting into the darkened halls before the gate slammed shut.

The fortress was deceptively large, with not one, but three great halls. Spires and turrets rose through the mist, the courtyards invisible beneath layers of fog. The courtyards dotted the citadel at various levels, with balconies built to overlook the swamp.

The corridors were a labyrinth of networking passages that intersected around, above, and below the great halls. Personal chambers, training rooms, and storage spaces lined the halls, the doors recently replaced, the rotting wood removed in favor of fine elven cedar.

Beams extended across the hallways, permitting a vaulted feel to the corridors, while also hanging the countless light orbs, all bright and new. As Shadow crept across the beams he noticed even the metal brackets had been replaced, the rust absent, the paint bright. Gendor had spent a fortune to repair the hidden fortress, and it looked as new as it had in the Age of Oracles. Then he frowned, and realized that it was likely not Gendor, but Serak that had done so much.

When the fortress had been covered in moss and steeped in ominous shadows, he'd thought it beautiful. Now it gleamed like the gold on a king's crown, gaudy and shiny. Shadow shook his head in annoyance.

As he explored the fortress, he crafted traps out of the shadow magic, all set to trigger if the light orbs were broken. In the halls, corridors, and even the bedchambers, he set the traps, passing unseen as he prepared the next stage of their plan.

Many of the corridors and chambers were well lit, and those he avoided, but he found one corridor that was also guarded. He paused and surveyed the hallway from the shadows of the intersection.

At the end of the corridor a dark elf stood. Dressed in dark armor and a white mask, she stood like a statue, a disturbingly dark blade in her hand. The mask was not the silver of the Bloodsworn, but all white, with a single red claw marks across an eye. From a distance, Shadow examined the dark elf, wondering why a member of the Queen's Hand would be here.

Beyond the soldier, the corridor terminated at a single room, the bars suggesting it to be some sort of cell. Shadow wondered who was beyond the door, but there was too much light to find out. Shrugging, he turned and descended to the lowest level of the fortress.

From a perch on one of the beams, Shadow watched the prison wagon being guided down the wide corridor. A steed of fire pulled the wagon around a curve and then straight into a series of cells. The wagon was attached to a cell door, and finally opened.

The Bloodsworn prodded Lorica into the cell with long spears, but she grabbed a spear and yanked it from its wielder. Spinning it, she stabbed through the gap. The man Shadow had seen with dozens of kills marked on his arm died in his own fortress at the hands of an assassin, his scream rattling the remaining Bloodsworn.

Lorica smirked as they shouted, forcing her into the cell and slamming the door. Then they retrieved the dying man and retreated with the prison wagon. Shadow expected guards to be present and was not disappointed. No less than six stood guard in the hall, watching the barred door.

Shadow worked his way around the room and picked up a pebble, which he tossed down the hall. It rattled against the wall and all six turned to look. Shadow used the moment to morph to his shadow form and dive headfirst through the tiny window in the door, entering her cell. Turning corporeal once again, he pressed a rune on his gauntlet, preventing their conversation from leaving the room.

"How was your ride?" he asked with a smile.

Chapter 30: A Dangerous Ambition

"Did you have to antagonize them?" Lorica asked.

"I got bored," he said.

"You could have gotten us caught," she said.

He stepped to the door and eyed the guards. "But I didn't."

"Barely," she said. "But I have to admit, the flies were funny."

He grinned. "Did you see the one smack his own face?"

She grinned and then pointed upward. "We need to find Gendor. Did you see him?"

"I actually think you should stay in here," he said.

She scowled. "That wasn't part of our plan."

"Plans change," he said.

She took a step toward him, her hands balling into fists. "I thought I could trust you."

"You can," he said. "This fortress is formidable, and there's more Bloodsworn than we thought. The moment I release you it's only a matter of time until the guards discover your absence. When they do, we'll be trapped in the fortress and they will hunt us down."

She stepped to the door and peered through the bars. "Six guards?" she asked, her tone filled with surprise.

"You're the Angel of Death," he said. "Can you blame them?"

"I'll never get out without being spotted," she said.

"Isn't that what I said?"

She released an irritated grunt. "You said you were going to leave me in here."

"Only for a few hours," he said. "I need to find Gendor before we strike."

"We won't need to," she said, peering through the window.

"Why?"

"Because he's here."

He looked through the bars and cursed. With Relgor at his side, Gendor advanced on the cell and barked an order. One of the six guards stepped forward and began unlocking the door, the key clanking in the mechanism.

Shadow scanned the room, searching for a place to hide. Like the rest of the fortress, beams across the ceiling held light orbs. At fifteen feet off the cell floor they would be out of reach for most anyone, but Shadow pulled on the gloom and sent a thread into the rafters. He disappeared as the door swung open.

Lorica had retreated to the back of the room, her hands wide, ready for a fight. Her cloak swirled open, the wings partially unfolding as if they too were eager for blood. Gendor smirked at her position.

"You have no blade, no friends, no allies, yet still you stand defiant."

She whipped a dagger from a sheath on her back and hurled it at Gendor. He swerved to the side, the blade grazing his cheek and plunging into a Bloodsworn standing behind. The man stared in shock at the dagger in his chest and then groaned as he fell to his knees.

"Now I'm out of blades."

Gendor wiped at the blood on his cheek. "Somehow I doubt that."

"Why don't you come and find out?"

Gendor wiped the blood from his hand. "I think I'll keep my distance."

He motioned to the door, and a guard outside pressed his palm on a rune. Chains of anti-magic burst from the wall and coiled around Lorica's wrists, pulling her back to the wall. Lorica rattled the chains.

"You must be truly afraid of me, to kill me when I'm unarmed."

Gendor laughed, the sound filled with menace. "I could kill you as easily as I did your sister. But, unfortunately, Relgor wished to meet you."

Shadow shifted closer to the edge of the beam, peering down at the krey, who surveyed Lorica with a great deal of interest in his black eyes. Shadow held a dagger in his hand, but Relgor's expression did not herald violence.

"I know who you are," Lorica said coolly. "You're Wylyn's son."

"One of many," Relgor said, eyeing Lorica like she was a prized bull.

"How many sons does she have?" Lorica asked.

"Hundreds," he replied with a laugh.

Shadow leaned down on the beam, watching the conversation. Relgor's presence with Gendor here was not unexpected, but his desire to meet with Lorica was. Why would a member of the krey wish to speak to an assassin?

Lorica scowled at Relgor's attention. "Keep looking at me like that and I'll cut your eyes out."

"You must understand my position." Relgor stepped to the side and looked her up and down. "Wylyn is the head of our house, and there are tens of thousands of direct descendants. Each is given a position of authority."

"I take it you don't care for yours."

Relgor's lips curled into a sneer. "I deserved a higher position, but I was relegated to the position of house slavemaster."

"How very vile of you."

Relgor sniffed. "I control the slaves in the house, and the sale of new stock when a world like yours is harvested."

"There is no world like ours."

Relgor's black eyes spun, a flicker of gold appearing. "Indeed, and for the first time, I saw an opportunity to escape my station. The value on this world is a thousand times that of any other, but there are some of you worth even more."

Lorica bristled. "I'm not a slave."

"You will be," he said, striding forward and examining her up close. "An assassin with wings, the Angel of Death. I know just the buyer for you."

"I'm not for sale."

Relgor continued as if he hadn't heard. "There is an arena renowned as the graveyard of the mighty. Imagine an island filled with killers more dangerous than you, with millions paying to watch you hunt . . . and watch you die." He smiled and reached out to flick her wings. "Survive long enough and you get your freedom, but no human ever has. I think you could be the first."

"Does this arena have a name?" Gendor asked.

Relgor never took his eyes away from Lorica. "They call it The Bone Crucible."

Lorica's wings spread wide and curved toward Relgor. He leapt back, but one struck him in the chest, knocking him sprawling into the dirt. Lorica spit on his boots as Gendor raised a sword to her throat, lightning crackling on the blade.

"Take her wings," Gendor barked to the guards outside.

"No," Relgor said. "A bird in a cage is all the more saddened when they can fly."

"I said I'm not for sale," Lorica said.

Shadow shifted to stand above Gendor. If a strike came, it would come from him. His blade hung ready, his grip tightening. With a start Shadow realized he was angry, not for himself, but for another. The emotion surprised him. Aside from the fragments or Elenyr, he'd never felt such a compulsion to protect someone else.

Relgor rose to his feet, wiping the blood from his nose with a laugh. "She's almost worth as much as the others. Don't damage her."

"Before you take her there is one thing I require," Gendor said. "I want the ring."

"*I'm* the guildmaster," Lorica snarled.

"The guild is dead," Gendor said.

He stepped forward and reached for her hand, but she clenched her fist. Even chained, she fought him until he put his sword against her throat, his dark eyes conveying a desire to strike deep.

Lorica's eyes filled with hatred and flicked up to Shadow. Then she allowed Gendor to pull the ring from her finger. He smiled as he examined the ring—until Lorica brought her head forward, bashing him in the face with her forehead.

Gendor recoiled and reached to his nose, which had broken, blood falling down his tunic. Shadow snorted a laugh, the sound lost in Gendor's bellow of pain. He retreated, grasping his nose and cursing Lorica.

"You shouldn't have come so close," Lorica said, a smile of triumph on her lips.

Relgor clapped with delight. "I will have to bet on you myself."

"Tell me," Lorica said, looking to Gendor. "What's to stop him selling *you* to the Bone Crucible?"

"I serve him," Gendor snarled.

"You are still a slave," Lorica said.

Relgor chuckled and shook his head. "Slaves serve out of fear, servants serve out of loyalty."

"I made a choice," Gendor said, his face a mask of pain. "I chose the side destined to win."

"An intelligent servant," Relgor said.

Gendor scowled at the term but remained silent, and Shadow realized the man had indeed chosen a side. Gendor inspired hatred, but he'd made his choice out of self-preservation, truly believing it was the smart route. Shadow wondered how he could use that, for if he could turn Gendor's desire to his own aims, he might become an ally. Of course, Lorica still wanted to kill him, and Shadow was not inclined to betray her.

"You have your ring," Relgor said. "Now go. I have other business to attend to."

Gendor scowled, clearly reluctant to leave the krey with Lorica. Then he swept from the cell. She'd managed to contain her fury, but her eyes glittered with hatred. Relgor regarded the bound assassin for several moments and then called out to the Bloodsworn at the door.

"Leave us."

"You saw what happened to Gendor," he said.

"She will not harm me," Relgor said.

"Yes I will," Lorica spat.

Relgor laughed and motioned them away. Disliking the look on Relgor's face, Shadow shifted his position so he could drop between them, if necessary. When Relgor glanced to the door, Lorica looked up and gave a tiny shake of her head. Shadow reluctantly stayed in place.

"What do you want?" Lorica asked.

"I want to know about the fragments."

"Who?"

"You were seen in the Raven's home," he said with a smirk. "And Water and Shadow were both present."

"Allies of circumstance," she said. "I know nothing about them."

"Come now," Relgor said. "We both know you were traveling with Shadow."

"He wouldn't shut his mouth," she said, raising her chin. "I killed him."

Her words were so convincing that Shadow felt a chill, and realized she'd considered the prospect enough that her voice had the ring of truth. Relgor too, regarded her with surprise in his eyes. Then he began to laugh.

"I would have been sorely disappointed if you had, but I suspect even you could not kill a fragment of Draeken."

"What do you want?" she repeated, her tone annoyed. "You have your friends for answers, so why don't you speak the truth?"

"Very well," he said. "Keeping one such as yourself contained would prove . . . problematic, and I do not care for the cost. I know what happened to your sister, and I know what you really want. So I ask you, would you join me of your own accord . . . if I let you kill Gendor?"

Shadow's eyes widened in surprise. Relgor was offering what she wanted most, a chance to avenge her fallen sister. It wasn't his only goal, that much was clear, but Shadow recognized the seriousness to his tone. He meant the offer.

"Why choose me over him?" she asked warily.

"Gendor is a killer and a survivor, but he lacks a certain . . . gravity. Thorg was the same, and you already killed him. You, on the other hand, are no servant. You may be born a slave, but you have the eyes of a slayer."

"Gendor will kill you if he finds out you want to replace him."

"Are you going to tell him?" Relgor laughed. "He would not believe you."

232

"I'm afraid I have to decline," Lorica said.

"Are you certain?" Relgor asked. "I know you seek to protect your companion, but I wonder what you will think when he is also in a cage."

Shadow's eyes narrowed, and he scanned the cell. Relgor spoke as if he knew Shadow was present, and Shadow rose to his feet, retreating further into the darkness of the rafters, tightening his grip on the hilt of his dagger.

"I came in a prison wagon," Lorica scoffed. "You think I have a friend here?"

"You were very clever," he said. "But then, I expect nothing less from one of your caliber. Isn't that right . . . Shadow?"

He turned and looked into the rafters, directly at Shadow. Before Shadow could respond, a hidden door swung open in the wall above the beams, and light filled the cell. Shadow recoiled at the blinding light and didn't see the incoming blow. It struck him in the skull, knocking him to the floor below. He grunted when he was struck, his vision swimming. He managed to see a man drop from the opening and alight at his side, his smile one of triumph as he hefted chains of pure light.

Serak.

"Welcome to Mistkeep," Serak said. "I hope you like it, because you're going to be staying a while . . ."

Chapter 31: Shadow's Cage

Shadow lurched awake, groaning at the immediate ache in his skull. He reached up and touched his head, his fingers coming away bloody. Wincing, he rolled to his knees and then rose to his feet.

He stood in a cell, only the chamber was not like the room that caged Lorica. The floor, the ceiling, the bars, all were made of pure, solid light, the white material just bright enough to ensure no shadows could exist in the room.

He looked down and realized his shirt was gone, leaving just his tunic. The heat from the light washed across his skin, causing sweat to glisten. As Shadow's vision settled, he realized two things. First, the cell had taken decades to build. And second, it was built for him.

"I hope you like the accommodations."

Shadow turned and looked beyond the bars. In the gloom beyond, two figures approached. Serak and Relgor came to a halt outside the cage, and Serak swept a hand to the cage, the pride in his gaze suggesting he'd been the architect.

"I hope you will consider this place your home," he said. "For you will be here until Relgor can craft a Gate to return home."

"How long were you standing there?" Shadow asked, his tone one of reproach. "I was just unconscious without a shirt on, and you were what, watching me? That's a little creepy, you know that?"

Serak shifted uncomfortably. "You could have used your shirt to leave shadows."

"So you stripped an unconscious man?" Shadow snorted derisively. "Now it's even more creepy."

Relgor chuckled at Shadow's tone. "You have a talent for words, one that I find—"

"Valuable?" Shadow finished. "Curse my good looks and my wit. Would that I lacked such attractions."

His tone elicited a sneer from Serak. "Of all the fragments, it is you I despise the most."

"Yet you built a cage for me," he said, and winked. "I think you like me."

Serak's scowl deepened, but Relgor cut him off. "It is important that you understand your predicament. The other fragments do not know your location, and your only real ally has betrayed you."

"Lorica?" he jerked his head. "She would never join you."

"She realized her fate was sealed when you were captured, and has accepted my offer while you slumbered," Relgor smiled. "She now serves the Order."

Shadow laughed, the sound low and mocking, so laced with scorn that both men flushed. If he'd just met Lorica he might have believed them, but over the last few weeks he'd grown to trust the woman. Friends do not betray friends.

Serak stepped to the edge of the cage and pressed a hand on a rune. The light within began to brighten, the walls and ceiling turning white, the bars glowing. Shadow grimaced as the light scorched his flesh, burning lines across his skin. More shadows curled off him like smoke, burned away by the searing light.

Shadow fell to his knees but fought the urge to cover himself with his arms. The pain continued to rise, ripping a growl from his lips. Then Serak reduced the light back to normal, leaving steam rising from Shadow's flesh.

"Can you direct me to the bathing chamber?" Shadow asked, looking about the cell. "I like to take a dip after being tortured."

Relgor's jaw tightened. "Do you not understand the danger you face? You are—"

235

"Famished," Shadow said. "Potatoes, a nice seared steak, and steamed vegetables sound delightful."

Serak glowered. "I'll give you—"

"And dwarven fire ale."

"I'll—"

"And perhaps some roast pig haunch," Shadow mused.

Serak reached for the rune. "*I'll roast you until you—*"

"No," Shadow said, tapping his chin. "That all sounds delicious, but I think it needs cheese. But what type?"

Shadow began to list the types of cheeses, wondering aloud what would go best with his meal. Serak stared at him, his hand inches from pressing the rune. Relgor's expression blackened, his black eyes spinning with red until he snapped.

"SILENCE, SLAVE!"

Shadow smiled, and Serak slammed his hand onto the rune. Again the light brightened, burning Shadow's body. He kept his feet, laughing through the pain, the sound so mocking that Serak pressed the rune harder.

"Enough!" Relgor barked. "Bring her in."

The light diminished and Shadow sucked in his breath, smiling through the pain. Relgor glared at him, his amusement gone, leaving fury in its place. Shadow blew a kiss, daring him to press the rune again. A door opened at the back of the chamber, briefly lighting a circular room and a pedestal at the center. Lorica entered and advanced to join Serak and Relgor.

"Lorica," Shadow said in surprise.

"I'm sorry," she said quietly. "But they made an offer I could not refuse."

"So you betrayed me?" Shadow demanded.

236

"I was here for Gendor," she said, grimacing. "My oath is to my guild."

Shadow stabbed a finger at her empty finger. "I see you have yet to claim the guildmaster's ring. Does Gendor yet live?"

"For now," Serak said. "We must ensure Lorica's loyalty before we grant her reward."

"So you trust *them*?" Shadow asked.

"I have no choice," she said, and looked away. "I'm sorry."

"Your reunion is touching," Serak said. "But we have a schedule to keep."

Relgor, obviously still seething, pointed to Shadow. "We want you to cast a messenger to Elenyr. We want her to dispatch Fire to help you."

"You think I'm going to help you?" Shadow snorted in disbelief.

"Of course," Serak said. "Because if you don't, we're going to kill Lorica."

Lorica rounded on them, just as Gendor appeared behind her, his barbed dagger at her throat. Her features contorted with fury, but the blade was tight on her neck, and she trembled in helplessness.

"You really thought Serak would trust you?" Gendor asked.

"I'll kill you for this," Lorica spat at Relgor.

"I did speak the truth," Relgor said, yellow replacing the red on his dark eyes, his tone shifting to amused. "I would rather have you on my side. But better to have a devil I trust."

Serak never took his gaze from Shadow, as if he knew victory was at hand. Shadow glared back, wanting to dismiss Lorica as easily as she had dismissed him. But he remained silent, the words failing to reach his lips.

"That was all it took to silence you?" Relgor asked, chuckling. "We should have brought her in sooner."

"Will you let her go?" Shadow asked.

"I swear it."

"You can't trust them," Lorica growled.

"*You don't get to talk to me,*" Shadow hurled the words at her. "Not anymore."

"You have no choice," Relgor said.

Shadow clenched his fists. "I'll do it."

Serak smirked, and touched the rune, lowering the darkness in the cell enough that he could craft a messenger. He crafted a jungle cat out of the darkness, and when Serak gave him parchment, wrote a brief message. He wanted to shape the message to his own aims, but they gave him the exact words.

As he wrote the message, he subtly crafted a dagger out of shadows and tucked it behind his back. When he was finished, Serak opened a section of the bars and the cat padded out. Then the bars shut and the room brightened again, disintegrating the dagger.

Relgor's smile was sickening. "You have my gratitude."

He motioned to the darkened room and Bloodsworn appeared from the gloom with shackles, which they placed on Lorica's wrists. At no point did he permit her an escape, and Gendor kept the blade on her throat. Then the shackles locked shut and the pair dragged Lorica from the room.

"I'm sorry," Lorica called as she disappeared, her tone filled with anger and regret.

Relgor went with them, leaving Shadow alone with Serak. The father of guardians regarded Shadow for several moments and then pressed the rune, burning Shadow anew. This time Shadow did not laugh.

"I sent your message," Shadow said, wiping blood from his mouth. "Will you let her go?"

Serak inclined his head. "I will spare her life as agreed. But I admit I'm surprised. I did not think you would feel compassion for another's pain."

"I'm surprised as well," Shadow said. "Surprised that anyone thought you attractive enough to love. Tell me, was Elsin blind? Or just desperate?"

Serak reached to the rune on the bars, and the illumination in the cell brightened. Shadow cringed away from the brilliance and raised a hand, but the effort was futile. The bars, the floor, even the walls and ceiling were all imbued with light, burning away every patch of shadow, and scalding his flesh.

His chest and face were scorched and cut, blood dripping to the floor. Shadow grimaced but laughed anyway, the sound low and mocking, daring Serak to brighten the room further. He knew it was foolish, but he refused to let Serak see him vulnerable.

"I do like long walks on the beach," Shadow said.

"You won't like this one," Relgor said, returning and joining Serak.

The krey stood as tall as Serak, his body lean, his black eyes gaining flecks of gold. His smile suggested he found pleasure in Shadow's pain, and Shadow managed to make a rude gesture to the krey.

Relgor did not take his gaze from the cell. "You have no idea how much you are worth," he said softly. "With you and your fragment brothers, I could even buy a marriage into the empirical line."

"You cannot trap us all," Shadow said.

"Actually, I can," Serak said.

He reduced the illumination in Shadow's cell, not enough to create darkness, but enough so Shadow wasn't bleeding. Then Serak stepped to the center of the circular chamber and touched a rune on the pedestal.

Four walls descended into the floor, revealing four additional cages. One was crafted of bright blue flames, another absent of all light. The third was built of water so cold that frost vapors curled off the aquaglass

239

wall. The last was a traditional cell, with hardened steel and mithral walls. Serak smiled at Shadow's expression.

"You see, I've been preparing to cage you for thousands of years, ever since I found the Gate chamber and sent a message to Relgor."

"I thought you sent the beacon to Wylyn," Shadow said.

"That's what my mother thinks," Relgor said, his smile turning smug.

"You lied to your mother?" Shadow feigned indignation. "How beastly of you."

"I wonder if your buyer will cut out your tongue," Relgor said. "Or maybe he will enjoy your crassness. Either way, it won't matter to me. I will already have my reward."

"You cannot cage what you do not understand," Shadow said.

Serak swept a hand to him. "I've spent my entire existence studying you. I know everything you are capable of, and what you cannot do."

"We shall see," Shadow said.

Serak regarded him for several moments and then motioned to the only entrance into the cell. "Come, Relgor. We must prepare for Fire's arrival."

"Enjoy your final days here," Shadow called. "You won't like how they end!"

Serak and Relgor departed, leaving Shadow in his glowing cell. He listened to their footfalls diminish. Then he stepped to the bars of his cage and leaned against them, examining the other cages.

He always appreciated how much men divulged when they thought themselves in power. Shadow had learned a great deal in the last few minutes. And for all their gloating, Shadow would have the privilege of seeing their triumph turn to despair.

"Your plans are good," he murmured, a faint smile spreading on his face. "But my plans are better . . ."

240

Chapter 32: Unbound

Gendor shoved Lorica into her cell, knocking her to her knees. She rose and spun, ready for a fight, but Gendor remained in the doorway, his lightning sword in hand. She kept expecting them to take her wing cloak, but they would pay for the effort in blood. Even without a weapon, she was dangerous as long as she had her wings. But not against Gendor. The urge to charge burned in her chest, but without a blade the effort would be lethal.

"Tell me," she said. "Is there anyone left that cares about you? Or have you killed them all?"

"You despise me for being smart?" Gendor asked.

"I despise you for killing the innocent," she snapped.

"No one is innocent," Gendor said. "Have you not realized that yet? They all deserve to die, and I'm just smart enough to see the coming storm. Only a fool would sail into a hurricane."

"Does that help you sleep at night?" she asked. "Kill anyone to survive?"

"That is all that matters," he said.

"You can't lie to me," she said. "You *love* to kill, to have the power to take someone's life. Give me my blade and see if you can take mine."

He twitched as if he wanted to agree, and then shook his head. "Goodbye, Lorica. When you die in The Bone Crucible, know that I'll be watching."

He turned and left, the door slamming shut. Lorica listened to the key turn and then his footfalls echoing into stillness. Then she stepped to the opening and peered into the hall. As before, six guards stood in the hall, all staring at the door.

241

Lorica retreated into the darkened interior of the cell and sat on the bed. Although the urge to escape was overwhelming, she held herself in check. Right now, the guards were watchful and wary, and she was still on Gendor's mind. She needed an advantage.

The guards checked on her every few minutes. It was maddening to know how to escape but be forced to wait, but she resisted the impulse. The guards had likely been warned to watch her carefully, but her unmoving silence eventually caused them to check on her less and less often.

As she waited, she pondered her brief moment of freedom and what she'd learned from Relgor and Serak. The pair thought themselves triumphant and in that victory had gloated. Exactly as she and Shadow had planned. But they had not planned for how well prepared their foes would be, and now they were both in cages.

A meal arrived, the tray shoved through a small flap in the base of the door. The food was better than expected, and although she wanted to ignore the meal, she eventually caved over the savory scents. She picked up the tray and retreated to the bed to eat. When she was finished she kept the tray and continued to listen.

She thought often of her sister and wondered what she would think of her predicament. She was caged by a member of the krey and destined to fight in an otherworldly arena for the amusement of the Krey Empire. If she failed.

"Would you have liked our plan?" she wondered aloud.

Loralyn had always been methodical in her craft, both as a soldier and as an assassin. In that regard she was much like their brother. Zenif would plan the design for a piece of cloth to the utmost detail, while Loralyn would plot an entrance and escape for every target. The actual blow was delivered with solemnity, almost apologetically, and Loralyn had always mourned those she'd killed. Her honor had been above reproach.

Lorica knew exactly what her sister would have said about her plan with Shadow. It was bold and risky, with many variables that could result in ruin. It also counted on Shadow's cooperation, but she reminded herself that he'd saved her life, more than once now.

A faint swell of voices outside the cell indicated her time had come, so she stood and approached the door. A glance through the small window proved that the guards had grown restless. Only one continued to watch the door, while the other five had fallen into conversation about Gendor and the krey.

Lorica smiled faintly and then spread her wings. Leaping into the air, she flapped once and alighted on the rafters above. Then she crept along the beam to the end, where Shadow had been when Relgor entered the room. Behind a beam where the shadows were darkest, she reached down and found a solid object clinging to the back side of the beam.

A key.

She smiled as she palmed the key and dropped back to the ground. After Shadow had been taken, she'd found the key in seconds, but decided to leave it there in case Gendor returned. Just when she'd been contemplating using it, Relgor had returned and repeated his offer. Realizing it was a chance to survey the castle, even if the offer was false, she'd accepted.

She chuckled in the darkness, pleased with how much she'd learned. Relgor's offer had sounded genuine, but Lorica had never believed he would let her live. By accepting, she'd learned what she most needed, the way to Shadow's cell.

Lorica stepped to the door and inserted the key into the lock. Shadow had crafted it out of darkness, so she was careful to keep her body between the key and the light orb in the cell. The lock creaked as she turned the key, drawing the gaze of one of the guards. She tensed, but another guard spoke and he turned away.

She eased the key around, rotating the lock until it opened in a whisper of steel. The wary guard looked again and frowned, and then began to walk towards the door. Lorica grasped the handle and ducked below the window.

The man reached the window and stared into the cell. He scowled and scanned the room before he struck the wood with his fist, calling her name. The other guards heard the concern and fell silent, their boots clicking on the floor as they joined him.

"Where is she?" one demanded.

"Does it matter?" another asked. "She can't go anywhere."

"We were not supposed to let her out of our sight," the first one said.

"She's just trying to bait us into—"

Lorica kicked the door open, smashing the guard into his companions. She darted into the open and used the food tray to hit a man in the face, sending him into the wall. Cursing, the remainder managed to draw their swords.

"Nice blades," Lorica said. "Which one will I take first?"

One sliced high, the other low. Lorica spun and took two steps to the wall. Racing up the surface, she leapt into a back flip and spread her wings, soaring over them both. They spun as she landed, her wings stretching out.

She sidestepped a hasty lunge and caught the man's wrist, wrenching his sword free. Raising the weapon, she blocked the blow from the second and then sent her wing to knock him into another guard who'd managed to get to his feet. Both crashed into the wall.

Now with sword in hand, Lorica dived into the fray. They were trained well, their swordcraft sufficient to inspire fear among normal soldiers. But in their disorganized ranks she flitted from one side to the other, her blade cutting deep, claiming one life, then two.

When the third slumped to the ground the one with a broken nose retreated, stumbling backward. He filled his lungs with air, but she filled his lungs with a sword. He stared in astonishment at the sword extending from his body. His shout died on his lips and he too fell to the floor.

The remaining two struck on both sides, driving her back from the blade, leaving her hands empty. Without a weapon, she was hard pressed. Steel split her skin, cutting her stomach, shoulder, and cheek. Their confidence mounted and they pressed the attack, forcing her back toward her cell.

The one on her right cried out in triumph, driving his sword toward her stomach, a tactic meant to force her back into the room. Instead she caught the door, swinging it outward to accept the blow. The blade dug deep, the wood momentarily binding the weapon. The second Bloodsworn came at her other flank, his sword swinging across her waist.

Still with her hand on the door, Lorica pulled herself above the flashing sword and kicked out, her boot connecting with his jaw. He tumbled backward, and she spun around the door. She caught the hilt of the bound blade and kicked the door, wrenching it free.

"Would you really kill someone so helpless?" he asked, raising his hands to placate her.

She whirled and launched the stolen sword. It spun end over end and plunged into the guard she'd kicked, the blade knocking him into the wall. He died before he hit the ground. Then she turned to the final guard.

"Better?"

"Much," he said.

He darted in and leveled a punch that would take her eye. She caught a glimpse of the steel around his knuckles as she ducked and sent her wings outward. The tips of the winged cloak wrapped around the man's throat, lifting him off the ground and slamming him into the stone wall.

"Where's Gendor?" she demanded.

The man struggled to speak, his hands clenched around the cloak. "The central tower, top floor."

"And Serak?"

"Left an hour ago," he groaned. "Went into the Deep."

"Why?"

"I can't—"

245

She retained her grip on his throat as she turned and slammed him into the opposite wall, where he hung above two of his dead comrades. Her voice turned to ice as she leaned in, her face just inches from his.

"Last time I'll ask."

"Someone was impersonating Serak," he growled.

"Who?"

He squirmed in the grip of her wings. "I don't know, I swear. But he got far enough into the Order to learn a great deal. They're setting a trap for the imposter."

Lorica considered the idea that they might have an ally against the Order. Donning Serak's persona was a bold move, and bespoke someone both powerful and daring. If they'd also learned about the Order, it could prove useful. It also meant that Gendor was alone in the fortress.

"And Relgor?"

"With Gendor," he said.

"How many are in Mistkeep?"

The man fought to breath. "More than—"

He pulled a blade from a hidden sheath in his sleeve, a motion he'd obviously waited to do until she was distracted. He sliced for the cloak, forcing her to release him. He dropped the blade and caught it with his other hand, knifing for her throat.

Lorica retreated from the flashing knife, ducking and twisting to avoid his evident skill. He switched hands, and then rolled the blade along his forearm, flicking it out to nick her already bloody cheek.

She winced and kicked a fallen blade. It clattered off the man's boots but he kept up the onslaught, driving her back, forcing her against the wall. She twisted, redirecting her retreat toward the last one she'd killed, toward the blade protruding from his chest.

The knife cut again, drawing blood across her upper arm. She retaliated with a blow from her wings, but he endured the buffeting and surged forward, driving for her heart, a shout of triumph on his lips.

She reached back and caught the sword hilt. Yanking it from the dead man's body, she raised it forward, using her retreating wing to hide the blow. He did not see the raised blade until it was too late, his own momentum driving the steel into his heart.

He gasped, his jaw working in pain and disbelief. Lorica reached out and plucked the knife from his fingers, then she stepped around him and walked away. His body struck the ground, his dying shout weak and empty. She picked up a discarded sword on her way down the corridor and spun both weapons in her hands.

It was time to get Shadow.

Chapter 33: Imposter

Laying in the center of his cell, Shadow heard a muffled grunt and then a thud. A smile crossed his features but otherwise he did not move. He listened as a creak of steel indicated the door was opening and then soft footfalls crossed the space.

"I see you found the key," he said.

"You could have left me a weapon," Lorica said.

Shadow rose to his feet and stepped to the bars. "That wouldn't have made it fair."

She grunted in irritation and reached for the rune that opened the door, but Shadow shook his head. With a smile on his face he produced a tiny, elven made crossbow. No longer than his finger, the weapon pointed at her. She frowned, but when he fired the bolt it veered to the side and struck the rune. The bars dropped into the floor and he stepped free.

"Where did you have that?"

"In my boot," he said, returning the weapon to the hidden cavity of his bootheel.

"You could have escaped anytime?" she demanded. "Why wait?"

He yawned and motioned to the cell. "I've never been absent my magic. I found it quite refreshing."

She snorted in disbelief and turned toward the door. "We don't have much time. I killed my guards and it's only a matter of time until the alarm is raised."

"Wait," Shadow said. "There's something I need to do first."

"We can't wait," she said, but he was already turning toward the cells.

He stepped to the center pillar and pressed the runes that lowered the bars on the other cells. Then he darkened the room, the lights fading and granting him a return of his power. He breathed in the shadows and shaped them to his will, fashioning ropes and a winch.

By necessity, the cells for the fragments of Water and Fire were on opposite sides of the room. Bringing such extreme magics together would have been volatile, and Serak had obviously taken precautions to ensure the cells were kept apart. In total darkness, Shadow used large machines to dig into the floor, ripping the stones apart.

"They're going to hear that," she growled.

"Doesn't matter," he said. "I have to destroy this prison."

A shout came from without, followed by the thudding of footfalls. Cursing, Lorica leapt to the door and engaged the two guards, cutting them down before they could cry for aid. Holding position, she called to Shadow.

"We don't have time for this."

"My plan is working perfectly," he said. "Just give me a minute."

"Our plan didn't work at all," she protested. "We didn't know they had a cage for you, and Relgor forced you to send a messenger."

"That was rather irritating," he said. "But no matter. We'll find them soon enough."

"Serak isn't here," she said. "He went into the Deep. Seems someone is walking around with Serak's face."

Her voice was hard to hear over the crunching of rock. Shadow coughed in the dust as his machine ripped into the supports beneath the cells. Dirt and chips of stone flew about the room, the cacophony eliciting another curse from Lorica, who had to fight three that rushed the door.

"*Shadow . . . ,*" she called in a rising tone.

249

"Almost there," Shadow said.

The cell of fire teetered forward, its moorings broken. A moment later the cell of water did the same. Shadow lashed both cells to ropes of shadow, coiling them onto a winch that began to turn. A grinding of stone echoed as the two cells began to approach each other. Shadow's eyes lit with delight as he gauged the distance. Then he turned and swept past Lorica into the lit corridor beyond.

"Ready?" he asked.

"I was ready *before* you told everyone we were here," she said. "What were you even doing?"

"We have thirty minutes until those two cells come together," Shadow said. "When they do . . ."

Her eyes widened. "It's going to take out half the fortress."

"Exactly."

A man rounded the corner and shouted in surprise. Shadow and Lorica sprinted towards him but he was too far away, and the guard reached the end of the corridor. He slapped a rune embedded in the wall, causing a keening wail to rise within the fortress, the sound echoing down every corridor and in every chamber, the sound magic signaling that the fortress had been breached.

Lorica glared at Shadow and he shrugged apologetically. "Let's find Gendor and finish him."

She spun her blade. "It's about time."

They sprinted down the corridor and up the stairs at the end. The door swung open into a great hall, where forty Bloodsworn were closing ranks, leveling swords and crossbows, which they aimed at the two escapees.

Lorica leapt into the air, avoiding a volley of crossbow bolts that thudded into the wall, just missing her feet. She caught an arch and swung out of sight onto a higher level, and sprinted around the curving balcony, firing at the light orbs. The tinkling of shattered glass punctuated the shouting men as the room fell into a flickering light.

Shadow dived behind a couch. Crossbow bolts pierced the leather and passed through, the steel heads poking out the back. Shadow rolled beneath the couch as the gloom mounted, and then turned to his shadow form.

Pulling himself free, he leapt into the midst of the soldiers, a shadow among shadows. Swords swung at him, clattering off the helms of their companions, while crossbow bolts filled the air, flying in all directions.

Shadow ducked an arm and attached a thread of darkness to the man's wrist, and then fastened it to the foot of the man next to him. One turned, and both went down cursing. Shadow weaved past the captain and thumbed his nose, before lashing the man's sword to his trousers.

The man swung at Shadow, ripping the pants right off his legs. He tripped in the tangled cloth, losing his sword and his dignity. Shadow caught the captain's shirt and stripped it from his body. He turned and ducked, avoiding swords as he donned the tunic, but paused in front of a mirror, admiring the look. He liked the look of a uniform, even if he hated the trappings of obedience that came with it. Then he leapt over the man's falling form and rolled under a swinging blade. It crashed into a table instead.

Shadow leashed a line of darkness to the nearest man's neck and sent a thread above, yanking him all the way to the ceiling. Another cried out when the man next to him flew upward, and Shadow took advantage of his distraction to lash his wrist to the waist of the woman behind. The man caught sight of Shadow and swung, knocking himself and the woman into a tangle of struggling arms and legs.

An elf appeared from a corridor and skidded to a halt, his eyes going wide at the chaos. Then he pulled from the dim light to cast a light in his hand, partially repelling the darkness. The raging melee unfolded before him and his eyes widened, his angry orders dying on his lips.

Men and women fought to stand, the shadows lashing them to each other, the wall, the furniture, and even the ceiling. One woman hung upside down, her feet bound to the wall. She furiously yanked on her legs, but they refused to budge. Shouts and howls filled the dark hall.

The light from the elf's hand gradually burned through the shadow ropes, and one by one the Bloodsworn came free, only to be met by the falling men and women that had been lashed above.

From the balcony on the second level, Shadow leaned against a pillar and surveyed the scene with a smile of pleasure. The Bloodsworn had been well trained, but all their talent was for naught in a darkened room. Then Lorica caught his elbow and dragged him away.

"We must hasten."

"Do you have to spoil *all* my fun?"

She grunted in irritation. "You're just making them mad."

"Don't tell me that wasn't fun to watch."

"I can't say that," she said, her lips twitching.

She shoved him into an alcove as Bloodsworn raced by. When they were gone she stepped out and into a stairwell, hurrying upward. Shadow fell into step behind her, and the two raced higher into the fortress.

"Have you forgotten you set a trap that's going to destroy half the fortress?"

"No," he said. "But I want to see the explosion."

"You've lived a long time for someone so reckless."

They reached the top corridor and darted behind a cabinet of weapons, allowing another patrol of soldiers to rush by. Orders were being shouted, but they contradicted others he'd already heard, suggesting the Bloodsworn did not know how to react.

"We need to hurry," she said. "We can't fight the Bloodsworn *and* Gendor."

"Then stop playing around," he said.

He darted past her and hurried down the hall. A pair of guards rounded a corner and Shadow surged forward, drawing the dagger he'd pilfered from the melee below. Sidestepping the lunge, he knocked the blade upward and then struck the man's arm. He stumbled back, allowing Shadow to drive the dagger into his stomach.

Lorica stood over her fallen foe and shook her head in disapproval. "You're getting slow."

"Are you turning this into a competition?" he asked, raising an eyebrow.

"Maybe," she said.

He grinned. "I took out six below."

"Seven," she said smugly. "Eight including this one."

He spotted movement behind them and spun, hurling the dagger the length of the corridor. The guard that had just appeared met the blade, his shock matched by his dismay as he tumbled down the stairs from which he'd appeared.

"Eight," he said, picking up a sword and stepping past her. "And counting . . ."

"That doesn't count," she protested.

"Does too," he replied.

They heard approaching footsteps and separated to opposite sides of the corridor, both striking as a patrol appeared. The quartet of Bloodsworn went down in seconds, unprepared for the ambush.

"Still tied," Shadow said.

"For now," she replied.

Shadow stole a look at his companion, surprised to find her enjoying the conflict. When they'd met she'd been set on killing Gendor, and now she stood just feet from reaching him, and she bore a smile on her face.

"I fear I've ruined you," Shadow lamented.

"How so?" she replied, peeking up a stairwell before ascending.

"You've lost sight of your target," he said. "And what he did to you."

She came to a halt, surprise appearing on her features, as if she hadn't realized the distraction. Then she frowned and shook her head, accelerating up the steps. Regretting the choice to bring it up, Shadow followed.

"I'll see Gendor soon enough," she said.

"Wait," he said.

"For what?"

Recognizing the room at his side, Shadow swung the door open and darted in. Lorica hissed his name but he ignored her as he sifted through a rack of weapons. Finding the one he wanted, he returned to the hall and offered the weapon to Lorica.

"I think you'll need this," he said, presenting the red blade.

"My oathsword," she said in surprise.

"I saw it when I searched the castle before," Shadow said. "I figured you'd want it for Gendor."

"Thank you," she said, discarding the Bloodsworn blade.

A pair of hurried footfalls came from the stairs they'd just exited, and Shadow grinned. "Ready for another?"

"Always," she replied.

They flanked the steps, and Shadow claimed the position affording a view down the stairs. When the two appeared, Shadow blinked in surprise. He'd expected more guards, but instead it was a dark elf woman he recognized, standing next to Serak himself.

"Willow?" he blurted, stepping into the open and pointing his sword at her. "What are you doing with him?"

Serak's eyes lit up with delight and he rushed up the steps, avoiding the blade with ease to engulf Shadow in an embrace. Startled, Shadow fought to release himself from Serak's grip, but Serak gushed into his ear.

"Shadow!" he cried. "I've missed you so much, and there is so much for me to tell you. You wouldn't *believe* what I've seen in the Deep."

Shadow finally disentangled himself and put his sword between them. "A few hours ago you wanted me dead. Now you act like you love me?"

Serak giggled, and then passed a hand over his face, his features fading. The haughty gaze, the cruel lilt to his lips, were replaced by wide eyes and a beaming smile, revealing the fragment of Light.

Chapter 34: The Unguarded

"Light?" Shadow exclaimed. "What are you doing here?"

"Looking for—"

"We should get out of sight," Willow exclaimed.

Lorica nodded in agreement and retreated to the room across the hall. Barely lit, the chamber contained crates and barrels, the dust thick on the wood. Shadow shut the door before turning to Light.

"I thought you were with Water and Lira."

"I was," he replied, speaking in a delighted rush. "Then I met up with Elenyr and she sent me into the Deep with Willow. And who is your companion?"

"We don't have time for tales," Lorica said. "And I'd rather not be inside when that trap explodes."

"Right," Shadow said, and pointed to Lorica. "Assassin. Dead sister. Betrayed. Revenge. Fun. More fun. Want to kill Gendor." He raised an eyebrow to Lorica. "Did I leave anything out?"

She snorted a laugh. "I think that covers it."

Light grinned. "Became Serak. The Deep. Tired. The Queen's Hand. Battle. Willow is beautiful. Kiss. Another Kiss. Mistkeep. See Shadow."

He beamed like he'd accomplished a challenging task, and Shadow sorted through the wealth of information. Willow smiled at the description, and Shadow noticed Lorica eyeing the woman's copious tattoos.

"What do you need?" Shadow asked.

"We're hoping the queen of the dark elves is here," Willow said. "She was taken by the Order."

Shadow recalled his searching the fortress before he'd found Lorica. He'd covered the entire fortress except one corridor, the one with the dark elf guard. He grimaced as he realized the corridor's location.

"It's on the east side," he said. "But in a few minutes that entire wing is going to explode."

Light and Willow exchanged a look. "Then we'll hurry," Light said.

Willow's jaw set and she swung the door open. A roving patrol appeared on the stairs at the same moment, the three men looking up to see Willow standing in the door of the storeroom. All three reached for their weapons.

Willow grabbed her bare shoulder, where the hilt of a crossbow was tattooed onto the flesh. The weapon curved down her back, the bow extending onto her stomach. At her touch the ink turned liquid and poured into her hand. The crossbow rose from her body, leaving clear skin behind as she pointed the weapon.

The weapon triggered three times, the bow snapping so fast that the three bolts seemed to fly as one. Black bolts pierced the Bloodsworn armor, knocking them into the wall and down the stairs, the clatter of their fall drowning out their dying groans.

Willow pressed a rune on the crossbow and a thread of ink appeared between the crossbow and the bolts, yanking the three bolts back into the weapon. Nodding in satisfaction, she returned the crossbow to her shoulder, the ink sinking into her flesh and returning to a tattoo.

"Let's go," she said to Light, and then darted into the corridor.

"Isn't she incredible?" Light whispered to Shadow, his voice tinged with awe as he slipped out the door and followed her out of sight. "Good luck!" he called back.

Willow nudged Light and his features returned to Serak. Then they were gone. Shadow turned to find Lorica staring, her expression stunned

257

at what she'd just witnessed. Shadow smirked and stepped into the open.

"I take it you'd never heard of Willow?"

Lorica fell into step beside Shadow. "That's not a magic I've ever heard of."

"Elenyr said it's a unique," he said. "Willow got a tattoo of a dagger as a young woman and found that she could draw the weapon and make it real. It can never fully leave her skin, but she's a walking armory."

"Indeed," Lorica mused. "She would make a good assassin."

"Already trying to build your new guild?" Shadow asked.

"Perhaps," Lorica said. "You want to be part of it?"

The comment was said in jest, but Shadow faltered in his steps. He'd never considered a life outside of the fragments, but the prospect of being an assassin with Lorica appealed to him. For an instant he imagined hunting dangerous prey, instilling terror in the hearts of the corrupt and cruel.

A broad smile spread on his features as he imagined the fun of such an occupation, of targets and assignments where he could go as he pleased, hunt as he liked, never having to report back to Elenyr . . .

His smile faded as he imagined a life away from Elenyr and the other fragments, and uncertainty stilled his amusement. Was that a fate he desired? He'd always said he preferred to be alone, but was it true?

A Bloodsworn appeared and Lorica dispatched him with ease. Shadow told himself her comment was not serious and forced the idea aside. Then he accelerated to the end of the corridor, reaching it at the same time as the assassin.

They slowed and came to a halt at a second great hall. More lavish than the first, it contained adornments fit for a king. A large fire crackled in a giant hearth, with gilded couches set around the fine stonework. Arches of stone reached to the peak of the chamber, the carvings suggesting they'd been made by dwarves.

Tapestries and paintings lined the walls, some so ancient they were encased in aquaglass, the worn material depicting moments from the Dawn of Magic. Others showed the krey standing over kneeling men and women of all races.

Twin staircases ascended to a balcony above, where Shadow spotted Relgor and Gendor. The heated argument brought a smile to Shadow's lips, and he hoped he was the cause. He always liked infuriating a foe before their defeat. It made the victory so much sweeter.

"There are no guards," Lorica whispered.

Shadow scanned the great hall and saw that her words were true. Not one Bloodsworn stood in the hall, in the doorways, or on the balcony. From the distant shouts, it seemed the Bloodsworn were still hunting for Shadow and Lorica, and dealing with all the traps he'd left behind. Lorica took a step forward but he put a hand on her shoulder, holding her in check.

"We need to move," she hissed. "We don't have much time."

"Wait," he said. "I want to hear their conversation."

She scowled, obviously reluctant to wait now that her foes stood within reach of her blade. But she inclined her head and the two leaned against the wall, listening to Relgor and Gendor argue.

Although Shadow caught only snippets of conversation, he heard enough to understand what made Gendor angry. He wanted to ship Lorica away before she escaped, a wise tactic, considering they were already out of their cells. Of greater importance was Relgor's response.

"It won't be long until Wylyn raises the tower. When our army arrives it won't matter if the slaves are in a cage or free. They will all be taken."

A slight tremble came through the stones under Shadow's feet, and he looked downward. As the cages got closer together their magics would react, and he guessed only fifteen minutes remained before the explosion. His thoughts turned to Light, and he hoped his fragment brother would escape.

"Worried about Light?" Lorica asked.

"Maybe," he said.

"Good," she said, nodding in approval. "It's good to see you care. Now can we please kill Gendor?"

He shrugged and then motioned into the room. She drew her sword and then stepped forward, leading them into the great hall. The two crossed half the space before Gendor spotted movement and his eyes widened in surprise.

"How did you escape?"

"I'm the fragment of Shadow," he replied. "It's kind of what I do."

"It's true," Lorica said.

Her chuckle was tinged dark, her jaw set in a determined line. Her eyes were fixed on him, her knuckles white on the hilt of her sword, which she raised to point to the one who'd killed her sister.

"You should have killed me when you had the chance."

"I won't make that mistake again," he snapped, and glanced to Relgor.

The krey man regarded Shadow and Lorica as if seeing them for the first time. Shadow had seen that look before, on a soldier deciding if he should sell his prized bull or kill him because he refused to be obey.

"I must say, I am disappointed. Serak assured me the cage would hold you. But it lasted less than a day. Your value is immeasurable, but only if I could bring you to market. And you said yourself, escaping is what you do."

"I also kill," Shadow said, and looked meaningfully at the krey.

Relgor sighed and waved his hand to Gendor. "As you desire. Kill the assassin."

Gendor's eyes glowed in triumph and he stepped to the railing and drew his sword. Locking eyes with Lorica, he loosened the latch on his cloak—and it began to spread. Lorica sucked in a breath when the cloak swung outward, feathers appearing on the shimmering material as they became wings.

"Do you like them?" he said. "I admit I was always envious of yours, but it took a lifetime to track down their creator. It's too bad she won't be able to make another set for you."

"Sentara," Lorica's voice trembled with anger. "Did you kill her?"

"Of course," he said. "Dropped her off the Giant's Shelf. Even on her way down she talked to that orb of hers. She was truly mad. Gifted," he ruffled the wings. "But mad."

Trembling with rage, Lorica began to stalk forward. She didn't speak, and her wings flared wide. Gendor smirked and launched himself off the balcony but banked to the side and flew down a corridor. Lorica leapt into the air and flew in pursuit.

"Have fun!" Shadow called, and then turned his gaze on Relgor. "I guess it's just you and me, now." He scanned the room again, but there were still no guards.

"Tell me," Relgor said. "Is there any price I could offer that you would accept?"

Shadow cocked his head to the side and then nodded. "One."

"Do tell," Relgor said, leaning forward.

"Slit your own throat," Shadow said. "Do that, and I give you my oath that I'll let Wylyn sell me to whoever she wants."

"You go willingly . . . but I do not get to reap the benefits?" Relgor chuckled, the tone one of admiration. "Such a clever tactic. A pity. I think if the circumstances were different, you would relish all the Empire has to offer."

"Probably," Shadow said. "Will you pay the price of my loyalty?"

"I'm afraid your offer is too high," Relgor said, touching his throat. "I do like my life, after all."

Shadow shrugged, his smile turning smug. "Either way, I get to watch you die. You really should have posted more guards."

"I don't need them here," Relgor said. "For Serak has his own protections, and I think he must have thought of you when he crafted this particular sentry."

Relgor didn't move, but the balcony where he stood grew brighter, the light mounting to the point of blinding. Then a massive frame stalked into view. As tall as a horse and twice as long, the scaled reaver padded to Relgor's side. Cast from pure light, the sentient was so bright that Shadow squinted, but he could not tear his gaze from the beast.

Its jaws were long like a wolf's, with hundreds of teeth visible. Its body was scaled, small fins extending from the powerful legs, granting the reaver speed when underwater. The long tail contained a barbed tip, the barbs flattening and straightening as it stepped up to the balcony and dropped to the floor. It rumbled a warning, its lips lifting into a chilling snarl.

Shadow began to retreat from the sentry, glancing to Relgor in doubt. The reaver had obviously taken years to create, a little magic added every day, until the mind was finally finished, granting the sentient flesh a purpose.

Relgor settled into a chair and picked up a glass. "I may not get to sell you, but at least I'll get to watch your final battle." Then he looked to the reaver. "Make certain I get to witness the kill—"

The wall next to Shadow exploded, stones clattering onto the floor as Light tumbled into the room. His clothes were rent and torn, his hair in disarray. He rose to his feet and spotted the reaver of light, his eyes widening in delight. Without noticing either Shadow or Relgor, he strode to the reaver.

"You shall do nicely," he said.

The reaver snarled, but the moment Light put his hand on the creature's flank, it dropped to its knees, allowing Light to climb onto his back. Then Light rode his new mount back the way he'd come, the reaver blasting through the too-small opening before he disappeared. Light's laughter echoed back.

"Willow!" he shouted. "Look what I found!"

Relgor's features were frozen in disbelief, and he looked between the broken wall and Shadow, his jaw working as if he wanted to speak, but words failed him. Shadow shrugged helplessly.

"You should have had more guards."

Relgor's shock faded to fear, and then he turned and fled. Shadow, a smile on his face, followed. Relgor was a man used to power, to control, and now he fled like a frightened rabbit. He was the best type of prey, and the hunt was on . . .

Chapter 35: Wings of an Assassin

Lorica flew down the corridor, banking through a tight turn and running along the wall, surging to catch up to Gendor. A Bloodsworn appeared and cried out in surprise, but she flew past before they could draw a blade.

"Do you flee out of fear?" she taunted.

Gendor swerved up a staircase, his momentum bleeding away as he turned up the turret. She did the same, folding her wings as she reached the top, and sprinted after Gendor's fleeing form. She surged forward, closing the gap and swinging her sword.

Gendor turned and parried the blow, their swords ringing in the corridor. She struck high and then low, driving to breach his defenses, but he knocked her sword wide and leaned into a kick. She sidestepped and struck him in the knee with her free hand. He stumbled back, spinning off the wall to avoid another strike.

She followed the blow with her blade, but he switched his grip and blocked. They stood so close she could feel his breath on her face, and see the hatred burning in his eyes. They twisted and turned, each attempting to breach the other's defenses, until Gendor leaned in and struck her face with his forehead.

Stars exploded in her vision and she recoiled, instinctively darting back. The air whistled as Gendor's lightning sword sliced in front of her stomach, cutting into her armor and drawing a shallow line into the skin.

"The Angel of Death," he wiped the blood off his lip. "A name you do not deserve. The people should not love an assassin."

"Do you even know how many innocents you've killed?" she asked.

"Does it matter?" he shot back. "Everyone dies anyway."

She saw Zenif's face and her blood boiled. "When you kill it leaves a scar," she growled, attacking with such ferocity that he was forced to retreat. "Every life taken, every death, hurts *everyone* in their life. We don't just kill, we leave a wake of carnage."

She lunged and then twisted, bringing her sword on his opposite flank. He narrowly blocked, but again was forced to retreat when she used her wings to strike a cabinet. He dived away when the cabinet crashed to the floor, scattering the displayed blades.

"My *sister* understood that," she spat. "She *knew* that the assassins choose targets for where they will do good, not harm. And what do you do? Kill the most honorable person you've ever known."

"Your sister was a fool," he said.

He flared his wings and jumped into the rafters, and she followed, leaping to the beams and dancing across them, maintaining the onslaught. Gendor sneered as he fought for an advantage, but her anger would not be bound.

He scored several hits, but each was shallow, and the sting only drove her to greater lengths. As if realizing he needed space, Gendor turned to a window and dived into the night. Unwilling to let him escape, she leapt after.

From a ledge just below the window, Gendor swung his sword, slashing across her leg as she soared by. She gritted her teeth to prevent a shout and spun, her wings flapping for altitude. Gendor, his wings also spread, stood on a tiny ledge, flicking the blade free of her blood.

"You were always so impulsive," he said coldly. "Without your sister, you would never have become an assassin, yet you think you deserve to be guildmaster."

"Has the ring opened for you?" she challenged.

His lip curled into a sneer. "It opens with an act of honor, an antiquated requirement. It's only a matter of time until I find a mage that can force it to obey my will."

She hovered above the center of the fortress, the mist creeping over the battlements. A sliver of a moon hung in the night, providing just enough light for her to make out the towers and battlements of Mistkeep.

Windows glowed from the light within, and voices rang out. Punctuated with the sounds of battle, she had no idea if it was Shadow, Light, or Willow that was the cause. Stone cracked and smoke billowed out of a pair of windows on another turret. A body flew out of a nearby window and the man screamed as he fell.

"Your Bloodsworn are dying," she said.

He walked along the ledge, eyeing her position as he twirled his dagger. "I admit you and the fragments are stronger than I anticipated. But you have no idea how powerful Serak is, and how much he has plotted. He and the krey are certain to win."

"If they do, you won't be there to see it."

She'd gradually risen through the air, and now she dived forward, sacrificing height for speed. Gendor sprinted along the ledge and leapt away, his dive taking him into a courtyard steeped in mist.

Lorica banked against the wall and kicked the stone before inverting her fall and dropping after him. Like a cauldron of smoke, the courtyard was filled with the greenish mist, and Gendor disappeared into its embrace. She pursued, the mist filling her vision as she followed the flapping of his wings.

A flicker of motion came at her side and she wrapped herself in her cloak. Gendor burst into view, narrowly missing her as she fell. Unfurling her wings, she swept upward and followed, her sword cutting only mist.

"This is *my* keep," Gendor's voice seemed to come from everywhere. "And you think you can defeat me here?"

She flapped for altitude until she came above the mist. Battlements and turrets rose above her, while other sections of the castle blocked the horizon. No one was in sight, and she turned and twisted, scanning the mist for Gendor.

A faint flapping was the only warning, and again she folded her wings, diving into the mist to avoid Gendor. His blade plunged into her shadow and he growled in dismay, before he too disappeared into the mist.

"You cannot hide forever," she called.

"I'm not hiding," his voice seemed to float upward, dark and sinister.

The hair of her neck raised and she flapped again, soaring upward. A clanking of steel signaled another threat, and a pair of ballistae bolts exploded from the mist, trailing a wide net. She avoided the first but the second came inches from entrapping her wings. Then the mist filled with more, all rising to claim her.

She bared her teeth as she swerved, fighting for the freedom of height. The clouds briefly cleared, and for a moment the moonlight pierced the mist, revealing the quartet of ballistae on the floor of the courtyard. Manned by Bloodsworn, the weapons were quickly reloaded and fired again, the view fading as clouds blocked the moon anew.

"Come and get me," Gendor's voice taunted from the dark mist. "Or are you too—"

A large shape plowed through the courtyard wall. Broken stones clattered across the war machines and their operators. Lorica blinked in surprise as the reaver of pure light streaked through the courtyard, its body knifing through the ballistae as if they were made of parchment. Evidently chasing a fleeing quarry, the reaver had a rider on his back that looked like Serak, but his peeling laughter indicated it was the fragment of Light.

"Sorry!" he called back as he disappeared.

The illumination from the reaver and the distraction were all Lorica needed, so she dived into the green mist. A pair of ballistae managed to fire but she veered past the volley and flared her wings, her speed taking her below the angle of the weapons. Spotting Gendor, she turned toward him and raised her blade.

The assassin snarled in anger and spit toward the departing reaver, which blasted through another wall on its way back into the castle. His trap spoiled, Gendor flapped his wings and raced up the beam of a broken ballistae before launching himself skyward.

Lorica realized the man had prepared the trap just for her, rightfully attempting to negate Lorica's greater experience in the air. But now he had no choice, and the two battled for dominance in the sky above the fortress.

Both fought for altitude, attempting to use the height to gain the advantage. More in tune with her wings, she continued to ascend above, her blade cutting into his wings despite his efforts to keep her at bay.

He curved wide, attempting to flank her, but she twirled in the air and knocked his dagger aside. Then she swooped in, again cutting his wings. The shining material became torn and ragged, each cut damaging his ability to fly.

They tangled again, and although he cut her hand, she again sliced his cloak. She caught his wrist with her free hand and twisted, throwing him wide before slashing him across the chest, drawing blood. His wings flapped hard, struggling to hold him aloft.

"Die at my blade," she called, "or die on impact. I don't care which."

Gendor scowled and went into a dive, attempting to return to Mistkeep before his wings gave out. She pursued him, and Mistkeep filled her vision, growing larger as they both plummeted from the sky.

She angled her body, accelerating to catch his right wing. Flaring her wings, she slowed them both and flipped him onto his back. His sword came for her throat and she struck his hand, knocking the lightning blade from his hand, sending it spinning into the mist. He drew his dagger and slashed, but she parried with her sword and kicked him in the chest, slamming him into a roof.

She'd slowed their fall but he landed hard, the impact driving the air from his lungs. She landed above him, using her speed to drive her sword through his cloak, pinning him to the roof. Fighting for breath, he swung his dagger, but she caught his wrist and put her boot on his hand. She pressed him against the roof and reached for the ring.

But it was absent.

"Where's the Guildmaster's ring?" she demanded.

He held open his other hand. "Go and get it."

He released the ring and it tumbled down the slope, bouncing off the edge before falling free. Scowling at the choice, she leapt to the edge and dived, chasing the glittering object as it fell outside the fortress, towards the mist and the lake.

She flapped hard, her hand outstretched, her fingers reaching. The ring passed into the mist and she followed, stretching her entire length, following the ring by the faint glimmer in the mist. In a final burst of speed, her fingers closed around the ring, flaring her wings to come to a stop . . .

Deep in the fortress, the cage of fire and the cage of water pressed against each other, the enchanted flames pushing against the water, causing the ice to burst into steam, the heat rising as the two contrasting magics were forced together. Cracks in the bars appeared and spread, and then both cells detonated, the blast shredding the entire chamber, the ball of fire consuming the corridor beyond and the surrounding stone.

The Bloodsworn in the nearby halls felt a rush of air before the fireball claimed their lives, the blast ripping through the supports, exploding outward to shatter an outer wall. Lorica, just feet from the shore of the lake, was knocked into the water, the blast singeing her wings.

She groaned, her vision and mind swimming, and just managed to make it to shore. Her face speckled with dirt and blood, she looked blearily up to the castle. Bereft of its supports, an entire wing of the castle groaned, and then collapsed into the raging flames. Struggling to focus, her ears ringing, she did not notice Gendor step out of the smoke and raise his dagger, until it sliced across her back.

Chapter 36: Fear of the Hunted

Shadow followed Relgor, leaping to the beams above the corridor and following them along the ceiling. He cast a shadow crossbow and fired several bolts at the krey's back. The light blunted the weapon, but he cried out each time they struck. He glared back, and Shadow chuckled in delight.

Shadow dropped into the corridor just as Relgor ducked into a room. Shadow caught a glimpse of the Gate on the opposite side of the chamber before Relgor slammed the door shut. Shadow came to a halt at the barrier.

"Do you mean to flee?" Shadow taunted. "From a *slave*?"

Like many of the doors in Mistkeep, this door had a small, barred window at the top, allowing Shadow to see the interior. Relgor stood with his hand on the edge of the mirror, one foot inside the Gate. He cast a look back, the black in his eyes spinning red.

"Your kind cowers before mine," Relgor said haughtily. "I would never run from you."

Shadow heard the slight tremble in his voice, the sound of one attempting to control their fear, and not entirely succeeding. Relgor was rattled and alone, but now that he was partially safe, he would return to his former scorn, and seek to erase the memory of his terror. An idea came to mind that appealed to Shadow, and so he leaned against the wall opposite the door.

"Gather your forces, then," he said. "And let us see if you really are the superior race."

Relgor's gaze would have scorched steel, and he shouted into the Gate, his tone that of command. Seconds later, a dakorian stepped through the Gate and rose to his full stature. Five others followed, the last of which was Tardoq himself, Wylyn's Bloodwall.

"Come and get me," Shadow said. "If you can."

He turned and sprinted away, his mocking words galvanizing the dakorians and Relgor in pursuit. Shadow guessed that Relgor would have preferred to send the soldiers to kill him alone, but the sting of fleeing before a slave needed to be eradicated, and so Relgor joined his soldiers.

Shadow turned a corner to find a dozen Bloodsworn hanging from the traps he'd set. Others fought to disentangle them, with some also getting trapped for their efforts. All looked to Shadow at his appearance, rightfully guessing he was the culprit.

A grin on his face, Shadow stepped onto a man bound to the wall, using his shoulder to leap into the rafters above. Curses and crossbow bolts were hurled at him, but he leapt across the gap, dodging those hanging by their feet.

Relgor and the six dakorians rounded the corner and charged through, shoving the Bloodsworn aside. Relgor barked an order and a handful joined him, the group accelerating after Shadow.

He dropped to the floor of the corridor, avoiding a blast from a dakorian hammer as he rolled through the door. The wood shattered, the power of the weapon sending the bent hinges into the corridor beyond.

Shadow raced through the entrance hall and turned to his shadow form, leaping straight through the portcullis at the entrance. Like smoke, he passed through the barrier and then turned solid before darting onto the bridge that would take him into the Evermist.

Relgor screamed for someone to open the portcullis, and a pair of dakorians caught the bars and heaved them upward, allowing the army through. Dropping the portcullis behind, the entire group charged the bridge.

Relgor slowed as he reached the end of the bridge. In the night and within the swamp, Shadow would have a great deal of power, and

Relgor seemed to recognize his disadvantage. He scowled and slowed, glancing back towards the safety of the fortress.

Shadow, having entered the Evermist and circled back, ducked beneath the bridge and traveled back towards Mistkeep. The thudding of dakorian boots came from above, fading as the group reached the swamp. Then Shadow caught the darkness and flipped onto the bridge. Alighting inches from the krey, he leaned in and whispered in his ear.

"How does it feel to be afraid?"

Relgor nearly leapt from his skin. Anger replaced Relgor's fear, and he sprinted to his forces, joining the dakorians and Bloodsworn on the bank of the lake. They lined the bank, aiming their weapons at Shadow.

"Kill him!" Relgor cried.

Shadow leapt to the side of the bridge and caught the railing, swinging into the welcome darkness beneath. Blasts of dakorian hammers and crossbow bolts streaked across the bridge, filling the night.

The supports of the bridge curved down and out, and Shadow leapt from end to end. Ahead, the soldiers barred the way, leveling weapons at him, but Shadow reached to the underside of the bridge and used the darkness to swing to the opposite side. From there he leapt to the bank and into the swamp.

He immediately took to the trees, lashing himself to the darkness above and ascending from view. By the time Relgor and his group appeared, Shadow was safely perched in a crook of a branch.

"Give us light!" Relgor barked. "His magic will be useless."

The dakorians struck the trees, their hammers empowered by the impact. Glowing runes appeared on the shaft and on head of the weapons, illuminating their faces. The Bloodsworn used pocket light orbs, holding them aloft to shine into the gloom. Shadow activated the rune in his gauntlet that threw his voice, his voice seeming to come from everywhere and nowhere.

"Look at the little krey . . . isn't he adorable?"

"I want him found," Relgor spat.

"Alive?" Tardoq asked.

"Dead," Relgor snapped.

". . . your fear is pleasing to my ears . . ."

"I'm not afraid of a slave!" Relgor bellowed.

Shadow's mocking laughter came from ahead, and the group charged into the trees. The dakorian in the lead swung his hammer—and tripped over the line of shadow at his feet. His growl ended as his body fell upon a bed of shadow spikes. Some were made ethereal by the glowing hammer, but enough were solid that they pierced his bone armor, leaving him mortally wounded.

Tardoq scowled at the dying dakorian. "Spread out, groups of three. One dakorian each. Find and flank him!"

The group split up, but all kept close enough to each other to take advantage of the light. It was a smart tactic, especially when Tardoq barked another order, and one of the dakorians pulled a small sphere from a pouch in his armor. Standing behind a trunk close to the fallen dakorian, Shadow frowned, and recalled the spheres the Bloodsworn had used in the assassin council chamber. Instead of using it like a weapon, the dakorian tossed the ball into the air and it floated upward, where it began to glow. Instead of exploding, the energy within turned to light, flowing outward to fill the swamp, illuminating a large swath. Fortunately for Shadow, it cast a multitude of shadows behind trees and brush.

Shadow smiled in anticipation, and then dropped behind the trunk of a dead tree. He crept close to a trio and pulled on the darkness, the shadows wrapping around his arm to form a giant claw. From the night he swung, slashing the Bloodsworn from cheek to chest.

The scream rattled the others, and they converged on the spot. The one in the rear passed into the shadow of a tree and did not emerge. His companion turned, his eyes going wide as the killer was carried aloft.

"Here!" he cried. "He's here!"

273

The body tumbled to his feet, and he recoiled in fear. The dakorian jumped into the tree, the limbs groaning as he sought to reach the height. But the action put him into the shadowy limbs. Even as Tardoq bellowed at him to descend, great jaws appeared from the mist, and devoured the dakorian. The dakorian's shouts were punctuated by the snapping of bones, and then he fell silent. In the shocked stillness, the broken body of a dakorian landed heavily, and all eyes stared at the corpse.

"Do *not* step into the shadows," Tardoq bellowed. "He is not a foe you know!"

Their fear turning to terror, the Bloodsworn rushed to the safety of the light orb, while the dakorians spread out, and at Relgor's order, tossed more lights into the air, flooding the swamp with illumination.

"More!" Relgor barked.

"We only have one left," one of the dakorians said.

Tardoq stepped to Relgor. "We should retreat," he murmured. "This is his battleground, and we are at a—"

"We do not retreat from *slaves*," Relgor snarled.

"This is no normal slave," Tardoq hissed. "It is unwise to—"

The krey rounded on him. "Do not tell me what is unwise. Or have you forgotten your place?"

"The light will not last," Tardoq growled. "The deton spheres will expire soon."

"Then I suggest you find him quickly."

"Are you just going to talk?" Shadow called.

He leaned against a tree at the edge of the pool of light, his pose languid, his smile amused. The dakorians spun, unleashing blast after blast from their hammers. Others charged the spot, reaching the burning trees to find the trail curving away, his mocking laughter daring them to follow.

"Go!" Relgor barked.

Tardoq growled in dismay and ordered a pursuit, and the Bloodsworn reluctantly followed. Racing down the dark path, they did not see Shadow flit into the trees above and toss a rock into the nearby lake.

The ripples of the impact faded, and then a large shape shifted underwater. In the gloom it surfaced and darted into the trees, passing over the carcasses of crocodiles that lined the shore. Its passage may have been silent, but the animals of the swamp went still.

The great predator followed the second thrown stone, and then veered toward the sounds of Relgor's force. It slowed as it came alongside the trail, and then leapt across, so quickly its giant shadow passed through the light. A Bloodsworn disappeared, his scream cut short.

"Use the deton!" Tardoq barked.

The dakorian tossed the sphere into the air, and the scene glowed to life, revealing a giant shape partially hidden in the brush, the body in its jaws. The group turned to fight, but this was no figment of shadow, and it released a dark rumble as it stepped onto the trail.

"Scaled reaver!" one of the Bloodsworn shrieked, and fled.

"It's just a beast!" a dakorian roared and aimed its hammer.

The scaled reaver darted around a tree, and then charged. He cut through the dakorian, its jaws snapping just once, nearly tearing him in two. Relgor screamed and those that remained attacked the beast, but it swung its tail, the barbs standing on end, impaling a Bloodsworn and knocking others from their feet.

It caught sight of Relgor and accelerated, its fluid body gliding across the ground. A dakorian stepped into its path, its hammer striking the reaver's head. The beast rocked to the side, and then whipped its tail, knocking the dakorian into a tree, the brutal impact reverberating in the swamp. Another dakorian struck the reaver's flank, but it whirled, its jaws clamping shut on the dakorian's horned skull. With the agility of a cat, it yanked the dakorian from view, dragging him into its pond.

The remaining Bloodsworn fled, evaporating into the mist. Alone with Tardoq, Relgor cursed their cowardice and turned to the Bloodwall. His voice tinged with hysteria, he huddled at the dakorian's side.

"Kill them both!" he shrieked. *"I want them dead!"*

There was no answer, and he looked up to the hulking dakorian, demanding answers. Tardoq, his eyes on his dead companions, scowled, and then leveled a glare so filled with hate that Relgor retreated.

"You are my mother's Bloodwall," Relgor barked. "You *WILL* protect me!"

Tardoq regarded him for several moments and then retreated, his large frame evaporating into the mist. Shadow watched the soldier abandon the krey, recognizing the act as a silent rebuke of Relgor's leadership. It was the first time he'd seen a dakorian disobey a krey, and Relgor's shock indicated it did not happen often.

"I AM YOUR MASTER!" Relgor roared.

Tardoq did not respond.

Shadow stepped into view, and the krey whirled, yellow swirling in his black eyes. "I'd say screaming was unwise," Shadow said.

Shadow retreated as the reaver appeared but stayed close enough to witness. The krey spotted the large beast slink into sight and froze, his chest heaving as he stumbled behind a tree. Then the reaver snarled and Relgor bolted, desperation filling his voice as he called out to Shadow.

"I know you could save me!"

"Why would I do that?" Shadow asked. "After all, I'm just a slave . . ."

He retreated into the night, listening for Relgor's final scream. It came quickly, the sound punctuated by sheer terror. Shadow smiled and took to the trees, pleased with the victory. Elenyr had wanted Relgor dead, and despite the legends regarding a krey, he'd perished as easily as any man. Of course, he'd tried to survive against a scaled reaver, and ignored the wisdom of Tardoq, a foolish—

The earth rocked from an explosion at Mistkeep, and Shadow clung to the tree branches as heated air washed over him. He hurried to the canopy, clearing the leaves in time to see a giant ball of fire rising above the fortress, illuminating the night. Smoke billowed, darkening the mist as it curled skyward.

"Blast," Shadow said, annoyed. "I missed it." Then he thought of Lorica and leapt forward.

Chapter 37: Lorica's Vengeance

The wings absorbed the brunt of the blow, saving Lorica's life. She screamed as her skin split, her wings tearing and tumbled away. Sparks burst from the break, and Gendor slashed again and again, obliterating the wings in a fury.

On the ground, Lorica heard the death of her wings and knew she was next. Gritting her teeth against the fire on her back, she pulled her knees under her, willing her body to stand, to fight. She sucked air through her teeth as sparks from her wings rained down on the shore of the lake, and grabbed a section of rock at her side, using it to rise.

She turned, and found Gendor watching her, his tattered wings partially flared, his spined dagger low and ready. Lorica's bright wings lay scattered at his feet, still sparking, a section struggling to flap.

"You were never a match for me," Gendor said, his voice muffled through the ringing in her ears.

"Why did you kill him?" she mumbled, her thoughts spinning too fast to control.

He circled her position. "You do not ask about your sister?"

"My brother," she said.

"I killed your brother?" Gendor asked, a trace of surprise in his voice, followed by recognition. "That's why you hated me."

Lorica spotted the oathsword nearby and eased towards it, the motion igniting the cut along her back. She could move, indicating it was shallow, but it ran from shoulder to hip. She grimaced and slid another step, working her way along the boulders of the shoreline.

"I didn't know it was you," she said, grateful her ears were beginning to recover. "Not at first."

278

"What was his name?"

"Zenif," she said.

"Target?"

She shook her head and took another step. "He was a simple weaver, in a corridor when you escaped a kill."

"A tall man," Gendor said slowly. "I remember he stepped into my path, refused to let me leave. Even unarmed, he barred the way."

"Sounds like him." She managed a pained laugh. "The heart of a warrior, the hands of a weaver. He made my cloak, before Sentara made me fly."

She took another step and agony lanced across her back. She slumped to her knees, groaning, and found her hand on a section of the wing. The fine thread touched her fingers, soft and bright, woven with traces of mithral thread, the texture reminding her of her conversation with Zenif.

"I'll never need mithral in my cloak," she'd said, irritated at the expense.

"Let a big brother take care of his little sister," he replied. "I may not have a blade, but I can build you armor."

Tears escaped her eyes and dropped onto the wing. Even in death, her brother had saved her life, yet she'd failed to avenge him, or Lyn. Gendor had slain her entire family, all because they'd been in his way.

The fire on her back seemed to sink into her bones, burning with a heat that compelled action. She reached for the hilt of her sword and rose, turning to face her adversary. Gendor stood, watching her with the soberest expression she'd ever seen.

"I didn't want to kill him," he said softly.

"Every action has a price," she said.

The fire in her bones mounted, burning into her limbs. She embraced the pain of her wounds. They brought clarity, and she fixed her gaze on Gendor, not with hatred or rage, but the steel of one willing to die.

She began to walk forward, and Gendor looked up from the fragments of her wings. He raised his dagger and deflected her sweeping strike. He lunged, driving for a quick kill, as if eager to end the fight, to walk away.

She barely deflected the blow, and then struck again, her blade coming from below. He parried and struck back, seeking to use her weakness, her pain, to find a gap in her defenses. She managed to block again, and then sidestepped the next blow. Leaning in, she punched him with her free hand, rocking him back on his feet. She hissed as pain crackled in her hand, but the burning fire drove the emotion away.

Unleashing her blade, she attacked with every ounce of skill she possessed, yearning to end the one that had killed her family. His features twisted in disbelief, Gendor retreated a step, and then another.

She saw it in his gaze, a weakening of his will. The man killed to survive, and the coin was just an excuse. Without her wings, injured and limping, Lorica fought like a lion, and Gendor foresaw his death.

He turned and sought to fly, but she stepped on a protruding rock and leapt, catching him by his feet. His tattered wings could not support them both, and she brought him down, slamming him into the shore. Darting in, she brought her sword down upon his chest.

He rolled to the side, the oathsword cutting his side and burying into the sand, severing Gendor's left wing. The material had not been made to the same quality as hers, and it rent in two. He rolled to his feet and flung it away, before retreating again. But there was nowhere to go. The explosion had taken out a section of the battlements and shore, with great stones blocking his escape, beams burning above them. He came to a halt and brandished his dagger.

"I'm not letting you kill me."

"You don't have a choice."

She slapped his dagger with her sword, knocking it up. He flipped the blade over his hand and caught it with the other, slicing across her arm. She retaliated in kind, reversing her grip and hiding her attack, flicking the oathsword out to cut him along the side.

Grimacing, he held the wound, and she lunged. He sidestepped and swung the dagger at her throat, but she leaned back, allowing the blade to swing above her face. She caught a glimpse of her dirty and bloodied expression before rotating and slashing him across the back. He cried out and swung his dagger backwards.

She blocked his wrist with her forearm, the dagger's tip stopping an inch from her eye. Catching his wrist, she brought it down on her knee, snapping his fingers open and sending the dagger into the sand. Then she rotated his arm and brought his wrist behind his back, trapping it painfully. Swinging her sword forward, she placed it along his throat. Gendor froze when cold steel touched his flesh.

Lorica held him bound, the kill within her grasp. Her chest heaved from the exertion, from the triumph. She yearned to slide the blade across his neck, to spill his blood down his tunic and watch him fall.

But her hand did not move.

"Why do you stay your hand?" Gendor asked.

She kicked the back of his knees and used the grip on his hand, forcing him to twist and fall on his back. Then she stood with her sword on his chest. She'd expected fury and hatred in his gaze, but instead it was regret.

"I'm sorry I killed your brother," he said softly.

"I'm not going to spare you," she said.

"I know," he replied.

She knelt, and again put her sword on his throat. Their eyes met and she saw his fear, and realized again that he didn't want to die. The fire that had burned in her bones evaporated, leaving her aching and weak.

She pushed the blade until a drop of blood appeared, dredging up images of her fallen sister and brother, both dead at his hand. Her fingers trembled, but the sword did not move. She tightened her grip, but the desire to kill abandoned her, and she wilted.

"You're not going to kill him?"

She looked up and found Shadow sitting on a nearby boulder. "How long have you been there?" she asked.

"Long enough to get bored."

She looked down at Gendor. "I don't understand. I still hate him, but I can't do it."

Gendor smiled in relief, a glint of his previous cunning appearing in his expression. "I knew you—"

She smashed her sword hilt into his skull, and his eyes rolled back. Rising to her feet, she stared at the unconscious assassin and clenched her eyes shut, anger flooding her body. Why did she not kill him? Why would she spare his life?

"I don't understand," she repeated.

Shadow hopped down from the boulder. "I've corrupted you."

"You?" she asked, incredulous.

"I taught you a higher purpose."

"Having fun is not a higher purpose."

"I'm not talking about *my* higher purpose," he said. "I'm talking about yours. Revenge doesn't bring peace, and that is what you seek."

She cast her eyes to the burning fortress. The Bloodsworn had fled, to where she knew not, nor did she care. She and Shadow had won, escaped their cages, and defeated those that had destroyed the guild. So why did she feel such conflict?

"He deserves to die," she said. "And that is what I do. I kill those that do not merit life."

"He does deserve to die," he said. "But killing him now would be for revenge, and the Assassin's Guild kills for honor."

"What do you know of honor?" she asked.

"Nothing," he said with a shrug. "But that does."

He pointed to her hand, and she looked down to find light glowing from the ring, the ring of the assassin guildmaster. To her astonishment, it threaded up her arm. Purple and bright, the threads sank into her flesh near the shoulder.

She sucked in her breath, but the magic did not sting. Instead it seeped up her neck and throat, filling her mind and thoughts. Her eyes widened and she turned to Shadow, but he was absent, replaced by a wall of books.

The burning walls, the lake steeped in mist, even the sky and moon, all faded as the library appeared about her, closing above her head into great windows. The sun appeared, and a carpet of flowers appeared on the ground.

Bookcases extended away from her, each containing tomes and archives, the records of all the past guildmasters, not written in parchment, but inscribed in the memories of her predecessors.

"I take it you can now access the archives?" Shadow asked. His voice was smug.

"You knew I wouldn't kill Gendor."

She clenched her fist and the archives faded, to reveal Shadow still standing at her side, and Gendor still at her feet. His smile gave the answer, and he shrugged as if it didn't matter. She shook her head.

"But how did you know?"

"Because I'm your friend," he said.

She groaned, the sound washing over her, and she inclined her head. "You are indeed. The most annoying friend a person could have, yet better than I deserve."

"Don't tell my brothers you said that. I have a reputation to uphold."

Lorica stared at the unconscious body of her foe. The desire to plunge her sword through the man's heart was still present, but she knew she couldn't kill him, not now. But the question remained, what to do with him?

A shift of motion drew her eye to the edge of the lake, where two figures stepped into the open. Both resembled Shadow in looks, and they raised their eyes to the still burning fortress. Shadow noticed them as well, and a smile brightened his face.

"It looks like my brothers got my message."

Chapter 38: Shadow's Brothers

Lorica eyed the two fragments as they crossed the lake, recognizing them from the battle in the assassin guildhall. They'd come to Mistkeep from the east, but instead of circling to the road, the pair approached the shore of the lake. To Lorica's astonishment, two alligators approached and turned, providing a ride.

"I didn't think Mind would come," Shadow said.

"That's the one controlling the beasts?" she asked warily.

He swept a hand to them. "Mind has his name for a reason, and I'd suggest you guard your thoughts, or he'll know your darkest secrets."

Disliking that prospect, she closed her mind, a technique she'd learned on one of her earliest assignments as an assassin. Many regarded memory magic as a commodity, but some memory mages used their ability as a weapon to see into the minds of others.

As the pair crossed the lake, Lorica resisted the urge to raise her sword. From what she understood, they were fragments of a single guardian, powerful like him. And likely even more dangerous. The alligators came to the shore and the two fragments stepped off. Mind walked with a stiffness to his body, as if he had recently been injured. She noticed Fire had speckles of red in his dark eyes, and he smirked and pointed to the fortress.

"I thought you said you needed firepower."

"I took care of it," Shadow said.

"I approve," he replied.

Shadow grinned. "I thought only Fire would come."

"You've never asked for aid before," Mind said, folding his arms. "Elenyr decided to send us both. She thought you were in trouble."

"Nothing I couldn't handle," Shadow said.

"Fire," Mind said, "search the fortress, make certain there are no more threats."

Fire inclined his head and departed, and Mind's gaze settled on Lorica. Although he hadn't looked her way until then, she got the impression he knew everything about her, and the feeling only heightened when his dark eyes met hers.

She retreated a step. "Mind, I presume?"

He didn't respond, only regarded her with a strange curiosity. "You may have learned of us from Shadow, but speaking the truth to another would invite swift reprisal."

"He's joking," Shadow said.

"I'm not," Mind said.

Shadow grinned and swept a hand to Lorica. "This is the Guildmaster of the Assassin's Guild."

"Lorica," Mind said with a curt nod.

"You know my name?"

He gave a faint smile. "Your mental shields are admirable, but not formidable."

She scowled, but Mind turned his gaze on the unconscious Gendor. "You defeated the Blade Ghost. Impressive."

"Stay out of my head," she said.

The faint smile returned and Mind turned to Shadow. "Tell me everything."

"Why don't you read my memories?" Shadow asked. "Or are my mental shields . . . formidable?"

For the first time, Mind betrayed a hint of irritation. "Just tell me what happened."

Shadow grinned, and then began to speak. As Shadow detailed the events of what had occurred, Lorica fought the desire to retreat another step, irritated that Mind made her feel small. It was like he knew everything about her, and he inspired a touch of fear as none had before.

Although Shadow described the major events that had brought them to Mistkeep, she noticed he shared little of her, and did not mention her sister, or Zenif. His eyes flicked to her, confirming he chose to withhold that information for her, another reminder of their friendship.

"Light was here?" Mind interrupted. "Why?"

Shadow shrugged and motioned to the keep. "How should I know?"

"Elenyr will want to know of this."

Lorica realized he'd spoken Elenyr's name with ease, like he didn't care if she knew it. Had he done so because he knew Shadow had spoken of her? Or was it an oversight? A lapse in his thinking—

"It wasn't an oversight," Mind said absently.

Lorica scowled and gripped her sword. "I told you to stay out of my mind. I won't warn you again."

Shadow laughed and leaned against a rock. "As much as I would enjoy witnessing a fight between you, I'd rather not see my friend die at the hand of my brother."

"You don't think I can defeat him?" Lorica demanded.

"He's trained for five thousand years with a sword," Shadow said. "He could defeat Mox, first of the Bladed, even if he doesn't really have the magic the rest of us—"

"Shadow," Mind said, his tone gaining the hint of warning. "You have the freedom of sharing your own secrets, not mine."

Fire appeared on a boulder above and dropped to the ground. "The fortress is deserted except for the dead, and the fire has spread."

"Did you do the spreading?" Shadow asked.

Fire grinned. "Of course."

Lorica looked up to the structure and saw flames burning in the windows above, spitting sparks into the mist. Before long the entire citadel would be on fire, and only the stone structure would survive. It would require a fortune to renovate, and she doubted the Bloodsworn would return.

"Did you see the cells for us in the basement?" Shadow asked.

"What was left of them," he said, his tone darkening.

"That room had to have been filled with fire," Lorica exclaimed. "How would you have seen them?"

He raised a hand and his hand turned to pure, liquid flame. "One made of fire does not feel the heat."

"Serak was prepared to capture us all," Mind said, his forehead creased in thought.

"He made a deal with Relgor long before Wylyn's arrival," Shadow said. "But we don't need to worry about him anymore."

"Why not?" Fire asked.

"He was killed by a lesser being," Shadow replied, and finished the tale of their battle in Mistkeep. By the time he was done, Gendor had begun to stir.

Lorica stooped and used a section of Gendor's torn wing to bind his hands behind his back. Then she raised and leaned him against the rock. His eyes fluttered open, rising to see Lorica and her companions. He yanked his arms, but when he saw they were bound, he scowled.

"Why do you keep me alive?"

"Who says we will?" Lorica asked.

Gendor snorted derisively. "You're not going to kill me. You know your honor now."

"But I will," Shadow said.

"As would I," Fire said, a blade of fire appearing in his hand.

"Not yet," Mind said, and crouched before Gendor. "Tell me of Serak."

Gendor regarded Mind, and then shivered. The motion was subtle, and for the first time, Lorica sympathized with the man. Looking into the eyes of Mind left one feeling cold, and it seemed Gendor, too, felt small.

"You don't want to know of Wylyn?" Gendor asked.

Mind's smile was as disturbing as his gaze. "Wylyn is a threat, Serak is our foe."

"Serak has been hoarding records from the ancients for ages," Gendor said. "But I don't think he has found what he seeks."

"Why?"

"Because his search continues," Gendor said. "All I know is that he is looking for an ancient tower called the Shard of Midnight."

"Relgor spoke of a rising tower," Shadow mused.

"How do we know you're telling the truth?" Lorica asked.

"I always know," Mind cast over his shoulder, and then looked to Fire.

"Ever heard of it?"

Fire shook his head. "Perhaps the Hauntress knows."

"What will Serak do with Relgor dead?" Mind asked.

"Wylyn already thinks Serak is her ally," he replied. "And Serak always has a plan. Even for this." He jerked his chin towards the destroyed fortress.

"And the Bloodsworn?" Lorica asked. "What will they do?"

Gendor hesitated, and then shrugged. "I don't know. Thorg is dead, and without me they lack a leader. I suspect the Raven will absorb some of the killers into her ranks, while others will probably join the Order."

Mind searched his face and then stood. "We have what we need."

"I told you everything," Gendor said. "You'll still kill me?"

"Without hesitation," Mind said, drawing his sword.

Lorica's gut clenched, but she couldn't tell if she wanted him dead or alive. Before she could speak, Shadow began to chuckle, the sound tinged with a trace of excitement. Mind looked to him in irritation, the expression exactly like an older brother annoyed with a younger.

Lorica was surprised to realize that Mind's chilling demeanor was not constant. Rather he chose to instill fear, using it as a weapon. In that glance to Shadow, Lorica saw a wealth of history, for Lorica had seen that same look on Loralyn, and Zenif. He may have sought to intimidate, but he also loved his brothers.

Mind's scowl deepened, as if he'd heard her thoughts about them being brothers. If he had, he chose to ignore it, and spoke to Shadow. "You have another idea?"

"Of course," Shadow said. "You may have missed the fun, but perhaps there is some amusement yet to be had." His eyes settled on Gendor.

"Do what you will and be done with it," Gendor spat. "I'm not a means of your humor."

"Remember Hosin?" Shadow asked.

Fire inclined his head. "It is a clever tactic."

Mind grunted in annoyance and sheathed his sword. "You know such magic can be broken. Are you certain you wish to leave him alive?"

"We can always kill him after Wylin is dealt with," Shadow said with a shrug.

Lorica looked between them, confused and irritated. "Will you stop talking like I'm not present?"

"Let her decide," Shadow suggested.

To Lorica's surprise, Mind turned to her. "He is your enemy. Would you have him dead, or alive with no memory of his past?"

"You can do that?" she asked.

Mind flashed his faint smile. "It's powerful memory magic, but it could be broken. If it is, he will know everything of his former self."

"Will he return to being an assassin?"

Fire shook his head. "New memories change people. He could return to being an assassin or forsake that life altogether."

"We've seen it before," Shadow said with a nod.

"Lorica," Gendor said. "You can't let them do that to me. I'm an assassin, not some blasted farmer."

Lorica didn't hear him. Instead she heard Loralyn's voice when they'd decided to join the Assassins' Guild. "Assassins deliver justice, whether it be by death, or other fate, that is our code."

Gendor had begun to struggle but Lorica nodded. "Do it."

Mind sheathed his sword and grabbed the man's shoulder, dragging him to his feet. Gendor sought to flee but Mind pushed him against the boulder and reached to his throat, holding him pinned as he used his other hand to cover his mouth.

Gendor fought as purple light appeared in his eyes, leaking down his cheeks in large, purple rivulets. The light glistened in the night and fell into the sand, more and more, each drop sizzling on the ground.

Mind pulled on Gendor's face like he sought to remove it—the purple light swelling across his features. Gendor screamed as a second face appeared, a mask of purple light that Mind pulled away.

Lorica retreated a step, her mouth agape as the purple mask was pulled from Gendor's flesh. Mind released his grip on Gendor's throat,

291

but the assassin stood frozen, his features bright with horror as the mask was pulled from his skin, and he stared at his reflection.

Swirls of purple magic spun around Gendor and his reflection, pulling at Lorica's clothing, the wind whipping across the sand. She raised her palm and squinted at the bright light, but Mind continued to separate Gendor from his mask.

The Gendor of purple light opened his mouth to scream, but the sound came from Gendor's throat. In the midst of a cyclone of magic, Mind squeezed on the mirage, crushing it in his grip. More light burst from the mirage's eyes and mouth, shining as if in agony, until it shattered into sparks of magic.

The cyclone faded and Gendor dropped to his knees, gasping for breath. In the darkness he looked up to the foursome and retreated like a frightened youth, his eyes rolling in fear. He came to a halt against a boulder and curled up, raising his bound hands.

"Who are you? Why am I here?"

"We saved you from the fortress," Mind said, his voice comforting as he pointed to the burning citadel. "Don't you remember? You were kidnapped from your farm outside of Herosian and taken here."

Gendor shivered and trembled, his eyes wide with unfeigned terror. "Do you mean me harm?"

"No," Mind said softly. "We are here to take you home."

Chapter 39: Farmer

Shadow leaned against the tree, watching the man work in the field. He hacked at the weeds with surprising vigor, before pausing to take a drink from the waterskin at his side. He looked to the evening sky and smiled, the expression one of contentment.

"He looks happy," Lorica said.

"You sound annoyed," Shadow said.

Shadow watched Lorica. His friend. He was still getting used to the idea of having one but found that he liked it. He would not have any more, of course, but he liked trusting Lorica. And not just because of her lethal occupation.

"It is not what he deserved," she said.

"Sometimes we spare a life to save our own," Shadow said.

Lorica glanced his way and raised an eyebrow. "That doesn't sound like the Shadow I know."

Caught, he grinned. "Water likes to say it—an irritating number of times, in fact."

"So you think I did the right thing?"

"I would have killed him," Shadow said with a shrug. "But as we've established, I don't really care about other people."

"You care about me," Lorica said. "Or you wouldn't have hidden the truth about Zenif from the other fragments."

Shadow recalled the conversation outside Mistkeep. He had indeed avoided speaking of Lorica's brother, not because Mind wouldn't know, but because he didn't want to be the one to share it.

"It's your secret," he said.

"Thank you," she said. "For everything."

"You helped me kill Relgor," he said. "I'd say we're even."

"Are you certain he is dead?"

"Mind found what was left of his body," he said. "But I do wish I could have seen his end. Unfortunately, a castle exploded and I thought a friend was in danger."

"I wasn't," she said.

"As I discovered," he replied.

She smiled and turned back to watch Gendor. After leaving Mistkeep, the group had traveled to Herosian, and Gendor had been terrified to silence the entire journey. Without any memories of combat or killing, he only remembered his youth, and the time of living alone on a distant farm, the memories Mind had implanted.

In truth, the farm was owned by Elenyr, and she occasionally liked to vacation there. Gendor had taken to the soil as if he'd been born to the plow, while Lorica had insisted she stay and watch her former adversary. Shadow thought watching a man toil in a field excessively dull, but Lorica never departed her vantage point.

"What will you do without your wings?" he asked.

"I'll miss flying," she replied. "But it seems the Angel of Death is gone."

"Can you not craft more?" he asked.

She pointed to Gendor. "I believe he ensured I could not."

Shadow glanced into the trees. Through the trunks of the small stand, he spotted a small fire, where the other two fragments waited. Mind had agreed to stay until nightfall, and with the sun setting, Shadow was eager to depart.

"I'm not going," Lorica said.

"How did you know I was going to ask?"

She motioned to Gendor. "I'm going to watch him for a while. Then I have a few things to do."

"Like visit Zenif's wife?"

She nodded but did not speak, her jaw tightening with regret. "I need to rebuild the guild. The world needs those that kill for honor."

Shadow withdrew a small figurine from his pocket. It resembled a jungle cat, its flanks sleek and dark, its jaws open in a snarl. She accepted the gift with a look of confusion, and then noticed the symbol of shadow magic inscribed on the right flank.

"It only works at night," Shadow said. "But if you need me, that will send me a messenger."

"And if you need me?" she asked.

He laughed. "I'll have no problem finding you."

She turned and wrapped her arms around him, the embrace catching him by surprise. When he recovered he hugged her back, the contact warm and close, like returning home after a long journey.

When they parted she smiled, "Good luck, Shadow. If you haven't killed Wylyn by the time I've gathered my guild, let me know."

"I promise," Shadow said.

Recognizing it was time to go, Shadow turned and strode away, leaving Lorica to watch the farmer toil in the field. He made his way through the trees, wondering at the touch of sadness that marred his excitement. Relgor was dead, but foes abounded, so why was he sad?

He reached the campfire to find Mind already on his feet and Fire extinguishing the flames in the ring of stones. The trio turned away and stepped onto the nearby trail, making their way towards Herosian.

"Ready for more?" Mind asked.

"Always," Shadow said, and cast a look back to the trees.

"You called her your friend," Mind said.

"So?"

"You don't have friends," Fire said.

"I do now. Why is that so strange?"

Fire and Mind exchanged an amused look, and Mind said. "It's not. It's just nice to see."

Shadow frowned. "Just tell me about my next assignment. I assume I'm to travel to the Deep?"

Mind pointed downward. "From what you say, Serak is aware there is an imposter, and Light will be in danger."

Shadow smiled at the prospect of traveling to the Deep. Nowhere did he have such power, and the idea of hunting Serak would make it even more fun. He recalled the room of many Gates that he'd found in the Raven's house. He would wager a fortune that one of them connected to the Order of Ancients in the Deep.

"And you?" Shadow asked. "I noticed you did not speak of your own travels while Lorica was present."

"We are glad she is your friend," Mind said. "But you cannot trust her completely. She is still an assassin."

"Of course," Shadow said, and smiled to hide the lie.

Mind watched him, but Shadow had far too much practice lying to be caught, even by the fragment of Mind. Fire too, seemed to accept Shadow's answer, and Shadow wondered if their faith was due to how little Shadow trusted everyone else.

"We've learned much since your departure," Mind said.

As Mind described the events at the Stormwall Arena, and the reunion at Cloudy Vale with the fragment of Water, Shadow found himself still thinking of Lorica, and her casual invitation to join the Assassin's Guild. Then Mind spoke of becoming Draeken, and the battle with Histikor, king of dragonkind.

"And I missed it?" Shadow lamented.

"So. Much. Fun," Fire crowed.

Shadow reached out and flicked his ear. "You don't have to gloat."

"Why?" Fire said. "*You* would."

Mind swept a hand to Shadow. "It's true. You would."

"Still," Shadow said. "You got to fight a *dragon*. How long's it been since we got to do that?"

"Too long," Fire said. "But you'll just have to wait till the next one."

They passed out of the trees and into a sprawling village. Homes and farmland stretched for miles, with more cows than humans. The sun crept below the horizon, the light reminding Shadow of being trapped in Serak's cage.

"Serak will be prepared for the loss of Mistkeep," Shadow said. "He's as tactical as you." He pointed to Mind.

"It doesn't matter," Fire said. "You and the assassin dealt him a blow, and the loss of Relgor will infuriate Wylyn."

"True," Shadow said, imagining the woman's face when she found out her son was dead.

"I'm not so sure," Mind mused. "From what I've seen, the krey look at family more like partners in commerce than true kindred. I suspect she will be more angry than heartbroken. The greater question is Tardoq. He really abandoned Relgor?"

"He did," Shadow said.

"May I witness?"

Shadow shrugged and opened his thoughts to Mind while imagining the moment. He felt a tug, like a fishhook caught in a tunic, and then Mind frowned, his eyes distant as he recalled the memory that was now his.

297

"Tardoq could have killed the scaled reaver," Mind said.

"I doubt that," Shadow said. "The reaver killed the other dakorians with ease."

"Tardoq is a Bloodwall," Fire said. "And he's lived for many lifetimes, just like us."

Shadow recalled Tardoq's departure, the look of disgust on his features, disgust for Relgor. He hadn't fled out of fear, he'd abandoned the krey because Relgor had ignored his warning. Mind came to a halt.

"Can you show me more?"

"More than the memory?" Shadow asked, confused. Mind had never asked such a thing before.

"Please," Mind asked.

Shadow glanced to the setting sun and gauged the light. His magic would be greatly weakened, but he could depict the moment. Shrugging, he drew on the long shadows from a nearby field of corn, and in the road he shaped the trees and swamp.

Trunks of shadow rose around them, while brush and bodies appeared at their feet. The reaver stood frozen a short distance away, while Tardoq and Relgor stood in the center. When the image was complete, Mind stepped forward and reached up, adding a touch of purple magic to the shadows, enhancing their features until both Relgor and Tardoq looked real.

Relgor's eyes were wide in fear and fury, his face flushed. Tardoq looked down on him, his lip curled in disgust. He stood with his hammer in hand, but the look in his eye suggested he would rather use it on the krey.

"Do you see it?" Mind asked.

"See what?" Shadow asked.

"Oh," Fire said, stepping in and looking into Tardoq's eyes.

"It's doubt," Mind said.

"He doubted his master," Shadow said. "That's why he left."

"No," Mind said. "That is not the look of one abandoning a person. It is the look of one abandoning a *cause*."

"No," Fire said, jerking his head. "As you said, Tardoq is a Bloodwall, Wylyn's sworn protector, so loyal that she gave him the gift of a perfect body. He is ageless because he has proven his fealty."

"Perhaps he just doubted Relgor," Shadow said.

Mind extinguished his magic, and Shadow did the same. "Perhaps," Mind said.

Shadow heard the doubt in his brother's voice, and realized Mind wondered if Tardoq could be turned to their side. But Shadow had seen him fight, and from what they had said, Tardoq was a born killer, like Gendor if he lived thousands of years and killed millions.

"Tardoq will not betray Wylyn," Shadow said.

Mind scratched his chin. "I've looked into the minds of commoners and kings, thieves, knights, and even dragons. Do you know what they all have in common?"

Shadow glanced to Fire, but he was just as confused.

"Everyone has a point of pressure," Mind said. "And they all have the potential to break."

"You think that applies to the dakorians?"

"*Everyone*," Mind said. "Including us."

Darkness settled around them, and Shadow considered the prospect. The idea of turning Tardoq against Wylyn sounded amusing, but would it work? Ultimately, he realized it was worth the attempt.

"I guess we shall see," he said, "But before I leave, I need a favor."

"What sort of favor?" Mind asked.

Shadow described what he wanted, careful to keep his thoughts from revealing the truth. Mind shrugged and cast the requisite charm, a shard of purple magic that would link an object to one's consciousness.

"Am I going to regret this?" Mind asked.

"Of course," Shadow said with a chuckle. He pocketed the piece of magic and gathered the shadows around him to form his dragon.

"Be safe in the Deep," Mind said.

"I never am."

Fire burst into a laugh. "Fun is not safe."

"Indeed," Shadow said. "I'll see you after we finish in the Deep."

He gathered his wings and launched himself skyward. A farmwoman nearby was on her porch, tossing out the bath water. She screamed as Shadow passed above the house, but for once he was not inclined for mischief. Still, he found a smile on his face as he thought of Lorica. He had a friend, and if he could evolve, perhaps the other fragments could as well.

Flying north, he considered how the change in him would affect Draeken. From what Mind had described, Water and Lira were becoming close, and their attachment had changed Draeken. Shadow wondered if his newfound friendship with Lorica would help Draeken be whole? Or cause damage? He tossed his head, dismissing the thought. Instead he recalled what Mind had said.

Everyone has a breaking point. Even us.

But what would break Draeken?

Chapter 40: Finding Serak

Elenyr watched Mind and Fire depart, hoping they would reach Shadow in time. Shadow had never requested aid, not in such a fashion, and at the last moment she'd decided it would be best for Mind to go as well. She didn't say that she had an ulterior motive.

"You think Shadow will be well?" Water asked.

"It's Shadow," Elenyr said, hiding her worry behind a smile. "He has a way of getting out of conflict."

"That's true," Water said with a laugh.

"Still," Lira said, her eyes on Mind and Fire down the trail. "You did send two fragments."

"Better to be sure," Elenyr said. "But it's time for you to depart as well. Wylyn's forces are weakening, but the Order is much stronger than we could have imagined. We must prepare for the possibility that they succeed in opening a Gate."

"If that happens, we will not survive," Lira said.

"Perhaps," Elenyr said. "But it's important that we prepare, and if the rock trolls will come, the other kingdoms will as well."

Lira shook her head. "I'm here to find and kill Wylyn, not negotiate with kings."

"This is an assignment that you are best suited to complete," Elenyr said, "for the current king is not a king, but a queen, one that doesn't care for men acting like they know more."

"And you think she will listen to me?" Lira asked.

"That is my hope," Elenyr said. "When you return, go to Herosian and find Light and Shadow. They should be back by then."

301

"What about King Numen?" Water asked. "Will you search for him?"

"I have a more pressing concern," she said. "I will return to Cloudy Vale, and see if I can learn more of Serak."

Lira appeared uncertain, but in a testament to how much she'd come to trust Elenyr, the woman nodded, and Water cast his traveling wheel, widening it so it was large enough for both him and Lira. They said their farewells and then the wheel sped away, kicking up mud as it rounded a curve in the trail.

Alone, Elenyr turned away from the departing fragments and made her way south. Her gait slowed by the weight of her thoughts, she brooded on the revelations about Serak, and his anonymity since the Age of Oracles.

For a man to stay hidden for so long seemed unthinkable, yet when a powerful guardian was involved, she'd learned that anything was possible. She scowled when she thought of Guildmaster Elsin, the head of the guild of Verinai. She'd craved power and pushed the boundaries of magic as none had before. Serak must have been present during that time, although Elenyr had not known of him.

The leaves of the forest had turned to fall, the green fading into gold and brown, floating down when the breeze picked up. She glanced to the sky and saw the impending storm, and picked up the pace, her need to understand propelling her forward.

Lightning crackled above, and the clouds blackened, thunder rumbling across the rolling forest. Elenyr picked up the pace and turned ethereal, rushing through trees and brush, willing herself to fly across the earth.

The trees thinned when the ground proved too rocky, and Elenyr climbed the slope. Just as she reached the entrance, the storm broke, and rain poured upon her. Still ethereal, she leapt through the stone wall and then willed herself upward, toward Cloudy Vale.

To everyone else, the underground was solid, but to her it presented an open expanse, like an unmoving pond, each piece of earth bound in place, the harder stones murky, while lighter earth was clear. She floated upward, ascending past dark tunnels and empty chambers, past the ruins of Verisith, and continued to climb until she reached Cloudy Vale.

She rose through the ground, into the rain. The water washed through her ethereal body as she strode toward her house. Steeped in darkness, the hidden refuge brightened when lightning crackled in the sky, briefly illuminating the darkened doors leading to the fragment quarters and the meal hall. She passed them by and ascended the steps into her home, turning corporeal once she was under the porch roof.

Lightning crackled again, and thunder briefly overpowered the patter of rain. Elenyr, her thoughts ahead, entered her home and passed through the entrance hall to the library at the back. The circular chamber contained her archives, a multitude of books on the three balconies and the ground floor.

Elenyr reached to a light orb next to the door, and it brightened at her touch, the others in the room igniting as well. She turned ethereal and passed through the fireplace at the heart of the chamber, the black chimney briefly obscuring her vision before she crossed to the opposite side and ascended to an innocuous bookshelf on the second balcony.

While the rest contained records by historians, this particular shelf held memory orbs by herself or the fragments. Still ethereal, she passed through the bookshelf, entering the secret chamber beyond. Without door or window, the room was inaccessible from without and was the one space that not even the fragments knew about.

More memory orbs littered the space, most salvaged from the Requiem trees beneath Dawnskeep, the fortress that had been her home as high oracle. Many dated back thousands of years and included those created by her ancestors. Several of the collection drew her gaze, those of Elsin, guildmaster of the Verinai.

Elenyr stepped to the orb and activated it by touching the rune. Like all the memory orbs crafted by the Verinai, the orb did more than just show a memory inside the glass, it filled the room, light turning the walls into a training hall.

"Guildmaster Elsin," a woman said. "You have our gratitude for creating a memory orb for our training."

"It is my pleasure," Elsin said.

Elenyr gained little from the memory, so she sifted through the remaining memories of Elsin. On the fourth, she found what she sought, and her lip curled in disgust, for standing behind Elsin stood one with familiar features.

Serak.

He looked young and had yet to gain the cruel twist to his lips. Here he gazed upon the woman he loved with the utmost adoration, an affection that had been unrequited, since Elsin had married another. Elenyr watched the memory to its conclusion, and then selected another, scanning the memories for clues about Serak's fate.

She began with her own memories, carefully noted after each conflict. Being ageless did not grant perfect memory, and so she'd begun the habit shortly after starting Draeken's training. Selecting the events where an unseen hand might be suspect, she searched the orbs, several times reliving multiple memories at once.

The hours dragged by, the voices of Elenyr's past echoing in the secret chamber. Elenyr found signs of Serak but did not locate him in her memories. Irritated, she continued the search, until she found what she sought.

In a memory from three thousand years ago, when Elenyr and Water had gone to the orcs to resolve a dispute, Elenyr watched herself and Water speaking to an orc chieftain. Unlike his predecessors, he'd hired a multitude of mercenaries, and with the increased forces the orc was set to crush the other clans. Elenyr managed to talk him out of the plan, with her sword on his throat.

In the background of the memory, one of the mercenaries stood watching. Half in the shadows of a large statue, he did not take part in the conflict, where Water fought dozens of humans, orcs, gnomes, and dark elves.

Elenyr advanced to the edge of the memory and circled the man. He stood watching, his sword still in its scabbard, his eyes lit with dark intelligence. Just as the conflict had ended, he retreated into the corridor and departed.

304

Elenyr returned the image to the previous scene and watched it again, and again. The man had Serak's height and build, but his features were different, and he had a beard. But the eyes were the same, barely visible when Elenyr's gaze had swept the room, passing over the battle, the gaudy statues of orc wives, and teeth of slain beasts. She had not noticed the observer at the time, but now she did.

Now that she had found Serak, she continued her search, and found him again just a hundred years later, in a rebellion in Griffin. Then again, on a pirate ship on the South Sea. Each time his appearance was altered, each time the eyes were the same.

Elenyr paused and returned to the orbs, sifting through her memories of the events leading up to the conflict, and discovered snippets of tales, all suggesting someone had provoked them to anger.

Serak had been smart. He'd manipulated events but done so subtly, just enough to measure the magic of the fragments, to watch their temperaments. He was the Father of Guardians, and the possessiveness in Serak's eyes was evident.

Elenyr closed the memories and stared at the line of orbs she'd collected, each resting on a small stand along a bookshelf. There were likely dozens more if she looked hard enough, and likely even more where he'd been present, but she had not seen him in her memories.

"What do you want?" she wondered aloud.

It was obvious he wanted Draeken, but for what purpose? Elenyr's thoughts shifted to the secret she'd kept since Draeken had split, since the moment the fragments had been born. It was the secret she feared the most, and the one she had never shared, not with the fragments, not with Senia, not with anyone. Had Serak discovered the truth about Draeken?

She shook her head, doubting that possibility. He might be the Father of Guardians, but he could not have guessed such a secret. But what did he intend? In some of the memories she noticed Serak had an opportunity to strike at the fragments, but he made no move to attack.

Starting at the beginning, Elenyr parceled together Serak's past. He'd loved Elsin, a love she had not returned. He'd probably become the first guardian in an attempt to gain her attention. But Elsin had recognized his power and caged him in the abandoned krey temple in the north, in the secret Gate Chamber beneath. By the time he'd escaped, the Mage Wars were over, and he'd set out to find the last of the Verinai. He'd found Draeken.

Gathering the Order of the Ancients, he'd prepared them for the return of the krey, and even discovered how to contact Wylyn. All the while he studied Draeken's fragments, watching and waiting.

How were Draeken and the krey connected? Did Serak wish to ally himself with the fragments, as he'd claimed to Water, or did he want to give Lumineia to the Empire—including Draeken—and live like a king?

Realizing she'd gotten all the answers she could, she departed with her questions. Extinguishing the lights, she phased through the outer wall, entering the balcony of her archives. Although she'd been inside the secret room all night, daylight did not stream through the windows. The storm had picked up while she'd been inside, and the rattle of rain echoed from without. Elenyr crossed the threshold and made her way to the door. Closing it behind her, she stood on the porch, and watched the rain batter the refuge. Phasing to ethereal, she stepped into the rain . . .

She noticed the trap too late. Hiding in a puddle, it was nearly invisible, just a circle of white energy, crackling and spitting. She tried to shift her weight but her ethereal boot touched the water, and energy crackled up her body.

She screamed, her back arching as the lightning forced her to become corporeal, the trap cinching around her ankle. She scrambled backward, putting herself on the porch, fighting for breath. Once out of the water, the spell diminished, and she sucked in a grateful breath. Then her gaze lifted, and she spotted the figure striding out of the rain.

Serak.

Chapter 41: Execution

Others appeared behind Serak, a dozen Order members, all with blades in hand. The scars and tattoos on their flesh marked them as experienced, but it was the masked man at Serak's side that drew Elenyr's eye.

Dressed in white and blue, the man wore a mask of the same colors. No weapon rested in his hand, except for a sparkle of white energy between his fingers. Elenyr bared her teeth as she realized the man possessed lightning magic.

All at once she saw the last few years from a different perspective, of the assassin that had come for her. His failure had revealed her weakness, and the lightning mage had placed the magic on Gendor's sword, a magic that would have killed her without Loralyn's intervention. Elenyr had assumed the weapons were from a past lightning mage, for it was difficult to keep such a secret private. But it was clear the magic had come from a living lightning mage, one allied with Serak.

Serak lifted his hand and waved, orange light blossoming on the gauntlet, silencing the storm. The rain continued to fall, but it no longer roared in Cloudy Vale. In its absence, Elenyr heard the crackling of power from the ring of lightning on her boot.

"Elenyr," Serak said. "I have waited for this moment for ages. A pity that our first meeting will be our last."

Elenyr's eyes flicked to the lightning mage and returned to Serak, realizing his intent. He'd come to Cloudy Vale, sought her out when she was alone, and brought his secret lightning mage for a single purpose.

An execution.

She gritted her teeth and caught the handle of her door, pulling herself to her feet. The lighting continued to crackle, shooting pain up her leg, but she could walk. Serak wanted to enjoy the moment, not kill her outright. His desire to gloat gave her time.

"You must be so unused to being weak," Serak said, his voice echoing oddly through the silent rain. "I'll give you a moment to recover. One such as yourself deserves to die on your feet."

"What do you want with Draeken?" Elenyr asked.

"Ah, the most important question," Serak said, his eyes lighting with delight. "But I expect nothing less from the Hauntress."

"All your intrigue will be for naught." Elenyr grimaced as power coursed up her leg.

"Are you certain you know them?" Serak asked. "Because I have studied them as long as you have been their teacher, and it won't be long until all the fragments of Draeken are in my possession."

"He will never join you," Elenyr said.

"Is that what you think I want?" he asked.

"Is it not?"

Serak smiled, but the amusement failed to reach his eyes. He reached up and pointed to the sky, and the water abruptly parted, turning to either side and flowing across a dome. The dome grew, expanding to reveal the breadth of Cloudy Vale.

Elenyr's eyes widened when she saw collections of krey explosives set against the other buildings, each blinking brightly. She raised a hand as if she could stop the destruction, just as the first ignited.

The meal hall exploded, the stone shattering, fire filling the interior and belching smoke into the rain. Light's quarters exploded next, and then Water's, the blast shaking the porch beneath Elenyr, heat washing across her frame. Every room, every home, every chamber in Cloudy Vale disappeared in fire, the flames igniting the sodden trees, the smoke passing through the water barrier into the rain. Last to detonate, the chamber where the fragments had slept when they were young, the bunk beds and Shadow's secret exit, all filled with fire, spilling debris into the clearing. Only Elenyr's home remained intact.

"Why?" Elenyr demanded, watching in horror as her home burned.

"Last night your fragments destroyed Mistkeep," he said. "It's only fitting I return the favor." His features hardened. "And because you have guided the fragments long enough. You have trained them well, but it's time they were on their own."

"So you can take my place?" she spat.

"You are the wisest woman on Lumineia," he said, "yet still you know nothing about a true threat. And that is why the fragments need me."

"They will not follow you," she said.

Serak smiled again, the expression making her shiver. "Goodbye, Elenyr. Few know your identity, so few will mourn the loss." He motioned to the masked man. "I call him Carn. I think you'll see why."

Carn reached outward, and the lightning answered his summons, a bolt passing through the water shield to strike the earth at his side. Instead of knocking him away, the lighting swelled into a giant wolf.

Cast from pure energy, the beast snarled and pawed the ground, its jaws snapping, spilling lightning into the water. At Carn's command, it began to stalk forward. Elenyr's eyes widened in shock at the instrument of her execution.

An entity of lightning.

Elenyr spun and yanked the door open. She dived inside and slammed it shut. The lightning entity crossed forty feet in a heartbeat, blasting into the barrier. Fashioned of dwarven steel and hardened oak, it held, barely.

Wood crunched and steel bent beneath the onslaught, and the entity slammed into the barrier again, knocking dust loose from the ceiling. Elenyr stumbled into the hall, her gaze lifting to the painting above the hearth, the one of her daughter, Alydian, holding an infant girl.

Elenyr's fist tightened and she dropped to the floor. Grabbing the ring of lightning with her bare hand, she hissed in pain, and then began to pull it from her boot. It burned into her skin but she continued to pull, even as the door crunched behind her, and the lightning entity's jaws appeared.

She pulled with all her might, and the ring moved across her ankle, shifting across her foot towards her toes. Then the door crunched and the wolf charged again, more wood clattering to the floor. Energy crackled in the steel and Elenyr realized she was out of time.

Leaping to her feet, she limped into her archives, reaching the hearth as the door shattered. The lightning entity leapt into the opening, its snarl like thunder, the lightning crackling off its frame to ignite the room.

Elenyr leapt into the hearth and jumped, catching a stone within. The entity crossed the space as quick as thought, raking its claws down her leg. She cried out but managed to pull herself into the chimney. Soot filled her hair and covered her face and clothing, but she fought for height.

The wolf entered the chimney and clawed its way upward, power crackling off its flanks, striking the stones and her. Blood from the wound on her leg dripped into its jaws, and its thundering snarl reverberated in the confines of the chimney.

Elenyr scrambled upward, only saved by the tightness of the space, which made passage difficult for the large wolf. Its speed made up for it, and the entity closed the gap, inch by inch bringing its jaws closer to her foot.

Elenyr spotted her goal, a side chimney leading to another room in her home. The wolf's jaws snapped shut a hairsbreadth from her feet, so close she felt energy crackle into her flesh. Crying out, she lunged and caught the edge of the smaller shaft, and dragged herself into the curving channel. She squeezed her way into it, while the wolf clawed his way after.

Elenyr fell ten feet and landed in a heap on a pile of wood. Bleeding and limping, she caught the hearth and pulled herself to her feet as lightning from above ignited the wood, and the wolf forced his way into the chimney.

From inside the room, the stones of the chimney crackled with power, and bulged as the wolf pushed his way downward, its claw appearing in the fireplace. Elenyr limped across the room and reached upward, to the staff hanging on the wall.

A gift from Water, the staffblade was the same he favored in combat. Lightning may have been powerful, but its weakness was water, which would dilute the magic. She gripped the weapon that could kill the wolf, knowing she had to first land a blow. She retreated to the closet of the guest chamber, entering as the fireplace crumbled. The wolf landed on the carpet, burning holes as it stalked forward. It shook itself, and stones clattered to the floor.

Elenyr held the staffblade pointed at the wolf. An entity of lightning was faster than even the fragment of Light, but he was forced to attack through the narrow aperture into the closet. He slashed with his paw, testing her defenses, and she flicked the staff blade. Too slow.

Its snarl was tinged with triumph, and it prepared to lunge. Elenyr braced herself, and then the wolf darted forward, closing the gap in the time Elenyr tightened her grip. The beast struck the staff blade, driving her into the closet, his claws raking the air, clawing her from shoulder to wrist. But the blade had cut into its chest, forcing it to withdraw. Drops of lighting blood spilled to the floor, sparking and spitting.

In the closet, Elenyr screamed at the beast. "Come and get me!"

Although the wolf would not hear, its caster would, and the wolf dropped low to the ground before surging forward. But Elenyr was off the ground. Leaping to the ceiling, she caught the wood paneling above the door and swung herself over the wolf, landing in the room beyond, crying out as the impact sent pain spiking from her wounds. The wolf collided with the back of the closet, power arcing into the clothes and setting them on fire. Rebounding back into the room, it lunged for Elenyr.

She sprinted to the window and jumped free. She flew over the porch and landed in the wet ground between the house and Serak. The wolf exploded through the window and fell toward her, its claws wide, its jaws open. She turned and jammed the staffblade into the earth under the falling beast, and aimed the blade towards its throat.

Pointed upward and held against the ground, the entity could not turn aside, and the blade entered its jaws and passed through its body. Both exploded, the lightning crackling in all directions, forcing Serak and Carn to retreat. On her knees, blood seeping from her wounds, Elenyr glared at Carn.

"Is that all you have?"

"Impressive," Carn said. "But so is this."

He reached skyward and lightning crackled above Elenyr. She snatched a section of the destroyed staff and slashed across the band of lightning on her foot. It split in two, the energy scattering, and Elenyr morphed to ethereal.

"No!" Serak roared.

As the lightning bolt dropped toward her head, she fell into the earth, her eyes filled with the blinding light. Her waist disappeared, as did her torso, but the lightning came for her skull. She sucked in her breath and willed herself into the earth, her hair passing beneath the surface . . . and the lighting struck.

It blasted the earth, the energy spreading in all directions. Just inches below the surface, the current arced around her, and filled her ethereal form. Her flesh sought to become corporeal but inside the earth she could not, so she endured the full agony of the blow. The last thing she heard was Serak's furious bellow, and then darkness claimed her . . .

Chapter 42: A Brother's Home

Lorica listened to Shadow depart, a small smile on her face. After Loralyn had died, she'd felt a shattering within. She never would have imagined the events that would follow, or the one she would call friend.

She continued to watch Gendor until the sun set and he made his way into the cabin. Darkness fell around her, and she half expected Shadow to appear, but the stars turned in the heavens, and she knew he was gone.

When the light went out in the cabin, she turned and left the former assassin behind, and returned to the campfire. The embers had gone cold, the fragments long since departed. After traveling with Shadow for so long, she found that she missed him.

She rekindled the fire and slept. Rising with the dawn, she hurried to her previous vantage point, a rocky outcropping shaded by trees. From there she surveyed Gendor as he exited his farmhouse and went to work in the field.

Leaning against a tree trunk, she regarded her foe. Mind had made clear his magic could be broken, and so she remained on watch, unwilling to let Gendor return to his former knowledge, and enmity.

Part of her wanted him to do so, because it would mean she would be forced to kill him. But as the hours bled into days, and days into weeks, she found a measure of peace in watching the man's honest labor.

Each day Gendor exited and stepped to the barn, gathering tools for the field. Lorica expected him to trudge to the fields, but there was an eagerness to his step, and he tackled the soil with a passion.

Elenyr's previous caretaker had planted a crop, and Gendor began the harvest with a will. She expected him to hesitate, to pause as if he'd forgotten a past life, but he betrayed no hint of his former life, and even his eyes were bright and clear. She watched the change wrought upon him, and realized that he was not alone, that she too felt lighter.

After a decade of conflict and blood, Lorica found her heart gradually easing, like a bow being unstrung. An autumn storm came and went, and she watched Gendor care for his animals, the touch of tenderness surprising.

She departed only to replenish her stock of food, and hastened her return, worried that she'd find him gone. But each time she arrived, he was still there, in the field with his crops. After her fourth return, she realized it was time to depart.

A month after the battle at Mistkeep, she left Gendor behind and returned to her campfire for the final time. As she stared into the flames, her thoughts turned to what she was avoiding, a weaver hall in Herosian.

"Where are your wings?"

She lurched to her feet and spun, to find two figures standing in the shadows. The voice was female, and both were shorter. Lorica lowered her sword when she recognized the voice and shook her head in disbelief.

"Sentara?"

The aged woman stepped into the firelight with Rune at her side and smiled. "It's good to see you too."

Lorica sheathed her sword and embraced the woman. "I thought you were dead."

"It takes more than a fall to kill me," Sentara said, brushing her white hair out of her face. "Besides, I couldn't die before I heard of Gendor's fate."

"Tales are rampant that Mistkeep has been destroyed by the Angel of Death," Rune said, taking a seat by the fire. "They say you were among the dead."

314

"Just my wings," Lorica said, resuming her seat before looking to Sentara with hope. "Could you make a replacement?"

"Sadly, I cannot," Sentara said. "But I suspect you will not need them." She flashed a cryptic smile.

"How did you find me here?" Lorica asked.

"Sentara's friend can find anyone," Rune said with a laugh.

Sentara touched the pouch at her side, the one containing the orb she spoke to, but did not withdraw the object. Then she leaned back against a fallen log, her smile fading as she regarded Lorica.

"What can you tell me of Elenyr?"

"The Hauntress?" Lorica asked. "I saw her when my guild was destroyed in Herosian, but not since."

"Yet you traveled with Shadow."

Lorica raised an eyebrow. "How did you know?"

"She knows much," Sentara said, motioning to the pouch containing the orb. "But I wish to know of Elenyr. How fares the battle with the krey?"

Lorica flashed a toothy smile. "Only one remains."

Rune grunted in irritation. "I wish I could have been there."

"You are an accomplished warrior," Sentara said absently. "But still young."

"You always say that," Rune said.

"Don't rush into battle," Lorica said. "It carries a cost you cannot fathom."

Sentara looked about as if just realizing Lorica was alone. "Loralyn did not survive?"

"Gendor killed her," Lorica said.

"Yet he still lives?" Sentara asked, shocked.

"The fragment of Mind stripped him of his assassin memories," she replied. "Made him think he was a farmer . . . are you well?"

Sentara's features had darkened, her eyes gaining a frightening rage. Lorica reached out to her but Sentara came to her feet and stood rigid, her hands clenching and unclenching. Lorica cast a look to Rune, but the girl, too, seemed mystified.

"You let him shatter a mind?" Sentara ground the words out.

"I didn't see the harm—"

Sentara stabbed a finger at Lorica. "You have no idea the damage such magic can cause."

"You've seen it before," Lorica guessed, rising.

"Rune," Sentara said. "Come, we have an assassin to watch."

Rune cast Lorica an apologetic look, and then the girl followed Sentara into the shadows. Lorica shook her head in disbelief, confused at the sudden turn in Sentara's behavior. Just as the weapons master exited the firelight, Lorica called out to her.

"Wait," she said. "Who did he hurt?"

Sentara regarded her from the darkness, the firelight flickering across her face. "Me," she said.

"But what happened—"

"Don't you have a task to get to?" Sentara asked. "One you've been avoiding?"

She turned and left, and Lorica could have sworn the pouch at her side was glowing bright red. Then the woman and her charge were gone, leaving Lorica to her questions. She considered following Sentara and Rune but knew that Sentara would not appreciate the intrusion.

Taking solace in the fact that the pair would be watching Gendor, Lorica tried not to consider the prospect of what Sentara had implied. She reclined to sleep near the fire and lapsed to slumber.

She woke with the dawn, her thoughts turning ahead. Rising, she kicked dirt onto the coals and turned away from the ring of stones. Pondering the exchange with Sentara, she headed north, to Herosian.

Although it was Sentara's past that dominated her doubts, she could no longer avoid what lay ahead. She'd been hunting Gendor for so long that she hadn't given thought to the future, or the oath she had made with her sister.

She'd pursued killers and beasts, targets of fearsome power, but never had she felt such fear, the emotion slowing her steps and accelerating her heart. She reached Herosian before dawn and passed through the gates unchallenged.

The bustle of street urchins and travelers, the scent of bread and roast eggs, washed over her, unnoticed. As if sensing the pall over her, none approached. Her clothes were still rent from the battle at Mistkeep, but her wounds were healed. Children veered away from her, looking up in silent awe before scurrying away. They did not know she was an assassin, or the guildmaster of an empty guild. But they knew to fear.

She passed through the circles of Herosian and took the road north and west, towards the weaver hall on the small hill. Her footsteps further slowed as she imagined what lay ahead, of seeing Irenae, of speaking to Zenif's son. Would she be angry? Would she scream profanities and slam the door?

Lorica's heart tightened in her chest, a lump of steel that struggled to beat. She passed homes and factories, the workers already set to their labors churning out cloth and refining wheat to flour. The sun crested the city wall, bathing the streets in light and shadows. She wished one of them contained her friend.

Lorica rounded a corner by the warehouse and took the final steps to the gate, to the rickety barrier that had prevented her entry for a decade. It came to her waist, just a few boards fastened to a beam with rusted nails, the wood warped and grey.

Like so many times before, she came to a halt, her eyes lifting to the door. She'd never visited during the day, afraid she would be recognized. The structure looked different, more alive.

Although worn, the exterior wall showed signs of repair, and new wood had been installed on the eaves. The coloring indicated it was a few years old, and she wondered how she'd never noticed.

A handful of discarded toys littered the patch of grass in front of the house, while the weaver hall adjacent to the home smelled of cloth and linen. Sunrise filled the building with light, an invitation, a beckoning.

Lorica reached for the gate, a chill sweeping through her flesh, her hand trembling. Her fingers settled on the wood. The rough texture was exactly as she'd imagined, but she'd always seen a second hand on the gate.

Her features fell, emotion clogging her throat, and the loss of Loralyn was as bitter as the moment she'd died. But another emotion was also present, a soft relief, a yearning to see Zenif's child. And she could almost imagine the second hand resting on the wood beside her own.

Drawing a stuttering breath, she eased the gate open, the hinges releasing a creak. The barrier broken, she stepped through, and her boot settled onto the path, the gravel crunching. Tears filled her eyes, and she took another step, and another. Her slow stride carried her to the door, and she lifted her hand to the knocker.

The heavy metal struck the door, the sound reverberating into the interior. The hum of a weaving machine came to a stop, and then footfalls approached the floor. Lorica nearly bolted, the urge to run so powerful and sudden that she took half a step toward the street. Then the door opened and Lorica found herself facing Irenae.

Lorica saw the same door but ten years in the past—Lorica and Loralyn standing in the doorway, their uniforms still dirty from the road, both in silence as Zenif's wife crumpled on the threshold. The young child clung to his mother as she wept, unaware that his father would never return.

Lorica struggled to speak as Irenae blinked in shock. She froze, the cloth in her hands tumbling to the floor. A young voice called out in curiosity, but she failed to respond, and Lorica struggled to speak.

"Irenae . . ."

318

Lorica's voice abandoned her, and her throat closed up. Tears blossomed in Irenae's eyes and she shook her head. Lorica thought it was anger that twisted her features, but abruptly Irenae released a laugh.

"What took you so long?"

The woman closed the gap in a rush, engulfing her in a crushing embrace. Lorica clung to the woman, and tears wet her cheeks, leaking from her eyes despite her effort to stop them. She smelled the dust and linen on the woman, mixed with a faint scent of cinnamon and apples, the smells of a mother.

"I'm sorry," Lorica whispered. "I'm so sorry."

Irenae's grip tightened. "*You* didn't kill Zenif."

"The one who did has paid for his crime."

Irenae finally retreated and wiped at the tears wetting her cheeks. "I never cared about that."

"We did," she said.

Irenae cast about. "Where's Loralyn?"

Lorica shook her head.

Irenae's smile faded and she motioned Lorica inside. "Come in. It's past time we shared a meal."

Lorica crossed the threshold, shivering but not from a chill. She'd been to war for a decade, and stepping into Zenif's home was the first time since his death that she felt such an emotion. Despite the time, it was easy to recognize.

She was home.

Chapter 43: Shadow's Gift

"Off to bed."

The boy groaned, and Lorica looked to the window in surprise. The entire day had passed, and the light orbs had grown dim. Irenae ignored the boy's protests and ushered him upstairs, and Lorica surveyed the table.

A day with Irenae had softened scars not of the flesh, and she only wished Loralyn had been present. Irenae was not the best of cooks, but her food was warm and comforting, the bread seeming to fill the room with heart.

Lorica's gaze swept the room, the tapestry on the wall, woven in Zenif's hand, the simple cabinets, the handmade table. The dishes were few and old, but well cared for, as was the vase on the counter, the one containing flowers picked by the boy.

Lorica withdrew a coin purse and slipped it between the books on a small shelf near the stairs. All had been well read, the pages yellowed with age, the bindings frayed. She saw the stains of fingers and imagined Irenae reading to the child.

Irenae smiled as she descended the stairs. "The Ballad of Ero and Skorn," she said. "One of his favorites."

"I've never read it," Lorica said.

"You should," she said, and set to clearing the table.

"He is wonderful," Lorica said, picking up a plate.

"He is his father's son," she said, "and has his father's gift with thread."

"Then Lumineia is fortunate."

They'd spent the day talking about the weaver hall, its position among the other halls, and tales of the past decade. Zenif had left a legacy in the guild, one of quality that his family had managed to maintain, despite the competition.

Zenif's son had asked repeatedly about Lorica's past. Evading the truth, she'd claimed being contracted to Griffin's northern army. Tales of Bartoth's attacks on caravans were rampant, and Lorica entertained the boy with stories of the villainous rock troll.

"I thank you for not talking of your exploits with my son present," Irenae said.

"I doubt Zenif would have liked his son following my example."

"Did you kill many in your quest for Zenif's killer?" she asked.

The question was quiet, almost afraid, and Lorica shook her head. "That is not the question that matters. What matters is, have I killed anyone that did not merit death?"

Irenae remained silent, and then sighed. "It is hard for me to understand your chosen life."

Lorica thought of Shadow, of how he was, of what he did. He was a fragment born to magic, and many current mages would regard him as an abomination. Yet he'd probably saved Irenae's life, or the lives of their ancestors. He would not think of himself as an abomination.

She drew her sword and set it on the table. The steel clunked onto the wood, the sound heavy, as if the blade knew the history of blood it carried, the mantle it shouldered. The weapon was not the oathsword, which she'd hidden near the old guildhall on one of her trips away from Gendor. The blade was her old sword, the one that had been hers upon becoming an assassin, and the hilt was as familiar as her own flesh.

"This is my loom," she said softly.

"My loom does not kill," Irenae replied.

"I did not choose my talents," Lorica said. "But I can choose my fate. The one who killed Zenif was like me, gifted with a sword, willing to take a life that needed taking. But he wielded his talents for a darker purpose, just as you could, just as any could."

Lorica swept a hand to the bookshelf. "A historian could use his talent to inspire hatred and fear, while a weaver might create clothing and decorations that instill jealousy and anger. It is not what we possess that defines us, but how we choose to wield the blade we have been given."

Irenae regarded her with curiosity, her features warm, like a mother, or a sister. All at once Lorica realized the woman saw her as such, and worried for Lorica as if they were blood. They may have been joined by marriage, but Irenae saw her as kindred.

"Do you not feel pain when you take a life?"

"One of my targets was an elven noblewoman that beat her children," Lorica said, recalling the kill. "She stole from the poor and whipped a human youth because he had the audacity of looking her in the eye. He died, and the family sought recompense, but the crime was overlooked because of her status. Loralyn gave the contract to me, and I felt pride upon its completion."

"Surely the family could not afford your guild."

"The contract was issued by the queen of the elves," Lorica said.

Lorica hadn't known that part until recently, when she'd browsed the assassin archives while watching Gendor. She'd learned a great deal in her time of observation, including the identity of the patron.

"Justice was bound," Lorica said. "So the queen used us."

"You speak with eloquence," Irenae said. "And I believe I understand. I assume this means you will continue in the guild?"

Irenae's back was to Lorica, her tone light, but Lorica heard the note of worry that went beyond curiosity. She'd obviously wanted to ask all day, but her son had bombarded Lorica with questions, preventing the question from being voiced.

"I must," Lorica said. "For if I do not, the guild will disappear."

"Would that be so awful?" she asked, rotating to face her.

Lorica sighed and motioned to the castle at the heart of the kingdom, its spires visible through the window. "Throughout Lumineia, the nobles reign, held only in check by their own sense of morals . . . and the assassins. If we did not exist, I fear they would rise to tyranny, and you would suffer."

"A difficult burden to bear," she said.

Lorica thought of Loralyn. "We became assassins to find Zenif's killer. I never anticipated we would become the aspect of justice."

Despite her words, Lorica was drawn to Zenif's home, and the simple life it offered. She'd spent her life fighting, and for a moment, she imagined relinquishing the ring of the guildmaster and simply fading into obscurity.

The knocker on the door thudded, and Irenae stepped to the portal, swinging it open. When she did not speak, Lorica joined her, surprised to find the steps empty. Steeped in darkness the grass and the street beyond were also empty. Then she noticed the box.

The crate on the doorstep was not overly large, nor did it contain markings of any kind. Lorica eyed the empty street and glanced to Irenae, raising an eyebrow. The woman shook her head, a trace of fear in her gaze. Then Lorica noticed a faint script on the text, almost as if a shadow of words . . .

"Dim the lights," she said.

"Why?" Irenae asked.

Lorica smiled reassuringly. "Do it. I know who it's from."

Irenae did as requested and touched the light orb above the table. Darkness engulfed the room, while illumination spilled down the staircase. In the gloom the words on the crate were clear.

A gift for a friend.

Lorica chuckled as she pulled the box inside and shut the door. The box was lighter than expected, and she set it on the table to remove the lid. When she saw the contents her eyes widened, and she caught the clasp to withdraw the cloak.

Irenae sucked in a breath and squinted in the gloom. "That's not made of cloth."

"I know," she said.

The cloak was sheer black yet shifted like smoke in a faint breeze. She reached out to touch it—and her fingers passed through, as if the material lacked substance. The cloak re-solidified when she withdrew her hand.

"What sort of magic made that?" the woman asked.

"Shadow magic," Lorica said.

She reached up and wrapped it around her shoulders, felt the touch of consciousness, like a whisper in the back of her mind. The cloak rippled at her will, and then arced outward, rising and shaping.

Into wings.

Irenae squinted and raised a hand to the light orb. Lorica saw the motion but her word of warning came too late. Light flooded the dining room, and she expected the wings to fade. Instead the darkness swept aside, and wings of white took their place.

Irenae gasped in surprise, the sound matched by a young boy's shout of joy. Then Irenae rushed up the stairs, calling for him to return to his quarters. Lorica stood in place, marveling at the gift.

She recognized that Shadow had crafted the wings, and likely enlisted the aid of Light and Mind to complete them, making it possible to be an extension of her mind, as well as able to withstand daylight.

She spread her wings and they responded to her slightest thought. Her heart filled with gratitude. It was a gift fit for a king, and would have taken time to craft, even for the fragments of Draeken. The ring containing the assassin archives glowed on her finger, as if it too, recognized the act of honor.

Shadow could have waited to prepare such a gift, yet he'd done so now, and she understood the unspoken invitation. He didn't want her to forget her place. She was the head of the Assassins' Guild, and it was time to replenish her ranks.

Chapter 44: Leashed

Through the open door leading to the weaver hall, Shadow listened to Lorica describe her purpose, the words reminding him of Elenyr, and how she spoke to the fragments. He reclined on the stack of fabrics and stared at the ceiling, considering the idea that the conflict of self was not exclusive to the fragments of Draeken. The way Lorica spoke, as if she'd once been uncertain about her talents and purpose, seemed an echo of Shadow's own doubts.

"This is my loom," Lorica said.

In the darkness, Shadow cast a dagger, and smiled. In his youth, many had scorned his magic, claiming it to be a devil's skill. Useful to assassins, criminals, killers, and thieves, his magic was sought after by those of nefarious intent. He couldn't blame them. He frequently had nefarious intent of his own.

But were the fragments of Draeken only pieces? Or could they be more? More importantly, did he want to be more? The questions were uttered in the darkest recesses of his mind, never to be voiced. Doing so would be the pinnacle of vulnerability, and he didn't do vulnerable.

Still, he recognized that his current predicament had been created due to his attachment to Lorica. But Wylyn's leverage was significant. He'd actually considered killing Lorica himself, just to end Wylyn's hold over him. But the mere thought of harming the assassin was worse than the idea of his will being trapped.

On impulse, he leapt to the rafters of the weaver hall, and to a window fastened in the bedroom of the boy. The opening allowed the child to view the workings of the weaver hall from his room. As expected, he was not in his bed, and instead had crept down the stairs to listen. From the window, he watched the child, whose eyes were bright with wonder.

Shadow cared nothing for the boy. He could die or live, it mattered not, but if the child died it would devastate Lorica, as would the death of Irenae. Shadow settled back in the rafter, wondering how his desire to protect the assassin extended to this simple woman and her child.

He pondered the question and then he cast an elf out of shadow, dispatching him to the front door. It lifted the knocker and then dissipated. Dropping to the floor of the hall, Shadow slipped into the portal between the weaver hall and the home and watched as the assassin discovered the crate.

Drawn to Lorica's impending discovery, Shadow advanced to the limit of darkness, risking discovery as he watched the assassin don the new wings. His smile was one he would never have shown to anyone, and he realized that he had never given a gift. Elenyr did, and some of the fragments had, but Shadow never had. As he watched Lorica's delight, he could not recall ever feeling such a strange emotion.

Reluctantly he retreated. He still had work to accomplish this night, and it would not do for Lorica to discover the note in the crate before he was ready. Striding to the door, he morphed to his shadow form and slipped away. Then he circled the pools of light in the street and plunged into the city.

A ghost of a smile appeared on his features as he wove his way into the dark streets of Herosian. As he left Lorica behind, his thoughts turned to the last three weeks and the events that had led to his current situation.

He made his way from the seventh circle all the way to the first, passing the noble circles and even the military district. The guards never saw him, only a flicker in the shadows as he breached their vaunted defenses to reach the castle at the heart of the city.

The fortress was even larger than Mistkeep, with enormous towers, several great halls, and curving courtyards. King Porlin had expanded on the work of his predecessors, and smaller turrets clung to the larger, providing hanging balconies that connected to suspended bridges. Like a city in and of itself, the castle was the largest on Lumineia.

He passed the guards by the door, pausing only to tie the boot laces of the haughty captain. Then he ascended through the fortress, winding

327

up stairs and through guarded doors, finally reaching his destination, a chamber in the largest of the towers, and formerly the king's own quarters.

The door was shut and flanked by two very observant men in guard uniforms. Neither were actual soldiers for Talinor, but they looked the same. Shadow allowed himself to be seen and the first caught the handle, swinging the door open.

"She's expecting you."

Shadow offered a mock salute as he stepped through the portal, the guard shutting it behind him. The receiving room was occupied by several more guards, including the hulking, bone armored dakorians on either side of the entrance.

The guards drew their swords and blades, the sheer number suggesting they feared Shadow. He was tempted to show them why they required such caution but resisted the urge. This time. Instead he faced the woman standing at the window where she could survey the city. At Shadow's entrance she turned and regarded him with a cold stare.

"Wylyn," Shadow said, "You always look so pleased to see me." He winked. "Be careful, I bite."

"You were not supposed to depart," she said coldly.

"I didn't speak to a soul," he said, and then gestured to the room, which had an abundance of light orbs. "Were you worried I might kill you?"

He cast a dagger of shadows, the action causing the Order members to bristle and raise their weapons, but the blade withered under the glare of so much light. He watched it crumble and then his eyes flicked to Wylyn, a smile forming on his features that made even Wylyn scowl.

"I do not need the darkness to kill," Shadow said. "I simply prefer it. The terror of one used to arrogance is indeed the sweetest, as Relgor would know."

"Need I remind you the price you will pay for betrayal?"

328

She reached to the orb at her side and tossed it to him. Shadow caught the orb, and although he ignored it, his touch activated the image, showing Irenae and her son working in their hall, the memory taken from a false buyer. Unwilling to permit the tug in his chest to show on his features, he flicked the orb to the side, letting it shatter, as if it didn't matter.

"I have not forgotten," Shadow said easily.

"Serak was wrong, you know," she said, circling the room. "He said you would never have friends."

"Is this about Mistkeep?" Shadow scratched his chin. "I did leave quite a mess. I would say I'll clean it up, but I have no intention of doing that."

"The Angel of Death taught you of friendship," she said. "But I wager she never told you the price."

Shadow groaned. "You lecture more than a mother—and I never had one."

The krey's lip curled into a sneer. "Friends may support you, even believe in you, but they can be used against you."

"I already told you I would do your bidding," Shadow said, folding his arms with an irritated sigh. "Why do you feel the need to gloat like a spoiled child." His eyes lit with understanding. "Or is it because I killed Relgor? Tell me, did you even like your son? Or was he simply . . . one who could be used against you?"

She came to a halt and stared at him. "I think it's time you know the truth."

"Please don't tell me you favor me." Shadow feigned panic. "I'd rather die than receive a krey kiss."

She ignored his comment, and instead she flashed a knowing smile. "I believe you are under the assumption that Relgor negotiated a deal with Serak long before my arrival. Indeed, you believe he sought to work behind my wishes, without my knowledge or approval. In truth, I learned of Relgor's deal with Serak only days after it was made."

"You sound like one who has lost," Shadow said. "Can you not admit Relgor was smarter than you?"

"I allowed him to believe his little ruse," she said. "After all, those who believe they work for their own fate are always more willing than servants. The *illusion* of free will is a powerful motivator."

Shadow began to laugh, his tone low and mocking. Although her words were persuasive, he'd lied enough to recognize a liar. This particular lie sounded legitimate because it was believable. The more Shadow laughed, the more Wylyn's black eyes swirled with red.

"Don't insult me," Shadow said. "We both know your son bested you, and if I hadn't killed him, he probably would have killed you."

Her glare seeped with cold fury, but she could not speak. He'd caught her in a lie, and anything she said now would merely bring more amusement to Shadow. The guards shifted their feet, disliking the tension in the room. Ultimately, she sought to retain her dignity and swept her hand away.

"You bore me. Speak to Tardoq about your assignment. I assure you, it will not be pleasant."

"I assure you it *will* be pleasant."

Shadow mimicked her voice to perfection, eliciting a scowl. Smirking, he strode to the side chamber that had once been the king's private training hall. He stepped inside and the door was shut behind him, leaving him alone with Wylyn's Bloodwall.

Tardoq stood in the center of the circular room, examining a giant war axe. "The weaponry on this world is impressive," he said. "I will have to add it to my collection. I also keep the bones of my foes, you know."

"Sorry," Shadow said. "I don't think I have any bones."

"Then you—"

Shadow groaned and pushed the rune on his gauntlet, cutting off all sound from the chamber. "As much as I enjoy threats, they are growing tedious, especially when you know what I saw."

"You saw nothing."

"I saw that you could have saved Relgor," he said.

The dakorian regarded him, his eyes like orbs of obsidian. Then he snorted. "Wylyn would not believe you," he said, his tone of dismissal.

"Don't you want to know why I have kept your secret?"

"The thoughts of a slave are meaningless to me," he replied, sweeping the blade. "I have been tasked to tell you of your next—"

"Why did you let Relgor die?" Shadow said, folding his arms.

Tardoq regarded him for several seconds, and then surged across the room, closing the gap in the span of a second. Grasping Shadow about the throat, he raised him up and slammed him into the wall.

"I am a Bloodwall," he snarled. "My loyalty is *absolute*. Question it again and I will kill you myself."

Shadow managed to keep his words to himself. He had his answer. Such an enraged response meant only one thing, Shadow had spoken the truth. When he remained silent, Tardoq tossed him across the room and stabbed a bony finger to the window.

"Return to the Hauntress and discover her plans. Wylyn wishes to know where she will journey next, and when."

Shadow came to his feet and strode to the window. He smirked and swept his hands wide. "As you order." He leaned back and fell out the window.

Wind buffeted him as he fell down the side of the turret. Then he cast his wings of darkness and banked around the turret. He swooped under a high bridge, startling a guard before turning around another. Passing outside the fortress, he soared above the city, and then folded his wings and dropped to the roof of a noble's house, the House of Runya.

Owned by the only elven family in Herosian, the house had risen to gain a great deal of respect among the populace, and the head of the house was a friend of Elenyr. Shadow alighted on a balcony and let the light from within destroy his wings. When he stepped inside, a dozen elven blades turned on him. Then the guards recognized him and the captain motioned him up the stairs.

"They are above."

"You have my gratitude, good lady," he inclined his head to the beautiful elf and winked, before climbing the stairs to the large room situated on the top floor of the house. Upon opening the door, Thorilian, head of the House of Runya, and his wife, Venia, both in battle armor, stood around a map of the castle. Two other elves were also present, one dark, one light.

Willow and Jeric.

Chapter 45: Unleashed

"You're late," Jeric said.

"They had to threaten me," Shadow said, a smile lighting his features as he recalled their ignorance. "They think I'm still loyal to them."

"Are you?" Jeric asked.

Shadow feigned a wounded expression. "Of course not."

He strode across the room. Built of elven wood and stained dark, the polished flooring would have been at home in a palace, yet few knew it had been made by Thorilian's own hand. He and his wife had been outcasts of other houses and had built the House of Runya from nothing. Now their home commanded attention, even if it did not reside in the elven kingdom.

Also of wood, the walls were lighter in tone, and contained aquaglass ovals, each depicting a member of the family, the three sons as handsome as they were lethal. One was a member of the Bladed, while another a captain in the royal guard in Ilumidora. The third resided in the house, and Shadow guessed he was gearing for combat as well.

On the opposite side of the room, a massive map of Lumineia hung from gilded brackets. Crafted by Venia, the scene depicted the great castles of Lumineia, the scene so lifelike it appeared real. And it was. The image actually connected to the fortresses, a spell the fragment of Light found fascinating, permitting a view of the current weather at each castle.

"You like to play both sides," Thorilian said, folding his arms.

"He is always on our side," Willow said with a nod.

Jeric nodded his agreement. "Is it set? Is Wylyn in the castle?"

"She is there," Shadow said.

"Light's information was accurate, then," Willow said. "And Wylyn has not told Serak of her deal with Shadow. If he had . . ."

"Serak would likely have stopped her from coming to Herosian," Shadow said. "He is too clever for his own good."

"Then Wylyn's distrust is our advantage," Jeric said.

"We strike now," Thorilian said. "Before she can slip away again."

"Light has yet to arrive," Willow said. "And he should have been here yesterday."

Her tone was worried, but Shadow swept his hand to the room. "We have enough. Wylyn will not survive the night."

"Are you certain you wish to do this?" Jeric asked, looking to Thorilian. "If it is discovered you aided our attack, the consequences could be devastating."

His wife leaned in, her eyes forceful. "We did not claim our home out of fear. Is this so different? We will not stand idle when such a threat has risen."

"Indeed," Thorilian said. "Our guard is ready."

Willow folded her arms. "We should wait for Light."

"Your concern is admirable," Shadow said. "But he is a fragment of Draeken. He is more than capable of watching his own back. Literally. You should see him cast magic to watch his own back." He tapped his chin in consideration. "Actually you might not want to witness such a thing. It's rather disturbing."

Jeric grinned and turned to Willow. "I know you are concerned, but if we wait, we risk losing our best chance. Wylyn moves often, and with her network of Gates provided by the Order, we have no way of knowing where she will go."

Willow looked away, her eyes dark. "Light would not miss this."

334

"You think him in danger?" Thorilian asked.

"That is my fear," the dark elf said.

Jeric and Thorilian exchanged a look, and then Jeric shook his head. "If he is in trouble, killing Wylyn will only help. Doing nothing merely serves our foe."

Willow regarded her surface cousins, and then finally dipped her head. "There is truth to your words."

"Then gather yourselves," Jeric said, turning to Thorilian. "We have everyone we need so the assault may begin—"

"One more," Shadow said, and stepped to the window.

"We cannot wait," Thorilian said. "No doubt Wylyn has a Gate up there. If she even hears us coming she'll—"

"Husband," Venia said, placing a hand on his arm. "Patience, my love."

He scowled, and Jeric turned to Shadow. "Who are we waiting for? Fire and Mind are occupied, as are Lira and Water. We cannot wait, especially after what happened to Elenyr . . ."

Jeric's jaw tightened and he looked away. Shadow too, scowled, hatred welling within him for what had occurred at Cloudy Vale. Serak had destroyed his home and set an execution for Elenyr. The least he could do was take Serak's pet krey.

"One more," Shadow repeated.

"The assassin?" Jeric asked. "What makes you think she will come?"

"Because I extended an invitation," he replied.

"And that is enough?" Willow asked.

Shadow caught a glimpse of dark wings flashing through a column of moonlight. The direction was unmistakable, and it was clear she was following the note he'd hidden in the base of the crate.

"She's already here." Shadow said.

He opened the window and cast a giant hand of darkness that pointed to the balcony. Jeric snorted as the hand lead Lorica to the top floor of the House of Runya. She alighted, her wings folding into the cloak on her back, her eyes sweeping the room.

"Shadow," she drawled. "Did you have to point the way?"

"I wouldn't want you to miss this," Shadow said, motioning her into the room.

"What if I decided not to be an assassin anymore?" she asked.

He pointed to the wings and winked. "If you were no longer an assassin, you wouldn't be wearing those."

Jeric looked her up and down, nodding his approval. "Then let—"

"Wait," Shadow said. "Can I say it?"

Jeric sighed. "As you will."

Shadow pulled a cowl of darkness to cover his features, unable to keep the delight from his voice. "Then let it begin."

The Chronicles of Lumineia

By Ben Hale

—The Shattered Soul—
The Fragment of Water
The Fragment of Shadow
The Fragment of Light
The Fragment of Fire
The Fragment of Mind
The Fragment of Power

—The Master Thief—
Jack of Thieves
Thief in the Myst
The God Thief

—The Second Draeken War—
Elseerian
The Gathering
Seven Days
The List Unseen

—The Warsworn—
The Flesh of War
The Age of War
The Heart of War

—The Age of Oracles—
The Rogue Mage
The Lost Mage
The Battle Mage

—The White Mage Saga—

Assassin's Blade (Short story prequel)
The Last Oracle
The Sword of Elseerian
Descent Unto Dark
Impact of the Fallen
The Forge of Light

Author Bio

Originally from Utah, Ben has grown up with a passion for learning almost everything. Driven particularly to reading caused him to be caught reading by flashlight under the covers at an early age. While still young, he practiced various sports, became an Eagle Scout, and taught himself to play the piano. This thirst for knowledge gained him excellent grades and helped him graduate college with honors, as well as become fluent in three languages after doing volunteer work in Brazil. After school, he started and ran several successful businesses that gave him time to work on his numerous writing projects. His greatest support and inspiration comes from his wonderful wife and six beautiful children. Currently he resides in Missouri while working on his Masters in Professional Writing.

To contact the author, discover more about Lumineia, or find out about the upcoming sequels, check out his website at Lumineia.com. You can also follow the author on twitter @ BenHale8 or Facebook.

www.ingramcontent.com/pod-product-compliance
Lightning Source LLC
Chambersburg PA
CBHW020904200626
46814CB00001BA/169

9 781945 580147